THE DRYGULCH TRAIL

When Will Curtis rides into Junction City on a cold rainy night, all he wants is a shot of whiskey and a place to dry off. Instead, he finds himself dragged into a feud between a land-hungry banker and the tough homesteaders who are desperate to keep their ranches. But when rich bully Clem Dawson brings in hired guns to force the ranchers off their land, Curtis decides there is only one thing a decent man can do under the circumstances — and that is to fight . . .

NED OAKS

THE DRYGULCH TRAIL

Complete and Unabridged

LINFORD
Leicester

First published in Great Britain in 2016 by
Robert Hale
an imprint of The Crowood Press
Wiltshire

First Linford Edition
published 2019
by arrangement with
The Crowood Press
Wiltshire

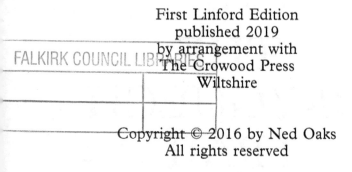

A catalogue record for this book is available
from the British Library.

ISBN 978–1–4448–4012–4

Published by
F. A. Thorpe (Publishing)
Anstey, Leicestershire

Set by Words & Graphics Ltd.
Anstey, Leicestershire
Printed and bound in Great Britain by
T. J. International Ltd., Padstow, Cornwall

This book is printed on acid-free paper

off his slicker and shook the water from it, then did the same with his hat. It was the first time he'd been out of the rain all day.

The man pushed through the batwings into the saloon. It was a surprisingly clean establishment, albeit a small one. There was a bar along the far wall, the length of the room. The tables and the chairs appeared new. There was a large and ornate mirror behind the bar. The brass lanterns had been polished recently. To the man's left, a staircase led up to a landing on the second floor. A pair of closed doors opened onto the landing.

Apart from the stranger, there were two people in the saloon. One was a man sitting on a stool at the far right of the bar, his back turned to the man standing just inside the batwings. The other was a young woman standing behind the bar. She was wiping a glass, her eyes cast down, when the man stepped into the room. The hinges of the batwings creaked and she raised her

2

1

It was nearly midnight when
stranger rode into town.

The rain assailed him as he made h
way up Main Street. His horse's hoo
made squishing noises in the thicl
mud. The man wore a slicker against
the relentless rain, and water streamed
off the brim of his Stetson, which he'd
pulled down low over his lean face.

Only one lantern burned in the
street, dangling from a pole in front of
the saloon. The man pulled reins in
front of the saloon's hitching post and
looked up and down the street. Apart
from the area where he was sitting, the
town was completely dark.

He dismounted and wrapped his
reins around the post. One other horse
was tied there. He climbed the steps
wearily and stood under the awning in
front of the batwing doors. He peeled

eyes toward the stranger.

He was a tall man, somewhere around twenty-five years old. He was lean but sinewy. He had light-brown hair and several days' worth of stubble bristled across his jaw. He unbuttoned his sheepskin coat with his right hand and began to walk toward the bar, holding his slicker and hat in his left hand. His coat fell open as he strode forward, revealing a large Navy Colt strapped to his right hip.

When he reached the bar he placed his slicker and hat on one stool and sat down on another.

'Evening, ma'am,' he said amiably. Fatigue was evident in his face. He fingered the makings from his pocket and began to construct a cigarette on the bar.

'Good evening, sir,' the young woman said. 'You look like you've had a hard day.'

He grinned crookedly and poked the cigarette between his lips.

'It's been a long one, that's for sure,'

he said, the cigarette bobbing as he spoke. He thumb-snapped a match and held it to his smoke.

'Would you like something to drink while you dry off?'

He nodded. 'Yes, please. Whiskey.'

She brought out a shot glass and filled it with the dark liquid.

'That should warm you up,' she said with a smile.

The man tossed the whiskey back and put his glass back on the bar. She quickly refilled it. He sipped slowly at this one and smiled back at her.

She was a pretty girl, a little over twenty, the man thought. She had lustrous red hair, with a sprinkling of freckles across her nose and under her eyes, which were green.

He extended his hand. 'Name's Will Curtis,' he said.

She shook his hand. 'Sally Bannerman.'

'Pleased to make your acquaintance, Miss Bannerman.'

She released his hand and he went

back to sipping his drink.

'You just passing through?' she asked.

'Yes, ma'am,' he said.

'What brings you to this part of Oregon? The constant rain?' There was a twinkle in her eye and Curtis laughed.

'The rain I could do without,' he said. 'But I don't mind the company.'

She smiled again and was just about to say something else when a fist pounded hard on the counter at the other end of the bar. Sally Bannerman and Will Curtis turned their heads in that direction simultaneously.

'Sally!' the man at the end of the bar bellowed. 'Another drink!' There was no friendliness in his tone. His statement was an order.

Curtis watched Sally walk toward the man, who was meticulously dressed in a pinstriped suit with a massive gold watch chain across his vest. He was a little older than Curtis, with light-blond hair and a small build. When he saw Curtis looking at him, he turned his

5

head and looked back, his lips curled in a sneer.

'What're you looking at, stranger?' the man snarled, his tongue thick from the alcohol he'd consumed.

Curtis shrugged. 'You,' he said simply. His gaze didn't waver.

The man held Curtis's eyes for a few more seconds, then lowered his own to his glass as Sally Bannerman poured whiskey into it.

'Now Alvin, you remember what your father told me,' she said, her voice clear. 'After five drinks I'm to cut you off.'

'Yeah, yeah,' the man said, waving her away.

She hesitated for a moment before walking back toward Will Curtis.

'He seems fun,' Curtis said drily.

She coaxed a faint smile to her lips.

'Not especially,' she said. She flicked her eyes quickly down the bar and then looked back at Curtis. 'That's Alvin Dawson. His pa owns most of this town.'

Curtis arched an eyebrow. 'That

explains his courtesy toward ladies.'

The batwings creaked behind him and he looked at the doorway's reflection in the mirror. A huge man stood there, his eyes rapidly scanning the room. When he espied Alvin Dawson at the corner of the bar he moved toward him.

Curtis watched in the mirror as the man walked across the room. He wore a dark-brown trench coat and large white Stetson. A long black beard descended from his face down to the center of his chest. Curtis discerned a brutality in the man's immobile features. He sat down beside Dawson, who seemed startled to see him for a moment. Then Dawson smiled.

'Evans,' he said, a little nervously. 'What're you doing here?'

Evans cuffed his hat toward the back of his head and sighed, a smile tugging at the corners of his mouth.

'You know why I'm here, Alvin. Your pa sent me.'

Dawson guffawed. 'It's past the old

man's bedtime,' he said.

'Well, he ain't asleep,' Evans retorted.

Sally Bannerman carried a glass and the bottle of whiskey down to where Evans was sitting. She poured him a drink and he downed it in one gulp.

'Another,' he said.

She complied and he dispatched the liquor quickly. He belched loudly and rose.

'I got to piss,' he announced. He stood up and walked around Alvin Dawson. A door in the corner of the room led outside to the alley. Evans opened it and stepped outside, leaving the door ajar behind him.

Dawson looked up at Sally and pushed his glass across the bar toward her.

'More whiskey,' he said.

'Alvin, your pa gave strict orders that I'm to cut you off after five drinks. You know that.'

Will Curtis turned his head to watch the exchange.

'Aw, don't go starting that again,'

Dawson moaned. 'Just shut your mouth and do as you're told.'

The woman's face flushed. Curtis continued to watch, saying nothing.

'Alvin, I don't think — ' she began, but her words were cut off when Dawson slammed both hands down hard on the bar.

'Goddamn it, you bitch! You just don't know when to leave it alone, do you?'

He reached across the bar and gripped Sally Bannerman's arm, wrenching it painfully. She gasped and dropped the bottle onto the counter. Whiskey spilled out. Dawson grabbed the bottle and turned it upright, still holding tightly to the woman's arm.

'Alvin, stop! You're hurting me,' she said. Outrage suffused her voice.

Alvin Dawson laughed harshly and then shoved her back toward the wall behind her. He lifted the bottle and was about to refill his shot glass when a shadow to his left caused him to turn his head.

Will Curtis pulled the half-empty bottle from Dawson's fingers.

'I don't know who your pa is, smartass,' Curtis said through teeth clenched with anger. 'But it's too bad he never took the time to teach you some manners. Now I guess I've got to do it for him.'

Dawson's mouth was agape as Curtis spoke, as if no one had ever dared to speak to him in such a manner. His nostrils flared with rage.

'How the hell are you going to teach me, you lowdown sheep-herder?' Dawson asked.

'Well, like this, for starters,' Curtis responded.

He raised the bottle and brought it down with all of his strength across Alvin Dawson's brow. The bottle shattered and blood spilled out from the man's hairline, flowing freely down his face. Dawson fell against the bar and then toward Curtis, who kindly stepped aside and allowed him to fall hard onto the plank floor of the saloon.

Curtis raised his eyes to Sally Bannerman's.

'You won't have to worry about him having a sixth drink,' he said. 'He's done for the night.'

He turned and walked back to his stool in front of the mirror. He resumed sipping slowly at his whiskey.

Sally Bannerman stood perfectly still, watching Curtis with widened eyes.

'Mr Curtis, I think you're going to have to leave,' she said, her voice trembling just slightly. She looked toward the door through which Evans had disappeared. 'Right now.'

Curtis polished off the last of his whiskey and wiped his lips with the back of his hand.

'What's the rush?' he asked.

Sally realized that his nonchalance wasn't an act.

'If Evans comes back and sees this — ' she began.

The door burst open all the way and Evans's massive frame filled the doorway.

'What the hell is going on here?' he exclaimed. His eyes fell upon the inert form sprawled on the floor. He stepped into the room and nudged Alvin Dawson with the toe of his boot. There was no response. Blood dripped from the wound on Dawson's forehead onto the floor.

'I think your little friend is having a nap,' Curtis said. 'I guess learning to treat a lady with respect exhausted him.'

Evans raised his head, raking his eyes across Will Curtis.

'What'd you say?' he asked.

Curtis turned sideways to face Evans, resting his left elbow on the bar as he did so.

'So you're deaf as well as ugly?' he asked.

Evans's eyebrows shot up incredulously. He stepped past Dawson and stared hard at the drifter at the other end of the bar.

'You just hit Alvin Dawson,' Evans explained. 'Do you know who his pa is?'

Curtis emitted a threadbare chuckle.
'No, I don't. You his pa's errand boy?'

Evans stiffened. 'Let's just say I handle things for Clem Dawson,' he said. 'He's a big man around these parts. He don't like strangers.' He paused for a moment and looked down again at the man on the floor. 'Especially strangers who beat up his kid.'

'Has Clem Dawson met his kid?' Curtis asked sarcastically. 'He might end up wanting to slap the brat around a little, too.'

Evans moved back the sides of his trenchcoat, revealing a Colt .44 in his holster. Curtis pushed himself away from the bar. He moved a chair out of the way so that the space between himself and Evans was unobstructed. His right hand dangled near his holster.

'What's your name?' Evans asked.

'Will Curtis.'

'You ready to die, Will Curtis?'

Curtis smiled sourly.

'Ready as I'll ever be.'

Evans's eyes narrowed. Curtis expected him to draw at any moment, but the man stayed still. Curtis decided it was fear. Like Alvin Dawson, Evans wasn't a man who was used to being challenged. He seemed confused by the turn of events in this quiet little town where he intimidated almost everyone.

Curtis was tired of waiting.

'Make your move. Otherwise quit wasting my time,' he said, his tone clipped.

Evans waited a moment longer, then his hand blurred toward his gun. By the time he cleared leather, Curtis had already dragged his Navy Colt from its holster and leveled it with the other man's chest. The pistol roared and flame erupted from the muzzle.

Evans stumbled, his gun tumbling from his fingers onto the floor. He looked down at his chest. Blood was spreading from a hole in his sternum. He clawed desperately at his shirt, ripping off a couple of buttons, then his eyes rolled back and he collapsed awkwardly, toppling over a table with a loud crash as he fell.

He was dead before he hit the floor.

2

The smell of powdersmoke was thick in the air in the seconds after Evans fell to the floor. Curtis slid his pistol back into its holster and slowly exhaled. He swiveled his head toward Sally Bannerman, whose face was contorted with horror at what she'd just witnessed.

'Sorry, ma'am,' Curtis said sincerely. 'The man was going to draw on me no matter what.'

Her green eyes regarded Curtis for a moment. She seemed to regain her composure.

'Mr Curtis, I thank you for coming to my aid. I'm sorry it led to this,' she said, gesturing toward the two men lying motionless on the floor.

'Some people just want to have a quarrel, come hell or high water,' Curtis asserted.

One of the doors opened upstairs

and Curtis turned to see an elderly man descending the steps in his pajamas, a shotgun clutched in his hands. The man looked from Sally to Curtis, and then to the men on the floor.

'What in God's name happened?' he cried.

'Pa, this is Will Curtis,' Sally said, pointing at the drifter. Curtis nodded at the man with the shotgun. 'Alvin Dawson got rough with me and Mr Curtis stepped in. That's when Evans came in and started the gunfight.'

'He lost,' Curtis said, deadpan.

'You better hit the trail, and quick,' the old man said to Curtis. 'Someone's bound to have heard that gunshot. We'll have visitors soon.' The man came the rest of the way down the staircase and extended a hand toward Will Curtis. 'I thank you for coming to my daughter's aid. Not a lot of men around here who would stick their necks out like that. My name's Cecil Bannerman.'

Curtis took the man's hand and shook it.

17

'Pleased to meet you, sir.'

The old man looked down at Evans's corpse.

'Tabor Evans,' he said. 'I always figured he'd end up this way. No-good sidewinder for as long as I've known him.' He glanced at his daughter. 'You doing OK, honey?'

She nodded. 'I'm fine, Pa. Probably just have a bruise on my arm where he squeezed me.'

Sally Bannerman had barely finished her sentence when the batwings parted and a baldheaded man looked through. He took in the situation at a glance and backed out of the doorway into the night again.

'Earl Jackson,' muttered Cecil Bannerman. 'Damnit. It won't be long before more of Dawson's boys show up.' He gestured toward his daughter. 'Sally, you get ready right quick and take Mr Curtis out to your uncle's place.'

Without a word, Sally came out from behind the counter and ran up the steps. Curtis heard a door open upstairs. Bannerman faced him.

'My brother died a couple months ago,' he explained. 'Left us his property. There's a cabin there where you can hole up.'

'My horse wouldn't make it far right now anyway,' Curtis noted. 'I'll be happy to borrow your cabin for a brief spell.'

'Good,' Bannerman said. He sighed heavily. 'I'm afraid you rode into town at a bad time, Mr Curtis. Lot of bad stuff happening around here these days.' He pointed at Alvin Dawson. 'Mostly because of him and his pa.'

'His pa's got a lot of money, huh?'

'Yes, he does. But he wants more. Lots more. And he figures the people of this town are either going to help him get richer or pay for his failure.'

Curtis frowned. 'What's his game?' he asked.

'He owns the bank and almost half of the businesses in town,' Bannerman said. His face was somber. 'Now he

19

aims to go into the ranching business. He's been putting the squeeze on a lot of the local homesteaders, including my brother.'

Just then they heard the door close upstairs and watched Sally Bannerman race down the steps. She wore a flannel shirt, Levis, and a dark floppy hat, along with riding-boots.

'Ready?' she asked Curtis coolly.

'Hell, yes,' he responded. He shook hands with Cecil Bannerman again. 'Thank you, sir.'

'No, thank *you*,' Bannerman replied. 'Something like this was bound to happen, with the men Clem Dawson's been bringing to town. You just happened to be the match that lit the fuse, so to speak.' He shook his head quickly. 'All right, enough jawing — you two head out. Sally, after you get Mr Curtis settled, head on out to your brother's place. I'll come over tomorrow afternoon.'

She nodded and led Curtis through the batwings. He donned his slicker and hat again, then unhitched his horse from the post.

'This way,' she said, leading him to an alley between the saloon and the livery next door. He cast a quick glance down Main Street and observed lights in a large house several doors down from the Bannermans' establishment.

'That Clem Dawson's house?' Curtis asked.

She looked where he pointed.

'Yep,' she said. They both saw human shapes stirring in the shadows in the front yard of the Dawson place. 'We got to get going.'

She walked rapidly down the pitch-dark alleyway. It was barely wide enough for Curtis's horse, which he led by the reins, following closely behind the young woman. They emerged into a much wider alley that ran along behind the buildings on Main Street. She led them across the alley to a small stable where she and her father kept both of their horses. A little over two minutes later she had saddled her horse and was ready to ride.

They both mounted after she led her horse from the stable and closed the door behind them. Loud voices were coming from the front of the saloon.

'Looks like Pa has company,' Sally said. She neck-reined her horse around and touched spurs to its flanks. The animal took off quickly, cantering back in the direction from which Will Curtis had come to town. He spurred his animal to follow her and they rode into the darkness, the only light coming from the silvery moon that loomed above the forested peaks around the town.

★　★　★

It was about an hour before they reached the cabin.

Sally Bannerman led Will Curtis out of town and through the foothills, taking a circuitous route that avoided the main road. They emerged from the trees and pulled leather on the edge of a misty forest pasture. The cabin was a dozen yards from the rim of the trees. It was completely dark, with shuttered windows.

'This is it,' she said. 'There's a little barn around back where you can put your horse.'

They dismounted and led their horses by the reins to the barn. She tied her mount to a pole outside while Curtis led his into a stall. He unsaddled his horse and rubbed it down with a handful of hay. He removed a bag of oats from a saddlebag.

'I'll go in and build a fire while you do that,' Sally said.

'I'll be just a minute,' he said.

She left and before he had finished with his horse he could smell wood smoke coming from the stone chimney at the back of the cabin. He closed the stall and then shut the door to the barn. She had lighted an oil lamp in the kitchen and he could see her through the window as he approached the back door, carrying his bedroll with him.

He opened the door and stepped into the cabin. It was very clean, although a little musty. He closed the door behind him and grinned faintly.

'This is a pretty nice place,' he said.

She was looking in a cupboard near the woodstove and turned around when Curtis spoke. She pushed a stray lock of hair from her face.

'Thanks,' she said. 'My uncle was a very tidy bachelor. I come out every few weeks and air it out, get rid of the dust and cobwebs.'

'I'm sure he'd appreciate that.'

She turned back to the cupboard and removed a tin of coffee. There were also a few cans of beans and a can of strawberries.

'Well, there're a few things here you can eat. And there's plenty of coffee. I'm sure Pa will bring some food out for you when he comes tomorrow.'

Curtis sat down on one of the two chairs by the kitchen table. He removed his hat and laid it over his knee. His eyes were red and weary as he scrubbed a hand down his face.

'You know,' he said with a grin, 'I don't even know the name of your town. I didn't see any signs when I rode in.'

'It's Junction City,' she said. 'Where are you from originally?'

'Hard to say,' he said. 'I've lived in lots of places around the Oregon and Idaho line.'

'What brings you around here?'

'Oh, just drifting around mostly. Never been to the Willamette Valley and always heard about it, so I thought I'd check it out myself.' He wiped some dirt from his palm onto the leg of his pants. 'My sister and her husband own a place down by the California border. I figured if I didn't find anything to do around here then I'd mosey on down there a spell.'

'What do you think so far?' she asked with a sardonic smile.

'It ain't boring, that's for sure.'

'Not right now, anyway,' she said. 'It

was different before Clem Dawson came to town.'

'How long ago was that?'

She considered the question. 'Probably around five years ago, now.'

Curtis took out the makings and began to roll a smoke.

'Where'd he come from?'

'Portland, I think,' she said. 'I got the impression he wanted to be a big fish in a little pond, if you know what I mean.'

'I do,' Curtis said. 'Looks like he succeeded.'

Her mouth tightened. 'Not in an honest or decent way, he didn't. He did it by bullying people and hiring thugs to get what he wanted.'

Curtis licked the cigarette paper and scraped a match down the heel of his boot. Cigarette smoke billowed out of his mouth as he listened to Sally speak.

'Alvin's just as bad as his pa, but in a different way,' she continued. 'He's always pawing after girls, whether they like him or not.'

Curtis blew a smoke ring and poked

his finger through it.

'Who in hell'd like that little yellow belly?' he asked.

'Good question.'

He chuckled and took another drag.

'How did Evans fit into all this?' he asked. 'Or is he paid to be Little Alvin's nanny?'

'He is — er, was Clem Dawson's enforcer. Part of his job was keeping Alvin under control.'

'He a drunk?'

'Not always, but he has his moments. Especially when he and his pa are fighting. That's when Evans stepped in to keep Alvin in line.' She arched an eyebrow. 'As you saw tonight, it didn't always work.'

Curtis grunted inscrutably, pondering the situation into which he'd wandered.

'What about the law?' he asked finally. 'Ain't there a sheriff around here, or a town marshal?'

'There are deputy sheriffs in Eugene,' she said. 'But they don't come out to

27

Junction City very often. Plus, Clem Dawson has deep pockets. He's become a good friend to the sheriff. It's an open secret around here — the bribery, that is.'

'Well, what are the locals around here going to do about it?' There was a tinge of exasperation in Curtis's voice.

'I don't know,' she said tentatively. Her face darkened slightly. 'Now that Dawson's planning on becoming a big landowner, the people out here in the hills are starting to feel the pinch, too. Used to be he limited his harassment to the city folk, like my pa. The farmers and ranchers turned a blind eye most of the time. Now they can't afford to do that, unless they're willing to let Dawson ride roughshod over them.'

'How many of them stand up to him?'

She shook her head sadly. 'Not many. My uncle did, when Dawson came out here and made him a cash offer. Uncle Chuck told him to go to hell. Not long after that they tried to burn down the cabin with him in it.'

'I'll be damned,' Curtis said quietly.

'Luckily he was a light sleeper. He came out with his rifle and scared Dawson's men away before the fire spread. He was able to put it out himself.'

'So Dawson's willing to murder innocent people to get what he wants?' Curtis asked in a grim voice.

'Oh, he won't hesitate to murder someone if that's what he thinks needs to be done.'

'What are you and your pa going to do?'

Her even white teeth tugged pensively at her bottom lip.

'I don't know,' she said. 'Especially after tonight. I think we might just have to sell up and leave town.'

'I'm sorry I made it worse for y'all.'

She met his gaze. 'There was going to be a confrontation with Clem Dawson or his son one way or another, Mr Curtis. Please don't apologize. I'm just relieved that you weren't hurt or killed.'

Curtis's face brightened. 'Mighty kind of you, ma'am,' he said. He stifled a yawn and looked down the hallway. 'Well, I better be getting some shut-eye. I got to be ready for anything come morning.'

'Yes, of course,' she said, slightly embarrassed. She stepped toward the back door. 'Please just make yourself at home. You might want to keep the windows shuttered and only build a fire at nighttime. Dawson's men might come snooping around here.' She turned the handle on the door. 'My pa will be here in the afternoon to check in with you. Take care, Mr Curtis.'

Curtis rose and smoothed down his greasy hair.

'Thank you, Miss Bannerman. I hope to see you again, real soon.'

She smiled shyly and stepped out, closing the door behind her. Within twenty minutes Curtis was asleep in his blankets on a cot in one of the bedrooms. His rifle was leaning against the wall beside the bed, and on a table nearby was his Navy Colt.

*   *   *

Cecil Bannerman came early the next afternoon. His face wore an anxious expression. Will Curtis came out from the back door to meet him.

'Morning, Mr Bannerman.'

'Call me Cecil,' the old man said, dismounting a few feet from Curtis. 'As long as I can call you Will.'

'I wouldn't have it any other way,' Curtis said. He noticed Bannerman was wearing a pistol on his belt. 'Everything all right in Junction City?'

'For the time being. A couple of Dawson's men showed up right after y'all left last night. They took Alvin home, and then Clem Dawson himself made an appearance. I told them a stranger had come and killed Evans and knocked out Alvin, and that I didn't know anything more than that.'

'Did they ask where Sally went?'

'Yeah, they did. I said she was so upset by the gunplay that she'd ridden out to her brother's place. I told them you lit out right after shooting Evans and that I thought you were headed for the California border.'

'Has Alvin woke up yet?'

Bannerman smiled. 'Just this morning. Evidently he doesn't remember anything about last night.' He tied his horse to a pole outside the barn and removed a burlap sack containing biscuits, jerky, and bacon from one of his saddlebags. 'I brought this for you. Should keep your belly full for a couple of days. I don't think it'll be safe to ride out before then. Dawson's got some of his men combing the hills looking for you. They won't check here, though. It's too far out of the way.'

He hefted the sack and handed it over to Curtis.

'Thanks, Cecil. I appreciate it.'

'Not a problem. And by the way, I was thinking about something ... ' Bannerman said a little tentatively.

'What's that?' Curtis asked.

'Well, I figure you've probably done quite a bit of ranch work.' Curtis nodded. 'My son has a hundred-acre spread a little east of here. I know he's been needing some help, but he has a hard time finding it because Dawson's men tend to run off strangers — especially strangers who are good with a gun and know how to run a ranch.' Bannerman paused and cleared this throat. 'Anyway, what I'm getting at is maybe you'd like to stick around a while and do some work for my boy. What d'ya think?'

Curtis pursed his lips thoughtfully. 'I don't want to bring Dawson's men down on your son.'

'Don't you worry about that,' Bannerman said confidently. 'Abe can handle himself.' He held up a hand. 'Just let me talk it over with him today. I have to go out there and get Sally. I'll come back by in a few hours and let you know. You can think it over in the meantime.'

'All right,' Curtis said. 'I got no problem with that.'

'Good. Now you get yourself something to eat.'

Bannerman untied his horse and clambered up into the saddle. Curtis watched him ride out across the yard and disappear into the trees. He went back into the cabin and made himself a meal while he waited for Bannerman to return.

Hours passed. Curtis was sleepy after his meal and took a nap on the cot in the bedroom. He was surprised to awake and find that Bannerman still hadn't returned. He lay in the cot for a few minutes, dozing lazily, then decided to make some coffee. He was boiling water in the kitchen when some movement in the trees across the yard caught his attention through the grimy kitchen window.

It was a horse. More importantly, Curtis realized after a moment, it was Cecil Bannerman's horse. There was no sign of the saloon owner, although the animal still had a saddle cinched around its middle.

The hair was already bristling on the back of Curtis's neck when the horse halted near the back door. Curtis opened the door to take a closer look. He saw thick smears of wet blood on the empty saddle, leading in a stream down a strap to the right stirrup. Drops of blood fell from the edge of the stirrup onto the grass.

'Judas priest!' Curtis whispered to himself.

His hand flashed to his hip and palmed the Colt in one smooth movement. He backed into the kitchen and kicked the back door closed. He stepped toward the kitchen window and moved into the shadows by the wall. He had a good view of the south side of yard then, and he was in a position where no one outside could get a good view of him.

His eyes scanned the trees across the yard, where Bannerman's horse had emerged. It wasn't long before he saw movement among the branches. He sucked in a sharp breath when he saw two horsemen ride into the yard and walk their horses toward the back of the cabin.

They moved out of Curtis's line of sight and he took the opportunity to cat-foot down the hallway into the living room. He was glad that all of the windows were shuttered except for the two in the kitchen. Once in the living room, he stood in a position in which he could see down the hallway without being observed by the men in the yard.

There was a window in the back door and through it Curtis observed the two horsemen pull reins by the woodpile. He could see them more clearly now, and he recognized their breed instantly. They were hardcases, hired guns. Curtis had no doubt whom they worked for and why they were here. They were Dawson's men, and they must have been following Cecil Bannerman.

Judging from the amount of blood on Bannerman's saddle, the old man was either dead or dying. No one could lose that much blood and still be on his feet.

He watched the men tie their mounts to the pole outside the barn. One of them took the reins of Bannerman's horse and looked it over, saying something as he did so that made the other man chortle. Curtis couldn't hear what they were saying, just the mumbling of voices.

Adrenaline flowed through Curtis when he saw them approach the back door. The first man leaned toward the window in the door. He shaded his eyes with his hand and looked into the kitchen. Then he reached down and opened the door.

Curtis, lurking in the shadows of the living room, knew what was coming. If these men found him, and he assumed they soon would, then they would try to kill him. He had been around and seen enough professional killers to know these men's methods. He would have to kill them if he wanted to get out of this cabin alive. Curtis thumbed back the hammer and waited, unconsciously holding his breath.

The door pushed open and the men stepped cautiously into the kitchen. Curtis backed further out of sight. His pulse pounded in his ears and everything seemed to be moving slowly.

'Anyone here?' one of the men called. 'We're looking for Cecil Bannerman. He around?'

Curtis was silent, his body tensed for whatever was about to take place.

The men were in the first bedroom now. He heard them move a few things around and then step back into the hallway. They were moving toward the second bedroom, where his bedroll and rifle were. They would know someone was in or around the cabin when they saw Curtis's things. He decided to act while there was still an element of surprise in his favor.

He swiveled away from the wall toward the hallway and raised his pistol.

'Afternoon, gentlemen,' he said evenly. 'Out for a little bushwhacking?'

The men froze in place, staring at Curtis in shock. Neither had a pistol in hand. Curtis suspected they hadn't tangled with anyone around Junction City who gave them a run for their money. That was why they'd gotten sloppy.

'Who the hell are you?' the first man asked with a sneer.

'This is private property,' Curtis said. 'Trespassing is against the law, you know.'

'We ain't stealing nothing,' the second man said. 'Like we said, we're just looking for Cecil Bannerman.'

'Shut up,' Curtis commanded. 'You're lying. Now pull out your pistols and throw them on the floor, nice and slow.'

The men exchanged glances before moving to obey Curtis's order. The first man pulled out his pistol and lobbed it a few feet ahead of him onto the wooden floor.

'Now you,' Curtis said to the second man.

'You got it,' the man responded.

He was dragging the pistol out of its holster when he made his move. His partner crouched and leapt forward onto the floor while the big man behind him drew. The man was confident of his abilities, probably mistaking Curtis for a local cowpunch without much skill in the gun department.

Curtis was momentarily distracted by the man on the floor, and the second gunslinger was able to get a shot off. It hit the wall inches away from Curtis's face, shearing off shards of wood. Curtis fired without aiming and made a lucky shot. The bullet went straight into the second man's throat, causing a grotesque spray of blood to spurt across the wall in the hallway. The man dropped his gun into the bedroom doorway and grabbed for his throat, trying to stop the bleeding with his hands. Blood oozed between his fingers, flowing freely from the severed artery in his neck. He fell forward onto his knees, held steady there for a moment, then collapsed onto his partner's legs just as the latter reached desperately for his own pistol. Pinned by the dead weight of his partner's corpse, the drygulcher screamed in helpless terror, his outstretched fingers falling short of touching the gun by mere centimeters.

'Golly, you really want that gun, don't you?' Curtis asked. He stepped forward and brought the heel of his boot down on the man's fingers.

'No!' the killer said. 'Oh, please!'

Curtis crushed the man's fingers under his boot, feeling the snap of bone and cartilage. He lifted his other foot and put all of his body weight on the man's hand. The man released a wail of pain such as Curtis had never heard in his life.

'Where's Bannerman?' Curtis asked coldly, releasing a bit of the pressure from beneath his boot.

'Let me go, please! Oh, God — my

fingers!' the man bleated.

Curtis leaned down a little closer.

'I guess you didn't hear me,' he said. He pressed down with his boot and felt something crunch in one of the fingers beneath it. The man howled, tears streaming down his face.

'I don't know where Bannerman is,' he cried. 'I swear! Just let me go — I'll give you anything!'

'I got all I need,' Curtis said casually. 'And you're a liar. I won't ask you again, feller. Where's Bannerman?'

'He's out there in the woods.'

'Alive?'

'I think so.'

'You shoot him?'

'No,' the man said, jerking his chin toward his partner, whose lifeless body still clung to his ankles. 'He shot him. Got him somewhere below the ribs. I can show you where Bannerman is. You get him to a sawbones in Junction City in a hurry and I bet he pulls through.'

'That's awful Christian of you,

friend,' said Curtis witheringly. 'You must have a lot of love for your fellow man.'

He leaned down and picked up the man's gun from the floor, then stepped back, his pistol still fixed on the pinned man, who now held his mangled fingers to his chest, moaning quietly.

'Get up,' Curtis said.

The man pulled himself forward on his elbows, thrashing his legs out from under the corpse. He used his uninjured hand to push himself up and stand before Curtis. A thick film of sweat was layered across the man's face and neck.

'You're going to show me where to find Bannerman,' said Curtis.

'Then you'll let me go?' the wounded killer whined.

'Hell, no. You'll be lucky if I don't plant a bullet in your brain, you slick little weasel. I'd turn you over to the law, but I've been told what little law there is around here is owned lock, stock and barrel by Clem Dawson. So maybe I'll turn you over to Bannerman's son. I heard he lives not far from here.'

'Honest, sir — I wasn't going to hurt Bannerman. I was just doing what I was paid to do.'

'Which is?'

'Dawson wanted Bannerman followed.'

'Why?'

'Because . . . he thought Bannerman might lead us to whoever it was that killed Evans and smashed that bottle over Alvin's face.' The man looked down at Curtis's gun. 'I guess it was you, wasn't it?' Curtis said nothing, and the nervous man continued speaking, trying to calm his own nerves. 'We looked for Bannerman earlier in the afternoon but didn't find him until about a half-hour ago, heading this way.'

Curtis wondered where Sally was.

'Was Bannerman alone?' he inquired sharply.

'Yeah, he was.' The man's mind was

racing, searching for any kind of angle that would get him out of the situation. 'I'll show you where to find the old man. I've tried to help you. I've just been doing my job when it came to Bannerman. I didn't know anyone was going to end up dead.'

'Sure you didn't,' said Curtis, not altogether reassuringly. A thought occurred to him. 'Any more of Dawson's boys running around besides you and your late friend?'

A second passed, then the man said, 'No, just us.'

Curtis didn't believe him. He swung the barrel of the gun toward the back door.

'Git,' he said.

The man stepped over his partner and walked toward the kitchen. Curtis followed close behind, the muzzle of his pistol pressed firmly into the man's back. Curtis's shoulder brushed some of the dead man's blood-spatter on the wall as he stepped over the body.

'What's your name?' Curtis asked.

'Kantor,' the other man said, once more holding his injured hand gingerly against his chest. His teeth gritted with pain. 'Mack Kantor.'

'Open the door, Kantor.'

The man did as he was told and seconds later they were standing in the grass behind the house.

'Stop right there,' Curtis said.

He had decided to tie Kantor up before they went to search for Bannerman. He was stepping toward the barn to fetch a rope when the gunshot sounded from the trees. He felt the burn of the slug as it passed his left shoulder, digging a groove through his flannel shirt before passing into the barn wall a few feet away. Curtis swore as pain shot down from his shoulder through the length of his arm.

He pivoted and saw a burst of flame from among the trees. Another bullet came toward him, thudding into the grass near his feet. He dived behind a stone trough by the barn door. A third bullet ricocheted off the trough and lodged into the barn.

'Kill him!' screamed Mack Kantor. 'Kill that son of a bitch!'

Kantor turned and ran toward the trees, although not in the direction from which the gunfire was coming. Curtis swiped his pistol from the holster and observed Kantor's legs through the gap beneath the trough. He carefully took aim and fired, a wry smile creasing his face.

The bullet hit Kantor in the back of his right ankle, tearing through his Achilles tendon before lodging somewhere in his foot. Kantor leapt into the air, yelling frantically. He hit the ground clutching his ankle with his one good hand and rolled in the grass, howling in pain.

That's for Cecil Bannerman, Curtis thought. Then his grazed shoulder throbbed and his brief moment of satisfaction ended.

3

The gunmen had been distracted by Kantor's flailing in the grass, but not for long. Bullets started to pepper the trough and the barn wall above it. From the angle where the gunmen were positioned they were unable to hit Curtis under the trough. The firing went on for a few more minutes, during which Curtis saw Kantor drag himself into the trees on his elbows. Between the crushed hand and the shattered ankle, Kantor probably wouldn't be doing much bushwhacking for a while. Curtis was pleased.

Curtis's ear was near the ground, so he heard the other riders approaching. They were coming from the east, and there were many of them; at least five, he figured. In less than a minute the men in the trees became aware of them, too. The firing ceased and Curtis heard confused voices chattering. Shortly thereafter the men who had been shooting at him were mounted and riding away. Curtis could see some of their movements through the trees. They were heading west, toward Junction City.

Curtis rose cautiously, his eyes peering over the rim of the trough into the maples and firs where the gunmen had been hiding. There was no sign of them, or of Mack Kantor. Curtis assumed that Kantor's friends had helped him mount his horse and leave with them. The appearance of Dawson's other men confirmed Curtis's earlier suspicion about Kantor's veracity when the man had claimed there were no other men in the hills looking for Cecil Bannerman. Lying, however, was probably the least of Mack Kantor's crimes.

The horses were close now. Curtis rose and took a step toward the back of the cabin. The riders burst out of the trees to his left before he could take another step. His hand moved toward his hip but the leader of the riders already his pistol in hand and pointed at Curtis.

'Stop it right there, feller,' the man yelled, pulling on his horse's reins. The other riders followed suit and stopped close behind the leader. 'Put those hands up.'

Curtis cursed silently and obeyed the order.

'What's your name?' the rider asked.

A woman's voice responded before Curtis did.

'Will Curtis,' it said. Then Sally Bannerman rode around to the front of the pack of riders. 'It's all right, Abe. This is the man I told you about.'

The leader of the riders stared hard at Curtis, suspicious of any new faces in the Junction City area, particularly those of strong young men such as Curtis. Newcomers who fit that description tended to work for Clem Dawson.

'Howdy,' Abe Bannerman said. His

expression softened but only a little. Curtis could see a resemblance between Abe and his sister, now that he looked at the man more closely.

'Is my pa here, Mr Curtis?' Sally asked anxiously.

Curtis had a sinking feeling as he shook his head.

'No, ma'am, I'm sorry to say he ain't. His horse rode in alone a while back.' He looked around but didn't see Bannerman's mount. It must have wandered off into the trees. 'I was going to put it in the barn, but then some of Dawson's hired guns showed up.'

Abe Bannerman's mouth fell open. 'You know who it was?' he asked.

'One of them was named Mack Kantor,' said Curtis, who noticed the change on the rider's facial expression at the mention of the name. 'He had a partner with him.'

'Probably Butch Muller,' Sally said, looking toward her brother. He nodded.

'Well, he's still here,' Curtis explained. He pointed toward the cabin. 'He's in there, in the hallway.'

'Tied up?' Bannerman asked.

'Dead,' Curtis said plainly.

Abe Bannerman dismounted, handed his reins to his sister and stepped into the cabin through the back door. Presently he came back out.

'It's Butch Muller all right,' he said.

'They came here asking about your pa,' Curtis said. 'But they knew his horse was running around. They saw it in the yard.' He frowned. 'Did Cecil make it out to your place today, Abe?'

Bannerman shook his head.

'We were expecting him but he never came. That's why we rode out here to look for him.'

Sally was visibly fearful.

'Abe,' she said, 'we need to find Pa. Now.'

'I know it,' he said deliberately. He introduced the three other riders to Curtis. 'Mr Curtis — '

'Call me Will.'

'All right, Will — this is John Wilson, Phil Shirreffs, and Jake Douglas.

They're neighbors of mine. They've been having problems with Clem Dawson, too.'

'Pleased to meet you, gentlemen,' said Curtis with a nod.

'Will, would you mind staying here with Sally while we search the woods for my pa?'

'Now, just a minute,' Sally replied, her face flushed with anger. 'That's my pa, too. I don't need to be left behind here like a kid.'

'Sally, there are men still hiding out in the woods. Dawson's men. If we took you along and something happened to you, you know Pa would never forgive me.'

Sally Bannerman was quiet, then nodded reluctantly.

'Fine,' she said. She glanced at Curtis. 'You don't mind staying here?'

'Not at all.' Curtis pointed to the trees on the west side of the barn. 'That's the direction your pa's horse came from.'

Abe Bannerman put a foot in a

stirrup and swung up into the saddle. He pulled the reins and turned the horse around to face where Curtis had pointed.

'All right, fellers,' he said to the other horsemen. 'Let's take a look around.'

The group touched spurs and rode across the yard into the trees.

'I need to reload,' Curtis said, pulling his pistol from the holster. 'I got my rifle in there, too.'

Sally dismounted and led her horse into the barn while Curtis went back into the cabin. When she came out a short time later she saw Curtis dragging Butch Muller's body out of the house. He laid it in the grass behind the barn and covered it with a tarp he found in a lean-to near the woodpile.

Sally got water from the pump and cleaned up the blood in the hallway while they waited for the riders to return. Then she made coffee and sat down at the table, watching Curtis as he looked periodically out the windows for any sign of approaching horsemen.

More than an hour passed before Abe Bannerman returned with the other riders. His blunt features were drawn and grim, telling both Curtis and Sally everything they needed to know.

Sally ran from the back doorway to her brother, who stepped down from his horse and put his arms around her.

'Tell me it's not true, Abe,' she said desperately, tears streaming down her face.

The muscles in Bannerman's jaw clenched, as if to keep him from telling her what he'd found.

'I'm sorry, Sally.' He put his hand over his eyes for a moment and took a deep breath. Having regained his composure, he held his sister against his chest.

Curtis stood by in silence, observing the scene. Anger was rising steadily within him as he thought of Cecil Bannerman, a man whom he had barely known. The brevity of their relationship didn't matter to Curtis. He had liked Bannerman and seen him as a man of integrity. Now that man was dead, killed by Clem Dawson. Beneath the anger and sadness, Curtis also recognized that it had been his own actions in the bar in Junction City that had brought the conflict out into the open. He felt a responsibility to stick around and help Abe and Sally Bannerman — and hurt Clem Dawson.

Sally Bannerman's voice cut through Curtis's somber reverie.

'Where is he, Abe?' she asked. She looked toward the other horsemen. 'What happened to him?'

'He's about a mile from here,' her brother responded carefully. 'I want you to go with Phil and head back to my place for the night.'

'No!' she hollered. 'I want to see him. What if he's not dead, Abe? I can help him, maybe — '

'You can't do anything for him, Sally. I wish you could, but it's too late. And I don't want you to see him like that. Please, just do as I ask.'

'He was my pa, too,' she said, tears streaming anew.

'I know, Sally,' Abe Bannerman said soothingly.

Phil Shirreffs cleared his throat.

'Miss Sally, your brother's just looking out for your feelings,' he said. 'We all respected your pa. I don't think he'd want you to see him like that.'

Her eyes darted to Shirreffs.

'It's that bad, is it?' She looked at her brother. 'It's that bad?'

He nodded slowly and then removed a handkerchief from the inside pocket of his coat. He handed it to her and she wiped her face.

'All right, Phil,' she said finally. 'Let's go back to Abe's.'

'Yes, ma'am,' Shirreffs said.

She brought her mare out of the barn and mounted.

'Thank you, Will,' she said to Curtis, using his first name now. 'We'll all understand if you want to leave after everything that's happened.'

Curtis made a dismissive gesture.

'Miss Bannerman, I'll stick around as long as y'all will have me. It's personal to me now. Your pa wouldn't be dead right now if I hadn't come into your saloon last night. And a man who was paid by Clem Dawson pulled a gun on me last night. He would've killed me if he'd been a little faster. That don't exactly make me take kindly to Dawson.'

Curtis thought there was a new element of respect in the way Abe Bannerman looked at him.

'We're much obliged to you, Will. If my pa thought highly of you, then that's all I need to know. We'll be glad to have the help. We're going to need it.'

Phil Shirreffs led Sally Bannerman across the yard to where the trail vanished in among the trees. The remaining men watched them depart.

'I'll get my horse,' Curtis said. He returned shortly and mounted.

Abe Bannerman led the way, followed closely by Curtis, Wilson, and Douglas. They found Cecil Bannerman's horse not far away, idly munching grass. Douglas tied a rope to it and brought it with them. It was late afternoon when they emerged from the trees into a small forest clearing and pulled leather. As they did so Curtis observed Cecil Bannerman's body near the edge of the clearing, lying beside the base of a massive maple.

The old man's death had been far more painful and gruesome than Curtis had expected.

He was bound with barbed wire, the spikes cutting into his parchment-like flesh. His throat had been slashed so deeply that his head lolled at an awkward angle. Curtis counted three bullet wounds in his chest.

'My God,' he murmured. 'Who the hell would do something like this?'

'Dawson,' Abe Bannerman said.

'Or the men Dawson pays,' said Jake Douglas. He was a big man with enormously broad shoulders. His clean-shaven features glowed in the late-afternoon sunlight. 'Those hired guns he brought to town will do anything for the right price.'

Curtis nodded. 'I can see that.'

The body was covered in blood, the throat having been cut so deeply that the result had almost been decapitation. This wasn't a typical level of range violence, such as Curtis had encountered at various times in his wanderings. Usually that entailed no more than a bullet to the head or the heart. This was different. Any person who would order a murder like this was interested in more than taking over other people's land — that person wanted to instill terror in anyone who considered resisting him, and was more than willing to employ even the most brutal methods to attain what he desired.

The men dismounted and removed the barbed wire from Bannerman's body. Then they wrapped him in a blanket from John Wilson's saddlebag and secured the blanket with a rope. Curtis helped Douglas secure the body over the late man's horse.

'We'll bury him back at my uncle's place,' Abe Bannerman said.

Dusk had fallen by the time the men completed their task and departed for Abe Bannerman's ranch.

★ ★ ★

Sally was waiting for them on the porch when they rode in. Wilson, Douglas, and Shirreffs left for their respective homes not long after.

Curtis went into the house and looked around. It smelled like cooking. Abe Bannerman's wife came out from the kitchen to greet the men. She was a tall, handsome woman with a friendly disposition, although Curtis also detected signs of strain in her prematurely lined face. He wondered how long Clem Dawson had been making things hard for the local homesteaders.

'Pleased to meet you, Will,' Maggie Bannerman said. 'I hope you're hungry.'

Curtis grinned. 'I've never had much trouble rustling up an appetite.'

'Good,' she said. She gestured toward her husband. 'Abe don't eat nearly as much as he used to, ever since these problems with Clem Dawson started.' She searched Bannerman's face. 'God, Abe. It's your pa, isn't it?' She clutched a kitchen rag in her hand, twisting it in her fingers as she waited for Bannerman to answer her.

'Maggie, Pa is . . . dead.'

She gasped and shook her head.

Bannerman looked at his sister. 'You didn't tell her?'

She shook her head. 'I didn't want the kids to hear,' she explained apologetically.

'Where are the boys?' Bannerman asked his wife.

'Down at the creek. They should be back any time now.' She dabbed at her eyes with the cloth. 'Jesus help us, Abe. They killed Cecil.' Curtis could tell that the woman's mind was having a hard time believing it. 'What are we going to do?'

'We're going to fight,' Bannerman said curtly. 'We're going to fight hard, and when we're done old Clem Dawson will wish he'd picked another little town to try to take over.'

'He'll kill us all,' Maggie said. 'Or at least he'll try.'

'He won't succeed,' Curtis said. 'I swear I'll do whatever I have to do to help keep that bastard from running y'all off your land.'

'You see?' Bannerman said to Maggie. 'We've got a little extra help now. Will's good with a gun. He outdrew Evans and shot him dead in a fair gunfight. No one else around Junction City would have had the guts to try that, let alone pull it off. That's why Dawson is panicking.'

* * *

Clem Dawson leaned back in the plush chair, carefully toasting the edge of his cigar with a match before fully lighting it. He puffed luxuriantly and released a creamy plume of cigar smoke into the air above his head. He tossed the used match into a metal wastebasket by his chair.

Five men stood across the desk from Dawson. They lingered in uncertain silence, waiting for him to speak. He lifted his eyes and stabbed them at the men, then regarded the tip of his cigar for a moment. Finally, he spoke.

'Where's Mack Kantor?' he said softly.

He liked to speak quietly in moments of tension; it made the men who worked for him listen a little extra carefully.

'He's at the sawbones' place,' one man said. His name was Cal Hamilton and he was one of the newest of Dawson's hires. He was a large man with a grim visage and, as far as his employer could discern, no sense of humor whatsoever. Not that Dawson cared. He didn't pay them to laugh at his jokes.

And at this moment, he wasn't in a joking mood.

'What kind of shape is he in?'

'His ankle was damn near blowed apart,' Hamilton said. 'Wouldn't be surprised if Doc has to amputate.'

Dawson raised an eyebrow and shook his head.

'A damn shame. Couldn't have happened to a nicer feller.'

Four of the five gunmen smiled at Dawson's joke. Hamilton was the exception.

'And Butch Muller?' Dawson asked.

'Dead,' said Hamilton simply.

Dawson sighed heavily and organized some papers on his desk. He sat back and folded his hands across his stomach.

'This will not stand, gentlemen,' he said, rolling the cigar from one corner of his mouth to the other. 'I pay you all well, I think you'll agree.' He paused. 'Am I right?' He looked from man to man. There were no complaints about compensation. 'In exchange for the wages I pay you, I expect a certain level of professionalism in return. I don't think that's too much to ask. And yet, I seem to be mistaken.' He removed the cigar from his mouth and regarded it for a moment. 'Evidently it is too much to ask, given the carelessness with which Kantor and Muller acted today.'

One of the men appeared like he was going to say something, but a frigid glance from Dawson cut him off.

'Now,' Dawson continued between puffs on his cigar, 'Cecil Bannerman is dead. That makes one of their men for three of mine, if we remember the late Mr Evans. The important thing is that the conflict has now moved out into the open.' He tapped the thick ash off the end of his cigar into an ornate ashtray on the desk. 'We will have to seize the initiative, if you will.'

The office door opened and Alvin Dawson stepped in, his head still bandaged from his encounter with Will Curtis. He closed the door hurriedly and sat down in a leather chair across the room from his father, who gave him a brief stare laced with contempt.

'Mr Hamilton, I have designated you to be the leader for the time being. Your pay will increase according to your level of success.' Hamilton nodded curtly, his features inscrutable. Clem Dawson felt a twinge of irritation at the man's permanent poker face. 'I don't want any mistakes from now on. If you fail, I'm sure one of your . . . colleagues will be ready and willing to take over.' He stubbed out his cigar carefully and leaned forward on the desk, his fingers interlaced before him. 'I want you to ride out to Abe Bannerman's place and burn it to the ground. Tonight. I'm not telling you to kill anyone, but if any fools decide to get in your way, then you do what you have to do. Am I clear?'

There was a faint glimmer in Hamilton's eye as the man nodded.

'I have tried to be reasonable with the people in this town, but my attempts have fallen on deaf ears,' said Dawson, examining his fingernails as he spoke. 'If the people around Junction City won't listen to reason, then maybe they'll listen to force. If you pull this off properly, Hamilton, then this will likely be a one-time deal. The homesteaders will see the light and I can start building a real future for this town.' His eyes narrowed as he met Hamilton's gaze. 'Don't let me down.'

'We'll take care of it,' Hamilton said evenly.

Dawson made an impatient gesture.

'All right then, hit the trail. Time is money.'

The gunmen exited through the office door and left the Dawson house. Clem Dawson turned his attention to his son, who sat in silence across the room.

'You made quite a mess, Alvin. I've had to take drastic measures to maintain our family's name.'

'That man insulted me, Pa. And that bitch Sally Bannerman did, too.'

Clem Dawson flinched. 'You know,

Alvin, sometimes the sheer depth of your stupidity appalls me.'

A dark crimson color spread from Alvin Dawson's throat up into his cheeks. He clenched his teeth together but lowered his eyes to the carpet. He despised his father, but he feared him even more.

'Here's what you're going to do, Alvin. You're going to go upstairs and get in bed. You need rest to recover from your injury. You're not going to come out for a few days. I don't want you causing any more problems than you already have.' Dawson pushed back his chair and stood up. He was a portly man, with silver hair that was mostly gone on top. His thick mustache was neatly trimmed and combed. 'Just stay out of the way. I'll deal with you soon enough.'

Clem Dawson strode out of the room and his son could hear his footsteps recede down the hallway.

Alvin Dawson remained seated for a few minutes, rage and humiliation coursing through him so powerfully that his chest felt tight. He had felt anger against his father many times before — indeed, more times than he could count. But this was different. This was two humiliations: the one he received from Will Curtis at Bannerman's saloon, and now the command from his father to stay hidden in bed while *real men* cleaned up the mess Alvin had made.

I wouldn't care a bit if the old man died, Alvin Dawson thought. *I wouldn't shed a single tear for that son of a bitch.*

An image flashed through his mind, and part of him recoiled from it. He saw himself standing over his father. Blood trickled from Clem Dawson's mouth, and he cringed in fear of his own son. He saw himself raise a pistol and, ignoring his father's pleas for mercy, fire a shot into the elder Dawson's heart.

He shook his head and scrubbed a hand across his face. Then he climbed upstairs and went back to bed.

4

Will Curtis and Abe Bannerman stood in the darkness of the latter's front porch, smoking cigarettes and talking quietly. Maggie, Sally, and Abe's two young sons had all gone to bed, their moods somber. The shadow of Cecil Bannerman's death was like a dark cloud over the family. Curtis, too, was pensive.

'We're going to have a meeting in the morning at Phil Shirreffs's place,' said Abe Bannerman. He flicked the remains of his cigarette into the darkness beyond the porch. 'We're going to have to get organized.'

'Sally going to stay out here for now?' Curtis asked.

'Yeah. I think that's best.'

'Probably so,' agreed Curtis. 'What about the place in Junction City?'

'I know my pa would've locked up

the saloon real careful, so I'm not worried about it right now.'

'Good.' Curtis stifled a yawn. 'I'll take the first watch, like we discussed. You look like you could use some sleep.'

Abe Bannerman rose. In the silvery moonlight, his features were downcast but stoical. He put a hand out toward Will Curtis.

'Thanks for everything,' he said. 'It's probably going to get pretty hairy around here. I'm glad to have your help.'

Curtis rose and gripped Bannerman's hand.

'I'm happy to help. I got a taste of the way Dawson wants to run that town, and I didn't like it.' He hesitated momentarily. 'Also, I'm real sorry about your pa, Abe. I can't pretend to have known him well, but what I did know, I liked.'

Bannerman looked off into the yard, memories of his father crowding his weary mind.

'He was a good man,' he said.

'Always took good care of his family.' He exhaled a breath slowly. 'Anyway, I'll be up in a few hours to take over.'

He went into the house, leaving Will Curtis alone in the cool night air. A light rain began to fall a few seconds later.

★   ★   ★

Three hours passed. Curtis had made his rounds about the property roughly every thirty minutes. He walked around the cabin itself, scanning the woods around the property as he did so. He walked around the stable and over to the bunkhouse, where the two men who worked for Abe and Maggie Bannerman slept. He could hear them both snoring loudly inside the small building.

There was no sign of anyone lurking in the shadows.

Curtis knew that Abe Bannerman would soon be appearing, ready to take over the watch. He decided to take one last lap around the property before he was relieved. He moved quietly, staying in the dark areas as much as possible.

A cold wind stirred the grass as he passed around the back of the cabin. He was rounding the corner of the bunkhouse when he saw the two men scurry into the trees. His big Navy Colt was in his hand and he aimed where the men had run, firing off three quick shots.

Curtis backed up beneath the eave of the bunkhouse near the woodpile, his eyes scanning the rim of the forest. He heard movement in the bunkhouse and knew his shots had awakened the two ranch hands.

Then he smelled the smoke.

It was coming from the other side of the bunkhouse. His lips tightened. So that's what those two had been doing.

He turned and shouted over his shoulder toward the house.

'Abe! We got a fire out here.'

The door of the bunkhouse burst open and two men came out in their

74

underwear. One had a Winchester in his hands, the other a pistol.

The smoke was thicker now.

Curtis ran toward the back of the bunkhouse, followed by the ranch hands. Flames were swirling across the entire back wall of the building. The fire had already reached the roof and was spreading rapidly. He was relieved that neither man had still been sleeping inside. They would likely have died in the fire before they knew what had happened.

The heat and smoke repelled Curtis and the two others. As he backed away from the fire he noticed the door of the cabin fly open. Abe Bannerman emerged from the house, pulling on a shirt. A pistol was tucked into his waistband. He ran toward Curtis and had nearly reached the back of the bunkhouse when gunfire erupted from the trees beyond.

Curtis swore. They'd been so distracted by the fire that he'd nearly forgotten about the men who'd set it.

The bullets tore into the wall near Curtis, sending shards of wood raining down on his shirt. Both of the ranch hands went down. The older of the two, an elderly man with a long white beard, was clearly dead. The other rolled around on the grass, clutching his abdomen and moaning in agony. Curtis pivoted and stepped toward the fallen cowpunch, despite the bullets hammering into the ground at his feet. He reached out toward the man and had just clutched his arm when a bullet sank into the man's right temple, spurting blood and brain matter across Curtis's shirt. He released the man and followed Abe Bannerman around the building, the roof of which was now completely engulfed in flames.

They raced across the yard away from the bunk-house. After a short respite, the gunfire once more followed them. Curtis was a feet few behind Bannerman when a bullet blurred past his left shoulder, missing him by no more than an inch. They barely made it to the porch before the full firepower of Dawson's men was unleashed on the cabin. Windows shattered and bullets ricocheted around Curtis and Bannerman as they dived through the door into the dark living room.

The smell of gunsmoke was thick in the air. Bullets pounded into the walls above them.

A voice came to them over the roar of the firing guns. Maggie Bannerman's voice.

'Abe! Are you all right?'

'I'm OK.' Bannerman moved forward on his hands and knees toward the hallway across the room. Will Curtis followed. A stray bullet smashed into a picture on the wall above. It tumbled down, smashing Curtis on his right ear and drawing blood. He ignored the pain until he was safely in the hallway.

On the floor outside one of the bedrooms were Maggie, Sally, and the two young Bannerman boys, Ben and Sam. Abe Bannerman crawled forward and embraced his wife. The bullets kept coming, hammering relentlessly into the cabin.

'Who is it?' Sally Bannerman cried, holding her hands over her ears.

'Dawson's men,' Curtis said. 'No doubt about it.'

'What about the men in the bunkhouse?'

Curtis shook his head soberly. Sally Bannerman understood his meaning.

'The evil bushwhackers,' she said.

Curtis turned to Abe Bannerman and leaned close so that he wouldn't have to yell as loud to be heard.

'You got any ideas? They don't seem like they're going to let up any time soon.'

Bannerman wet his lips with his tongue and looked around the cabin, his face a mask of concentration. He focused on something on the kitchen floor, and Curtis twisted around to see what he was looking at. There was a large rug on the floor there, between the dining table and the wood stove. Curtis turned back to Bannerman, who met his gaze.

The gunfire diminished for a moment, as several of Dawson's men reloaded at the same time.

'I've got a tunnel to my spud cellar,' Bannerman said. He pointed at the rug on the kitchen floor. 'There's a trapdoor under that rug. It leads to the tunnel.'

Curtis frowned. 'When did you put in the tunnel?'

'It was already there when we bought the place,' Bannerman explained. The gunfire had increased again now. 'Never thought I'd be using it to escape from my own house.'

He looked again at the rug, then motioned for Curtis to follow him. They bellied across the floor into the kitchen. A bullet pinged off a skillet hanging on the wall near the stove and both men paused, covering their heads with their hands, before moving on to the rug. Bannerman pulled the edge of the rug back, revealing a plank door in the floor, about three feet square.

Just then the firing stopped entirely.

Powdersmoke drifted on the night air and the sudden silence was eerie. A voice called to them from outside.

'You in there! Listen up and listen good. We know you had something to do with killing Tabor Evans in Junction City. We also know you killed Butch Muller. Come out and have a talk with us. There's been enough killing. We just want to talk.'

Curtis and Bannerman exchanged sardonic glances. Abe Bannerman leaned on one elbow and cupped his hands to his mouth to project his voice.

'Y'all killed my pa,' he called. 'You also killed two of my men out there. Did you forget about that?'

There was a pause before the voice outside responded.

'Either way you look at it, there's been enough killing,' the voice said. 'Let's work this out without any more blood being spilled.'

Bannerman reached out and pulled the latch on the trapdoor, which he swung open, revealing a pitch-black void beneath the floor. The hair bristled on the back of Will Curtis's neck as he pondered crawling through the tunnel. He ignored the anxious sensation when he considered the alternative.

Bannerman called again to the band of killers waiting outside.

'Y'all can rot in hell! Do your best, you bunch of lowdown sidewinders. Anyone who comes close to this house will end up eating lead!'

He looked at Curtis and grinned, then waved the women and children over into the kitchen. When they reached the trapdoor he reached up and pulled an unlit lantern down from the kitchen table.

'Have it your way, Bannerman,' the voice called from outside. 'That was your last chance to be reasonable.'

A few seconds later the barrage of gunfire erupted again, assailing the cabin anew.

Bannerman handed the lantern to Curtis.

'You go first,' he said. 'Don't light the

lantern until you're at least five feet into the tunnel. We don't want anyone outside seeing the light.'

Curtis nodded. The moonlight was sifting through a shattered kitchen window, illuminating the entry into the tunnel a little better. He could see the sturdy-looking wood that helped support it. Whoever had built this tunnel had known what he was doing.

Curtis lowered his feet into the tunnel and then stood up. Only his shoulders and head protruded from the kitchen floor. He took a match from his shirt pocket and knelt down, moving forward into the musty darkness in a crouching position. He had probably gone forward seven or eight feet when he paused, thumb-snapped the lucifer alight, and lit the lantern, keeping the wick turned down low.

When he turned back toward the entrance he could see two legs coming down as the gunfire continued to thunder through the house above him. The legs made the small jump onto the dirt below and Curtis saw Sally Bannerman's nervous face in the dim lamplight. She moved down toward Curtis and was quickly followed by Ben and Sam Bannerman and then their mother.

'They're lighting the house on fire,' Maggie Bannerman said. Her scared eyes glinted in the lantern light.

'Bastards,' said Will Curtis bitterly.

Abe Bannerman dropped into the tunnel and pulled the trapdoor closed above him. Will Curtis turned up the wick on the lantern. He saw two pistols in the waist of Bannerman's pants, and the rancher held a rifle in his hands.

'Let's move,' Curtis said, turning and moving forward on his hands and knees. The others followed closely behind. He could hear them scuffling through the dirt as he crawled. Bright light spilled through the cracks in the trapdoor.

'The house is burning down,' Abe Bannerman said.

Curtis heard Maggie cry out quietly,

although she didn't slow down. The crackling sound of burning wood had replaced the sounds of gunfire.

There was a dank smell in the tunnel, and the dirt was a little moist. There was a tight constriction in Curtis's throat, but he powered through his innate claustrophobia, almost irritated with himself for having such a serious physical reaction to the enclosed space. The tunnel seemed endless, and Curtis had to force himself not to ask Abe Bannerman how much further it was to the spud cellar.

'It's not much further, Will,' Bannerman said, as if reading Curtis's mind.

Curtis held the lantern directly in front of his face and saw the end of the tunnel about a dozen yards of ahead of him. He crawled a little faster, eager to reach his destination.

At the end of the tunnel was another trapdoor.

'Go ahead and open it,' Abe Bannerman said. 'But for God's sake be quiet about it.'

Curtis pushed his hands against the trapdoor, which moved up, revealing a small cellar containing several burlap sacks filled with potatoes. Curtis climbed out of the tunnel and reached down to help the others. He had turned down the lantern again.

Abe Bannerman closed the trapdoor after emerging from the tunnel. He and Curtis moved toward the solid wooden door. The walls and ceiling of the cellar were dirt. It appeared to Curtis that they were standing inside a small hill, somewhere on the Bannerman property. He had no idea where he was relative to the house.

Bannerman pulled the door open a couple of inches and Curtis looked out with him. Now he knew where he was. The spud cellar had been built in the side of a tree-covered foothill on the west end of the property. The house was between him and Dawson's men, whose yelling voices carried over the sound of the fire. By this time the entire roof of the cabin was aflame.

'As far as those sons of bitches know, we're all still in there,' said Bannerman, his voice suffused with icy rage.

'They're goddamn child-killers,' Curtis said, shaking his head.

His eyes flicked to the two young boys sitting close to their mother against the far wall of the cellar, then back to the burning house across the yard from him.

Clem Dawson evidently wasn't a man to quibble over minor details like children dying in a fiery inferno. That was clear. And for what? Curtis thought. To be the king of Junction City, a piddly, isolated little town that no one had ever heard of?

A man on a large gelding rode around the cabin, careful to keep his distance from the burning structure. Bannerman stiffened and pushed the cellar door a little more closed. He and Curtis regarded the rider, who was silhouetted against the flames, in silence for a moment. Then the rider finished his lap around the house and disappeared on the other side.

'You got any ideas?' Bannerman asked.

'You got any neighbors nearby?'

Bannerman nodded. 'Phil Shirreffs lives about two miles south of here.'

'Let's send the women and the boys to his place. I take it Maggie knows the way.'

'The boys do, too.'

'Good.' He turned to Sally, who had stepped up behind the two men. 'Sally, you and Maggie are going to take the boys over the Shirreffs place.'

Sally Bannerman raised an eyebrow.

'What're you two planning to do?' she asked.

'We're going to make these gunslingers wish they'd never heard of Junction City,' said Abe Bannerman.

'What if they kill you?' Sally asked incredulously.

'Ain't going to happen,' Curtis retorted.

'I can shoot as well as either of you,' Sally said. Curtis turned and looked at

87

her. 'You think I'm kidding?'

Something about her face brought Curtis up short.

'No, ma'am,' he said. 'I don't think you're kidding.'

Abe Bannerman pulled one of the Colt pistols from his waist and handed it to his sister.

'Sally, you are a damn good shot,' he said. 'That's why I need you to go with Maggie and the boys.' When Sally began to protest, Bannerman held up a hand to quieten dissent. 'What do you think Pa would want you to do?'

Sally's hard glare softened. She looked down at the pistol in her hand, which was trembling slightly.

'All right, Abe,' she said. 'You win.'

'There's a first time for everything,' Bannerman said with quiet exultation. Curtis and Sally smiled, grateful for at least one moment of levity.

'I won't let it happen again, you can bet on that,' Sally said.

Bannerman waved his wife and children over.

'Y'all are going over to Phil Shir-reffs's place,' he said. 'Sally has a pistol.'

'What about you two?'

'Don't worry about us. We're going to be careful. You know that.'

'I know,' Maggie said. Abe patted his boys on their heads. 'Boys, you take care of your mother and your Aunt Sally, y'hear?'

'Sure, Pa,' said Ben Bannerman. Curtis figured the boys were eight and ten years old, or thereabouts. They looked like serious boys.

Curtis peered through the doorway, his shoulder throbbing. He saw men on horseback pull reins on the side of the house, sinister in the firelight. One reached into a saddlebag and removed a bottle. He used his teeth to remove the cork, which he spat toward the flames. He drank deeply, then passed the bottle to his friend. Neither looked toward the spud cellar.

'Those fellers ain't from around here,' Abe Bannerman observed. 'They don't know about this cellar.' He looked at his wife and his sister. 'Y'all ready?' They nodded and he turned the lampwick almost entirely down as Curtis opened the door.

A few birch trees stood not far from the cellar door. They obscured the movements of the women and the children as they exited the cellar and moved off in darkness toward the forest beyond the edge of the yard.

They were stealthy and silent in their movements. The two horsemen continued to pass the whiskey bottle back and forth, oblivious to the movements in the trees. One of them tossed the empty bottle into the house just as the roof collapsed. The riders laughed uproariously and heeled their mounts back toward the barn.

Curtis and Bannerman made their move. They cat-footed out through the door, closing it behind them. They moved into the trees to their right and used the cover of the dark forest to move around to the other side of the yard, between the bunkhouse and the barn. Here they had a complete view of the front of the incinerated house.

Curtis was relieved that the buildings were far enough apart for the barn not to have caught fire. He could hear the horses stirring in their stalls, terrified by the sounds of the gunfire and the smell of the smoke.

Bannerman handed his last remaining pistol to Curtis, keeping the Winchester for himself. He levered a bullet into the chamber.

There were five men in the yard, all mounted. Each had a rifle in his scabbard and a pistol strapped to his hip. They were sitting their horses, staring at the fire.

By now they must think everyone in the cabin had been killed, either by a bullet or by the fire, Curtis thought. He noticed that they almost looked bored by the entire process. This was not their first time killing people, he thought, or burning down houses. When Dawson hired gunmen, he chose real professionals.

'You take the two on the left,' Curtis said tightly, thumbing back the hammer on his Navy Colt. 'I'll take the three on the right.'

5

Will Curtis and Abe Bannerman aimed carefully. Because they hadn't been spotted by Dawson's men, they took their time and made their bullets count.

Bursts of orange flame erupted from the muzzles of their guns as they fired. Although it was an unspoken agreement, both men were shooting to kill. The horsemen across the yard from them were hired killers who had just attempted to massacre an entire family — for money. As far as they knew, they had succeeded. They had chosen their line of work, and now they would take the consequences of their actions.

Their first shots blasted two of the gunmen out of their saddles. They collapsed forward, face-planting onto the ground with the solidity of dead weight.

Curtis's second shot was a miss due

to the startled horses of the three remaining killers. Bannerman connected, however, hitting the middle rider in the back of the neck. The rider tumbled sideways out of the saddle and his horse reared, pawing at the air in terror before breaking into a run toward the trees across the yard. The man's left foot remained stuck in the stirrup, and he screamed as the horse dragged him like a rag doll into the shadows.

'What the hell?' the gunman on the left hollered, hipping in the saddle and looking toward Curtis and Bannerman's position. His hand streaked toward his pistol, but before he could clear leather his body jerked as one of Curtis's bullets tore into his collarbone. He gasped and leaned forward, clutching the saddle horn and trying to steady himself. He reached again for his gun but was cut down by a bullet that penetrated his skull just above his right ear. He crashed from the saddle onto the ground, further propelled by his fleeing horse.

Only one of the Dawson men remained. He neck-reined his horse and looked toward Curtis. For a moment the cowboy thought the man was looking right into his eyes, although he knew that wasn't possible. Curtis raised his pistol toward the gunman, but before he could fire he heard the report of Bannerman's Winchester from a few feet away. A large chunk of the brim of the horseman's hat flew off and drifted toward the grass.

The man dug his spurs deeply into his horse's ribs, sending the animal into a panicky, full-speed gallop away from the cabin and toward the forest. He disappeared through a dense plume of black smoke that was drifting across the yard from the burning cabin. No longer able to get a shot off, Curtis lowered his gun and looked toward the three unmoving shapes scattered across the Bannermans' yard. They were well illuminated in the light of the fire.

★   ★   ★

It was less than an hour later when Curtis and Bannerman rode into Phil Shirreffs's yard. Dawn had appeared above the tree-cloaked ridges that surrounded the property.

Shirreffs was standing on his porch sipping a cup of coffee. His expression was serious as he greeted the two riders.

'Morning, Abe.' He nodded at Curtis. 'Will.'

'Morning, Phil,' said Bannerman as he and Curtis dismounted. They tied their horses to a pole near the porch. 'I'm sure Sally and Maggie have filled you in.'

'They have. They're all asleep inside.' He lowered his voice a little. 'Did you fellers manage to turn the tables on Dawson's boys?'

Curtis smiled thinly. 'We got four out of five of 'em.'

'Good to hear that,' said Shirreffs. 'What're we all going to do next?'

Bannerman folded his arms and leaned against the porch rail. Curtis removed the makings from his pocket and began to build a smoke.

'I think y'all are going to have to take the fight to Dawson,' Curtis said as he twisted the end of his cigarette. 'You can be sure that he'll plan on killing anyone who stands in his way now. He's going to be real ornery when he hears how many of his hired guns bit the dust.'

Shirreffs glanced at Bannerman.

'What do you think, Abe?'

'I don't see how we have any other choice,' Bannerman replied. 'Unless you call getting run out of our homes a choice.'

'I don't.'

'Didn't think so. But Dawson's playing for keeps, Phil.'

'I can see that,' Shirreffs said thoughtfully. His eyes regarded Curtis appraisingly. 'You sure you want to get all mixed up in this?'

'I ain't got nothing else going on right now,' said Curtis in a relaxed tone. 'Once Tabor Evans pulled that gun on me, I decided to take a special interest in Clem Dawson.' He took a long drag on his cigarette. 'Not to mention his chickenshit son.'

Bannerman chuckled. 'That Alvin makes me want to retch. I've heard that even his own pa can hardly stand him.'

Curtis raised his head. 'That right?'

'Yeah, I've heard that, too,' Shirreffs added. 'Heard his pa bit the kid's head off in the bank in front of a whole bunch of folks a while back.'

'Maybe that's why Alvin likes his whiskey so much,' said Curtis.

'What do you mean when you say we should bring the fight to Dawson?' Shirreffs asked.

Curtis frowned. 'He's vulnerable right now,' he said. 'Almost every one of his bushwhackers is dead. He won't have had time to call in any reinforcements yet.' He smiled faintly. 'It might be a good time for one of us to pay a visit to Mr Dawson.'

'He's still got one gunslinger working for him,' Bannerman said.

'I know,' Curtis said. 'I can handle him, though.'

'So you're volunteering?' Shirreffs asked.

'Yeah, I guess I am. I know where Dawson lives. Sally showed me after I met Alvin Dawson and Tabor Evans.'

'You're going to need some help,' Bannerman said.

Curtis shook his head.

'Not for this chore I don't. Dawson won't be expecting it. That'll make my job that much easier.' He glanced toward the door of Shirreffs's house. 'You don't need to take any unnecessary risks.'

'What do you have in mind?'

A cunning smile tugged at the corner of Curtis's lips.

'Well, I was thinking I would ride into town tonight . . .'

★ ★ ★

It was a foggy night, with intermittent rain. Junction City was immersed in darkness when Will Curtis halted his horse in the alley behind Sally Bannerman's saloon.

He tied his horse to a pole by the back door and stood in the shadows, watching and listening. His eyes scanned the rutted alleyway for any signs of movement. After a few minutes he was satisfied that no one had seen him.

Curtis was glad Junction City was a small town without much in the way of nightlife. Now its sole saloon was closed and the streets were virtually deserted. Peering down the alley toward the south end of town, he saw no signs of life. He turned and started walking in the direction of Clem Dawson's house.

He had removed his spurs and left them in his saddlebag. He didn't want them chiming and betraying his approach to anyone who might be looking for him. His right hand gripped the butt of his Navy Colt, ready to swing it into action at the first sign of danger. But there were no such signs, even as he came upon the back yard of the Dawson residence.

He took cover behind a large apple tree at the rear left corner of the yard. His breathing was shallow and his heart pounded in his chest. The yard was well maintained, with rose bushes and neatly trimmed grass. A thick tangle of ivy climbed up the back of the house, showing clearly in the moonlight.

Curtis was patient. He knew Dawson still had one man left, and he figured that man was somewhere out here in the night air, waiting and watching just as Curtis was. After almost five minutes, however, he was beginning to question that assumption. Nothing stirred in the darkness behind Dawson's house. From where Curtis was standing, he could see the entire north side of the house and part of the front yard. He saw no movement there, either.

What if the last of Dawson's gunmen had skipped town? Curtis thought. Maybe he'd been so scared by seeing

Dawson's other men shot down that he'd lit out. This had turned into a more dangerous job than the man had anticipated, Curtis was sure. Men had abandoned jobs for less.

Curtis had just taken a step toward the back porch when he heard a cough. A tingle snaked down his spine and he hastily moved back behind the tree. He unconsciously loosened his pistol in its holster, all his senses attuned to the danger he sensed.

He tried to get an idea of where the cough had come from, his eyes piercing the pools of darkness around the yard. There was a large laurel bush near the back steps of the house. Curtis was watching it closely when he heard another cough. It was coming from behind the bush, which was well over six feet high.

Curtis fixed his eyes on the bush and tensed. A man moved out from behind the bush and paused near the steps. He was a big man with a cruel face. He scratched a finger along his jawline and moved his gaze around the yard. His glance passed over Curtis, who held his breath and rested his thumb on the hammer of his pistol. To his relief, he hadn't been spotted in the darkness beneath the apple tree, and the man continued scanning the rest of the large back yard with the dark eyes that looked to Curtis like bullet holes.

When he had finished looking the yard over, the man started walking toward the outhouse, which was located about ten feet from the tree behind which Curtis stood. Curtis examined the man closely. He was wearing a black trench coat and a big brown Stetson. Curtis noticed that a large chunk of the brim on the right side of the hat was missing. He knew exactly where the man's hat had been damaged.

Sure that he hadn't been seen, Curtis watched the man open the outhouse door and step inside. It was a few minutes before the man emerged, wiping his hands on the legs of his pants. He carefully closed the door behind him and was turning back to his position behind the laurel bush when Curtis stepped out from behind the tree, his pistol fixed on the gunman. The man froze.

'Hands up,' Curtis said softly. The man hesitated and Curtis knew what he was thinking. 'You'd better be real sure before you make a move. 'Cause I'm sure — you can bet on that.' Moonlight reflected off the barrel of Curtis's gun.

The man cast a murderous glare at Curtis and slowly raised his hands.

'Higher,' Curtis commanded, his voice still quiet but menacing. The man obeyed.

Curtis gestured toward the shadows behind the apple tree.

'Git,' he said. The man walked cautiously toward Curtis, who waved the pistol further into the darkness. 'Couple more feet.' The man moved forward, the tree blocking any possible view of the exchange from within the Dawson house.

'What's your name?' Curtis asked.

'Cal Hamilton.'

'You picked the wrong man to work for, Cal Hamilton,' Curtis said. Hamilton's mouth twisted into a smirk, and Curtis's anger intensified. 'Don't believe me? Ask your four friends. You know — the ones you left in the yard out at Abe Bannerman's place.' The smirk left Hamilton's lips. 'Boy, you rode out of there real fast like, Cal Hamilton. I wouldn't be surprised if you shit your pants on the way.'

Hamilton's face was harsh as his eyes bore into Curtis's. Curtis had no doubt that, if he could, Cal Hamilton would have blown him away right there where they stood.

'Pull your pistol and toss it on the ground, Cal Hamilton. You ain't going to need it any more tonight.'

Hamilton hesitated again. Curtis decided the man needed a little encouragement.

Before Hamilton knew what was happening, Curtis took a swift step toward him, swinging the heavy pistol up into the man's throat. Hamilton tumbled backward, gasping for breath and clawing at his throat. His trench coat fell open, revealing the ivory-handled Remington pistol inside the killer's fancy embroidered holster.

The fingers on Hamilton's right hand twitched and he made a move toward the weapon, his left hand still clutched at his neck. Curtis threw himself atop the man, thrusting his knee hard into Hamilton's chest and pressing the barrel of the Navy Colt against his nose, which bent and flattened awkwardly against his face.

'Just try it, friend,' Curtis hissed through his teeth, leaning in close. 'You tried to kill an entire family last night. You think I forgot that?'

Hamilton's eyes were wide with fear. He threw his arms out to show that he was no threat to Curtis.

'It wasn't my idea,' he said as he grimaced in pain. 'Honest. I didn't know they were going to light the cabin on fire.'

Curtis snorted with disdain. 'Yellow-bellied, lyin' dry-gulcher. You make me sick. You knew exactly what was going to happen. You just didn't figure we'd get the drop on you. I guess your dead buddies didn't figure on that either, did they?'

Hamilton was silent, warily watching Curtis, whose anger seemed to overflow from within him. Curtis's finger was on the trigger and the hammer was pulled back. Hamilton could feel his hot breath in his face. He was fairly sure that Curtis was going to kill him, right there by the apple tree in Clem Dawson's back yard.

Curtis struggled to tame the killing urge within him. He realized he was clenching his teeth so tightly that it hurt. He could see the naked fear in Hamilton, even though the man's face was partially obscured in shadow.

He reminded himself that he had come into Junction City this night to fulfill a task. If he shot Cal Hamilton here he would undoubtedly awaken anyone in Dawson's house, and probably several of the man's neighbors as well.

Curtis relaxed his jaw and some of the tension seemed to leave his body. He slowly put the hammer back down, and Hamilton exhaled with audible relief.

'Don't go celebrating quite yet, Hamilton,' said Curtis.

He swiftly raised the pistol away from Hamilton's head and then brought it down hard, cracking the gunman across the left side of his skull. The skin split and blood began to flow freely down Hamilton's neck and into his shirt. Hamilton's eyes rolled back in his head and his body went limp.

Curtis dragged him a little further back into the darkness and removed some pre-cut lengths of rope from the pocket of his sheepskin coat. He bound the unconscious man at the wrists and ankles, then stuffed a handkerchief into his mouth and tied another one around his face, gagging him.

He dragged Hamilton behind the outhouse, where he dropped him in some bushes. Then he turned and strode purposefully toward the back door of Clem Dawson's house.

He climbed the steps carefully. They didn't creak beneath his feet. He paused momentarily and looked back toward the outhouse. There was no movement in the bushes where he'd deposited Cal Hamilton.

Curtis tested the doorknob and was surprised when the door opened, revealing a dark kitchen beyond. His earlier supposition had been correct: Clem Dawson wasn't expecting anyone to make a move on him in his own house. Either that or he still had a lot of unwarranted confidence in Cal Hamilton's abilities. Whatever the case, Dawson's laxity had made Curtis's job much easier.

Curtis stepped through the door and closed it quietly behind him. He waited for his eyes to adjust. Pale moonlight spilled into the room through a large window near the stove. The kitchen was large and very clean. He could discern no sounds of movement within the house. He leaned down and removed his boots, tucking them under his left arm as he drew his pistol with his right hand.

He moved around the large cutting table in the middle of the kitchen and entered the hallway, where he again paused before continuing on toward the front of the house. There was no one in the parlor or the living room. A lantern burned dimly in Dawson's office beyond, on the other side of the living room. No one was in the office. There was a closed door across the hall from the parlor entrance. Curtis figured it was the maid's room; he listened at the door for a minute but heard nothing inside.

He moved toward the stairway in the hall. The steps had a thick carpet on them and Curtis smiled, glad that Dawson was so dedicated to comfort in his home. He climbed the steps noiselessly and peered around the wall into the dark hallway on the second floor. Three doors opened off the hallway; two on the right and one on the left.

The door on the left had to be Clem Dawson's, Curtis decided.

He stepped to the door and reached for the knob. He had barely touched it when the door slid open a few inches. Curtis couldn't believe that Dawson was sleeping with his bedroom door unlocked, let alone ajar. Suspicious now, he dragged his pistol from leather and leaned forward, peering into the dim room.

A lantern was turned down low on the end table beside Dawson's bed. A pistol lay beside the lantern on the table. Curtis's eyes swiveled to the bed. He could see a shape lying there. It was the bulky shape of Clem Dawson, sleeping deeply. Curtis could hear the slow rhythm of Dawson's breathing.

He watched the sleeping man for a moment, then entered the room, closing the door softly behind him. There was no change in Dawson's slumber. His right hand still held the pistol, which he held out toward Clem Dawson. For all he knew, the man had another gun hidden under his pillow. Curtis wasn't taking any chances. If Dawson tried any gunplay, he'd be dead before he could do any damage.

Curtis made his move. Within seconds, he had crossed the room and was standing beside Dawson. He lifted his Colt and brought it down as hard as he could onto Dawson's pasty right ankle, which protruded from the silk sheets.

Curtis could feel the crack of metal against bone. Dawson was suddenly wide awake, his eyes bulging. He opened his mouth to scream but Curtis moved forward and clamped his strong, rough hand over the lower part of the banker's face, stifling any cries. Curtis raised his Colt and pressed the end of the muzzle against Dawson's cheek. He leaned forward and spoke quietly.

'This would be a very bad time for you to scream,' he said menacingly. 'It could be bad for your health.'

Dawson nodded quickly.

'You're not a very nice man,' Curtis continued. 'I guess you think you own this town, don't you?' Dawson didn't respond, but kept his fearful eyes on Curtis's. 'You're going to learn a lesson, Dawson. You shouldn't have played around with the Bannermans or their neighbors. Are you starting to understand that?'

He pressed the muzzle deeper into Dawson's cheek, making an indentation in the man's thick flesh. 'You're going to pay for what you did to Cecil Bannerman. Only a lowdown yellow snake would hire gunslingers to do his dirty work for him.' He leaned in closer toward Dawson's face. 'You tried to kill Abe Bannerman and his entire family. Two little kids, Dawson. They'd have been burnt alive in that cabin. And why? What do the Bannermans have that you want?'

The reptilian eyes regarded Curtis, who pulled his hand away from Dawson's mouth to allow the man to answer the question. Curtis kept the muzzle in his face.

'You got it all wrong, Curtis,' said Dawson, his oily voice low. 'I never wanted Cecil dead. Those men did it without my authorization.'

'Why?' Curtis demanded skeptically.

'Because of Evans. He was their friend. They wanted revenge. I tried to call them off, but they wouldn't listen to reason.'

Curtis hesitated. 'Why didn't you contact the law in Eugene?'

'I want to, believe you me. But Hamilton won't let me out of his sight. He's obsessed with killing you now. He was hiding out there somewhere in the yard, waiting for you.'

'Yeah, I know. He's taking a nap in the bushes as we speak.'

'Please, Curtis. That's your name, isn't it?' Curtis didn't answer the question. 'Let me go, will you? I'll prove

I'm not behind all the violence that's been going on.'

'How?'

Before Dawson could answer, Curtis's ears pricked at the sound of a footfall in the hallway behind him. He turned his head just slightly and Dawson pounced, grabbing the barrel of the gun. He attempted to twist it out of Curtis's hand, bending Curtis's finger painfully.

Curtis smashed his left fist into Dawson's eye, forcing the man to release the gun. Dawson cried out in pain. Curtis turned on the bed and pointed his pistol at the door just as someone pushed it open from the hallway.

A gun blasted from the doorway before Curtis had time to fire. A slug slammed into the wall above Curtis's head. He ducked, spinning off the bed as he triggered a shot toward the door. The man in the doorway screamed and doubled over, then collapsed onto the rug.

Curtis leapt to his feet and looked

toward Clem Dawson, who was reaching desperately for the gun on his nightstand. He grabbed it and hoisted it toward Curtis, who fired from the hip without aiming and made a lucky shot, striking Dawson in his outstretched wrist. The gun flew from his hand and landed on the floor near Curtis's feet. Dawson clutched his arm and rolled into a fetal position, sobbing with pain and fear. Curtis kicked the pistol across the room and it disappeared beneath a large wardrobe near the window.

Curtis stared at Clem Dawson for a moment, rage swirling within him. He had never shot an unarmed man in his life, but he had to struggle mightily to keep himself from sending a bullet straight between Clem Dawson's eyes.

Boots pounded up the staircase, inadvertently saving Dawson's life.

A large shape filled the doorway.

'Curtis!' the shape yelled.

They had only spoken briefly, but Curtis recognized the voice of Cal Hamilton. How in hell had the man gotten loose? Curtis wondered. His mind went blank as Hamilton lifted his Remington and fired, narrowly missing Curtis's head. He heard the click as Hamilton's thumb pulled back the hammer for another shot. Raising his pistol, he fanned the hammer of his own gun with lightning speed, sending the rest of his bullets into Hamilton's silhouette before the killer could get off another shot.

Hamilton's body jerked and then fell like a pole-axed steer, directly on top of the other man on the floor. Neither gunman moved.

Noise from the bed attracted Curtis's attention. He turned his head and a bullet whizzed by him. Dawson was clutching a small pistol in his left hand. The drawer to his nightstand was open, and Curtis realized he must have kept a second pistol in it.

Dawson raised the weapon and fired again. The shot was wild, missing Curtis entirely. Curtis moved toward the bed with the intention of taking the weapon away from Dawson. Before the cowpunch could reach him Dawson fired again, and this time his shot was on target. It hit Curtis in the left side of his ribcage and passed through his back, sending him hurtling back against the wall. A thick streak of blood smudged the wall as Curtis slid down toward the floor.

Emboldened, Dawson steadied the weapon with his bloody right hand and squeezed off another shot, which hit the floor a few feet away from Curtis. For a moment, Curtis considered trying for one of the guns of the two prostrate men near the doorway, but this would leave him exposed to Dawson. Using every ounce of strength remaining to him, he heaved himself away from the wall and dived into the hallway. A bullet followed him, striking the door of the bedroom opposite that of Clem Dawson.

Curtis could hear Dawson moving off the bed and shuffling after him. He pulled himself to his feet and made for the stairs. Dawson sent yet another bullet after him, but Curtis had already descended the stairs and was making for the back door by that time. Adrenaline pushed him forward, despite the serious pain and bleeding in his upper abdomen. He crashed through the back door of Dawson's house and ran awkwardly down the alley in the direction of Bannerman's saloon.

He was out of the city limits within sixty seconds of mounting his horse. He had left his boots on Clem Dawson's bedroom floor.

6

Two days later fear came to Junction City. It looked like it had come to stay.

There were ten men this time, all bearing the unmistakable aura of the professional killer. Each bore a badge, too — the badge of a deputy sheriff of Lane County. Word had it that Clem Dawson had paid big money to have these men deputized. Everyone knew he had a lot of connections at all levels of government in the state of Oregon.

Weeks passed.

Dawson was taking no chances this time. His right arm was still in a sling from the bullet Will Curtis had sent through his wrist. Everywhere he went he was accompanied by three of the 'deputies' he'd brought to town. Every weekday residents would see him walk to the bank in the morning and then return home in the evening, three large, dark-visaged men walking with him, their eyes scanning the buildings around them. Two other guards were on permanent watch at the Dawson residence. The others patrolled the streets in shifts, looking for any sign of the local homesteaders who were opposing Dawson. The banker hadn't sent the gunmen into the hills to retaliate. Yet.

His son, Alvin, was bedridden, paralysed by another bullet fired by Curtis. The sawbones told Dawson that Alvin would never walk again. Although he never verbalized his feelings, Alvin Dawson bitterly regretted having taken his pistol and trying to defend his father that night. Where had it got him? A life sentence as an invalid. His father had never thanked him for the sacrifice Alvin had made on his behalf.

There was no dissent in Junction City. Local residents had been frightened of Dawson before, but now there was no question that it was his town, and that they would abide by his rules.

In the meantime, Clem Dawson was busy making plans. He knew Will Curtis was still around, hiding somewhere up in the hills among the recalcitrant homesteaders. The ranchers and farmers in the area were now united in their opposition to Dawson. Those who had wavered in the past about selling their land to him now stood firm. They wouldn't sell, no matter what the offer was.

It was now a battle of wills, and might.

But if there was one thing Clem Dawson believed, it was that every man has his price. His experiences in business and politics had taught him that, time and time again. So he planned his strategy, unworried by the opposition in the hills.

Because he had found a man — one of the homesteaders — and that man had named his price. He really had no choice.

Dawson set his plan into motion on a frosty night in late November.

★ ★ ★

Will Curtis had lost so much blood after Clem Dawson shot him that he almost didn't make it out to Phil Shirreffs's spread that night. It had taken the dedicated ministrations of both Sally and Maggie Bannerman to pull him through, along with some help from Abe Bannerman himself, who had some experience with dressing wounds.

Shirreffs had let the Bannermans and Curtis stay in his bunkhouse for a few days, and then the family had moved out to their uncle's ranch, taking Curtis with them. Abe and Maggie had decided against building a new house out at their own property. They had salvaged what they could from the charred ruins and taken it back with them to their new home.

The shot had taken out a chunk of the bottom rib on Curtis's left side. The bullet had passed through his back, somehow missing any vital organs. Curtis had slept for much of the first week after getting shot. It was early in the second week when he got up and began walking around, slowly building up his strength again. His appetite returned and at the end of the second week he began spending an hour every day at target practice, shooting tin cans off the fence at the edge of the property. A day or two later he rode his horse again for the first time.

There was a flinty determination in Will Curtis now. The women noticed it, and so did Abe Bannerman. The local homesteaders had set up patrols of their own. They rode in shifts at night, vigilant against any attacks by Clem Dawson's men. They had no doubt that the attack would come, sooner or later. Their only defense was to be prepared, and to meet fire with fire when hostilities finally did erupt out in the open. They travelled by secret trails known only to the homesteaders themselves. Shirreffs's house was the headquarters for patrollers. Curtis was determined to be part of those patrols as soon as he possibly could.

One afternoon Abe Bannerman rode into his yard after attending a meeting at Phil Shirreffs's place. He dismounted and looked past the corral. Will Curtis was there, diligently shooting at his tin cans. Bannerman watched him for a few minutes. At first when he started his shooting regimen, Curtis's aim had been shaky, albeit still better than that of most of the ranchers in the Junction City area.

Now it was more than improved — it was better than it had ever been. Over and over, Curtis knocked every can off the fence. Then he would set them up and repeat the process from various distances and positions. Bannerman thought that every time he shot a can Curtis was seeing the face of Clem Dawson.

That night over supper Curtis announced his readiness to take part in the patrols. Abe Bannerman looked at him from across the table. He dipped a roll in some gravy and chewed thoughtfully before responding.

'We'll be glad to have you, Will,' he said. 'We need every man we can get.'

That night Curtis joined Bannerman on a four-hour watch. They roamed the hills in and around the properties of their neighbors, taking care to stay away from the main trails. Every night there were at least three riders in the hills, sometimes four. They were looking for Dawson's gunmen, but there had been no sign of them so far. That was true on Curtis's first night, too.

Bannerman and Curtis discussed it as they rode home through the woods.

'What do you think, Will?' Bannerman asked.

'He's got something up his sleeve,' said Curtis. 'He's biding his time. Maybe he's in worse shape physically than we thought.'

Bannerman shook his head.

'I just don't know. But something's going to happen soon. I can feel it.'

*   *   *

Abe Bannerman's hunch turned out to be right.

It was the night after Curtis's first patrol when someone torched the Bannermans' saloon, which had been unused since the night Curtis had ridden into town. The fire started around midnight. There was no rain, and there hadn't been for three days. There was very little moisture to impede the flames.

The citizens of Junction City turned out to battle the fire. Thanks to their combined efforts they were able to prevent the fire from spreading to the hardware store next door to the saloon. Several of Dawson's gunmen stood by impassively, watching the saloon burn without making any attempt to help put out the fire.

It was the opening salvo in Clem Dawson's war against the Bannermans and Will Curtis. They were his focus now, although he had no love for the other homesteaders in the area.

Dawson had hoped that burning the saloon down would smoke out Bannerman and Curtis. It didn't work. Dawson was compelled to implement his secondary plan.

*   *   *

Jake Douglas rode out to the Bannermans' cabin the next morning and told them about the burning of the saloon. No one had any doubt about who was responsible for the arson.

'I'm surprised he didn't do it sooner,' said Abe Bannerman cynically. 'I didn't want you trying to run that place by yourself anyway, Sally. With Pa gone, it's just not a place for a young woman.'

Sally Bannerman dabbed her eyes with a handkerchief.

'I know you're right, Abe,' she said. 'Still — that place meant so much to Pa.'

'Junction City's not the same place it used to be. Pa didn't want to accept that, but it's true. Since Clem Dawson came to town it's become an ugly place.'

'He did this to test us,' Will Curtis said. He glanced at Abe Bannerman. 'He's hoping this will bring us into town. He's got a trap set, of course.'

'Knowing Dawson, I don't doubt it.'

'He brought all those hardcases to town. I guess he wants them to earn their keep.'

The Bannerman boys came out and joined their father in the yard.

'Where y'all going?' Sally asked.

'We left a few things in the barn at our old place,' said Bannerman. 'We're going to take the wagon and make a clean sweep.'

'You need my help?' asked Curtis.

'No, we can handle it. 'Sides, I'd feel better knowing you're here with Maggie and Sally.'

'All right with me,' Curtis said. He took a sip of the strong black coffee that Maggie Bannerman made every morning when the family rose just after dawn.

Bannerman and his sons went into the barn and emerged presently with the wagon. Curtis and Sally waved as they passed the house.

'Be back in a few hours,' Abe Bannerman called.

Curtis sat down on the steps. He gazed at the dewy grass in the yard. Sally sat down beside him and gathered her skirt around her legs.

'How're you doing, Will?' she asked after a time. She turned her head toward him. He kept his eyes on the grass.

'I'm fine.'

'You sure?'

'Yeah, I'm sure.' He laughed quietly. 'Why did you ask it like that?'

She shrugged. 'I don't know. You seem so serious lately. I guess I was a little worried.'

'Well, we're dealing with serious business here.'

Now it was her turn to laugh.

'You don't have to tell me that,' she said.

'I know. Sorry.'

He drank more coffee, draining his cup. He put the empty cup down on the step between him and Sally.

'What're your plans, Will?'

'I'm going to help Abe with some things around here after him and the boys get back.'

'No — I mean your long-term plans.'

'To be honest, I don't really know. I'm going to see this through. Haven't really considered what I'm going to do after that. If I'm still alive that is.' His attempt at humor fell flat.

'You like Junction City?' she asked.

He raised an eyebrow and looked at her. She met his gaze without wavering.

'I like *you*,' he said. 'I still haven't made up my mind about Junction City. You can't blame me there.'

She pushed a strand of hair out of her eyes.

'No, I can't. It hasn't exactly been hospitable to you.'

'It hasn't treated you too well either,'

Curtis said. 'You ever thought about leaving?'

'No,' she said firmly. 'I grew up here. I could never leave as long as Abe, Maggie, and the boys are here.'

Curtis hid his disappointment. 'I can understand that,' he said.

'Where were you before?' she asked. 'I mean, I know you came from Idaho originally . . . '

'I've been all around the Western states. Wyoming, Colorado, Nevada, Idaho, California, Oregon. Lived my first fifteen years in Idaho. After that, I did a lot of drifting.'

'How'd you make a living?'

'Mostly punching cows. Did some farming here and there, but never really had the stomach for it.'

'The way you've helped around here, we thought maybe you'd been a lawman or something like that.'

Curtis's face darkened.

'I have done a little law work,' he said. 'Nothing official. Got involved in a murder investigation in eastern Oregon a couple of years ago. Ended up almost getting me killed. I figured that was enough badge-toting for me.'

'I think you'd be good at it,' she said. She straightened out the edge of her skirt. 'Still, I can see how it could bring a man down, seeing all the ugly things a sheriff or a marshal has to see.'

'I'd never seen anything like what I saw over in Fillmore. People killing entire families, including little kids.'

'Terrible.'

'Yes, it was. I never thought I'd see anything like that again, till I came here.'

'I guess there're bad folks every-where.'

'Yes,' he said, troubled by the memories. 'There certainly are.'

They were quiet for a time, watching two horses drinking from a trough in the corral.

'You know, you could make a real nice life for yourself here, Will,' she said pensively.

'You think?'

'Yes, I do. I mean, Clem Dawson isn't going to be in power here for ever. Not with you and my brother and the other ranchers opposing him like you are.'

'Sally, he's hired professional gunmen. They don't play by the same kind of rules that me and Abe do.'

'I know that,' she said.

'Guys like Shirreffs and Wilson — they can shoot and they've got guts. But it will take more than that to finish off Dawson.'

'You sound like you don't think it can be done.' Her voice was soft, and Curtis realized that he was discouraging her.

'Now, Sally, I don't want you to go off getting that idea.'

'It's just — '

'No, no,' he said. 'Dawson ain't licked us yet. Not by a long shot. We ain't going to let that happen, let me tell you.'

He placed his hand on her shoulder and her face turned to his.

'Do you mean that?' she asked

plaintively. 'After all, they killed my father. This is all so much for me to take in.'

'I know it is,' he said. 'If I didn't think we had a chance, I'd tell you. I swear I would.'

'I believe you.'

'I just want you to understand that it ain't going to be an overnight thing. And it's going to take some luck along the way, too.'

Suddenly she leaned over and kissed him. He was startled by it, but a feeling of happiness and exhilaration came over him.

'You do what you have to do,' she said. 'I'll support you all the way.'

With that, she rose and walked back into the cabin.

* * *

Late at night, ten days after the burning of the saloon, Curtis rode over to Phil Shirreffs's homestead. He was going to meet Jake Douglas and John Wilson there. With Shirreffs, they would take the patrol for the night.

Abe Bannerman had showed Curtis all the back trails in the hills outside Junction City. Curtis took one of those isolated back trails to Shirreffs's place. The wind moved through the bare branches of the maple trees above him as his sorrel picked its way up an incline. The animal's ears perked up and it lifted its eyes toward the trees up ahead on the right.

Curtis pulled reins and moved to the side of the trail. His Navy Colt was in his hand and he thumbed back the hammer. Minutes passed, then he decided to proceed, but cautiously. He had gone no more than twenty yards when he heard the sound of movement in the branches where his horse had looked before. He raised his Colt.

'You got about three seconds to show yourself or I'm going to start firing,' Curtis said in a loud voice.

Moments later a man rolled awkwardly out of the trees onto the trail.

He had a pistol in his hand. There were dry, crushed leaves on his clothing and his hat was askew on his head. Curtis realized the man had slipped and slid down the side of the hill, revealing his position.

The man watched Curtis. He didn't raise his gun, because he was already looking down the barrel of Curtis's weapon. There was fear and a certain amount of confusion in the man's face. As Curtis watched him an empty whiskey bottle rolled down from the trees where the man had been hiding. It smacked up against one of the man's boots.

'Who're you?' Curtis demanded.

The man hesitated.

'Name's Ike Gibson,' he said. His eyes were bright from the liquor he'd consumed.

'That right?' Curtis asked sarcastically. 'All right, Ike Gibson, what the hell are you doing hiding in the woods with a pistol?'

Gibson cleared his throat, his mind

groping for an explanation.

'I — uh — I'm a cousin of Jake Douglas.'

'Yeah?'

'I was riding out to his place. Haven't seen him in a few years.'

Curtis's eyes narrowed. 'Why you taking this trail to get out to Jake's?' he asked.

'I heard there's been some trouble 'round Junction City. I didn't want to run into anybody who was . . . unfriendly, if you know what I mean.'

'That why you were hiding in the trees?'

Ike Gibson smiled sheepishly.

'Yeah. Didn't know if you were one of the hired guns I heard about. I don't want any trouble, just want to see my cousin.'

Curtis sat for a few moments, considering the man before him and the explanations he'd given. *There's one way to find out if he really is Jake's cousin*, he thought.

'Well, I'm heading to a meeting right

now. Jake's going to be there.'

'Oh, yeah?' Gibson replied. He appeared sincere, although Curtis remained wary.

'Why don't you tag along?' Curtis asked.

'Why, that'd work fine.'

'After you put your pistol away, that is,' added Curtis pointedly.

Gibson gave a short laugh, but put his gun back in its holster.

'Not a problem, mister. You have me at a disadvantage, though. You know my name but I still don't know yours.'

'Name's Curtis. Will Curtis.' He watched Gibson's face keenly but couldn't discern any change in it after telling the man his name. His suspicions eased, but only somewhat.

Gibson pushed himself to his feet and kicked the empty bottle off into the trees. He gestured up the trail.

'Got my horse tied up about a quarter-mile thataway,' he said.

'Lead the way,' Curtis said. 'I'll bring up the rear.'

Gibson nodded and began walking up the narrow, leaf-covered path. For all the whiskey he'd consumed, he was remarkably steady on his feet. Curtis watched him closely as they moved through the dark foliage. Gibson walked with his shoulders straight and his hands loose at his sides.

'So, you from around here, Will Curtis?' Gibson asked over his shoulder.

'Nah,' said Curtis. 'From Idaho originally.'

'How'd you get mixed up in this Junction City mess?'

'Rode into town and ran into one of Clem Dawson's strongmen. He forced me to shoot him. Left a bad taste in my mouth, I guess you could say.' A crease furrowed Curtis's brow. 'How you know about what's going on in Junction City?'

'Like I said, I got kin around here,' Gibson responded easily. 'I hear things.' He pulled his coat closed against the sharp night air. 'Still, this ain't your fight. Probably caused you a lot of trouble. You ain't thought of just lighting out and looking for greener pastures?'

'Not that simple. They tried to kill my friends. They were willing to kill little kids to get what they want. I'm stickin' around until this gets resolved, one way or another.'

'Dawson tried to kill kids?' Gibson asked.

'Yeah, he did. Abe Bannerman's boys. You know old Abe, don't you?'

Ike Gibson didn't skip a beat.

'Oh, sure. I know Abe. Damn shame there are men who are willing to kill like that, just for a little money.'

Curtis was tiring of the conversation. 'Where's your horse?' he asked impatiently.

'Right up here,' said Gibson, pointing off the trail to the right.

Curtis halted his horse and looked up into the trees. He thought he could see the shape of the back end of a horse between two big maple trees up a slight rise off the trail. He rested his right hand on his thigh, poised for any surprises. He would take no chances with strangers in these parts, particularly on such an isolated trail at this time of night.

Gibson turned and grinned thinly.

'I'll just run up there and get her, if you don't mind.'

'Not a bit. Hurry up, though. I don't want to be late for that meeting.'

'Sure, sure.' Gibson started up the incline, stepping cautiously on the slippery leaves. Curtis watched him untie the horse's reins and then lead the animal back down to the trail. He could see the horse clearly in the moonlight.

'That's a damn fine mount you've got there,' Curtis said. He had always been an unabashed admirer of quality horseflesh.

Gibson patted the horse's neck. Curtis could tell the man was proud of it.

'Thanks. You wouldn't believe the offers I've gotten to sell her.' He looked into the horse's eye and spoke to her affectionately. 'Ain't that right, girl? Everybody wants to take you off my hands.' He slid his boot into a stirrup and swung up into the saddle. 'I'll tell you one thing, though. She ain't for sale. I don't know what I'd do without her.'

'A good horse is worth its weight in gold,' Curtis said, quoting one of his father's favorite expressions. 'How long have you had her?'

Gibson squinted, trying to be precise despite his whiskey-sodden state.

'Uh, it'll be three years in February. Got her in a poker game up near Seattle. Feller really didn't want to give her up, even though I won her fair and square.' He shook his head at the memory. 'We had to settle it with pistols. No way I was riding out of town on any horse but this one.' He leaned a little closer to the horse's right ear. 'Ain't that right, girl?' He patted her neck again. Curtis reckoned the man asked his horse that question a lot.

'What were you doing up in Seattle?' Curtis inquired.

'Little of this, little of that,' Gibson said. He stopped patting the horse's neck. Curtis wondered if Gibson were tired of the conversation, too.

'All right. I'll follow you. We're going to Phil Shirreffs's place.'

Gibson's face was confused for a moment.

'I thought you said we were going to meet Jake,' he said.

'We are. Out at Phil's cabin. We always meet there before we start the patrols at night.'

'Huh,' Gibson said simply. He scratched at his ear for a moment. 'You know, I don't rightly know how to get to . . . Phil's place from here.'

'I thought you were from around here.'

Gibson was irritated, though he tried to hide it.

'I am from around here. Just never ridden out to Phil's from this trail. Been years since I been there.'

This was plausible to Curtis, although he remained wary.

'Well, just head straight up this trail a ways,' he said. 'The road to his ranch branches off from this one. I'll let you know when we get there.'

'OK, fine.'

Gibson neck-reined his mare and heeled her up the trail at an easy pace. Curtis followed a few horse-lengths behind. He kept his hand near the strap that tied his holster to his thigh. Gibson was clearly hammered but functioning none the less, like a true hardcore range hawk.

In his travels Curtis had known many men who could consume enough liquor to stun your average mule. Many of these men could be in a state of extreme intoxication yet still ride a horse, win at poker, and outdraw opponents in a gunfight. Ike Gibson was that kind of man, Curtis thought. It could be dangerous to underestimate a drunkard like him.

They rode to the fork without speaking. The only sound was the smacking of their horses' hoofs on the wet ground.

As they approached the road to Shirreffs's homestead Curtis thumbed his Stetson back on his head and called to Gibson.

'Road to Phil's spread is up ahead on the right,' he said.

Gibson raised a hand in acknowledgement but said nothing. He directed his horse off the main trail onto the path to Shirreffs's cabin. Curtis maintained his cautious distance from the man ahead of him.

It was a mile before the forest started to thin around them. Curtis could see the cabin up ahead through the trees. A lantern was burning brightly in the kitchen of the house.

'It'll be good to see Phil,' said Gibson suddenly.

'Yeah? You two old friends?'

'Yep.' Gibson paused, then clarified his affirmation. 'Well, we're more like friendly acquaintances, I guess you could say.'

'I see,' Curtis said absently.

They were emerging from the trees into the large forest pasture that was Shirreffs's yard. There was a layer of mist over the grass that obscured the hoofs of their mounts.

The trail they'd used brought them out behind the house. They rode around the corral and passed by the bunkhouse, which was in darkness. As they moved up toward the front porch Curtis was surprised to see that neither Jake Douglas nor John Wilson had tied their horses to the hitching post. They invariably arrived for the pre-patrol meeting earlier than Curtis did, in part because their homes were much closer to Phil Shirreffs's house than was the Bannermans' uncle's place.

This was the first time Curtis had arrived before Douglas or Wilson. He looked toward Ike Gibson.

'We can tie up here,' he said.

Gibson drew reins near the porch and then dismounted. Curtis followed suit seconds later. They twisted the reins around the post and Curtis put a boot on the bottom step. The front door was open slightly.

'Phil, you in there?' he said, feeling for the makings in his coat pocket. He removed the papers and the sack of tobacco and began to build a smoke in the light that shone out from the front door.

'You got an extra smoke there, partner?' asked Ike Gibson.

Despite his casual demeanour Curtis had kept a watchful eye on Gibson. The stranger hadn't made any suspicious moves.

'Sure do,' Curtis said.

He heard boots crossing the floor inside the house. The hinges groaned as the door was pulled open. Curtis looked up and his face went slack. His fingers froze in the middle of twisting the end of the cigarette.

A man stood in the doorway. In his hands was a shotgun. Both barrels were aimed at Will Curtis's head.

7

The man on the porch smiled, but his face was humorless.

'You go ahead and toss your pistol up here on the porch, Will Curtis,' he said.

Curtis swiveled his eyes toward Ike Gibson. He wasn't surprised to see Gibson aiming his pistol at him.

'You heard him,' Gibson said. He was smiling, too.

Curtis pulled his Navy Colt and dropped it on the edge of the porch.

'You're not as dumb as you look, Curtis,' said the man on the porch. He used the tip of his boot to bring Curtis's pistol closer. Then he bent down and picked it up. He leaned the shotgun in the doorjamb and examined the pistol. He nodded approvingly and looked back at Curtis. 'You take good care of your weapons, don't you?' he asked rhetorically. 'This looks like it was just cleaned and oiled.' He slipped the gun into his waistband.

Curtis glared at the man. 'Where's Phil Shirreffs?' he asked.

The man scoffed. 'Don't worry about Phil,' he said.

'Where're Jake Douglas and John Wilson?' Curtis demanded, undeterred.

'Like I said — don't worry. Don't worry about Phil, don't worry about Jake, don't worry about John.' The man looked at Ike Gibson. 'Tie him up, Ike.'

Gibson opened his saddlebag and removed a rope. He stepped up to Curtis, who put his hands behind his back.

'See?' Gibson said smugly. 'I like it when people cooperate. It makes things easier for everyone.'

'Shut up, you drunken ass,' Curtis said.

Both Gibson and the man on the porch laughed. Gibson pulled the knots painfully tight.

'I want to make sure your bindings

are real secure,' he said with a mocking sneer.

The man on the porch gestured toward the front door.

'Bring him in, Ike,' he said.

Gibson grabbed Curtis and propelled him up the stairs and into the living room of Phil Shirreffs's home. Curtis looked around as he stepped in. There were no signs of a struggle in the room. Gibson shoved Curtis onto the couch.

'Take a load off,' he said. He leaned over and removed the tobacco and papers from Curtis's pocket. 'Never did get that cigarette.' He sank heavily into a chair across from the couch and looked at the other man, who stood near the front door, shotgun slung over the crook of his arm. 'Cobb, you got any whiskey?'

Curtis raised his head.

'Cobb?' he asked quietly. 'You're Cobb McGillicutty?'

McGillicutty was visibly annoyed. He glared at Ike Gibson for a moment before answering Curtis.

'That's right.'

'I'll be damned,' Curtis said. He let out a low whistle. 'Clem Dawson's really scraping the dregs, ain't he?'

Gibson's eyes widened and looked at McGillicutty to see how the big man would respond. McGillicutty's lips curled into a sinister grin.

'Glad to see my reputation precedes me,' he said.

Curtis was quiet, his mind racing. He knew of Cobb McGillicutty — everybody did. Everybody in the Pacific Northwest, anyway. He was a notorious gunman who was said to have killed more than a dozen men. Some of these men he'd killed because of insults or fights in saloons. Others were men he'd been hired to kill, whom he'd hunted down and executed for money.

There were many lawmen in Oregon, Idaho, and Montana who wanted to hang Cobb McGillicutty. And here he was, standing casually across the room from Will Curtis. Curtis wondered how Clem Dawson had found the killer.

With his connections, it probably hadn't been too hard. Curtis hadn't doubted Dawson's commitment to wiping out the homesteaders of Junction City, but he was stunned by this turn of events.

'So how about it, Cobb? You got any whiskey hiding around here?' Gibson asked.

'There's some on the table in the kitchen,' McGillicutty said. 'I found it in a cupboard.'

That was all Ike Gibson needed to hear. He strode out of the room, leaving Curtis and McGillicutty alone. Curtis decided to try to get some information from McGillicutty.

'What's all this about, Cobb?' he asked.

McGillicutty regarded him coolly.

'What do you mean?'

'I mean, why the hell does Clem Dawson want to control Junction City so bad? This is a little village out in the sticks. Dawson's already rich. What's the point of all this?'

McGillicutty picked at a cuticle for a few moments.

'I guess it don't make much difference if you know or not,' he said. Curtis understood his meaning. It didn't make a difference what Curtis knew because Curtis would soon be dead. 'You see, Mr Dawson has big plans. He's going to build a railway station right here in Junction City.'

Curtis was incredulous.

'That's worth killing people over?'

McGillicutty shrugged.

'To Clem Dawson it is. And he pays good money to get what he wants.'

They were interrupted by Gibson, who walked back into the living room with a half-empty whiskey bottle in his hand. He stopped and took a giant swig, then wiped his sleeve across his lips.

'That's good stuff!' he proclaimed. He stepped back to his chair and was sitting down when the sound of approaching horses brought him back to a standing position. 'That must be them,' he said to McGillicutty.

'Bring him out,' McGillicutty commanded. He turned and walked out onto the porch to meet the approaching horsemen.

Gibson grabbed Curtis and yanked him roughly to his feet.

'Come out and say hello to your pards,' he said. He pushed Curtis forward and they joined McGillicutty on the porch.

There were six men on horses. As the riders got closer to the porch and the light shining from within the cabin, Curtis recognized Jake Douglas and John Wilson in the front of the pack. Their faces were swollen, bloody, and bruised, and their hands were tied together in front of them. The group stopped a few feet from the front steps. Gibson and McGillicutty walked down and helped pull Douglas and Wilson from the saddles. They let the two men fall into the dirt beside their horses.

Curtis scanned the faces of the other

four riders, but none was familiar. Clearly these were more of Dawson's hired enforcers. The men dismounted and tied their horses to the hitching post.

Douglas and Wilson struggled up to sitting positions, spitting dirt and stray blades of grass from their mouths. Douglas's beating had obviously been particularly brutal: probably, Curtis thought, because of the man's massive size. He was more of a threat than small John Wilson was, although Wilson was a fighter, too.

Jake Douglas looked at Curtis through swollen eyes.

'Howdy, Will,' he said.

'Damn, Jake,' Curtis said with concern. 'They really put you through the wringer, didn't they?'

Douglas coughed wretchedly and a stream of blood poured from his mouth. He leaned forward and let it drip into the dirt.

'Yeah, they're pretty tough,' he said. 'Well, when you get all four of them together. I don't think any of them wanted to tangle one on one.'

The look in Jake Douglas's eyes was savage and blood-thirsty. The four gunmen responded with a show of bravado, partly to save face in front of Cobb McGillicutty.

'Now don't go flattering yourself, Douglas,' one of the men said. 'You can't win 'em all.' The man raised a muddy boot and kicked Douglas hard in the side of his head, sending him toppling back onto his side with a groan.

McGillicutty observed this interaction without apparent interest.

'All right,' he said. 'Let's finish this job up.' He glanced at Ike Gibson and nodded.

'What're you doing?' Curtis asked, his pulse roaring in his ears.

'Watch and you'll see,' Gibson said with a snicker.

He stepped off the porch and the four other Dawson men stepped away, leaving a clear space around Douglas and Wilson. Gibson grabbed John Wilson's hair and yanked the man to his feet.

'Git up, you!' he snarled. Wilson struggled to maintain his balance and finally succeeded. Gibson turned and addressed himself to Will Curtis, who stood watching with his jaw set in a grim line. 'This,' Gibson continued, 'is what happens when you cross the wrong people in Junction City.'

Without further ado, he pulled his pistol from his holster, placed it up against Wilson's forehead, and fired. Blood spurted from the rancher's head and his body collapsed onto the ground.

'No!' yelled Curtis. He took a step forward but halted when Cobb McGillicutty gripped his shoulder. 'You sidewinding bastards,' he cursed. 'You just killed a good man.'

The gunmen laughed, some uproariously. Two of them lifted Jake Douglas by his shoulders and pushed him forward toward Gibson. Douglas's bloody face was resigned. He almost hadn't had time to begin despairing.

Gibson raised his pistol and pressed it up against Douglas's temple. Gibson pulled the trigger and Douglas's body joined that of Wilson in the dirt with a sickening thud. Blood poured from the side of his head. Gibson had a satisfied smile on his face as he slid the pistol back into the holster.

Curtis's body tensed and his wrists pulled against his bindings.

'You're going to pay for that, Gibson,' he said, his lips pulled tight against his teeth.

'Who's going to make me pay?' Gibson asked. 'You?'

'Why don't you take these bindings off and we can answer that right here. Man to man.'

Gibson laughed disdainfully. 'Yeah, sure,' he said.

When his fellow gunmen looked at him questioningly nervousness manifested itself in a strange twitch in Gibson's right eye.

'Y'all heard what Dawson said. He wants us to bring in Curtis in good shape. I wouldn't want to spoil his pretty looks.'

'Just like I thought,' Curtis said. 'A coward to the core.'

Ike Gibson was dangerously close to losing face in front of his peers. He decided he had to act. He stepped toward Curtis and grabbed the front of his shirt. He lifted his hand and brought it hard across Curtis's face in a dismissive, insulting slap. Curtis's head barely moved, and his angry stare remained locked on Gibson's face.

'Let's get outta here,' Gibson said angrily, as if he could recover his dignity by barking commands.

He turned and took a step toward the hitching post. With blinding speed Curtis struck out with his right foot, catching Gibson in the shins. Gibson's feet flew out from under him and he smashed face first into the hard dirt. The impact was powerful, and some of Gibson's colleagues stifled laughs.

'How'd that taste?' Curtis asked.

Dazed and still quite drunk, Ike Gibson stood up slowly and a little uncertainly. His rheumy eyes darted around the circle of men in the yard, then his hand went for the pistol on his hip.

'That's enough!' Cobb McGillicutty hollered. All heads turned to him. His shotgun was back in his hands, aimed at Gibson.

'What the hell are you doing?' Gibson asked hoarsely. He had a deep gash on his chin and two of his front teeth were bloodied and dangling from his gums at an awkward angle.

'We're getting paid to do a job, you pathetic drunk,' said McGillicutty. 'You get your hand off that gun. Curtis has an appointment in Junction City.'

Gibson's hands dangled once more at his sides. He was careful to keep them well away from his gun.

'Now y'all get back on your horses. Help Curtis onto his. We're running late.'

The men obeyed instantly. McGillicutty selected two of the men to stay at Shirreffs's cabin.

'Tomorrow there'll be homesteader scum coming 'round to see where the patrollers are and why they ain't come home. Close the shutters and be ready for them. You know the plan, so I shouldn't have to explain it again.' He paused and looked hard at the two who were staying behind. 'Right?'

'Oh, right, Cobb,' said one of the men eagerly. 'We know what we're doing.'

'Yeah, well, sometimes I wonder,' McGillicutty said, his words clearly directed at Ike Gibson. He descended from the porch and climbed up onto his horse. 'Let's get out of here.'

The men rode across the yard into the forest, with Will Curtis directly in front of Cobb McGillicutty.

A cold drizzle began to fall as the forest swallowed them. Ike Gibson, riding just ahead of Curtis, occasionally looked over his shoulder and shot a hateful glance at the man who'd humiliated him so badly. Gibson's entire livelihood depended on his reputation for toughness and action. To be kicked into the dirt by what the other gunmen considered a two-bit ranch hand was bad enough. To be kicked in the dirt by a two-bit ranch hand whose hands were tied behind his back was thoroughly beyond the pale for a man such as Gibson.

Curtis ignored him, his mind focusing on the changing situation that now faced the people of the Junction City hill country.

Jake Douglas and John Wilson, two of the most reliable and courageous of the local ranchers, were dead, shot by a hired assassin while tied up and unarmed. Phil Shirreffs was missing and Curtis presumed he was dead. Curtis had been captured and was being taken into town. He had no doubt that Clem Dawson had special plans for him. The banker's desire for vengeance after the earlier encounter with Curtis had overtaken virtually all other concerns in his life.

Mostly, though, Curtis thought of the Bannermans. Dawson now had a foothold in the hills from which to operate against his enemies. It was only a matter of time before the man struck, and now he had the element of surprise on his side.

8

Clem Dawson smoothed out his silk tie and flicked some stray cigar ash from his lapel. Then he looked across his desk at the man sitting opposite him and smiled unctuously.

'You really have gone above and beyond the call of duty,' he said, his voice smooth and confident.

'I didn't really have any other choice,' the other man said grimly.

'True,' Dawson said with a sly chuckle.

'I don't know why that's so funny.'

The smile faded slowly from Clem Dawson's lips. His eyes were like black, bottomless pools.

'I'm a business man,' he said. 'Sometimes I have to make decisions that others might find . . . unsavory. I have come to accept this as the price I pay for my success. Ultimately I think

I've been more than generous with you, all things considered.'

'Yeah? How you figure?'

'I could have simply thrown you out of your home with no kind of compensation. That would have been well within my legal rights as the holder of your mortgage.' He settled back in his chair and drew deeply on his fragrant cigar. 'Instead, I have compensated you handsomely.'

'Well, you got what you wanted in return, too. Don't forget that.'

Dawson nodded. 'Yes, the information you gave us was vital to turning the tables on your neighbors.'

'We'll see about that.'

'Oh, we will.' Dawson's eyes were slitted. 'And you'd better hope things go my way. I could make things very awkward for you.'

'We had a deal.'

'We did. As of right now, we still do.'

'You got what you wanted. I showed your boys where all the secret trails are. I told you when we were meeting and who would be there. Without that, you'd never have found a way to spring a trap.'

'Indeed. I'm not arguing about that.' He rubbed his eyes for a moment. The entire exchange had become distasteful and he wanted the man out of his office. 'You've received your payment?'

'Yeah.'

'Good. Did you count it?'

'Yeah, I counted it.'

'All there?'

'Yeah.'

'Good. Now get the hell out of my office and don't ever come back.'

'I couldn't come back here even if I wanted to.'

'You're right,' Dawson said. He examined the tip of his cigar as if it were a fascinating artefact. 'The name of Phil Shirreffs will be mud in Junction City for at least the next fifty years.'

Shirreffs's face reflected the impotent anger that welled within him. Without another word he turned and strode out of Clem Dawson's office, slamming the door behind him.

His horse was waiting for him in Dawson's back yard, where it was roped to a tree. He mounted and entered the alley behind the house, passing one of the guards who lurked in the shadows there. The man gave him no greeting, and Shirreffs didn't acknowledge him.

I had no other choice, he thought. *I could either lose everything and have nothing to show for all the years of hard work, or I could take Dawson's offer and have a chance to make a new life somewhere else. Besides, it was inevitable that Dawson would win in the end. He had all the advantages, and his men were committed to Dawson's cause. His money made sure of that.*

Shirreffs leaned over and spat tobacco juice into the bushes that grew along the left side of the alley.

He had had this same internal discussion with himself countless times in the two weeks since he'd received the formal legal letter telling him he was about to lose his home and property.

Along with the letter was a personal note from Clem Dawson.

Dawson had read his man well, Shirreffs thought with intense self-disgust.

He was out of town heading south within a few minutes of leaving Dawson's yard. He figured he'd just keep on heading south, out of Oregon. He'd spend a little time in California, then maybe continue on to Mexico. He'd heard good things about Mexico. The gold coins to the tune of $1,000 that he'd received from Dawson would go a long way, south of the border.

He'd only made it three miles out of town when the two riders emerged from the trees, one ahead of Shirreffs and one behind him. Shirreffs pulled reins, his heart pounding. In an instant he was soaked in sweat.

'Evening, Phil,' said the man in front of him. 'Nice night for a ride, don't you think?'

'What the hell do you want?' Shirreffs asked.

He wasn't a cowardly man, but his chest was filled with a stark terror he'd never before experienced.

'Mr Dawson was doing some thinking,' the man behind Shirreffs said. The rancher hipped in the saddle and squinted toward him. 'He thinks he overpaid you.'

'I was just in his office and he didn't say anything like that!'

'He probably didn't want to make a scene,' said the man in front.

'Yeah,' said the man in back. 'Mr Dawson just hates scenes.'

Both gunmen snickered.

'We had a deal,' Shirreffs said. 'Get out of my way and let me go.'

'Afraid we can't do that, Phil.'

There was no alternative. Shirreffs recognized this now. In desperation, his hand reached for the rifle in the scabbard beside him.

The two gunmen were thorough professionals. They sank six bullets into Phil Shirreffs's chest and back before he'd even got a firm grip on the butt of his rifle. He fell out of the saddle onto the cold ground and didn't move.

The gunmen dismounted and dragged his body deep into the thick brush beside the trail. One of the men opened one of Shirreffs's saddlebags and removed a bulky bag of coins from it. Then he slapped the horse on the rump and the animal broke into a gallop, heading south on the road toward Eugene.

The two men clambered up onto their mounts and rode back to Junction City.

★   ★   ★

Clem Dawson looked at the massive clock on the wall of his office. It was just after two o'clock in the morning. If everything had gone according to plan, he would soon be expected at the barn on the edge of town. He stabbed his cigar out in the ornate ashtray and rose. There was a bar set into the wall across the room and Dawson poured himself a stiff brandy. He finished it in two quick gulps and stepped out into the hallway.

The house was in silence. He listened for any sounds from Alvin's room upstairs, but there were none.

Dawson left through the back door. The guard was waiting for him there. Dawson retrieved his horse from the stable and the guard untied his mount from a pole near the fence.

Junction City was like a ghost town as they rode through its streets. On the north-western outskirts of the town, set a few dozen yards back from the street, was a large barn. Dawson kept several horses, a wagon, and two buggies there. Unless Dawson were going to Eugene or Salem, the barn was virtually never used.

Tonight, however, lanterns were burning in the wide aisle between the stalls. Two more guards met Dawson at the back entrance to the barn. He dismounted and entered the building. He saw that the mission had been a success and he was filled with a feeling of deep pleasure.

Will Curtis was tied to a chair in the center of the aisle. He was stripped to the waist and Dawson saw that his orders to the guards had been obeyed. Curtis hadn't been beaten or abused.

★   ★   ★

A door opened near Dawson and Cobb McGillicutty stepped out of the store room. He closed the door behind him and nodded toward Dawson.

'You did good work,' Dawson said. He reached into his breast pocket and pulled out a cheroot. 'Now I want all of you out of here. Wait outside and keep a good eye out. I'll call you when I need you.'

'Yes, sir,' said McGillicutty. He motioned to the two guards standing near the rear stalls and they followed him out into the yard behind the barn.

Dawson stepped out of the shadows and walked toward Curtis. He stopped a few feet away and struck a match on one of the stall doors. He lighted the cheroot and stared at Curtis through the smoke.

'Good to see you again, Dawson,' Curtis said sarcastically. His face was defiant as he glared at the banker.

'Yeah, I'm sure,' Dawson retorted with a smile. His right hand was still in a bandage from the bullet wound he'd received from Curtis that night in Dawson's bedroom. He looked at the bandage absently.

'How's that hand treating you?' Curtis asked.

Dawson's eyes glinted as he chewed on the cheroot.

'You got a real smart mouth on you, Curtis.'

'That's what people tell me.'

'Hmmm. I think after tonight you just might learn to tame that sharp tongue of yours.'

'You think so?'

'I do. I think you're going to be a different man in a few hours.'

Curtis glanced toward the door

where the guards had exited.

'I guess you better call in your boys, Clem.'

'Don't worry — I'll call them in when it's time.'

Smoke billowed out of Dawson's flared nostrils and Curtis regarded him curiously.

'What are you waiting for?' he asked.

'I just wanted to get a good look at the man who's caused all this trouble for me. You're not even from around these parts. What's your game?'

'I ain't got any game.'

'There must be some reason you've chosen to insert yourself in my affairs.'

'All this business that's been going on ain't just your affair, Clem.' Curtis spat contemptuously into the dirt near Dawson's feet, narrowly missing the man's polished shoes. Dawson stepped a little further back from Curtis.

'How do you figure?' Dawson asked.

'You can't just force people off their own land, or bully people into giving you whatever you want.'

'I made all those people very generous offers.'

'Sure you did. And if they chose not to accept, then you tried to burn them and their children alive.'

'As I told you before, that had nothing to do with me.'

'Spare me your bullshit. I ain't buying it.'

'Fair enough,' said Dawson.

He rolled the cheroot from one side of his mouth to the other as he regarded Curtis. The latter was puzzled by Dawson's desire to converse, particularly since it was plain as day that Dawson intended to have Curtis killed.

Why is he taking the time to have this little chat? Curtis wondered. The entire exchange was bizarre.

'Since you're in a mood to talk, why don't you tell me what your big plans are for Junction City? I asked your boy McGillicutty, but he ain't really the explaining type, if you know what I'm saying.'

'My plans for Junction City?' Dawson

asked innocently.

'Yeah. Whatever scheme you've got up your sleeve, it must be pretty big to justify killing so many people.'

'Like I said, that was an unfortunate — '

'You want to tell that to the families of Jake Douglas and John Wilson?'

Dawson shrugged. 'Those gentlemen had their chance to make the right decision . . . '

'And where the hell is Phil Shirreffs?'

'Mr Shirreffs? Last I heard he'd taken leave of Junction City. Headed south somewhere, from what I understand.'

'I don't believe you,' Curtis said. 'I'm sure he's dead, just like anyone around here who has the audacity to defy you. But go ahead — tell me about how you plan on building Rome in a day.'

Dawson looked down at the dirt floor. He moved some hay around with the tip of his shoe.

'I guess I might as well tell you,' he said. 'After all, you're going to be dead in a few hours, so you won't be able to throw a wrench in the works anyway.'

'Don't worry, Clem. I won't share any of your precious secrets.'

Dawson grinned. 'You know, you are amusing in many respects, Will Curtis. It's a shame you picked the wrong side in this fight.'

'I didn't have much choice. Your moron son made it for me.'

'Ah, yes,' Dawson said with a sigh. 'Alvin. He's never really been the same since his mother died.'

'Poor kid. I'm sure he's got a heart of gold.'

This time Dawson laughed out loud.

'No, not Alvin. He's too much like me.' He pulled his watch out of one of his breast pockets and checked the time. 'You wanted to know why I have such an interest in controlling Junction City. Well, I'll tell you now, and then our business will be completed. Junction City has the potential to be a major center for the cattle business. I intend to buy up all the land in the area and import cattle. Thousands of Herefords, shipped here directly from Texas. This kind of undertaking needs centralization and someone who knows how to, shall we say, manipulate the levers of power in order to get things done.'

Curtis watched Dawson carefully as the latter spoke. A thin sheen of sweat lay over the man's features. His eyes sparkled with enthusiasm as he detailed his ambitions.

'I must say, when I made my offers to the local ranchers and homesteaders, I figured they would recognize my generosity and be reasonable. The only way I can operate on the scale I have in mind is by getting the rights to the land and water around this town. As you know, this is a very fertile area, with almost unlimited resources. Why, I reckon I could recoup all of my investment in the first year after the cattle arrive. By the end of the second year, I guarantee I could bring in between two- and three-hundred thousand dollars. And that's just the beginning.'

'These hundreds of thousands of dollars — they going to benefit you or the entire town?' Curtis asked.

There was a hint of disappointment in Dawson's face as he answered Curtis's question, as if he had suddenly realized he was speaking to an idiot.

'I don't think you understand, Curtis. What's good for me is good for Junction City. I'm going to put this little podunk town on the map.' His chest puffed as he spoke. 'I'd say that's more than the people around here deserve.'

'There's one thing you seem to have forgotten while you were making all these plans, Dawson.'

'What's that?'

'How are you going to get all the cattle here?'

Dawson waved a hand dismissively.

'That's all taken care of,' he explained. 'We're going to build a railroad depot right here in Junction City. I have lots of friends in the railroad industry, you see. We're going to build cattle pens on a grand scale. That, too, will be a benefit to the ... local economy. Once we get the railway established here and bring in the cows from Texas, well — there's really no limit to what can be accomplished. A few hundred thousand dollars is only the beginning, you see.'

He removed another cheroot from his pocket and lighted it with the tip of his last one. 'In ten years, the cattle industry here will be worth well over a million dollars per year.' His eyes sparkled with expectant triumph. 'Just imagine that, Curtis. The profits will only increase, and they'll do so every year. And I will be the biggest cattle baron north of California.'

'You sound like Napoleon,' Curtis said. 'Your brain must be fuzzier than a grizzly's ass.'

The humor left Clem Dawson's face.

'We'll see about that, Curtis,' he said. 'Or, at least, some of us will see about that.'

In a swift movement that caught Curtis by surprise, Dawson stepped forward and grabbed Curtis's hair, yanking his head to the side. He thrust the fiery tip of his cheroot into the side of Curtis's neck and twisted it. Curtis howled as the scent of his own burning flesh filled his nostrils. Then Dawson stepped back, flicking the remainder of the small cigar into the seated man's face.

'You son of a bitch,' Curtis said, wincing from the searing pain of the burn.

'That's just the beginning,' Dawson declared. He buttoned his coat neatly and smoothed his hair. 'There's someone who wants to see you. An old friend, you could say.' He turned and looked toward the store room door from which Cobb McGillicutty had emerged several minutes before. Lantern light showed in the crack near the floor. 'You can come on out,' he said loudly, and then turned back to Curtis.

The door opened and a small figure

emerged, his body supported on the right by a crutch. Curtis couldn't make out who it was in the darkness near the back door.

'I think you remember Mr Mack Kantor, don't you, Curtis?' Dawson asked. 'He's been recuperating at a hospital in Eugene since last you met, but he jumped at the chance to renew your acquaintance.'

9

Mack Kantor moved slowly out of the shadows at the back of the barn, his crutch scraping in the dirt as he moved forward. It was only when he was about fifteen feet from Curtis that the latter saw the extent of Kantor's injury.

His right foot had been amputated right above the ankle where Curtis had shot him. A thick cloth bandage had been wrapped repeatedly around the lower part of his leg. He hobbled until he was a few feet away from Clem Dawson and then stopped, staring at Will Curtis with an oblique glance. The fingers on Kantor's left hand were splayed out in an awkward fashion where Curtis had stepped on them at the cabin.

'Well, would you look at that,' Kantor said. 'How the mighty have fallen.'

Curtis was still a little woozy from

the cigar burn on his neck. He had to concentrate extra hard in order to insult the crippled bushwhacker who stood before him.

'Boy, that's quite a job the doctor did,' he rasped. 'I guess you won't be winning any three-legged races any time soon, huh, Mack?'

'You smart-mouthed bastard,' said Kantor, his face contorted with loathing and a desire for vengeance. 'Keep flapping those gums. You won't be laughing for much longer, I promise you that.'

'I seem to recall you specialize in killing old men, Mack. I guess you also like it when the men you torture are tied to a chair, is that right?'

Kantor ignored Curtis's taunts and shifted his beady eyes to Clem Dawson.

'You all set, boss?'

'I'm finished with him,' Dawson affirmed.

'Good.'

'You have about four hours, Mack. I trust you can find some way to amuse yourself at Mr Curtis's expense.'

'Don't you worry, Mr Dawson,' Kantor said, looking again at Will Curtis. 'This is going to be a night that neither of us will ever forget.'

'Fine, then. I'll be off.' Dawson slipped his derby hat back on his head and grinned at the prisoner. 'Do try to die like a man, Will Curtis. I would be disappointed if you did otherwise.'

With that, Clem Dawson pivoted and left the barn through the back door, leaving Curtis and Kantor alone.

Kantor limped closer to his prey.

'My goodness, that is one nasty burn on your neck. Yes, indeedy. Must've hurt like hell, am I right?' he said with a laugh.

'Probably didn't hurt half as much when I shot you in the ankle. You were really running that time. Guess you ain't doing much running these days.'

'Shut up,' said Kantor.

He backhanded Curtis across the face viciously, then dug his thumbnail deep into the burn on the man's neck.

Curtis yelled with pain, and a smile of pleasure crossed Mack Kantor's face.

'Yes, yes — that's more like it,' Kantor intoned. His voice was oddly clinical as he began his work. 'You don't know how long I've been waiting to see you again, Will.' He used the crutch to move back a couple of feet and then, balancing on his left foot, he drove the end of the crutch into Curtis's throat.

Curtis gagged and then vomited on himself. His eyes welled from the pain as he struggled to catch his breath.

'Mm-hmm,' Kantor said. 'Been thinking about this little reunion of ours for months now. I had nothing better to do, sitting around in that hospital in Eugene. Every day I thought about you.'

'I'm flattered,' Curtis said.

'You should be. I've wanted to hurt people before in my life, there's no doubt about that. And I have killed a lot of people. But there ain't never been nobody I wanted to hurt like I want to hurt you.'

Curtis's arms were tied securely behind him, so that he was no threat to his tormentor. Kantor leaned in and punched him as hard as he could across the bridge of the nose. Bright lights exploded in Curtis's eyes as blood burst from his nose and streamed down his face, dripping off his chin onto his shirt.

'How you like that?' Kantor asked.

Curtis, barely conscious, didn't respond. Kantor brought his arm back and punched Curtis again, this time flattening his nose grotesquely. More blood flowed onto Curtis's shirt. His head drooped forward and the blood flowed onto his pants and then onto the dirt floor.

'Damn, you're bleeding like a stuck pig, Curtis!' Kantor exclaimed. There was exuberance in his voice. 'You're going to need to get the doc to check out that nose. It ain't looking so good.' He giggled at his own cleverness, and his power.

Curtis's brain reeled and he struggled

to stay conscious. He blinked a few times. He could see Kantor's foot and the crutch on the ground before him. Pain assailed him, from his nose, his throat, and the burn on his neck.

'Thaaaaat's right,' Kantor said, almost soothingly. 'It hurts, don't it? Pain like that can take some getting used to.'

Curtis tried to raise his head to face his tormentor but failed. He heard a low moan of agony. It took a few moments for him to register that he was the one making the noise.

'You know, I thought I understood what pain was until you shot me in the foot. That's when I learned a whole new lesson about pain. Yes, sir, I did. They took me into Eugene and dumped me at the sawbones' place. I mean it, too — they just dumped me right in his goddamn yard in the rain, middle of the night and everything.'

Curtis realized that Kantor was talking to himself as much as he was to his prisoner.

'I told the doc I'd kill him if he cut my foot off. I said I'd rather die than lose my damn foot.'

Through his hazy vision, Curtis saw something glinting in the lantern light. He couldn't tell what it was, but suddenly it moved from the right side of his line of sight to the left, then back again.

Still Mack Kantor droned on.

'Wouldn't you know, the varmint did it anyway. He cut my foot off! When I woke up he said if he hadn't cut it off an infection would've set in and killed me.'

The mysterious shiny object moved again.

'Thing is, I'm glad he did it now. Gave me the chance to come back to Junction City and spend a little time with my old friend, Will Curtis.'

Kantor emitted a maniacal laugh and the shiny object moved swiftly toward Curtis. He felt a hot, sudden pain on the side of his face, and then he was aware of more blood flowing, this time down his face and onto his neck and shoulder. The pain intensified and he realized he'd been cut, and pretty deeply, too.

It was a knife he'd seen moving in Kantor's hands. A very sharp knife.

His mind began to clear and, just as it did so, Kantor made another move toward Curtis, who felt a sharp pain along the upper left side of his chest, cutting through his shirt to pierce the flesh. Then the tip of the blade gouged into his collarbone, sinking through the flesh and gouging the bone itself. The mostly healed bullet wound in his ribcage began to throb for the first time in weeks. Curtis's vision cleared and he screamed in pain.

Kantor's smiled widened and he withdrew the blade. Curtis felt a few seconds of relief, but Kantor wasn't done. He drove the blade again into the wound he'd just made, harder this time. Again Curtis screamed, and again Kantor laughed.

Kantor removed the knife and took a deep breath.

'That feels good, don't it?' he asked.

He slipped the knife into his waistband. Again he balanced on his one good foot and struck Curtis with the crutch, this time in the mouth rather than in the nose. Curtis's head whiplashed back, spewing blood. His lips split and began to swell almost immediately.

Kantor was gleeful.

'Goddamn!' he exulted. 'You sure know how to bleed.'

He hit Curtis with the crutch, again in the mouth.

'You got anything to say, cowboy?' he taunted.

'Yeah,' Curtis said.

'Speak up.'

'Yeah . . . I got something to say.'

Kantor leaned forward slightly.

'Spit it out.'

'I wanted to tell you that . . . that . . . I never did meet a more sorry, lily-livered sack of shit in my entire life than Mack Kantor.'

Kantor's good humor evaporated instantly. He lifted the crutch again and smashed it with all his strength into Curtis's face. This time the chair tumbled over backward and Curtis crashed to the floor with immense force. The wind was knocked out of him and his hands were pinned beneath him. He wheezed and coughed, turning his head to the side to allow the blood from his mouth and nose to pour onto the ground rather than down his gullet. Hideous gurgling noises escaped from his throat.

'That's what your smart mouth will get you,' Kantor hissed. 'And there's a lot more where that came from. You better believe it.'

Kantor was interrupted when someone opened the back door of the barn and spoke to him.

'Hey, Mack — '

'You dumb bastard! I said nobody better interrupt me.'

'I know, but you also said you wanted

some whiskey. Well, we just got our hands on a bottle.'

Kantor's tone softened.

'All right, then. Bring it in.'

The man shook his head.

'Can't do that, Mack. We're passing it around. If you want some, you'll have to come and get your share.'

Kantor considered the offer.

'Fine. I'll come out,' he said. He looked down at Curtis. 'Don't go anywhere, y'hear? We ain't finished yet.'

Curtis said nothing. He could hear Kantor's crutch scraping through the dirt and then the back door of the barn slammed shut.

Instantly Curtis was in motion. He shifted his body weight with as much momentum as he could muster and the chair fell onto its side. When Kantor had knocked Curtis over he'd inadvertently broken the back of the chair. Curtis pushed against the ropes around his wrists and the back of the chair broke off cleanly from the seat, releasing the ropes from where they'd been tied to the chair.

Working frantically, he was able to loosen the ropes from his wrists, aided in part by the sweat that covered his entire body. Once his hands were free he began to work on the ropes around his ankles.

He could hear the men talking and laughing loudly outside, their high spirits lubricated by the jug of whiskey they were sharing. Curtis fought back a powerful urge to panic and kept his mind focused intently on untying the ropes at his feet. It took less than a minute to get his legs free, but it felt like an eternity, so acutely conscious was he of Kantor's imminent return.

Once his legs were free he got an unexpected burst of energy. He was working now purely on adrenaline and fear, driven by the will to survive. Barely conscious of his own movements, he found himself on his feet, moving toward the back of the barn where the store room door stood ajar.

He had nearly reached the store room when the back door of the barn opened.

10

It was two hours after dawn and the homesteaders had Phil Shirreffs's cabin surrounded.

Sally Bannerman lay in some brush between two large maple trees, her father's pistol in hand and a Winchester rifle in the grass nearby. Abe Bannerman bellied up beside her.

'Is everybody here?' she asked.

'Yep,' her brother said. He gestured at various points in the trees around the cabin. 'Mike Tancred's there, Gil Harmon's over there, and Dean Taggart's covering the back door.'

The bodies of Jake Douglas and John Wilson were still in the yard where Dawson's men had left them the night before. Both of the Bannerman siblings tried to avert their eyes from the corpses of their longtime friends and neighbors, but they weren't able to do so and continue to keep a watch on the front of the cabin at the same time.

It was a little after dawn when Abe Bannerman had ridden out to the Shirreffs property to see where Will Curtis was. He'd made it to within ten yards of the cabin when the shooting began. The men inside were so drunk they hadn't heard him approach. The liquor also affected their aim, and he escaped intact, although his favorite horse had a deep bullet burn across its chest.

There was no question now that Clem Dawson was making his move against the country dwellers around Junction City. Bannerman had alerted Tancred, Harmon, and Taggart, and now they were ready for anything Dawson's men had to offer.

Sally had insisted on joining them, and her brother had known better than to argue. He had no credible argument to make, since Sally was an excellent shot with both pistols and rifles. He could have tried to argue that women had no place taking part in gunplay, but that wouldn't have gotten far with his sister.

'I wonder where Will is,' she said. 'Phil, too.'

'They killed Jake and John right here in the yard,' her brother responded somberly. 'Didn't even bother to bury them.' He shook his head with disgust. 'You don't get much lower than that.'

'And their hands are still tied behind them.'

'Never seen anything like it in my life. Not to mention having to look at Pa's grave every day. Can't believe this is what things have come to in Junction City.'

Bannerman looked past the bodies and cupped his hands on both sides of his mouth.

'You in there,' he yelled. 'You're surrounded. There's no way for you to escape. Come on out and surrender.'

A voice bellowed from inside the cabin. 'Why don't you come on in and get us, Bannerman!'

'You really want to die for Clem Dawson?' Bannerman replied. 'You think that rich bastard gives a damn about you?'

A second voice responded from inside, somewhere near the front door as far as Sally Bannerman could tell.

'What are you going to do if we come out?'

'We'll just have ourselves a little talk.'

'Uh huh. Then what? You'll have yourselves a little hanging?'

'We'll turn you over to the law in Eugene.'

'We are the law.' It was the first voice again. 'We're deputy sheriffs, in case you forgot.'

'I've never heard of deputy sheriffs executing unarmed men with their hands tied behind their backs,' said Bannerman angrily. 'But we won't be taking the law into our own hands. We'll turn you over to the sheriff himself, just like I said.'

There was a pause.

'We had nothing to do with shooting

those two out in the yard.'

'Of course you didn't.' Bannerman's voice was thick with suspicion.

'All right, then — what was it y'all are wanting to talk about?'

'We want to know where Will Curtis and Phil Shirreffs are.'

'We don't know.'

'What d'you mean, you don't know? This is Phil's spread. I'm sure he didn't just invite you in.'

'See, that's where you're wrong, Bannerman. Phil Shirreffs is working for Clem Dawson now.'

The blood drained from Abe Bannerman's face. He and Sally exchanged glances.

'I don't believe you,' he yelled.

'It's the truth. If it weren't, his body'd be laying out there in the dirt with those other two.'

'Where's Will Curtis, then?' Sally interjected.

'We don't know. Dawson took him into town.'

'Where?'

'Don't know. Cobb said something earlier about some barn on the north edge of town.'

'Cobb?' called Abe Bannerman urgently. 'You mean Cobb McGillicutty?'

'That's the one.'

'He's working for Dawson, too?'

'That he is.'

Abe and Sally Bannerman conferred quietly before he resumed the discussion with the gunmen.

'Come on out. You got no other choice. Like we said, we'll treat you fairly and take you into Eugene, let the sheriff sort it out.'

'No tricks?'

'No tricks. You have my word.'

Nearly a minute went by as the two men inside considered their options. Finally they recognized the futility of staying inside the cabin.

'All right,' said the second man. 'We're coming out. We want to go to Eugene right away, y'hear?'

'Fine,' called Bannerman, who had

no intention of carrying out their request immediately.

The people surrounding the cabin could hear the plank being raised from behind the front door. Then the door opened slowly and a man appeared in the doorway.

'Coming out now,' he said.

He stepped out onto the porch and began to descend the steps.

'Where's your pard?' Abe Bannerman demanded.

'He's coming,' said the gunman.

'Get your hands up, you,' called Mike Tancred from his position across the yard.

The man halted uncertainly and started to raise his arms. Then he made his choice and drew his pistol. He raised it and began to fire toward Tancred.

'Get down!' Bannerman commanded his sister.

The words had scarcely left his mouth when the other gunman burst out of the cabin, two six-guns drawn. The men made for their horses at the hitching post. Mike Tancred fired at the first man, who doubled over for a moment, clutching his stomach. He raised his gun and fired again toward Tancred, but his shot was wild.

Tancred took careful aim and hit the man in the head. His body fell into the dirt only a few feet away from the body of Jake Douglas.

Desperate, aware of the futility of trying to shoot it out but also aware of the noose that likely awaited him if he surrendered, the other gunman turned to where the Bannermans were crouching in the trees. Pistols blazing, his aim was surprisingly accurate. Leaves and branches burst over the Bannermans' heads.

'I've got this,' Sally Bannerman said thinly.

She lifted the pistol and fired once. The man in the yard took a bullet directly to the heart. His arms fell to his side and his pistols fell from his fingers. He took a step backward, trying to keep his balance, then fell dead onto the steps of Phil Shirreffs's cabin.

Abe Bannerman let out a low whistle.

'By God, Sally,' he said. 'That was a damn fine shot.'

Sally lowered the pistol and smiled wanly.

'He earned it,' she said, her cheeks flushed.

Tancred, Harmon, and Taggart stepped out from the trees and began walking toward the bodies that now littered the front yard. Abe Bannerman stood up and helped his sister to her feet. He put out a hand and she gave him her father's pistol. She retrieved the Winchester from the ground and handed that to him as well.

'We're going to get a few more of our neighbors,' Bannerman said. 'Then we're going into Junction City to finish this.'

* * *

'That's some good stuff right there,' said Mack Kantor.

He was still facing outward, talking to the other men outside, as he backed awkwardly through the back door of the barn, pushing it open with his shoulder.

Curtis had taken cover against the wall. As Kantor opened the door, Curtis was hidden behind it. He held his breath, keenly aware that one word from Kantor would alert Dawson's men in the yard outside.

Kantor turned around and was still mumbling approvingly to himself as he looked down the aisle between the stalls. His eyes widened in alarm and he opened his mouth to speak.

'What the — ?'

Curtis slipped in behind him, shutting the door as he did so. His mind was remarkably clear now. Kantor turned his head and Curtis could smell the fresh whiskey fumes coming off the man. He clamped his left hand hard over Kantor's mouth and reached into the killer's waistband with his right hand. He pulled Kantor's knife out and drove it firmly into the side of his neck.

The crutch dropped away and thudded onto the floor. Kantor's body stiffened briefly, then went completely limp in Curtis's arms. Blood spurted across Curtis's sleeve and down his arm.

The entire exchange had taken less than fifteen seconds.

He dragged Kantor's body into an empty stall and dumped it onto a pile of hay. Then he went into the store room to look for weapons.

The room contained mostly livery supplies, with some barrels stacked against the wall. Kantor's gunbelt lay over the back of a chair near a rolltop desk in the corner. Curtis strapped it on, then removed the pistol and checked the cartridges. Satisfied, he wiped the blood off the blade of Kantor's knife with a rag from the desk. He put the knife in his belt and stepped back into the barn.

He could hear the voices of the gunmen outside. There was no indication that the men had heard Curtis kill

Kantor. He walked down the aisle, glancing into the stalls to find a horse. There were four horses in the barn. Each one was large, powerful, and obviously very well cared for.

Curtis chose a big black. He opened the door to the stall and spent a minute calming the animal. The violence that had occurred in the barn had spooked the horse. It didn't take long for Curtis to win her over, and he slipped a bridle over her head and brought her out into the center of the aisle. He chose a saddle and slipped it over the horse's back. He cinched it up and took another glance around the room.

The back door opened suddenly.

'Mack, we got — hey!' a man yelled. He groped for his pistol, but Curtis was already firing. The man took a bullet in the groin and another in the chest before he went down. Boots scuffled behind the barn as Dawson's men responded.

Curtis dragged the horse toward a side door between two of the stalls. He had his hand on the door handle and was just about to open it when a pair of Dawson's men leapt through the back door over the dead body of their friend. They took cover in the first two stalls by the door. The first man was in the stall that contained the body of Mack Kantor.

'Goddamn!' he yelled to the other killer, 'he killed Mack.'

Curtis peered cautiously around the corner of the stall wall toward the center aisle. He was greeted with a bullet, which hit a board a few feet above his head. He pulled his head back and knelt in place, thinking.

'You look like hell, Curtis,' one of the men yelled. 'Mack really did a number on you, didn't he?'

Curtis grinned wryly, despite the pain of his split and swollen lips.

'How's Mack looking, you chicken-shit?' he retorted. 'He's a damn sight worse off than I am.'

Curtis could hear footsteps at the back of the building near the door.

Another voice entered the conversation.

'All right now,' a man said. 'This ain't going to end well for you, Curtis. Be sensible and surrender. We promise to kill you quick-like.'

The other men laughed.

'That's mighty kind of you,' said Curtis. 'I think I'll stay here, though, if it's all the same to you.'

'Suit yourself. And by the way — if you're figuring on trying to get out that side door there, keep in mind we got a man outside covering it.'

Curtis looked toward the door and swore quietly.

'Y'all think of everything, don't you?' he said acidly.

'That's why Mr Dawson pays us so well.'

More laughs came from the back of the room.

'Take the money while you can,' Curtis advised. 'Dawson's luck is going to run out. When it does, he's going to take all of you down with him.'

'We'll see about that.'

Curtis stiffened when he heard one of the men make a dash down the aisle and dive into one of the stalls not far from Curtis's position. They had him cornered and were going to pin him where he was. He could try to make an escape through the side door, but he knew the man hadn't been lying when he said someone was out there covering it, waiting for Curtis to make a break for it.

There was no way around it; his options were bleak no matter what way you looked at it. His best bet, he thought reluctantly, would be to stand his ground and take out as many of Dawson's men with him as he could. He felt no self-pity or regret, only a fierce determination to make these men pay for what they had done, and what they were about to do.

He'd had no illusions about what the consequences might be for allowing himself to be entangled in the conflict between Clem Dawson and the ranchers of Junction City. He'd had high hopes for a positive outcome, but that appeared impossible now — at least for him. But if he could take two or three of the men in the barn with him, then he would give the Bannermans and their neighbors that much more of a fighting chance.

The man who'd moved a few stalls closer to Curtis made a break for the stall beside him. Curtis was ready. He leapt to his feet and raised his pistol. This time he didn't show himself in the center aisle, but stood up over the plank wall of the stall just as the man dived into the straw that was strewn across the hardpacked dirt floor. Curtis recognized Ike Gibson, who screamed in terror when he spied Curtis looking down at him. A blast from Mack Kantor's pistol silenced the scream instantly. Curtis returned to a crouching position behind the wall.

'So much for your friend,' he taunted.

Enraged, the gunmen responded with brute force. They sprayed the wall and floor around him with one bullet after another. One stray slug found its way into the horse's head. The animal made a strangled noise and fell onto the floor near Curtis, nearly crushing one of his legs as it collapsed. Fragments of wood burst around him and fell into his hair and onto his shoulders.

Finally the fusillade ended. Curtis could hear the men reloading their pistols.

'We're coming for you, you son of a bitch!' someone yelled.

Curtis opened the cylinder on his pistol and inserted another bullet. He wanted to be fully loaded when he made his last stand.

Then he heard the thunder of approaching horse hoofs and the eruption of gunfire outside. The horses drew closer and a man screamed in the yard.

Abe Bannerman's voice sounded and Curtis knew that the tables had turned.

11

Curtis heard the horses pull up in the yard, followed by the sounds of the riders dismounting.

'Will!' yelled Abe Bannerman. 'Will — you around?'

'I'm in here,' Curtis called back.

'Can you come out?'

Curtis looked toward the door. The dead horse's body had fallen in such a way as to block the door from opening. It had to weigh over a thousand pounds and Curtis knew he couldn't move it.

'No. I'm stuck in here. Along with three of Dawson's boys.' He called to the gunmen crouching in the barn. 'You hear that, gentlemen? You're through. There ain't no getting out of here alive if you fight.'

'Same goes for you, Curtis,' one of the men responded defiantly.

Despite the bravado, Curtis could tell

that much of the fight had gone out of whoever it was who'd uttered those words. Dawson's men were beaten and they knew it. The only question now was whether they'd listen to reason and surrender or decide to go out in a futile blaze of glory.

The answer came sooner than Curtis expected.

Shots were fired near the rear of the barn, and Curtis realized that Dawson's men were exchanging fire with Bannerman and the other homesteaders, who were now clustered at the back of the building.

He rose and looked over the top of the stall wall. He could only see one of the men, three stalls down on the opposite side of the aisle. The man was distracted, firing toward the back door. Curtis lifted his gun and shot him dead where he sat, his bullet entering the left side of the man's head. Now only two of Dawson's killers remained in the barn. When they saw their partner dead in the stall, they decided that discretion was truly the better part of valor.

'All right,' the man closest to the back door hollered when there was finally a break in the gunfire, 'we're ready to give up. No more shooting.'

'Throw your pistols into the aisle,' Bannerman said.

Curtis heard the guns clatter into the dirt.

'Get your hands in the air and step out of the stalls. Two of your pards died out at Phil Shirreffs's place this morning because they decided to make a last stand. Don't be stupid like them.'

Seconds later the men emerged from the stalls, their hands raised obediently. Bannerman had them turn around to prove that they didn't have other weapons on them. Once that had been confirmed, he came into the barn, a pistol in each hand. He was followed by Mike Tancred and Gil Harmon.

'Will,' he called, as Tancred and Harmon tied up the gunmen.

Curtis stepped out from the small passageway from which he and the horse had almost escaped. Bannerman was clearly shocked by his friend's appearance.

'Judas, Will! What happened?'

Curtis walked toward Bannerman and pointed at the body of Mack Kantor.

'I ran into an old friend,' he said. 'He had a little fun at my expense.'

'My God, I guess so,' Bannerman said. He looked at Kantor's body. The knife wound gaped in the dead man's neck. 'Glad to see you returned the favor.'

'It was the least I could do.'

Bannerman put his hand on Curtis's shoulder.

'Damn, Will. I'm glad to see you're in one piece, even if you're not looking so good.'

Curtis chuckled despite himself.

'Thanks, Abe,' he said. 'I think.'

'You know about Jake Douglas and John Wilson?'

'Yes. I saw it happen. You know Dawson hired Cobb McGillicutty to run y'all off your land?'

'I heard. Pretty hard to believe.'

'Believe it.'

They followed Tancred and Harmon out into the vard as they led Dawson's men, who were now bound. Four other of Bannerman's neighbors were sitting their mounts in the yard.

'Glad to see you brought reinforcements, Abe. How's Sally holding up?'

'She's doing fine. I made her head home rather than come into town. She wasn't too happy about that. She took out one of Dawson's bushwhackers out at Phil Shirreffs'.'

'What?'

'She's a hell of a shot, Will.'

'So you've told me.'

Curtis paused by a trough at the back of the barn. He stripped his shirt off and dunked his head into the frigid water, gasping as he pulled it back out. He repeated the process, and soaked his shirt in the water, getting some of the blood and most of the vomit off it. Then he put it back on and buttoned it up.

'Let's head over to Dawson's place and finish this thing,' he said.

★ ★ ★

The homesteaders split up, with half the group approaching Dawson's house from the alley and the other half approaching along Main Street. Tancred stayed at the barn with the two prisoners.

Alerted by the gunfire at the barn, several of the residents of Junction City watched the horsemen from their porches.

'God bless you!' one elderly woman called from the open second-floor window of her home. Abe Bannerman nodded at her, his jaw set with determination.

The men in the alley dismounted and left their horses tied to a fence a few doors down from Dawson's house. They approached the house with guns drawn, which was just as well, for they were greeted with gunfire from the back porch and the trees near the fence.

Curtis and Bannerman dismounted and tied their mounts to a hitching post at the bank. Curtis read the sign at the front of the building: Bank of Junction City, Est. 1876, Clement F. Dawson, President.

Not for much longer, he thought.

They had reached the edge of the fence in front of the house when they heard the gunshots in the back. Both men had already drawn their pistols.

'Cover me, Abe,' Curtis said.

He leapt over the fence into the yard and knelt behind some rose bushes. His eyes scanned the windows and the porch for any signs of movement. He saw nothing.

Still in a crouching position, he moved rapidly across the yard to the edge of the porch. He expected someone to take a shot at him anytime, but nothing happened. Cautious, he waited a little longer, looking toward Abe Bannerman to make sure the man was still covering him. He was.

Curtis relied on speed to get him safely to the front door. He flattened himself against the wall beside the door and then dared to take a peek through the ornate decorated glass into the entryway. There was no sign of movement there. He reached down and tried the knob. To his surprise it was unlocked. He looked one last time through the window in the door before he pushed it open and stepped into the house, his pistol extended in front of him.

Guns continued to explode behind the house, helping to muffle the sounds of movement inside. Curtis took a few steps and moved toward the wide-arched entrance to the living room. Right as he looked into the room, a large man pivoted from his position near the fireplace and fired at him. Curtis dived forward and hit the floor in the hallway, on the other side of the archway. The bullet smacked into the wall not far from where Curtis had been standing a moment before.

Curtis rolled over onto his back, his gun raised, and the gunman jumped through the hallway in pursuit of his quarry. Their eyes met and Curtis recognized the face of Cobb McGillicutty.

'Curtis!' yelled McGillicutty.

The killer was so shocked to find Curtis alive that he momentarily gave his opponent an advantage. Curtis brought up his left hand and fanned the hammer on his pistol, sending four shots into McGillicutty's torso before the latter could get another word out. McGillicutty gasped, his face distorted, and fell backward through the open front doorway onto the porch.

Curtis sat up and looked toward the killer. The acrid gunsmoke dissipated and he saw that McGillicutty was no longer a threat to anyone.

He also realized that the shooting behind the house had stopped. His mind was just registering the change when he heard rapid footfalls up on the second floor. He lunged to his feet and made his way to the staircase.

A feeling of déjà vu came over him as he ascended the steps, his pistol at the ready. He recalled a night just a couple months ago when he'd climbed these stairs in pursuit of Clem Dawson, and now here he was again. That time, both men had survived their encounter. This time, however, only one man would emerge alive. Curtis knew there was no other way.

No one stood at the top of the landing and Curtis covered the last five steps in two quick leaps. The hallway was empty, but the door to Clem Dawson's bedroom was wide open.

'Dawson?' Curtis called, his voice reverberating off the walls. 'You're finished. Come out and face the music.'

There was no response.

Curtis moved forward down the hallway toward Dawson's bedroom. He halted a few feet from the open doorway. He could see part of the room from where he stood. On a desk on the far side of the bedroom was an open leather valise, beside which stood two tall stacks of paper money. Clem Dawson was doing some packing.

Impulsively, Curtis jumped through the doorway into Dawson's room. He swung the gun from left to right, covering the entire room. Dawson was nowhere to be seen. Curtis parted the curtains and looked down into the back yard. He saw Gil Harmon's body in the alley, and the bodies of two of Dawson's men in the grass. Dean Taggart and three other homesteaders were moving out of their covered positions and moving toward the back of the house.

Hinges creaked behind him and Curtis twirled, thumbing back the hammer on his gun. In the doorway of his son's bedroom across the hall stood Clem Dawson, a shotgun gripped in his hands. His clothes were disheveled and his face glistened with sweat. His bloodshot eyes regarded Curtis with unalloyed hatred.

Curtis's hand was perfectly steady as he stared back at Dawson. The air between them seemed charged with danger.

'You're done,' Curtis said. 'Put the gun down or you'll be carried out of this house boots first.'

'You don't know what you've done, Curtis,' said Dawson, his voice trembling with barely controlled frenzy. 'You should never have gotten involved in my affairs.'

'Tell that to Tabor Evans.'

Dawson glared at Curtis and a drop of sweat fell from one of his pasty jowls. Then he bared his teeth and Curtis saw his finger tighten on both triggers of the shotgun.

A gunshot sounded and Dawson's eyes widened with horror and disbelief. His fingers loosened of their own accord and the shotgun fell onto the expensive rug on which Dawson stood. Dawson clutched the bullet wound in his side and turned to his right.

'You!' he shrieked to someone out of

225

Curtis's line of sight.

Another shot came from the place where Dawson was looking. Then another. The banker struggled to say something else, but nothing came from his mouth other than an anguished croak. He fell backwards onto a velvet sofa behind him before falling forward onto the floor. He didn't move again.

Curtis looked down at his gun, his mind not quite comprehending how Dawson had died.

'C'mon in, Curtis,' called a voice from the room across the hall. 'I'm all done shooting now.'

A pistol was tossed onto the rug in the room across the hall from Curtis, who stepped forward and looked in. Alvin Dawson sat in his expensive wheelchair, his legs covered by a blanket. The look he gave Curtis contained no rancor, and the latter realized that the younger Dawson wasn't a threat to him.

'I'm done,' Alvin Dawson said plainly, his eyes resting on the body of his dead father. 'I'm all done.'

Curtis took in the scene for a moment before he went down the stairs and called to Abe Bannerman to let him know it was safe to come in now.

12

Within a few weeks life had largely returned to normal in Junction City. The revelation of Clem Dawson's murderous activities made the front pages of almost every newspaper in Oregon, and the front pages of several out-of-state papers as well. The governor, stung by the accusation that he might have been inappropriately involved with the elder Dawson, had a new district attorney appointed in Eugene. Only one of Dawson's gunmen survived the shoot-out in the banker's yard, and he was convicted of a variety of crimes and sent up to the state penitentiary in Salem.

The new prosecutor declined to bring charges against Alvin Dawson for the shooting of Clem Dawson. Given the young man's physical and mental condition, it was doubtful he would have survived a trial to begin with. Also, his father's reputation was now so black that much of the public approved of the son's actions. He inherited his father's fortune but remained in isolation in the Dawson home. He had no visitors apart from his servants.

The former vice-president of the Junction City bank took over its operations. The sign with Clem Dawson's name on it was removed from the front of the establishment.

On a cold morning almost exactly a month after the shoot-out at Dawson's, Will Curtis sat on Abe Bannerman's porch, smoking a cigarette and chatting with Maggie Bannerman. He had mostly recovered from his last encounter with Mack Kantor, who was buried in an unmarked grave in the Junction City cemetery along with each of Dawson's other dead gunmen.

'Well, Will — what are your plans now?' asked Maggie, trying to keep her tone casual as she sat knitting in the porch's rocking-chair.

'I don't rightly know,' Curtis said.

He knew why Maggie was asking the question. He'd been back on his feet for more than a week now, and there was nothing keeping him in Junction City: no family, no house, no business. A private person, he hadn't felt comfortable broaching the subject of his plans.

'You still thinking about going down to your sister's place?'

'That probably wouldn't be a bad move for me,' he said. 'They say there're a lot of opportunities down there for people who want land of their own.'

Maggie was silent, her brow furrowed. She'd been confident before the shoot-out that Curtis would stay around, and maybe even marry Sally. Perhaps seeing the cold-blooded murders in Phil Shirreffs's yard, along with the torture he'd suffered at the hands of Mack Kantor, had changed Curtis's mind about Junction City.

The rumble of approaching horses ended the conversation. Curtis still felt a little tingle in his stomach when he heard that sound, something that had never been true before his arrival in this small Oregon town. He had to remind himself that Clem Dawson was dead, along with Cobb McGillicutty and the rest of the banker's henchmen. The sound of horses' hoofs was no longer a harbinger of danger in these parts.

Abe Bannerman emerged into the yard, followed closely by his sister. Maggie rose and put down her knitting.

'I'm going to put on some coffee,' she said.

Curtis stepped down into the yard as she went into the cabin.

'Morning, Sally,' he said with a smile.

The two riders drew reins and dismounted.

'Good morning, Will,' said Sally Bannerman.

'Abe, I'll be ready to help you chop wood any time you're ready,' Curtis said. 'First, I'd like to talk to Sally for a few minutes.'

Abe Bannerman glanced between his

sister and the cowboy, then nodded and headed for the front door of the house.

Sally gave Curtis a curious look, with just a hint of anxiety in her face. She, too, had noticed the brooding indecision in him over the last month.

'What did you want to talk about, Will?' she asked.

'Well . . . ' he began. There was uncertainty in his voice. 'Are you still thinking about rebuilding your pa's saloon?'

Sally thought that was an improvised question rather than what Curtis really wanted to discuss.

'Yes,' she replied. 'I'm thinking about it.' She waited a moment. 'Why do you ask?'

Curtis shrugged nonchalantly.

'That'll probably keep you real busy,' he said.

'It's a demanding job, running a saloon.'

'I'm sure it is.' He raised his eyes and met her gaze. 'Dangerous, too.'

She smiled.

'Sometimes, yes.'

'Kind of job where a woman might want to have a man around,' he opined, grinning. 'You never know who might come into a saloon and cause problems.'

'That's true,' she said, her heart pounding.

'That's why I've been thinking that, um — maybe it would be a good idea for me stay around Junction City. Just in case you need some help.'

Curtis reached out and took Sally's hand, drawing her close to him. He kissed her gently, then held his hands on her shoulders as they looked into each other's eyes.

'You just want to stay around in case I need help?' she asked, with mock coyness.

He laughed, relieved that they were finally having the discussion he'd been wanting to have with her since almost the first time he'd laid eyes on her.

'Maybe there are other reasons for me to stay. It's not right for a young woman to have to go through life on her own, without a pa to help her and all.'

'Well, I have Abe . . . '

'Yes, but Abe's got his own family and his own responsibilities.'

'So you mean a — a husband?' she asked plainly.

Curtis's face flushed and he held Sally's hand.

'I can think of worse things to do with my life than be your husband,' he said. 'Can you imagine yourself as my wife?'

Tears welled in her eyes.

'I think I can see that,' she said.

'I was hoping you'd say that,' Curtis said, a look of relief hovering over his features.

'Coffee's ready,' called Maggie from inside the house.

Without another word, Will Curtis and Sally Bannerman walked up the steps and went inside. They were still holding hands.

Gale Force 10

Gale Force 10

The Life and Legacy of Admiral Beaufort

1774 – 1857

Nicholas Courtney

review

First published in 2002
by REVIEW

An imprint of Headline Book Publishing

10 9 8 7 6 5 4 3 2 1

Cataloguing in Publication Data is available
from the British Library

ISBN 0 7472 7210 7

Typeset by
Letterpart Limited, Reigate, Surrey
Printed and bound in Great Britain by
Mackays of Chatham plc, Chatham, Kent
Designed by Anthony Cohen

HEADLINE BOOK PUBLISHING
A division of Hodder Headline
338 Euston Road
LONDON NW1 3BH

www.headline.co.uk
www.hodderheadline.com

Contents

AUTHOR'S NOTE

A s I HAVE QUOTED SO liberally from the letters, journals, and printed sources, I have only given source notes for the material actually quoted. To save peppering the text with even more indices, I have omitted the source of detail such as the weather on a specific day, or the description of a person or room, thus no detail has been invented. Likewise, the dialogue in the text is all reported speech taken from Beaufort's letters. In the main, the quotes are reproduced verbatim, except those instances in Beaufort's letters and journals where he uses code or shorthand for nautical terms. Force 10 on today's Beaufort Scale is classified as a storm but Francis Beaufort had it as a gale (see Appendix 2), hence the title.

ACKNOWLEDGEMENTS

WHAT HAS MADE THIS BIOGRAPHY of Francis Beaufort so enjoyable to research and write is the help and encouragement of all those who gave their knowledge and research so freely. As a 'breed', hydrographers and cartographers (especially those historians concerned with the history of hydrography and cartography) must rank amongst the most generous, in particular Dr Andrew Cook, Map Archivist, India Office Records, who steered me through Beaufort's early years and his relationship with Alexander Dalrymple and generously gave me his valuable research and contacts around the world. In the United States, Dr Mary Robinson and her admirable staff made my three visits to the Huntington Library, San Marino, both fruitful and enjoyable, while Ed Redmund in the Library of Congress, Washington

DC, produced some vintage material. Elizabeth Dunn, Dukes University N.C., came up with Beaufort's prize money and account book; Dr Darrack Danta of California State University, Northridge introduced me to Dr Arnold Court's great meteorological archive. In Ireland, Larry Conlon drove me around Beaufort's haunts, adding much local colour.

At home, Dr N. A. M. Rodger and Professor Roger Knight set me straight on the eighteenth-century Royal Navy, as did Claire Tomalin on the vagaries of early nineteenth-century courtship. Captain Rodney Browne RN explained the complexities of early hydrographic surveying. Liza Verity of the National Maritime Museum, Greenwich, provided a miscellany of valuable material and detail, as did Dr Gloria Clifton on instruments, while Jonathan Betts came up with a wealth of information from the Royal Observatory. At the Hydrographic Office, Taunton, the archivist Adrian Webb and his assistant Sharon Nichol ceaselessly plied me with thousands of Beaufort letters, charts and papers, while Lt Cdr John Blake RN gave me the idea for the biography of Francis Beaufort in the first place. Dr Michael Fisher and Dr Peter Fenwick both helped on Beaufort's many medical conditions and near-death experiences.

To all of these, and the many others (including Edith Stokes, the housekeeper of Mount Pleasant, Reigate, who provided a refuge when the builders next door grew too hard to bear), my heartfelt thanks. But most of all, I owe a deep debt of gratitude to my wife Vanessa, who did not overly complain at living so intimately with Francis Beaufort for two whole years, and it is to her that this biography is dedicated.

PROLOGUE

'In the name of God, Amen.'

St Andrew's Day, 30 November 1871. Gravesend

THE TINY MISSION CHURCH, with its pitch pine ceiling shaped like an upturned boat, was filled with the ringing tones of Bishop Cloughton, the Archdeacon of London. Around him in the chancel, the serried ranks of clergy were pinned against the walls below a large mosaic depicting *Christ calming the Tempest*, while the nave was tightly packed with a congregation that far outnumbered the 153 chairs – the exact size of the miraculous draught of fishes caught by Christ's disciples Simon Peter and his brother Andrew, after whom the new church was to be named that day. The weak winter sun shone through the stained glass windows showing the two Apostles. 'The said building now furnished,' the Bishop concluded, 'with all things needful and now necessary, I by Divine Permission do dedicate this church to the service of Almighty God and the memory of Rear Admiral Sir Francis Beaufort, Knight Commander of the Most Honourable Order of the Bath.'

Sitting in the place of honour beside the altar steps, Miss Rosalind Beaufort, the Admiral's unmarried daughter, listened demurely to the service. Although she had provided £1,000 towards the building of the church (Charles Dickens was a fellow benefactor), she wanted to remain anonymous. But Victorian tradition required a heroine. Miss Beaufort's involvement with St Andrew's Waterside had begun three years earlier when she had seen a snippet in the *Penny Post*, a sugary weekly journal. The advertisement, placed by the vicar of Gravesend, called for 'any pious mourner [to] purchase our Mission House now hired, and erect a Memorial Chapel to the memory of some lost friend'.[1] He believed that it would serve better than a costly marble memorial. So the church was built in memory of her adored father to whom she had willingly devoted so many of her spinster years. It would minister to a 'floating parish' of families living aboard the lighters, barges, shrimp boats, coal hulks – indeed every manner of craft – moored on the crowded river as far as the eye could see in both directions. That day, a little way from the shore, two ocean-going vessels swung at anchor on the turning tide as they waited to take on the last of the emigrants bound for a new life in Australia.

The ceremony of dedication over, the calm of the service gave way to the noises, smells and bustle of the busy waterfront outside. Fishwives, from their ramshackle shrimp market opposite the church, eyed the congregation as it snaked its way along the dockside and on through the pleasure gardens towards the Clarendon Hotel for a celebratory lunch. They walked slowly, muffled against the chill salt breezes from the North Sea that blew uninterrupted up the River Thames. Once inside the hotel, they climbed the stairs to the first floor dining room and warmed themselves by two blazing fires at each end of the room.

Lunch was a genteel affair, far removed from the insalubrious hotel surroundings. Course followed course until it was time to drink the health of the Queen Empress. Toasts were given to the 'Prosperity of the Mission', and answered in a predictable self-congratulatory manner. Flummery monologues followed until it was the turn of Admiral (later Sir Edward) Inglefield. He rose to his feet slowly. Like those before, he praised the work of the founders of the mission, then continued: 'It is doubly interesting to me that first the church was dedicated to Almighty God, and then in loving remembrance of an old brother officer, a great friend, and a gallant admiral, a man whom I had learned to esteem more than anyone on earth. Of all the men I have ever met, of all the officers I have sailed with, I never knew one who was a more sincere Christian, more modest and charitable, than Admiral Beaufort.'[2] Admiral Inglefield was clearly moved. Although born sixty years apart, Beaufort had not only been a great friend, but also his mentor. In the measured tones of the quarterdeck, Inglefield went on to describe Beaufort's career. He was talking to the converted. They all knew of the Wind Scale that bore his name, but few of his work as a cryptographer. Murmurs of approval and nodding assent, particularly from the Naval contingent, followed as the Admiral described Beaufort as 'the most accomplished hydrographer at the Admiralty in his own, or indeed any, time'.[3] He told of what his friend had done for the advancement of marine geography, and how he had transformed 'a mere map-office or chart depôt for the Admiralty' to a Hydrographic Office that was the most respected in the world.

He continued, extolling Beaufort's long and distinguished Naval career. He spoke of shipwreck and the many near fatal wounds, of valour in battle and how he had been the last surviving officer to fight at the Battle of the Glorious First of June in 1794. Then he enlarged on his prowess as a surveyor, particularly in charting the southern coast of Turkey. Although virtually self-educated, 'Beaufort,' he declared, 'was a savant in the true sense of the word, and a much respected member of the Royal Society.'[4] Inglefield turned and acknowledged Lady Franklin seated on his left as he spoke of Beaufort's involvement with the protracted search for her husband, Sir John Franklin, lost on his ill-fated expedition searching for the North West Passage. Inglefield had, in fact, commanded the yacht *Isabel* in a privately funded rescue attempt in 1852 (and HMS *Phoenix* a year later), and received a Gold Medal from the Royal Geographical Society from Beaufort himself. In conclusion the Admiral quoted the great American hydrographer Matthew Fontaine Maury that 'navigators of all nations owe him a deeper debt of gratitude than to any man dead or living'.

Speeches over, the guests departed. The Gravesend townsfolk walked back to their houses nearby, while a pinnace bore the Naval contingent to Greenwich. A special train had waited to take the Beaufort family and friends back to London. As they scattered in every direction, the *Star of Peace* of the Aberdeen Clipper Line weighed anchor and slipped downstream. As she passed the new little church of St Andrew on her way across the seas to Sydney, Australia, the bells (the gift of Admiral Inglefield) rang out – as they were to do for every emigrant ship bound for a new life.

CHAPTER 1

Master Beaufort

ON THE MORNING of 17 March 1789, the wind was in the right quarter to carry the Long Ferry from Billingsgate in the City of London down the River Thames as far as Gravesend in less than the usual six hours. When she finally tied up at the Three Crowns Causeway, her assorted passengers, mostly sailors and tradesmen, leapt on to the dock and were instantly absorbed into the crowded waterside street. Totally out of place amongst this rough company was a diminutive, though dapper, figure dressed in black doeskin breeches, a bottle-green coat with a clerical neck cloth and jabot beneath a heavy cloak. He was accompanied by a boy, doubtless his son by appearance and equally slight frame. The boy too was well dressed, except that his clothes were obviously for the sea. A porter hefted the boy's trunk on to his back and followed father and son along the main street to the Clarendon Hotel. The Reverend Dr Daniel Augustus Beaufort had come to see his son Francis off on his first voyage aboard the Honourable East India Company's ship the *Vansittart*.

Dr Beaufort had chosen to sail to Gravesend on the Long Ferry as it was cheaper than travelling by coach, even on the outside, and although the Clarendon Hotel belied its Royal origins (the site of a palace of James II and named after his father-in-law, the Earl of Clarendon) it was at least clean and comfortable. They dined there that night 'very agreeably with Captain Wilson [the captain of the *Vansittart*] by invitation'[1]. Lestock Wilson, a thorough going seaman in his late thirties, had agreed to take Francis on his forthcoming voyage to China. Also present at the dinner was Wilson's seven-year-old daughter Alicia, who thought Francis 'a remarkably clever, well-informed & well-behaved boy, although from bashfulness, somewhat brusque in manner'.[2] She liked his looks too. Though small, Francis was well proportioned. He had a pleasant, round face dominated by bright blue eyes and a firm set jaw, with a high, intelligent forehead: looks that were to remain with him until early middle age. The meeting was truly auspicious, for both Wilson and Francis took to each other immediately and they formed a close bond that was to last the whole of their lives. Francis was also to marry Alicia. But even more important to Francis was that Wilson was a first-rate surveyor and navigator, skills that would have the most profound influence on Francis' subsequent career.

For two days the Beauforts kicked their heels in Gravesend while the *Vansittart* completed the landing of stores from the East India Company depôt. They visited the grave of Pocahontas, the North American Indian princess; they dined with distant relations. Then, on the morning of 20 March, they looked out towards the familiar berth only to find that the *Vansittart* had weighed anchor at 6 o'clock that morning and slipped down the river without Francis. Consternation. At vast expense, a chaise was hired and they pursued the ship. Eventually they found her 'going well under sail'.[3] Fortunately, she anchored at 10 o'clock and Francis was able to go aboard 'to attend upon Capt. Wilson'.[4] The Reverend Beaufort watched the *Vansittart* weigh anchor at 2 o'clock that afternoon and slip down the River Thames on 'a stiff SW breeze'[5] before he returned to London. And so began, albeit a little late, a voyage that would shape the 14-year-old Francis Beaufort as a seaman, test him as a man, and confirm his passion for the sea that was to last the whole of his life.

The Long Ferry plied between the City of London and Gravesend.

Whatever decided Francis Beaufort on his career, it was nothing to do with his ancestry, nor his immediate family. His direct line can be traced to a François de Beaufort, the head of the Huguenot branch of a minor, but nonetheless ancient, noble family from northern France. After the anti-Huguenot Massacre of St Bartholomew in 1572, when all family records were burned, François de Beaufort abandoned his estates near Meaux in the Champagne country and settled in Sedan, then an independent Protestant stronghold. For four generations the de Beauforts lived there uneventfully, acting as agents for the Contes de Rouci, the local grandee family. With the Revocation of the Edict of Nantes in 1685, they were on the move again – as Francis Beaufort was to comment later, his was 'a strictly nomadic family'. The head of the family, another François de Beaufort, fled from his home and possessions disguised as a peasant with his son, 'Alexandre, who was then an infant, concealed in a pannier on the back of an ass'.[6] Heading west across the Rhine, they found asylum in the Duchy of Cleres, in Westphalia. François prospered and rose to become the Comptroller of the Court of Lippe-Detmold and a captain in the Dutch cavalry. In 1710, the Emperor Joseph I created him a noble of the Holy Roman Empire 'by a diplôme recognising his antecedent French nobility'[7] rather than for any gallant service. The title, however, devolved on his legitimate heirs in perpetuity, as did the Beaufort crest – a virago holding a looking glass rising from a castellated tower or *beau fort*. Their motto is also a play on their name: *La Vertu est un Beau Fort*.

It was Francis Beaufort's grandfather, Daniel Cornélis de Beaufort, the seventh child of François and Louise Marie de Beaufort who 'founded' the Irish branch of the family. Born in Wesel in 1700, he followed what by then had become a family tradition and joined the Prussian army. Military life was obviously not for him, for on the death of his father he instantly resigned his commission to read theology at the University of Utrecht. Newly ordained, he arrived penniless in England in 1728 to a parish in Spitalfields, at that time a poor Huguenot quarter in London of, mostly, silk weavers. Later ordained in the Church of England, he took the parish of East Barnet, then a fashionable London suburb.

The move to Ireland came through the statesman William Stanhope, Earl of Harrington. Daniel Cornélis had married Ester Gougeon, the daughter of a fellow Huguenot from La Rochelle in 1738 and a year later their only child was born. He was christened Daniel Augustus in the chapel at St James's Palace where Daniel Cornélis had often preached. It was there that he came to the notice of Harrington who had taken the lease on a house nearby. When Harrington was appointed Viceroy of Ireland in 1746, Daniel Cornelius Beaufort (he had Anglicised his Christian name and dropped the *de* when he was naturalised in 1742) accompanied him as chaplain. With such a powerful patron, Daniel Cornelius hoped for high preferment in the Church of Ireland, but was only given the benefice of Navan, a fine county town in Meath just 30 miles to the northwest of Dublin, together with the pastoral care of the large Huguenot community in the capital. Eighteen years on, his son Daniel Augustus not only inherited the family gifts of scholarship and a versatile and inquiring mind, but also his benefice of Navan. The nomadic Beauforts had once again adopted a new country.

By the time Francis was born in 1774, the Beauforts were regarded as a well-connected county family, largely due to Daniel Augustus' advantageous marriage to Mary, the heiress daughter of William Waller in Allenstown, County Meath, and the friendship and patronage of such notable landowning families as the Fosters, Packenhams and Stopfords. But Mary brought more to the marriage than mere social advancement. A devoted wife and mother, she was well read and intensely loyal, providing much of the family finances and all of the stability. She was a perfect foil to her mercurial husband.

The Earl of Mornington, a neighbour who admired Daniel Augustus' zeal and energy, thought 'Little Dr Beaufort would make a good terrier!'[8] But to Francis his father was a god, and throughout his life he never wavered in his admiration of him.

He invariably signed himself 'your devoted son, pupil and friend' as a measure of his esteem even when sorely tried paying off his debts, which he could ill afford. Daniel Augustus was known as 'Beau', although his close friends and adoring family referred to him as DAB, a particularly apt sobriquet for one who throughout life was a 'dabbler'. He had so many interests that he rarely devoted enough of his considerable talents and energy to excel at any of them. Had he concentrated on the church, he might have become a bishop, but he was invariably passed over at each vacancy. However, he was generally thought of as a cut above the average eighteenth-century parson, while the Irish novelist Maria Edgeworth considered him 'an excellent clergyman of liberal spirit and conciliating manners'.[9]

Apart from a disastrously cavalier attitude to money that led to debt throughout the whole of his life, DAB did have many fine qualities for his son to admire. He was 'a man of taste and literature',[10] a lover of the theatre and good music, and true to his Huguenot ancestry, a connoisseur of food and wine. Well versed in the arts and architecture, he was an architect manqué, designing houses and churches worthy of any professional. Yet as with so much in his life, he never fulfilled his true potential. He was innovative as a farmer, experimenting with breeding cattle and husbandry. Shortage of funds, however, prevented him from making a real mark on Irish agriculture. As a topographer he excelled, but the success of his *Grand Topography of Ireland* published in 1792, was never repeated. 'Little Dr Beaufort' was, however, excellent company – 'always serene, yet always gay, to the last moments he was the life and spring of his little circle'.[11] Noted for his ready supply of astute observations or topical anecdotes, he was as much at home in an Irish farmyard as a London coffee house. His breadth of knowledge was vast. 'Ask Dr Beaufort' was the general cry whenever any point on scores of diverse subjects needed clarification. Although Francis took after his father in so many of his eclectic interests, he rarely achieved his easy manner.

There was no rectory to go with his benefice of Navan, and the Reverend Daniel Beaufort was fortunate to take a lease on Flowerhill House when he married in 1767. The house was modest and unpretentious, and belied its idyllic position. With its formal gardens laid out in the Dutch style, Flowerhill was surrounded by a small park dotted with oaks and horse chestnut trees. A gentle wooded valley led down to where the River Blackwater and the Boyne meet at the bridge behind the Watergate – literally, a gate in the river – set in the remains of the town's medieval wall. A line of tall elms led to the ruined Blackcastle on the banks of the Boyne.

Into this magical setting, Francis Beaufort was born at Flowerhill on 27 May 1774. He joined his sister Frances Anne, always known as Fanny, and William Louis in the nursery – another sister, Anne Maria, had died in infancy. Francis was a 'delicate baby', the cure for which appears to have been 'sea-water baths'. But life at Navan was not to last. When Francis was just two, the family moved 60 miles south to his father's other parish of Mountrath in County Laois, leaving Navan in the hands of a curate, Philip Barry of Kilcane. The move, that took two whole days, was tedious. 'At 2 o'clock on 15 August we bid adieu to Flowerhill,' wrote Dr Beaufort in his diary. 'Mary, 3 maids and 2 children in ye coach; Father, Fanny, William and I in the chaise with Mr Waller's horses.'[12] The whole family began in lodgings before a suitable house with 'a yard and a garden attached, also a brew house' could be found. Eventually life settled down in the new vicarage after Dr Beaufort had 'hung the wallpaper and fixed the bells'.[13]

Life for Francis in Mountrath over the next three years was particularly happy, though he can have seen little of his father who continued to live his life at a frenetic pace – travelling, commuting to Navan, managing two farms, visiting grand houses, and sitting on the Bench as a magistrate. His mother taught Francis to read, and when he was considered old enough, he was allowed to sit in on his elder brother and sister's lessons in the schoolroom. Younger siblings came later. Mary Anne had been born in 1776 (she died aged 15), Henrietta (always known as Harry or Harriet) arrived two years later and Louisa Catherine in 1781. They were a close family, as they were to remain for all their lives. There was much ragging and fun, his father often describing Francis as a 'giddy whelp'. Nor was he short on courage, even at that age. As he was later to admit, he was rarely without 'a cut or a bruise, or a broken head'. There were the usual childhood diseases, with frequent recurrences of the 'itch', a particularly virulent form of scabies, a contagious skin disease marked by itching and livid red papules caused by the itch-mite.

When Francis was a little over four, the whole family went to Allenstown where Dr Beaufort was to officiate at the marriage of his sister-in-law, Leonora Waller to a Captain Robert Mayne RN. The occasion was to direct the course of Francis' life. Mayne suggested that he could enter Francis for the Navy, 'to give him standing'. It had long been an illegal, but nonetheless common practice for captains in the Royal Navy to fictitiously enter friends' sons on their ship's books in order for them to gain nominal sea-time without actually going to sea. Mountrath, set in bogs and heathland and overlooked by the Slieve Bloom Mountains, was geographically as far from the sea as possible, virtually the centre of present-day Eire. At that age, Francis can hardly have seen a ship, let alone known much about the Navy, other than from storybooks. Yet once this decision had been made for him, Francis embraced it wholeheartedly. In a testament written in 1801, his sister Louisa Catherine – declared that Francis 'at the age of five . . . had manifested the most decided preference for the sea, had even refused to learn Latin or any of the rudiments of a learned profession & uniformly persisted in choosing a Naval life for his department'.[14] For Francis, the sea was no longer a childhood fantasy.

By early 1779, in true Beaufort fashion the family was on the move again. With his mounting debts – 'no pay, no port' cried his Dublin wine merchant – and the political tension rising around Mountrath, Dr Beaufort 'conceived a scheme to retire to some cheap place in France or England for three years to save money and pay off debts'.[15] Leaving Mary Anne and Harriet with a relative in Ireland, the Beauforts set sail for Wales. After much searching, they found an adequate but remote house, Penylan, near Carmarthen, for 25 guineas a year. They stayed for three years, except that 'they' did not often include Dr Beaufort who characteristically spent much of his time travelling and dodging creditors. At Christmas 1781 he recorded in his diary, 'So ends this year disagreeably as it began and has continued.' Francis had anaemia caused by internal parasites.

The move the next year to Piercefield near Chepstow was a considerable improvement for the Beauforts, although they were just as isolated. Thrown together for their five-year exile, the Beaufort children became totally self-sufficient and fulfilled in their own company. With no proper schooling, as Francis was later to admit, 'the young Beauforts were admirably taught by their Father and Grandfather in these secluded places far from all society'.[16] Another house was found in Cheltenham for the winter of 1782. Dr Beaufort made himself 'pretty snug' with his books and papers, but his wife, by then more used to living in remote places, found the society of the spa town frivolous. Cheltenham was supposed to provide some schooling for William and Francis and contact with boys of their own age, hitherto missing in their lives. However, at The Hospital and Free School, founded by Richard Pate in 1578, the boys were sent home after just two days by the headmaster, Reverend

Fowler, who declined 'to undertake their tuition on account of their Hibernian accent'.[17] They never returned. Their father thought it a 'gross impertinence'.

At last Robin Waller, Mary Beaufort's brother, provided the funds for the family to return to Ireland at the end of April 1784. They settled in a fashionable quarter of Dublin, taking a house in Mecklenburg Street. In the decades before the Union, Dublin was a vibrant and bustling city, with plenty of distractions, both academic and social. Dr Beaufort was in his element. Francis was sent to Master Bates' Military and Marine Academy in Dublin as a dayboy, and the three years he spent there were to be his only formal education. Surviving amongst his papers from that time is a presentation copy of examples of a variety of geometric shapes and theorems drawn by him, with the areas of each figure worked out in a neat copperplate hand. It is a remarkable testimonial to the truly excellent draughtsmanship of the ten-year-old Francis and shows his natural bent and grasp of mathematics. To his fellow cadets, though, he must have appeared a spoilt and precocious boy. With their unusual family circumstances, Francis was indulged by Mary, his mother, and, in keeping up with his sister and brother (five and two years older respectively) he was naturally advanced for his age. In addition, he came under the influence of his father's friends, the intelligentsia of Dublin, who were constant visitors to the house.

One of Dr Beaufort's closest friends was Dr Henry Ussher, the first Professor of Astronomy at Trinity College, Dublin. A new observatory had been built for him at Dunsink, the highest point outside Dublin, coincidentally on an outlying estate belonging to the Wallers. In July 1788, Dr Ussher took Francis on for five months to 'complete him in astronomy for the sea'.[18] Francis was a committed pupil, meticulously recording his observations, as he would throughout his life. An early example, dated 12 December, reads: 'at a little after 11 o'clock, I saw a circle around the moon at the distance of about 8' or 9' . . . The breadth of it was a semi [half the diameter] of the moon. It consisted of three shades – the internal one, next to the ☾, was a lightish purple, next to that a light red, and next a greenish yellow . . .'[19] An impressive entry for a boy of fourteen.

At that time, Dr Beaufort was working on a new topographical survey of Ireland to be published 'upon two sheets, by the scale of six miles to an inch, from the best authorities and most authentic information'.[20] He had enough faith in Francis to send him 'out in a chaise with all Ussher's apparatus for Athlone and Galway to make observations for the latitude and longitude of those towns'.[21] For that, he gave credit to 'a pupil of Dr Ussher' in the *Memoire* that went with the map.

Dr Beaufort was never afraid to make use of his friends and contacts, just as they continually made use of him. He had been to the 'Navy Office to know what time Francis had served on board *Portland* and *Trespassy*', but found that Captain Mayne had neglected to enter him as promised at the time of his marriage. In fact, what Dr Beaufort did not discover was that, on 21 June 1787, Mayne had already arranged for his old shipmate Captain Hugh Clobberry Christian to enter Francis as a volunteer on his ship, HMS *Colossus*.

Undaunted, Beaufort went to Allenstown to discuss Francis' future with his well-off in-laws. Robin Waller and his father both agreed that he should give up the idea of the Navy, and enter the service of the Honourable East India Company, possibly as a tribute to his brother James Waller who had died in their service in India. The Navy could be expensive, even for a midshipman. A midshipman's pay was minimal – around £2 per month – and only went part way towards his uniform, laundry and mess bills, a shortfall that could be as high as £100 a year on a smart ship. It was too great a drain on the family finances. Also, 'prize money' – where the entire value of any captured enemy ship was divided up between the admiral, officers and crew once agreed by an Admiralty Court – could never be relied upon to make up that shortfall. In the East India Company it was possible for the officers to actually *make* money, something hitherto unheard of in the Beaufort family. Soon after the decision had been taken, Dr Beaufort went to dine with Philip Barry of Kilcane, his former curate at Navan. One of the guests, a Mrs Savage, promised to write to her brother John Nugent, a governor of the East India Company. In the meantime, The Reverend Henry Dabzac (Dr Beaufort's other close friend from Trinity College) canvassed his relation Daniel Corneille, the former Governor of St Helena. He was by then living in Ireland, having been removed from his post after a mutiny on the island.

All East India Company ships were obliged to stop at St Helena, both to and from the East. In the spring of 1780, Lestock Wilson had been chief mate on the *York* bound for Madras. One of the passengers was a Miss Bonne Boileau, the daughter of an influential Huguenot trading family from Madras. He married her when they reached her home. When she was found to be pregnant on the homeward voyage, she was put ashore in St Helena where she stayed for six months with Governor Corneille and his wife. Ten years later, Lestock Wilson was able to repay the favour, and readily agreed to take Francis at Corneille's request. Francis was an attractive proposition, for not only was there a fee of 100 guineas attached – hence the term 'guinea pig' for a supernumerary – he was also already a competent navigator and surveyor. In July, Henry Dabzac wrote to Mr Waller that 'Governor Corneille had got an answer from Capt. Wilson who will take Francis',[22] but it was not until Christmas Day that Dr Beaufort wrote 'to Robin [Waller] about Francis and the £200 needed for his outfit'. Four days later, Robin replied that he and his father would stump up the money. In the New Year, Francis and his father 'dined by invitation at Governor Corneille's' in Dublin to thank him for his commendation.

For Francis with a ship to join, home life was running down fast. Dr Ussher gave him extra tuition in advanced mathematics and astronomy. His mother and sisters fussed around, putting his sea chest together. There was leave taking of his friends and relations. At last the moment he was simultaneously looking forward to and dreading came, and he left home forever. At the end of February 1789, Francis and his father crossed the Irish Channel to Holyhead, and five days later reached London. There Dr Beaufort was in his element visiting relations and making and renewing old contacts. Francis acquitted himself well in the two weeks that he spent in London society. They 'attended Lord Courtown, where we met his Grace of Montague [*sic*] who expressed himself afterwards to Lord C that he was very favourably inclined to recommend Francis'.[23]

At last it was time to travel to Gravesend by the Long Ferry, and 'repair aboard the *Vansittart*'. When he finally made it on board, with a sinking heart Francis said a hasty goodbye to his beloved father. But ahead lay a voyage of excitement and adventure. Without hardly a backwards glance, Francis went below to stow his kit. The ship keeled over as the wind filled her foretopsail and the mainsail was shaken out, and the flow tide bore her swiftly down and out of the Thames never, as it turned out, to return.

That night, little Dr Beaufort wrote in his diary, 'God protect my boy.'

CHAPTER 2

Master Beaufort HEIC

F OR TWO DAYS, the wind blew hard from the southwest
sending in a heavy sea. The *Vansittart*, together with a
host of other Honourable East India Company and
Navy ships, was penned into the Downs, an anchorage off the
east coast of Kent behind the Goodwin Sands. She rolled
hideously laying at her single anchor. Then, on the evening of
23 March 1789, the wind veered round to the east allowing her
to escape and run down the Channel before a gale. For those
first seven days aboard, Francis Beaufort lay in his bunk,
debilitated by chronic seasickness. He was even too ill to write
home before the channel pilot left the ship to return to port on a
passing American brig.

But the *Vansittart* needed a good wind to push her along.
Built in 1780 and on her fourth voyage to the East, while not

that old, she was slow. At 829 tons, 146 feet long and with three decks, she was a generic East Indiaman. Although passed seaworthy by the Company surveyors, she was still making two inches of water an hour in her bilges, a rate that increased as the voyage progressed. But to Francis, once on the move, his first ship and her crew were perfection. He wrote to his father: 'on the whole, I think being at sea when I am not sick in such a fine large ship and having pleasant Gent[n]. on board is one of the most delightful places in the world.'[1] Francis settled down well, but occasionally admitted to bouts of homesickness – 'though I am a sailor, I can't help shedding some tears'[2] – understandable in one from so close a family. Although rated 'captain's servant' on the ship's books with a salary of £1 3s a month, he had some status as a 'guinea pig'. He was soon moved from 'a nasty dank hole at the upper end of the gun deck'[3] to a better berth in the corner of the great cabin. The officers liked and favoured him. Captain Wilson allowed him to stow his books in a drawer in the cuddy, a small cabin off his day room, while Walter Caruthers, the first mate, often invited him to his cabin. The third and fifth mates also allowed him the run of their cabins, which at least gave him some privacy aboard such a crowded ship. Francis, however, was contemptuous of the four midshipmen, whom he thought 'a set of Blackguards',[4] while his fellow 'guinea pig' Andrew Hardy was 'the most troublesome Brat that ever was'.[5] They doubtless found the captain's and officers' favourite somewhat priggish.

By mid-April, the *Vansittart* was bowling along at around 6 knots having reached the northeast Trades below Las Palmas. As the weather improved, so life on board settled to the unalterable routine of a ship at sea. Francis quickly fell in with the rhythm of the well-run ship, and the sights and sounds became second nature to him. After a while he barely heard the slap of the bare feet overhead well before dawn as the crew scrubbed and holystoned the already pristine decks and flogged them dry, or the hammocks being piped up and stowed by the quartermaster in nets around the waist. He was kept busy by the boatswain throughout the day learning his craft of seamanship. When the fine weather called for a change of sails, Francis was sent aloft to help rig the main topgallant masts and yards, and bend on the new sails. He had no fear going aloft, nor did he object to his initiation ceremony of climbing into the mizzen top (on the outside of the crosstrees), where he was lashed to the rigging by two sailors and left there until his promise of two gallons of beer for his messmates released him. He was, however, able to indulge his passion for navigation and mathematics. Just three weeks out of England, he joined the officers on the quarterdeck every day to shoot the noontime altitude of the sun and work out the ship's position. There he was in his element. At night, he made celestial observations, taking hundreds of moon and star sights with the Captain and chief mate in the clear tropical night sky: 'tell Dr Ussher that,' he wrote home with pride. He was fortunate to have such able navigators to work with, and they to have such a talented pupil.

He lived well in his own mess, breakfasting at 9, with dinner at 2p.m., tea at 6 and supper at 9 in the evening. Occasionally he dined with the Captain and the other officers. With the gusto of a hungry and enthusiastic boy, he faithfully recorded one such dinner in a letter to his father: 'roast and boiled mutton, soup, a goose, two fowls, some duck curry with rice, with potatoes and carrots, and an apple pie afterwards'.[6] Every-thing was new and exciting, and Francis delighted in it all. The arrival of 'Mr and Mrs Neptune over the bows, with the barber and his assistant' as the *Vansittart* crossed the Equator was, however, less to his liking. While 48 of the crew were subjected to the rituals of crossing the Line – 'shaving and ducking time' – Francis rather demurely bought himself off.

The fine weather lasted until the Cape of Good Hope where the *Vansittart* was badly battered by gales and 'heavy squalls with some seas almost as high as the mizzen top breaking over us every minute,' Francis wrote home. Despite the damage to spars and rigging, Captain Wilson decided not to put into Simonstown to re-provision and repair his leaking ship, although by that time she was making 6¹/₂ inches of water an hour with the pumps manned most of the time. On the China run, East India Company ships were always in a hurry. The earlier the ship made Canton, the better the cargo; the earlier the return to London, the better the price for the cargo. So Wilson pressed on to the Straits of Sunda that lie between Sumatra and Java, where he anchored on 11 July. Their position by then was critical. At a meeting, 'the commander stated to the officers that there was water barely sufficient to last the ship's company three weeks longer and in his opinion it would be improper to pass the Straits without at least 10 weeks consumption on board'.[7] Added to that, ten men had scurvy, 'others looked likely', and rations for all were down to a minimum, mostly salt beef and ship's biscuits full of weevils. The officers unanimously agreed that they should put into the port of Batavia (the present-day Jakarta), the headquarters of the Dutch East India Company.

But Lestock Wilson had another reason to stop at Batavia. On his previous voyage to Canton, he had successfully navigated the difficult Gaspar Straits with its myriad of tiny islands to the east of Branca, a large island off Sumatra, rather than the approved, but longer route west of Branca. On his return to London, Wilson submitted his observation and marked up charts of the Gaspar Straits to Alexander Dalrymple, then hydrographer to the Honourable East India Company. Dalrymple, who was later to have such a huge influence on Beaufort's career, was 'clearly of the opinion that this track proposed promised to be infinitely preferable to the old passage through the Straits of Branca, and only requires to be further known and described to be rendered essentially useful and generally adopted by our outward and homeward bound ships'.[8] He therefore directed Wilson to pass through the Gaspar Straits again, considering him 'to be a proper person to make the necessary observations'.[9] In order to carry out a proper survey, Wilson first had to have an accurate fix on Batavia and, mindful of Dalrymple's instructions, to check his chronometers.

Dalrymple thought that the survey could be done in a week to ten days, but so important was it to the East India Company that Wilson was told to take as long as was practicable. But as he would be 'unavoidably detained some days on this service', when he reached Canton he was 'to consider the ship as arrived there, and to place her, accordingly, in order of turn for dispatch for Europe, so many days previous to her actual arrival there as she was usefully employed on the service abovementioned'. In other words, he could jump the queue by the number of days his survey took. But first they had to reach Canton.

The officers, with Francis, took bearings and made soundings through the Straits of Sunda and, mooring up each night, continued their survey along Java Head towards Batavia. Francis was fortunate to gain such practical experience and be given so much responsibility early in his career. Wilson was well pleased with him, and wrote to Dr Beaufort that Francis 'was a very fine boy'.[10] The *Vansittart* reached Batavia Roads on 14 July and, having inched her way between two moored ships, stuck fast 'on a knowle and hung forward, and immediately foundered'.[11] The *Vansittart's* crew sprung into action. They backed the topsails, then 'handed the sails, hoisted the boats out and ran a 9-inch hawser out of the starboard quarter'.[12] The guns were manhandled aft and after five hours they managed to pull her off without any lasting damage. The next day, Wilson and Francis took the cutter to see where his ship had foundered and discovered that she had actually struck the buoy, now sunk, that the Dutch had moored to mark a shoal. Francis was indignant that they received no help from the resident Dutch, and, when they finally made port, was even more incensed that the *Vansittart*'s 11-gun salute was only answered with seven guns by the garrison commander. Wilson swore that he would not give any salute on his departure.

While the rest of the officers and crew refitted, watered and reprovisioned the *Vansittart*, Wilson and Francis were allowed the free use of the observatory built at the top of a town-house by the Dutch astronomer Johan Mohr. For three weeks they worked all day taking observations, although Francis complained bitterly about everything. The weather was sultry, the fruit tasteless, the turtle soup not as good as mock turtle, but above all, the instruments he had to work with and the observatory were sub-standard. 'In short, I never saw such a place in my life,' he wrote to his father, asking for his comments to be passed on to Dr Ussher 'to divert him'. However, despite the apparent defects in his equipment, Francis was able to fix the latitude of Batavia with a borrowed sextant, if not exactly, at least more accurately than the Dutch. In fact, he managed it within a mile. 'I make the Lat. From 6° 8' to 6° 8' 40" S. I am so conceited as to think that my Lat. is much nearer to the mark as I have got so many [observations] and none of them disagree more than 20" from each other.'[13]

At last the *Vansittart* left Batavia and sailed on a fresh breeze across the Java Sea, then crept up the coast of Sumatra and past the Island of Branca. She was now a little more seaworthy, with her decks recaulked and her broken spars replaced. The cutter with the third officer and Francis went ahead, taking soundings of the approaches to the Gaspar Straits. Slowly the *Vansittart*, with her cutter leading the way, eased into the narrow channel. Just before 4 o'clock on 24 August, the lookout hailed the deck and reported a shoal to windward. The *Vansittart* immediately hove to. The cutter, that had been taking soundings ahead, was sent to investigate – there had been a false alarm that morning when fresh spawn was mistaken for shallow water. The cutter returned and 'while the officer was delivering his report to the Captain on the Quarterdeck, the ship suddenly shoaled her water, although lying at 7 fathoms. The anchor was immediately let go, and in swinging to which, she was immediately brought up under her mizzen chains by some sharp, perpendicular rocks.'[14]. In his subsequent report to the Directors of the East India Company, Wilson wrote that these 'sharp perpendicular rocks upon which there is not the least break or sign by which it can be discovered and from whence land is only just visible from the top of the masthead'.[15]

Officers and crew worked frantically to save the *Vansittart*. The sails were furled and soundings made around the ship. When deeper water was found to leeward, an anchor was taken out by the cutter on a small bower cable, and the capstan manned. As the anchor took hold and the cable payed off to bring her head round, the headsails were set. Slowly, she inched off the rocks. The carpenter was sent to inspect the damage and reported that she was badly holed and making about four feet of water an hour. Francis was assigned to one of the pumps. With all chain-pumps flailing, they were just able to keep her afloat. Then, in the half-light of dawn, they could see the damage. The bread room was awash, and water was rushing in on the starboard side, 'where the outside plank was stove in and daylight appeared through her bottom'.[16]

Highly regarded by the directors of the East India Company, Captain Wilson had been entrusted by them with the letters for the 'Select Committee in Canton' and a cargo and treasure in chests valued at £90,655. As soon as Wilson had assessed the damage, he had these chests of specie brought up on deck. The crew tried to plug the hole with a large tree trunk, but to no effect. Then a sheepskin was prepared, and a seaman, for a reward, 'volunteered' to dive under the ship and place it in the hole, but again with no success. As the water was gaining 18 inches in two hours on the pumps, a joint decision was made to cut and run to beach the *Vansittart*. All plain sails were set, and she made 5 knots back towards Sumatra. An island was spotted from the masthead, but they could not 'fetch it'. The position worsened by the minute, and those who could be spared from the pumps were sent to rescue the provisions and fresh water, firearms and ammunition, and to rig the longboat.

With nearly ten feet of water in the hold, the *Vansittart* was run ashore 'at about 1/2 before 9 PM on the island in the Latitude 2 degrees 9' South and about 7 miles from the Coast of Branca ... on a bank of sand just within a reef of rocks and about 3/4 of a mile from the island from which the reef extended'. At daylight, the condition of the *Vansittart* was assessed. Wilson called the ship's crew together to outline their plight. Only a few casks of water were salvaged, along with eight casks of porter, enough for 20 days. No water was found on shore. Also, it would not be long before the notorious Malay pirates arrived in force (a 'prow' had already been spotted) and, while they could doubtless defend themselves while the *Vansittart* remained entire, they 'must fall to a conquest of numbers' once the ship started breaking up. As she was 'lying on a lee shore with a swell setting right against her, and her after part afloat as far forward as her Main Chains, her bows bumping in the water, deeper in the offside than the inner',[17] this was most likely. Added to that, they were beached on an unknown and unfrequented shore with little or no chance of rescue from a passing ship.

As Wilson saw it, there were two options, which he put to the ship's company. The first was for the main body of the crew to stay with their ship, while the cutter went for help. The chances of a small boat surviving the open sea with winds, currents and Malay pirates were slim. Also, those left on the ship would be 'greatly distressed', believing that they were never going to be rescued as their stores dwindled, and to remain would rightly indicate to the pirates that there was something of value on board that should not be abandoned. Privately, Wilson thought that the chests of specie would be too great a temptation to the crew. Put to the vote, they universally decided on the second option – to take the whole ship's company in all the small boats with the provisions, ammunition and water (and beer) and go in convoy to the Dutch settlement of Pelambang on Sumatra. There was just a chance that they would pick up a passing ship on the way.

The letter that Francis wrote to his father describing his part in the shipwreck has not survived, but the chances are that it was left to him to fix the position of the ship before they left and to pack up the ship's chronometers, which were formerly in his sole charge.

The decision to abandon ship was followed by frantic activity. The treasure chests were thrown overboard, together with the surplus ammunition and stores, and the guns on the quarterdeck spiked. Then, at around 4 o'clock in the afternoon, 26 August, less than 24 hours after the *Vansittart* first struck the rock, the boats set off for their epic journey. The Captain and chief mate took the cutter with 12 hands, including Francis, while the second and third mates had just over half the crew in the long boat. The remainder went with the other mates and the gunner in the pinnace and the yawl, except for eight hands in the jolly boat and the four with the boatswain in the gig.

A near disaster struck immediately when the longboat almost foundered on the reef. When the cutter sent down a line, 'drunkenness prevented them making proper use of it' – the ship having been abandoned, the crew, not under orders, had raided the spirit room of the *Vansittart*. However, the cutter 'immediately ran out another short warp' and the longboat partially brought herself off and anchored in deeper water. The rest of the boats anchored in the lee of the ship. At daybreak, the company returned on board and church was rigged on board the *Vansittart* where Lestock Wilson read Divine Service. The boats were then manned again, and the long boat finally pulled herself clear of the reef. They all made sail and headed northwards, coasting some way off the Branca shore 'to prevent the natives from seeing them'. They spent a wretched night at anchor, where Captain Wilson destroyed the company papers, then set off the next morning with a pleasant breeze behind them. They rounded the northern point of Branca, grouping twice that day for their allowance of water and beer from the longboat, before stopping for the night. The next morning, the gig with the boatswain and four crew were missing, and although a sharp lookout was kept, she was never seen again.

Once they reached the Straits of Branca, their spirits rose in the hopes of finding a passing ship only to be dashed when 'a large prow lay at anchor off Sanjang Panmambang and five others standing off, but they soon tacked as if to attack. The fleet therefore prepared to receive them as enemies'.[18] When the ships saw that the boats were armed and the crews ready to receive them, the pirates hauled their wind and let them well alone. Not long after, the masts of two ships lying at anchor were seen in a distant bay. The pinnace was sent ahead to investigate, while the rest of the fleet fought their way towards them through heavy squalls of torrential rain, thunder and lightning. Bedraggled but hopeful, the cutter hoisted her colours. A great cheer went out as both ships answered and broke out British colours from their mastheads. They were safe.

Captain Canning of the *Nonsuch*, an East India Company ship, and Captain Lloyd of the *General Elliot* made them most welcome. The 'Vansittarts' recovered quickly after their two-day ordeal. After a conference with his officers, Captain Wilson made an offer to the two captains to salvage the *Vansittart*. They should have a third of the value recovered, which should well compensate them for the time lost. If they were not interested, Wilson told them he would go to the Dutch. The two ships left the next day at dawn.

Due to his position with the Captain and chief mate, Francis was included in the party of Vansittarts who returned to their ship, while the other 80 members of the crew remained behind at Sangee Booloo Bay. The *General Elliot*, in convoy with the *Nonsuch*, made slow progress against adverse tides and moderate breezes. A sudden squall split the main topsail, foretopsail and jib. Seven days later they arrived at the *Vansittart* at dawn but they were greeted with a dreadful sight. The Malays had burned the *Vansittart* 'to within two feet of the water's edge in most places fore and aft, and the sea making a fair breech over her'.[19] They felled the burned foremast for safety, and then set about recovering the treasure. Divers brought up just three of the 13 chests from the bottom. The next day they returned and 'recovered 30 chests belonging to the Honourable Company and seven of private property'. For three days more they swarmed over the ship, but the rolling motion, currents and high tides defeated them and they returned to pick up the rest of the Vansittarts.

There were too many to fit into the two ships, so 23 men went in the longboat to the East India Company settlement at Penang, Prince of Wales Island on the west coast of the Malay peninsular. Francis went with Lestock Wilson and Walter Caruthers in the *Nonsuch* on what turned out to be a very slow voyage to Canton. They arrived on 14 October where they 'warped to French Island and struck yards and tops'. For nearly two months, Francis stayed in Canton until a berth could be found for him (and Captain Wilson) back to England.

Characteristically, he spent much of his time making astronomical observations. They sailed on the *Lascelles* on 16 December as 'cuddy passengers' with little to do aboard the well-manned ship. It was a slow and relatively uneventful trip. Francis went ashore at the Downs on 28 April. He had only been away a little more than a year, but was much grown in stature and experience. Despite his ordeal, he was even more determined to pursue his chosen career.

Mary Beaufort was in good spirits. For the first time in a month, the doctor had allowed her downstairs after she had slipped on the icy pavement outside their lodgings in Margaret Street, in London's West End, and fractured her leg just above the ankle. She lay on the sofa with her leg in a plaster and tightly bandaged splints. All that morning, Dr Beaufort had been reading to her from the novel *Ethelinde, or the Recluse of the Lake,* a new novel by Charlotte Turner-Smith. The passage dealt with the loss of a favourite son, castaway and drowned in India. It was a year to the day that Dr Beaufort had left Francis in Gravesend.

It was even more of a shock for Dr Beaufort later that day when his eye was caught by the headline 'Loss of the *Vansittart*' when idly reading snippets from *The Times* to his wife. He did not read the article to her, but scurried off instead to consult Mr Wheeler at the East India Company. There the report in *The Times* was confirmed, but Dr Beaufort was assured that Francis was safe and had gone with Captain Wilson to China. The news of the shipwreck had, in fact, been brought by Captain William Bligh following his epic open-boat voyage to Timor, after the mutiny of the *Bounty*. Bligh had run into James Davis, the second mate of the *Vansittart* in Cape Town and had heard the whole story first hand.

On his return to Margaret Street, Dr Beaufort found Mary in tears, 'much alarmed at his staying out so late'. When he explained the position, they 'mingled their tears of joy and terror and gratitude together'. They had to wait a month before a letter arrived from Francis, written the day that he reached the *General Elliot*, to learn the details of the shipwreck and hear that he had 'lost everything', but was 'in good health and spirit'. A few days after the Beaufort parents had digested his news, Francis turned up in person in London, to see them and to find another ship.

CHAPTER 3

Mr Midshipman Beaufort

I T WAS A SPLENDID DINNER PARTY. Dr Beaufort and Mary, her leg still in splints resting on a stool, Francis, and his elder sister Fanny, Lestock Wilson and his wife, all sat in the parlour in Margaret Street, off Cavendish Square. Dr Beaufort regaled family and guests with an account of Captain William Bligh, whom he had met that afternoon at the Royal Society when delivering some seeds that Francis had brought back from China to the naturalist and explorer Sir Joseph Banks. Beaufort and Bligh had talked of their respective adventures at sea, and the Doctor thanked him for bringing news of Francis' rescue. Francis then proposed a toast to the *Vansittart*, and another to her captain, who had just been totally exonerated of all blame in her loss – it was the Court of Directors, after all, who had put her in danger in the first place.

The conversation then turned to Francis' career. The loss of the *Vansittart*, far from damaging Wilson's career in the Honourable East India Company, had actually advanced it and they gave him another ship, the *Exeter*. Wilson offered Francis a berth in her, but as she was still on the stocks and would probably not be ready for another two years, he advised Francis to see some service in the Royal Navy. With the impending war with Spain over their claim on a British settlement on the Nootka Sound on the west coast of Vancouver Island, Parliament had ordered the Admiralty to bring the Fleet up to fighting strength. Thus, there was a good chance that there would be an opening for Francis if suitable patronage could be found.

Here Dr Beaufort was in his element, and rose to the challenge. He wrote to enlist the help of the Earl of Courtown, the father of the Reverend the Hon. Thomas Stopford, one of his closest friends from Trinity College Dublin, and suggested that he and Francis should call on him and the Countess. As Treasurer of the Royal Household, Courtown was admirably placed to be most useful, and although Francis had few social graces having been away at sea for the past year, he could at least hold his own in their company. Lady Courtown was charmed by him, and fascinated by the account of his shipwreck. Their efforts quickly bore fruit, and six weeks after returning to England, Francis was appointed to HMS *Latona*, a 38-gun frigate. He was rated Midshipman.

Once again, Francis travelled to Gravesend to join his new ship. This time he went on his own, and there was a certain swagger about him. He wore the full dress uniform of a midshipman – a dark blue frock coat with white facings on the collar, brass buttons up the front, three distinguishing buttons on each cuff, white waistcoat, ruffled shirt and black silk stock, nankeen breeches, and silk stockings. He carried his tricorn hat with its cockade under his arm. His midshipman's dirk hung at his left side. 'Tell William that he might well call me a handsome little fellow if he saw me in my full dress uniform,'[1] he later wrote to his father. With his first uniform, Francis had developed a foppish trait that was entirely at odds with his serious nature and fervent desire to succeed in the Royal Navy. Officially, Midshipman Beaufort entered the Service as able seaman in order to claim the £3 bounty due to volunteers. A week later, he was gazetted midshipman. His notional time on the *Colossus* combined with the year with the East India Company gave him the requisite two years' sea time to qualify for midshipman. Francis was termed a 'young gentleman', an apt description for one so worldly-wise just past his sixteenth birthday. As he went on board the *Latona*, saluted the Quarter-deck, and was taken below to the midshipman's berth on the orlop deck deep in the bowels of the ship, he was entering a very different world, and Francis had the good sense to recognise it instantly.

The next day, 24 June 1790, the *Latona* weighed anchor and made her way down the Thames to Sheerness, then paused at the Downs for two days to collect 200 pressed Londoners to transport to Portsmouth. There, Francis was summoned to dine with the Captain. Albemarle Bertie, a kinsman of the Duke of Ancaster, owed his promotion as much to his ability as his social standing. He was well liked. 'All officers agree,' Francis wrote to his father, 'he is the mildest and quietest captain in the service.'[2] In the same letter, he went into Bertie's family pedigree (incorrectly as it turned out). The aristocracy and titles undoubtedly impressed him, but unlike his father (and later to his chagrin) Francis never went out of his way to cultivate them for his own ends. Although Francis dined with Captain Bertie on a regular basis, as was usual on a man-of-war, his relationship with him and the officers was rather more distant than the one he had enjoyed on the *Vansittart*.

Life in the midshipman's berth for Francis was also very different, but in his letters home there are only minor hints of complaint. Being so short, the low 5' 7" bulkhead did not worry him, but the lack of space for himself and his belongings affected him deeply. He had just 21" to sling his hammock and only enough deck space for his modest sea chest, which he wrote, 'was so crammed that I cannot get at things at the bottom'. He had mild reproof for the food, where 'the salt junk [beef] is not quite so pleasant after living as well as I have done on board the *Vansittart* and the *Lascelles*'. The midshipman's berth on the *Latona* can have been little different from a contemporary account where 'the lingering effluvia of red herrings, bilge water, and fried onions, together with the airless stench of the place, dispelled what little appetite he might have brought to the repast spread upon a greasy tablecloth, and consisting of small beer, mouldy sea-biscuit and beef-steak. In every corner reigned confusion; a heap of soiled clothing, naval half-boots, wet towels . . . On the shelf that ranged the walls was a miscellany of plates, glasses, books, cocked hats, dirty stockings, tooth-combs, a litter of white mice and a caged parrot.'[3] Add to that, the midshipman's berth 'was the noisiest and most lawless place aboard, there being a good deal of horseplay, a good deal of vice and cruelty, and a little fun, and sea philosophy, to allay its many miseries'.[4]

For one formerly so spoilt at sea, Francis fitted into this bear garden remarkably well. He had the sense not to show off his undoubted mathematical and navigational skills to his messmates. Instead, he fell in with their obsession with their uniform, they being, he wrote, 'much smarter dressed than I ever imagined' – aristocratic captains tended to choose well-bred, moneyed officers. He lamented that his waistcoats were old fashioned and replaced them with darker ones. A broken clasp on his shoe, he whined, meant that his 'handsome buckles were of no use'; he needed a new sword knot. To indulge his new fashion sense, he kept writing to his parents for money – his allowance of 6 guineas a quarter was short lived: even the £5 his mother sent him went on laundry, save for 13 shillings. But as he was to do throughout his life, Francis sought the good opinion of his father. 'If I follow your advice about prudence, which I intend to do, I shall be well satisfied with myself if it requires some small degree of self denial to effect it if you are in a parcel of wild young men.' With no privacy in the berth, he rarely mentioned any of his messmates, who would undoubtedly have read his letters and journal.

But the greatest difference Francis found between the Royal Navy and the merchant service was in his newfound authority and discipline, which excited him. 'I find myself quite a different thing to what the midshipmen of an Indiamen are. There a sailor thinks nothing of striking a midshipman, but it is death to anyone who strikes me.' Soon after Francis joined the *Latona*, a landsman was 'seized to a grating' and given a dozen lashes by the boatswain's mate for drunkenness. It was the first of many floggings he witnessed throughout his career, (many at his own order) and the sight always affected him.

For the first month, the *Latona* went on a training cruise up and down the Channel. She 'exercised her Great Guns frequently', working up the gun crews, one of which was commanded by Francis. During that late summer, the weather was atrocious, with gales and squalls that taxed officers and crew. Conditions on board worsened, and at one time, the ship had to be completely fumigated with tobacco smoke. There were orders and counter orders. She was to go to the Baltic; she was to stay in the Channel. In mid-July, *Latona* was anchored in Portsmouth harbour. Francis was sent ashore with a press gang – in time of war, impressment of men and property for the defence of the realm was legal and commonplace (even far inland) until it was abolished in 1815. 'The other evening,' he wrote, 'I was sent ashore and I pressed about 19 men, and such work that was.' He was returning in the long boat to the *Carysfoot*, a holding ship for pressed men, when there was a near mutiny on board. Had he not made the ship, he would certainly have been thrown overboard. But Francis was both brave and resourceful. He had a pistol in one hand and a sword in the other, which he was prepared to use 'and take a life or two'. He bundled the men aboard the *Carysfoot*, ordering the skeleton crew to take charge of them. He then picked another 19 men who were quieter than the men he had pressed, 'and brought them to the *Latona* and got on board our ship at 1/2 past 2 in the morning'.

When at last she was up to strength and competent, the *Latona* was ordered to join the Channel Fleet lying off Spithead under Lord Howe, senior Admiral of the White and temporary Admiral of the Fleet. Francis was deeply proud of his ship and his squadron, reporting that 'I flatter myself that the *Latona* will cut a dash among this fleet.'[5] In early August it was reported that the Spanish fleet had put to sea. Lord Howe made the signal for his entire fleet to get under way. Howe's flagship, the *Queen Charlotte*, followed by 35 ships-of-the-line, sailing a cable length apart and escorted by the *Latona* with six other frigates, went to cruise between the Ushant and the Isles of Scilly. They ploughed up and down the Channel in a show of strength. There Howe 'exercised the fleet continually, both in Naval evolutions and in the new code of signals, which he had been elaborating for several years'.[6] The *Latona*, a frigate, served the whole Fleet. Being fast and manoeuvrable, her role was to pass on signals down the line, reconnoitre, and act as raiders and boarders. Twice she was sent off to board French merchantmen, one from Bordeaux, the other from Hamburg.

Just when Francis had been given his first responsible job as signal midshipman the news came the entire fleet was dreading. The sabre rattling had worked. Spain thought that the small island settlement at Nootka Sound was not worth fighting over, and the threat of war receded as abruptly as it began. Francis was beside himself with disappointment. He wrote: 'Alas! Alas! Alas! My dearest father. What is to be done? Go back to the Indian service? No I would rather stay a little time in His Majesty's service. It is I hear an equal chance that Capt. Bertie goes to the Mediterranean; if so I would like to go but I hear it is rather an expensive one, but you and I can talk more about that here-after.'[7] But the rumours came to nothing. The *Latona* returned to Portsmouth and the Commissioners of the Admiralty came aboard and paid off the ship's company at the end of November. Francis was again without a ship. What he did have, however, was a first class testimonial from Captain Bertie to offer his next captain and a taste for life in the Royal Navy.

Of his time aboard the *Latona*, there was one incident that he was to recall many years later when discussing a midshipman's appetite and the number of dinners he could consume. Francis Beaufort had managed three. One day off Spithead, he had messed adequately at Midshipman's table. When he had finished, the captain's steward came up: 'The Captain's compliments, sir,' he said. 'He desires the favour of your company at dinner today.'

'But I've dined,' said Francis.

'For mercy's sake, don't say that sir,' said he, 'for I shall be in a scrape if you do: I ought to have asked you this morning but I forgot.'

Francis said that he would go. Two hours later, he had 'his usual good dinner' with Captain Bertie. Just as he rose from the table, a signal was made by the Admiral to send an officer on board. As it was Francis' turn, he went off in the gig. Once on board, the Admiral addressed him: 'Ah, Mr Beaufort, I believe?'

'Yes sir,' replied Francis.

'Well, Mr Beaufort,' the Admiral continued. 'The papers you are to take back will not be ready this half hour; but I am just sitting down to dinner and shall be glad of your company.'

For a midshipman to refuse to dine with an admiral was unthinkable, there 'being no words for it in the naval dictionary'. So he sat down to his third dinner, and returned to his own ship just in time for tea.

For the first time in years, the nomadic Beauforts spent the Christmas of 1790 together as a complete family. Dr Beaufort had been given the living of Collon, County Louth, by his old friend from Trinity, John Foster, by then Speaker of the Irish House of Commons. With it came ten acres of glebe, a farmhouse, and a fine Queen Anne rectory. It was perfect for Dr Beaufort. Not only was it large enough to house his whole family, it was also grand enough to entertain and cultivate County society. Three storeys high and five bays wide, it stood in the fold of a valley overlooking its formal gardens that sloped down to the banks of the River Mattock.

Although Francis was happily reunited with his family, and enjoyed exploring the surrounding countryside with his brother William, he was impatient to return to sea. Once again, he turned to the Earl of Courtown, who had by then retired from Court and had gone live on his estates in County Wexford. Once again, the Earl obliged him, and introduced Francis to his third son, Captain the Honourable Robert Stopford, who, on 29 April 1791, had been given the *Aquilon*, a frigate of 32 guns. They liked each other well enough on meeting, and Stopford agreed to take him when his ship had finished refitting in Portsmouth. But that was not for another three months.

During this time, Francis and William devised a cipher for their own personal use, probably his sister Fanny as well. It was of the simplest form, being a straight one-to-one substitution of Greek letters, astronomical symbols, and made-up squiggles for the letters of the alphabet. As Francis' letters would have been

Pencil drawing of Collon Village by Francis Beaufort in 1820. His father's new church is on top of the hill, while the fine rectory, with its garden running down to the river, is on the right.

passed round all the family, the coded part would thus have remained private to William. Francis later wrote to his father 'never take it ill my writing things [to] William in a concealed hand or manner, for let me assure you 'tis only little jokes or trifles between us – and in general they serve to let one another see that we have not entirely forgot the hand'.[8] Francis also used this simple code in his diaries to the end of his life, even though by then he had developed far more sophisticated forms of cipher.

When Francis went to join the *Aquilon* in Portsmouth on 10 June, he was again rated able seaman to claim another £3 bounty, then resumed his rank of midshipman the next day. By that time, he had outgrown much of his uniform and his tailor's

37

bill left him with a deficit of £1 3s 6d on his first quarter's allowance. However, that was the very least of his worries. Soon after joining the *Aquilon* he was fooling about in the harbour in a small skiff when he was called back on board. As he went to tie up alongside, he stood on the gunwale and the little rowing boat capsized throwing him in the water. Unable to swim, he was floundering around trying to grab the boat or the oars. As he shouted for help, he swallowed great draughts of water. The marine at the gangway did not see him, and it was only when the tide carried him astern that someone in the foretop noticed him and raised the alarm. The response was immediate. Robert Dudley Oliver, the first lieutenant, jumped overboard, followed closely by the carpenter. The gunner pulled after them in the gig. By that time, Francis was exhausted. His struggling ceased and he began to sink below the surface of the water. As he wrote to the distinguished natural scientist William Hyde Wollaston thirty-five years later, 'I felt that I was drowning.'[9]

Francis partially remembered the details after his recovery or was reminded of them by witnesses 'for during the interval of such agitation a drowning person is too much occupied in catching at every passing straw, or too much absorbed by alternate hope and despair, to mark the succession of events very accurately'. But of the actual moment of drowning, however, he had perfect recall, even years later. 'From the moment that all exertion had ceased, a calm feeling of the most perfect tranquillity superseded the previous tumultuous sensations – it might be called apathy, certainly resignation, for drowning no longer appeared to be an evil – I no longer thought of being rescued, nor was I in any bodily pain. On the contrary, my sensations were now of a rather pleasurable ease, partaking of that dull but contented sort of feeling which precedes the sleep produced by fatigue. Though the senses were thus deadened, not so the mind; its activity seemed to be invigorated in a ratio which defies all description.'[10] Francis had total recall of those exact thoughts. It really was true that 'every past incident of my life seemed to glance across my recollection in retrograde succession; not, however, in mere outline, as here stated, but the picture filled up with every minute and collateral feature; in short, the whole period of my existence seemed to be placed before me in a kind of panoramic view, and each act of it seemed to be accompanied by a consciousness of right or wrong, or by some reflection on its cause or its consequences; indeed many trifling events which had been long forgotten then crowded into my imagination.'

What fascinated Francis was that although he had been 'religiously brought up', all his thoughts were confined to the past and nothing to the future. He was amazed that he saw so much during the space of what cannot have been more than two minutes between suffocation and rescue. The gunner hauled him aboard the gig and pulled over to a neighbouring ship. There he was ignominiously upended and the seawater pummelled out of him. He was bled and given some gin and, according to the onlookers, 'was very quickly restored to animation'. The reverse process then took over. 'Again, instead of being absolutely free from all bodily pain, as in my drowning state, I was tortured by pain all over me,' he wrote. Francis thought it worse than being wounded for pain and general distress. But as soon as he began to recover, he returned 'to a clear conception of my clear state'.

Although Francis made a quick and full recovery from his near death experience, his other worry was more pressing and lasted much longer. He, along with all the officers and crew, now cordially disliked his captain, Robert Stopford. 'I am unhappy aboard this ship,'[11] he wrote in cipher to his brother. His saviour, Lieutenant Oliver soon transferred to another ship, as did the second lieutenant, on the pretext of an injury but in reality 'he was tired of the disagreeable and ungentlemanlike behaviour of our captain (and not to him alone)'.[12] Oliver was replaced by a Lieutenant Fry. Francis did not take to him: 'the greatest bully, the greatest Tartar, and the most disagreeable man in the Service,'[13] he wrote to his father.

Officers at odds with their captain make for an unhappy ship. Part of the disagreement was born out of jealousy. Stopford had entered the Navy at the age of 12, and after serving as a midshipman where he saw action on the North American and West Indies stations, was soon made acting Lieutenant. As his father was a Lord of the Bedchamber, preferment came quickly. He was promoted commander, then Captain by the age of 20, with the command of the *Ferret*, a 14-gun sloop, and later the same year the frigate *Ambuscade*. On his appointment to the *Aquilon* he was given the post rank (of Captain). A 'post Captain' was one who held a commission as Captain as opposed to an officer of any rank who was always given the courtesy title of Captain when in command of a ship. Stopford was only 22 years old; his junior officers were considerably older. Francis, a midshipman and a mere six years his junior, shared the general dislike of his captain, citing his arrogance and 'imperious manner' in his letters home. This dislike filtered down to the crew. He did not have the reputation as a 'flogging captain' in the past, and his captain's log shows only a moderate amount of punishment. Yet Francis' own journal contains records of almost daily floggings of particular severity for all the usual misdemeanours, such as drunkenness, insolence, neglect of duty, and 'uncleanliness', a euphemism for indecency. The *Aquilon* was paid off on 7 September, 'to give those men an opportunity of leaving the ship who were pressed or have repented of entering – also we have a very miserable ship's company'.[14] Stopford tried to replace them with 'none but men of 5 feet 10 inches and complete seamen'.[15] Another cause for resentment of the crew (in particular the purser whose tobacco sales formed part of his income) was that Stopford forbade smoking on board. However, whatever the true position aboard the *Aquilon*, she was an efficient ship and was never found wanting in her duty.

For all September and October, Stopford worked up his crew in the Channel, cruising mostly from Torbay to Yarmouth on the Isle of Wight and back to Portsmouth, usually in atrocious weather. She lost spars and sails, and returned to Plymouth to 'repair our losses'. There was little excitement other than chasing a smuggler in a fast lugger for 24 hours. At last they were ordered to the Mediterranean, and the *Aquilon* sailed south, arriving at Gibraltar on 11 November. Francis relished being at sea, although his navigational skills were rarely put to use. Lestock Wilson wrote to Francis' father saying that he had complained to him of 'the idle life of a midshipman and that he is quite out of the habit of observing. I am sorry for it as such talents as his should be employed for the benefit of society.' However, he seems to have been included in the noontime observations by the time they entered the Straits of Gibraltar, as Francis recorded in his journal that when 'observing the latitude with a common quadrant, I perceived two very large spots upon the disc of the sun close to one another'.[16] He monitored them for the next three days, and lamented the death of Dr Ussher two years before, as he could not report his findings to him.

For months on end, the *Aquilon* made her relentless forays to sea from Gibraltar making observations, delivering messages to consuls, and generally 'showing the flag'. Despite the dirtiest of weathers, Francis was supremely happy and fulfilled. His initial antipathy to Captain Stopford had faded, and he settled down to the serious business of gaining advancement and promotion by 'doing his duty'. From the first, he delighted in everything. He greatly enjoyed exploring new places. At Leghorn, for example, Francis marvelled at the 'several curiosities to be found, such as the leaning tower at Pisa, some very fine statues and the finest shops in the world. Anything of English manufacture is very cheap here without any duty.'[17] But his observations were more usually confined to surveying details, as when sailing between the Isles of Elba and Stromente, he noted that 'the compasses vary greatly and are much affected by Elba, which I can not otherwise account for but for some iron mines which are on that island.'[18] He kept his hand in at surveying too. When the *Aquilon* was forced into the Bay of Especia on the Italian Ligurian coast by bad weather, Francis proposed to Captain Stopford that he should make a survey of 'one of the finest bays I have ever seen that is capable of containing the entire Navy of England'.[19] While the ship was being painted and the guns varnished, (it all washed off that night with fresh torrents of rain), Francis and Mr Kirby, the master 'took advantage of every interval of fair weather to sound about the west side of the bay and into the coves and by taking angles and bearings to correct the draughts in some measure which are mostly very erroneous'.

This first cruise was to concentrate so many of Francis' interests, from natural sciences to classical antiquity. With little formal schooling, he felt that his education was lacking. He begged his father to send him books on science and astronomy, philosophy and religion, which he devoured with enthusiasm. Just like his father, Francis had an inquiring mind and eclectic interests. He recorded his findings in meticulous detail – it took 20 pages of his journal to describe his visits to Pompeii and Herculaneum. He delighted in experiencing everything first hand. When returning from Mount Vesuvius with three ship-mates, they stumbled on the Lago d'Agano, a large lake that had once been a volcano. Behind was the Grotto del Cane, a small cave in the rock with 'a destructive vapour which rises from the bottom. Experiments were made with dogs who having had their noses put close to the ground immediately lose their senses and in two minutes are perfectly dead.' A door was put over the cave for protection but undaunted, Francis rashly put his nose to the ground, which gave him a shock that he 'did not recover from for the rest of the evening'. It struck him 'exactly in the same manner as by holding your nose too close to a lighted match only much stronger. This vapour will put a flambeau out, nor can you fire a pistol off it, or if you lay a trail of gunpowder from the outside and set fire to it, it will stop the instant it gets into this air.'[20] At Pozzuoli, after marvelling at the Roman remains, Francis went with his companions to Nero's baths, with a series of passages about four feet wide and twelve feet high cut out of the side of a hill. At the end, there was 'a well of boiling water. In it the thermometer rose to 202°, which only wants 10° of the hottest boiling water.'[21] Francis filled a bucket with the water and carried it back to his companions, where they cooked 'half a dozen eggs which were completely boiled in four minutes'.[22]

Having been finely tutored in the arts by his father, Francis had a true appreciation and a keen eye. While the other midshipmen went to explore the fleshpots of Naples, Francis joined a party of officers to visit Capodimonte, the run-down palace of the King of Naples. There he thought that the 2,000 paintings were 'placed without art, order or taste'. Although he admired the 'beautiful Holy Families by Raphael', the Titians and Caravaggios, he found the Guidos 'flat and uninteresting'. At this time, he appears intolerant and somewhat insensitive. He had been learning Italian and tried it out on the guards whom he found 'numerous and stupid'. When it began to rain heavily on the way back, 'all the party were wet except myself for I whipped a large greatcoat from off our old guide's back and put it on my own'.

The cruise continued to Palermo, Sicily and then on to Cagliari, Sardinia with plenty of shore leave and sightseeing. Shortly after their arrival, there was one piece of excitement when 'a shore boat rowed silently alongside and got the rope aft. They wouldn't answer, nor come on in, but on shoving off, one of them jumped aboard. The Marines fired several musket shots through her sail, but to no effect.' In the meantime, the man who came on board 'seemed greatly frightened, ran aft and caught hold of the ensign staff where he thought he was secure. He was in great distress.' Apparently, he was a Turk who had been captured at sea five years before and sold into the galleys. He had escaped by filing off his irons and giving all his clothes to the men who had brought him to the *Aquilon* 'to put himself under the protection of the English flag'. The Turk remained clutching the ensign until he could be persuaded that he was indeed safe, and remained with the ship until she returned to Gibraltar.

Throughout this early period of his life, Francis corresponded freely with his brother, but in matters of sex he resorted to code – when they first moved to Collon, County Louth, he inquired of William if he had 'got foul of any of the young lasses of Collon yet?'[23] Much of it was smutty, schoolboy stuff, as when the *Aquilon* went to Naples for the first time. Francis wrote that the Castel de Novo was built entirely from the tax called 'de Novo' extracted 'from a set of women generally known as prostitutes, which at the time the castle was built were extremely numerous'.[24] Later on in the cruise, he wrote from Leghorn that 'the whores here are very nasty yet you are secure from pox or theft as they are licensed.'[25] In Malaga, he again informed his brother that 'There are no females here but whores which are indeed in great abundance in this place but 9/10th of them have the pox. It is very common to take them into a gateway where they'll frig you for a rial.'[26] It would appear that Francis escaped the diseases common on board ship, as there are no stoppages for medicines against his pay in any of the muster books. Like the majority of the officers and crew, Francis was vigorously heterosexual. At that time, ships spent far longer in port, where women freely came aboard, than at sea. Contrary to the popular view of the Navy, homosexuality did exist, but was uncommon and disliked – it also carried the death penalty under the Articles of War. So Francis' fellow midshipman Thomas George Byng whose 'One great blemish in his character was that of frigging everybody who asked him'[27] was an exception rather than the rule. Byng, a kinsman of Vice Admiral John Byng shot in 1756 for losing the Island of Minorca during the Seven Years War, died of the flux, a common form of dysentery, and was buried 'in a very shabby manner indeed' in Gibraltar. Still the dandy, Francis bought his richly embroidered waistcoat at the sale of dead men's clothes at the mainmast, the £2 being stopped out of his pay. Another stoppage on Francis' pay was for a truss which he found most uncomfortable when he coughed. Hernias were common in the Navy with so much physical work in confined and awkward spaces.

During his spare time at sea 'in the hours not dedicated to writing, reading, drawing etc', Francis devised a simple method of surveying which he planned to use in a part of the Bay of Gibraltar that had been 'laid down pretty exactly'. His idea was to use a set of rods about seven feet long (AB in the diagram in his letter to his father), on 'which I will measure 6' very exactly from D to C'[28] the distance being marked with straight saw-cuts, ab and cd. The rods were to be laid alternately along the beach in a straight line, joining the saw-cuts together with a thin plate. 'I will then have a very exact base measurement' from which to make up the triangulation with a set of staffs. As usual, he asked for his father's opinion (and hopefully his approval) of his project 'which, though, will serve to keep my hand in, and will give you and me great satisfaction'.[29] However, like most of Francis' early 'inventions', it was fine in theory but totally unworkable in the field – the old surveyors' chain served the same purpose and was far easier to use than hauling planks over the beach.

On Christmas Eve 1792, Francis had been made up to 'Dickie' or acting Master's Mate, which earned him an extra ten shillings a month, not a fortune but at least he was on the promotion ladder and had the extra responsibility he craved. It also brought him a minuscule cabin of his own. He was elected secretary to the midshipmen's berth, and he flattered himself that under his care he and his messmates would eat better and 'live a little more like gentlemen than we did. I am neither the oldest nor the senior in the Berth, but I had the suffrages of almost all my shipmates, for I am the honestest, and as good a one as any of them.'[30]

Despite his outward show of bravado and self-confidence, Francis still longed for the good opinion of his fellow officers. Whatever his outward show of bravado, inwardly he was both sensitive and mindful of his fellow man. Once while ashore in Gibraltar, it was his choice to witness the execution of a soldier of the 46th Regiment for desertion. The wretched private had gone over the face of the Rock one night on a rope that was too short, and in the morning he was discovered dangling on the end. He was taken, court martialled, and sentenced to death by the end of the day. The firing squad next morning was made up by lot from his own regiment. Francis was horrified by the spectacle. 'Oh my dearest Mother,' he wrote. 'What an awful thing it was. 'Twas the first thing of the kind that I ever saw, and I assure you I was greatly affected by it. The tears, however, running fast from my eyes were reserved for the firing squad who had to shoot their comrade.'[31]

The New Year of 1793 brought the promise of war with Revolutionary France, and with the news excitement mounted amongst Francis and his fellow officers. The rumblings finally came to a head, and at last the moment they were all waiting for arrived, a signal for all captains to repair aboard Admiral Goodall's flagship anchored in Gibraltar Bay. There they learned that 'An American captain who took his oath before the Dutch, [said] that three days before he left Marseilles . . . war with England was publicly announced, and that all the English vessels there detained, their sails unbent, their masts unstruck and their rudders unhung, and the day he sailed, three privateers came out to sea in company with him.'[32] The moment Stopford returned to the *Aquilon*, she made ready and stood out to sea at 10 o'clock that night. His orders were simple and straightforward. 'To capture all French vessels, or at least to detain them until further intelligence.'[33]

CHAPTER 4

Master's Mate

THE FLASH OF A SINGLE GUN, 'NE by E, 3 leagues to westward'[1] of the *Aquilon* could clearly be seen from the quarterdeck despite the very dirty weather, a gale of wind, and a heavy cross sea. The master then 'tacked and wore' the ship, working her down towards it, in the company of the *Fury* and the *Lapwing*. They had been at sea for just two days when a French brig was sighted and the *Aquilon* gave chase. The Frenchman, the *Antoine* as they were to discover, was no match for the 32-gun frigate, and with a single shot across her bows she immediately struck her colours. There was too much sea in the Gut (the Straits of Gibraltar) to board the prize, so the master ordered in her foretopsails and reefed her main, then shadowed the prize for the rest of the night. The next morning the two ships lay under the lee of Cape Spartel on the Moroccan coast. The cutter was hauled out, and to Francis Beaufort's intense disappointment, it was Mr Ling, another master's mate, who was chosen as prize master, boarding her with four men. The cutter soon returned with the master of the *Antoine* and five of her crew. Francis recorded that the master was 'a very decent and well-informed man. He had heard nothing, nor even the probability, of war with England, and seemed much affected with the account of the poor king's [Louis XVI] horrid murder.'[2] They learned that she was carrying a cargo of lemons and sulphur from Messina. The *Fury* took a similar vessel and the two prizes returned to Gibraltar. Although the capture of the brig was far from heroic, it was at least a start and put officers and crew in good heart.

A week later, a large ship was spotted on the horizon and the *Aquilon* cleared for action and gave chase. Soon after, another five sails were spotted and the *Aquilon*, heavily outnumbered, fled. It was, in fact, Admiral Goodall, Commander-in-Chief Gibraltar, who was looking for the rest of his squadron. When the fleet was finally assembled, the Admiral made a signal for all lieutenants to repair on board his flagship. The lieutenant returned and the whole ship's company was mustered, officers and midshipmen on the quarterdeck, the rest of the crew in the waist below. Captain Stopford then read the paper from the Admiral. He began 'by informing the Squadron that for several very cogent reasons, he was determined to retaliate on the French by detaining and capturing all French vessels. But what they had done might have been the work of a few piratical fellows in the South of France and not authorised by government.' If that was the case, and war had not been declared officially, Goodall's orders would have amounted to piracy, and he would be personally liable to recompense every owner of each vessel taken. The choice thereafter was simple. Either the ship's captains would agree to sharing the whole risk with the

Admiral, or he would rescind the order allowing them to take prizes.

Captain Stopford told the ship's company that he thought it fair, but they in turn should share in his risk. The gunroom demurred, and the 'ship's company quibbled', while the petty officers said nothing. Then 'the Captain asked had we no opinion,' Francis wrote. 'Nobody answering, I stepped forward and gave my determined consent.'[3] The boatswain followed his example and too gave his agreement, followed by the other two mates, the midshipmen, and the warrant officers. Francis then explained the position to the men in greater detail. Did they want to 'remain at anchor in Gibraltar while the rest of the Squadron was at sea?' When the crew came round to his persuasion, they too gave their assent, 'The Gunroom, seeing they stood solus, gave their consent, more from that reason, as they said, than from any wish to promote the business.'[4] Stopford signed the document along with the first and second lieutenants on behalf of the other officers and all hands when it was returned to the Admiral.

To make such a stand was a brave, if not a calculated move on the part of an aspiring midshipman not yet nineteen years old. To side with the captain was obviously a good move, but to oppose directly the officers, with whom he worked, often messed, and hoped to join erelong, he ran the definite risk of alienation and retaliation. His relationship with the crew might also have been affected had the vote and circumstances not gone his way. However, the events were soon overtaken, and war was officially declared the next day. Francis did vote against the next proposal – that of sharing the prize money equally throughout the Squadron, as 'some of us,' he declared 'certainly have had bad cruising ground and some of us go with convoys etcetera'. It was fortunate for him that he lost the vote, for the *Aquilon* did not take another prize, but not for want of trying.

In company with all the officers and crew, Francis was frustrated at the lack of action and prizes. Over the next few months, both his journal and the Captain's log are filled with accounts of endless cruises out of Gibraltar – west as far as Cape Finisterre and east to Leghorn. All show disheartening lack of success. 'Spoke to several ships, but alas! all were friends. Really I believe we have had the luck of speaking to every Dane and Swede that has come past the Gut.'[5] Even when they found a foreign frigate that 'answered exactly to the description of a large French privateer who had been fitted out at Marseilles' she turned out to be friendly. However, that 'stranger showed Spanish Colours, but one of our officers confidently assisted that he saw French colours laying on her deck, so we continued to chase her'.[6] When the suspect ship was joined by two others, the Aquillons 'were a little alarmed, as our fleet could not possibly work up to us in less than 3 or 4 hours,'[7] so she turned and ran for the safety of Gibraltar. Another time, wearing French colours herself as a *ruse de guerre*, the *Aquilon* spoke to a Spanish brig who was much relieved and 'showed the most extravagant symptoms of joy on finding out who we really were'.[8]

The *Aquilon*'s ill luck continued. When Admiral Hood, to whose squadron she was attached, sailed in search of the French Mediterranean fleet that was rumoured to have left port, she was ordered elsewhere. Instantly, the mood of the ship changed from great good spirits to general gloom. 'In place of studdingsails actually flying up, the tacks would hardly come on board,' Francis wrote, 'everything seemed stiff and unwieldy and even the ropes and sails seemed to partake of our universal ill-humour.'[9] They chased French ships but failed to catch them. Cruising past Genoa, they saw a 40-gun French frigate lying with a 20-gun ship alongside the mole, 'with 25 sail of corn ships' preparing to leave for Toulon. 'What unlucky fellows we are,' Francis moaned. 'Had we but spent half a day longer on the road we certainly should have taken half the corn vessels and probably both men-of-war.' He railed at the French frigate, the *Impiniuse*, who 'was painted all black, seemed in extreme good order and carried a Tree of Liberty at her masthead and the Cap [of Liberty] nailed to her stern', anchored in the neutral port of Leghorn.

Despite their lack of success, the Aquillons did share in their squadron's prize money. The Prize Agents (civilians who collected prize money for officers and men from the Admiralty courts) paid out '1500 dollars to the commission'd officers, 750 to the warrant officers, 250 to the Petty's and 64 to the Foremast men – this is looked upon to be about a third for the prizes already taken amongst Admiral Goodall's Squadron'. Francis' share was nearly £300. Typically, he made a will leaving everything to his father with a note to say that if he wanted 'it now or ever that every farthing of it is heartily at your disposal'.[10] The *Aquilon* was further put out when she was ordered to return to Leghorn to pick up Prince Augustus Frederick, the sixth son of George III, and take him and his large retinue back to England. The Prince was a reluctant passenger for he had just secretly married his love, the Lady Augusta Murray in Rome five months before and was naturally loathe to leave her. 'Alas, a Breeze which they called favourable, swelled the sails of the *Aquilon*,' Lady Augusta wrote, 'and my darling was leaving his unhappy wife.'[11]

The passage took 48 days with a short spell in Gibraltar, from where they 'hurried away as fast as possible,' Francis wrote to his sister Fanny. 'The drinking, dissipation etc. agreeing but very badly with HR Highness who is in a very bad state of health.'[12] Francis liked the Prince enormously, finding him a 'most pleasing young man and in every respect the Gentleman. He is doted on by all officers and crew. The former he treats with almost too much condescension – the latter with greatest affability, several of whom, by his interception, were stayed from punishment.'[13] Stopford, who inherited him through his connections with the Royal Household, was less pleased with his royal passenger. He gave up his spacious quarters for the Prince and his staff, and to his further fury the Prince would tease him by blowing smoke from his cigar in his face, much to the amusement of the crew who were still denied tobacco.

With her continual cruising over the preceding eighteen months, the *Aquilon* was long overdue for a refit. The five weeks she spent in Spithead allowed Francis valuable time with his father and brother William in London. They all took lodgings in Conduit Street off Hanover Square. Although William longed to join the Foreign Office and travel, he bowed to his father's wishes and agreed to take Holy Orders. The three of them discussed theology and all manner of other intellectual subjects long into the night. Francis had devoured such theological works as William Paley's *Evidences of Christianity* and his *Moral Philosophy*, Gilpin's *Lectures on the Church Catechism* and Grotius' *The Truth of the Christian Religion*. He found them intellectually stimulating and rewarding, and while on one hand his belief in the Almighty was generally unswerving, these theological works served to fuel doubts in his faith at various stages of his life. These lapses were, however, for William's ear alone and not for his father. Besides theology, Francis had a hunger for other intellectual subjects: 'my dear sextant and my books, etc. for want of which food I am almost starving, for you know philosophy ought to be my principal and substantial food, and poetry and travels etc. etc. should be my banqueting stuff.'[14] Apart from his initial reading, predictably works on navigation, seamanship, the Bible and Shakespeare, he soon branched out requesting his father send him 'a general treatise on all parts of philosophy'[15] and a variety of scientific publications. He received such learned works as *Nicholson's Journal* and *Nicholson on Philosophy*, Simpson's *Geometry*, Bate's *Arithametic*, and Vine's *Astronomy*. The three men attended plays and lectures at the Royal Society, and went to church twice each Sunday.

What is even more remarkable about the nineteen-year-old Francis' thirst for philosophy, theology and science was that it was read entirely against the background and traditions of the midshipman's berth. The *Aquilon* can have been little different from a contemporary account of Edward Codrington, who as a midshipman was never 'invited to open a book, nor received a word of advice or instruction, except professional, from any-one'.[16] Add to that, it was the 'customary amusement to teach a lad to drink, and to lead him into their own habitual practice in that respect'.[17] In addition, the berth was lit solely by a 'purser's wick', a single lamp with a dim, smoking wick that made reading difficult, if not impossible.

During this visit to London, Dr Beaufort commissioned a portrait of Francis in his midshipman's uniform from Henry Edridge, a neighbour from the Margaret Street lodgings the last time he and his father stayed together in London. This water-colour shows a striking young man. His features are soft, almost feminine, with fresh pale pink cheeks and a full mouth. His nose is straight, though slightly large, while his whole face is domi-nated by deep-set, bright blue eyes. Although Beaufort would then have been aged about 20, his figure, quite remarkably, is pear shaped.

When the *Aquilon* carried Prince Augustus Frederick to England, he had been in good heart knowing that his new wife was soon to follow him. On his return to Leghorn in the middle of January 1794, the Prince was miserable having left his two-week-old son and sick wife in London, where she and her family bore the savage revenge of the King over their illegal marriage. Although he continued to be affable towards the ship's company, they were impatient to be rid of him and to return to the serious business of fighting the French. Francis was in charge of the boat party that took the Prince ashore. The 'fuss with regard to him and the impertinence of his numerous German sycophants and servants'[18] truly irritated him. He wrote to his father, 'I carried all his baggage, servants, etc. etc. and never did I do anything with greater pleasure except the landing of himself.'

On the voyage out, Francis had the second of his four narrow escapes from death. The *Aquilon* was battling against a head sea in a gale of wind in the middle of the Bay of Biscay. Shortly before dawn, the shrill boatswain's call piped all hands up to shorten sail. Francis was asleep in his flimsy cabin by the gunroom. He made his way forward mechanically in the dark, not even half awake. He clambered up the companionway to the upper deck, and, as he rushed on to mount the next companion ladder to gain the quarterdeck, the ship yawed, hit a huge wave and crashed down into the trough. The sudden jolt loosed a capstan bar, all twelve feet of solid ash. It fell about six feet, and caught Francis square on the head as he passed below. 'Blood gushed plentifully' blinding him and soaking his canvas jacket. Unseen hands took him back to his cabin where he passed out in his cot. The ship's surgeon could not believe that his skull was not fractured.

The Prince delivered to Leghorn, the *Aquilon* returned to Spithead. On the way back she had her usual run of bad luck. A French frigate was sighted off the Ushant. 'Never more a ship's company and officers in better humour for fighting,' Francis lamented to his father. 'What ardour was in every man's countenance? The studdingsails, tacks, sheets, clewlines, dunits, halliards etc. actually flew. What vexation and gloom ran throughout when we were necessarily obliged to give up the chase at 4. Oh Pellew, thy action would be forgot. My name sink into obscurity if that night Stopford and his noble, brave Aquillons had had their dearest and only wish.'[19]

The Aquillons dearest wish was answered in early April when she returned to Admiral the Earl Howe's Channel Fleet. After the ravages of the blockade of Brest hemming in the French Fleet the previous year, Howe was determined to keep his newly refitted fleet seaworthy by lying up for months in Torbay, the Naval base to the east of Plymouth. Francis, in common with most of the Fleet and the press, condemned 'Lord Torbay's' inactivity. 'How very imprudent of the Admiralty to permit such a valuable fleet to lie here at this time of year?'[20] he wrote to his father. Howe was biding his time.

At last the orders came to move. France, on the brink of starvation after a series of bad harvests, had sought help from the Americans. Intelligence had already reached the Admiralty that a convoy of 117 ships carrying grain and stores had left Chesapeake Bay on the Eastern Shore, and that the French Fleet, under the command of Admiral Villaret-Joyeuse, would rendezvous with them and their escort somewhere in the Atlantic to bring them safely to Brest. There was also a large convoy of over a hundred British merchant ships that needed protection on their passage to the East. By waiting, Admiral Howe hoped to combine these three objectives of sending the convoy on its way, then placing himself between the French fleet and the grain convoy in the Atlantic so that he could destroy one and capture the other. The *Aquilon*, with three other frigates, escorted the Fleet from Torbay to St Helen's Road on the Isle of Wight where the rest of the fleet and merchantmen had assembled.

From there, the cruise in early April proved unsuccessful, but on 2 May the British Fleet of 26 sail-of-the-line, with seven frigates and the merchantmen set off from Spithead, the anchorage in the Solent off Portsmouth. Howe kept his fleet well out into the Atlantic, but sent two frigates, *Latona* and *Phaeton*, into Brest and they reported that the French fleet was still there. Six ships-of-the-line were detached to escort the merchantmen south, then ordered to rejoin the Fleet once they were safely on their way. Two weeks passed cruising in the Bay of Biscay, and there was still no sign of the grain convoy. The *Aquilon*, in her role as a 'repeating frigate' was kept active throughout. Francis had been appointed signal midshipman, whose task it was to repeat signals up and down the fleet. Secretly he was delighted, although with a certain amount of swagger he wrote to his father that he would be 'not very glad of it as it will be very troublesome. But to tell the truth I should be, out of pride, much sorrier to see anybody else appointed to it.'[21] His was a vitally important job, although it kept him busy from before dawn to long after dark, with very short breaks for breakfast and dinner.

The fleet sailed back northwards to Ushant, and on 19 May the two frigates sent to reconnoitre Brest reported that the French fleet of 25 ships-of-the-line had sailed three days before. Howe turned south, but fortunately ran into the *Argo*, a brig from Newfoundland that had been taken by the French fleet. From the information gained from the English crew left on board, the French had turned westward.

In the forenoon of 24 May, the *Aquilon* was granted 'leave to chase a ship and a brig which were passing some miles to leeward of the fleet, standing to the eastward'. The Aquillons were in their element, treating their permission as 'a very great indulgence' as there was the possibility of both distinguishing themselves in front of the fleet and bringing back news of the French. Also, it was a chance to boast, 'in sailing which we greatly prized ourselves,' Francis added. The *Aquilon* was renowned as a fast sailer, part due to her Captain who had experimented with her trim over the years. As Francis had observed, 'a couple of ton of water out of the foretopsail hold made a very considerable alteration in her rate of sailing for which we were obliged to fill with salt water frequently, for when in her exact trim we always found, especially in a small breeze, that nothing could touch us.' The Captain also raked the mizzenmast back to greater effect. The ship turned out to be a French frigate, and a 'brig very much a prize' lay astern. The *Aquilon* was cleared for action and could have 'spoke to the frigate in less than half an hour' but Captain Stopford obeyed the signal to board the prize. Mr Eaton, the first Lieutenant, and Francis were pulled over to the prize, the brig *Tiber of Yarmouth*. She had been taken some days before by the *Patriot*, a French ship-of-the-line, and sent back to France with a prize crew. 'There was only one Englishman in her, the Mate who from stupidity or fear could give us but little intelligence,' Francis noted. 'There were six men and the quartermaster of the *Patriot* all of whom but the Quartermaster were lying sick on the deck when we boarded her.'[22] The quartermaster proved more cooperative and told him that the French fleet were not carrying much sail.

Francis was confident that he would be the prize master of the *Tiber* with her cargo of '250 pipes of Tenerife wine on board' and was 'proceeding with the prize when the signal had been made to destroy her' – the Admiral believed that the *Aquilon* could not afford to lose the seaman needed to take the prize home. When the signal was repeated, 'Mr Eaton and myself,' Francis admitted 'with a great deal of glee set fire to her.' On board the *Queen Charlotte*, the Admiral remarked to the junior officers on his quarterdeck, 'It must be very unpleasant to see your promotion burnt: but I will shortly be able to make you amends for it.'[23]

The British fleet continued westward, shadowed by the frigates. As dawn broke on the morning of 25 May, Francis was in the main top intent on discovering the French fleet first. From there he spied 'a large ship, apparently a man-of-war, at least two or three miles to windward of the *Queen Charlotte* under her three TS [top sails] upon the leeward tack, indeed edging away a little'. Francis hailed the deck and Lieutenant Eaton joined Francis in the top. Slowly, they were able to make out her poop and part of the hull, enough to convince them that she was a French ship-of-the-line. As the *Queen Charlotte* was two miles closer to the stranger than the *Aquilon*, they 'thought it ridiculous to make a signal for her'. They watched the French ship repeating private signals, continually altering and shifting the flags from one masthead to the other, then discovered four rather smaller sail to windward of her. To Francis' amazement Howe took no notice of them until the late afternoon, when the *Thunderer* gave chase, only to be recalled a little later. Francis had discovered the part of the Fleet they 'were seeking, for *sans doubte*, he [Admiral Villaret-Joyeuse] mistook us for the French Fleet. He immediately let the second reefs out of his topsails and set topgallants on the larboard tack' and was gone. The fleet sailed westward before Howe realised that he was too far west and turned back. The quartermaster of the *Tiber*, who had been interrogated by Francis, had been right. 'I fear that we have overshot the mark, as we have been carrying a press of sail all the time.'

At last the 'long-wished' signal 'prepare for battle' was passed down the fleet. On the morning of Wednesday 28 May the French fleet was sighted. Francis' journal record of the three days leading up to the battle known as the 'Glorious First of June' is a testament to his powers of observation, but then being in a frigate, moving up and down the line he was in a position to see far more than most. 'About 8,' he wrote 'I first saw the leeward ships from the *Aquilon* then I went up into the main top and could count about 29 sail with the glass – the farthest off were laying to, and the nearest were coming down to us with all sail set, mistaking us, no doubt, for some rich convoy perhaps their own. The body of them bore about South by West. About 9, they began to discover their mistake and brought to gradually in a line making a variety of signals. We could now just distinguish their ports from our decks. The wind began to freshen up and to raise a short heavy sea and the sky had a gloomy aspect.'[24]

Having checked the run of his fleet, the French Admiral now had the weather gage. From this advantageous position he could attack in his own time, an option soon discounted when his frigates reported the size of the British fleet. Instead, he held his wind to keep position, and be in the right place to protect the convoy when it arrived. The initiative, however, was taken by Howe, who made the signal to 'harass the rear of the enemy'. The *Aquilon* herself 'instantly complied with the signal,' Francis wrote, 'setting all the sail we could show to the breeze. The quality of sail that we carried will gain but the idea of the state of the wind and sea. We set courses, double reefed topsails and jib.' The first shot was fired by the *Bellerophon*. Five ships-of-the-line 'kept up an incessant fire on the rear of the enemy's line, in particular on the sternmost who was a large three-decked ship without a poop. The prisoners told us that she was the *Révolutionnaire* from Bretagne.' The engagement ended at dusk with the *Audacious* severely mauled, but the much larger *Révolutionnaire* was knocked out completely and only just managed to limp back to port. The *Aquilon* had been immediately ordered out of the action and sent back on her station. As Francis noted with a certain pride, 'Never did a ship display her superiority of sailing so satisfactorily as did the *Aquilon* that afternoon', coming from a position behind the Fleet to leeward, to far ahead of it to windward in four hours.

The night of 28 May the *Aquilon* was detailed to shadow the French fleet, where they 'continued at quarters all that night and carried a vast amount of sail'. In the morning, Howe ordered the van of the fleet to break through the French line. The initial attack, bungled by the ineptitude of the *Caesar*, the leading ship, was noted by Francis from his position in the main top, but he applauded the action of Howe's flagship, the *Queen Charlotte* as she led the way through the French Fleet towards the end of the line. Howe now had the weather gage. That night, and for the rest of the next day, the weather closed in. Blankets of swirling mist obscured the French fleet as they slipped away to leeward. Francis thought, correctly, that they meant to 'draw us off the track of their convoy even at the hazard of an action, which though I by no means think they wish for, yet I believe their orders are to risk it rather than the loss of their convoy'.[25] At midday on 31 May, the *Aquilon* was ahead of the fleet. Then the mist cleared enough and lookouts spied the French fleet at '1/2 past one PM'. Francis, *The Signal Book for the Ships of War*[26] to hand 'made the signal for the French fleet' giving their position to Howe aboard the *Queen Charlotte*. But the Admiral was content to bide his time, and prepare his fleet for battle the next day. The *Aquilon* 'was sent to each division with some particular orders which could not be communicated by signal.'

For a great sea battle, the Captain's log of the *Aquilon* is surprisingly precise and merely factual. 'Light breezes and hazy. The French fleet bore to Leeward. 1/2 past 7, the British Fleet bore down upon the enemy in three divisions.'[27] Although the *Aquilon* was not engaged in any of the action, her role in the battle was indispensable. As signal midshipman, it was Francis who ordered the hoisting of the exact signals from the Admiral to the leading division, sailing close to each ship so as to be seen through the smoke once the battle commenced. His first hoist was No. 34: 'Having the wind of the enemy, the Admiral intends to pass between the ships in the line for engaging them to leeward.'[28] Howe's tactics were brilliant. Instead of attacking on a parallel course from a long range, his idea was to advance almost bows on, (at right angles to the French line) so posing a narrow target. Each ship would therefore pass between two enemy ships hopefully taking out one of them. To this end, Signal 36: 'Each ship independently to steer for and engage her opponent in the enemy's line' was carried down the line. The resulting action was devastating. *Queen Charlotte* and five other ships carried out Howe's orders to the letter. Six French ships were captured and one, *Venguere du Peuple*, was sunk after a tremendous duel with the *Brunswick*.

In the mêlée, the *Marlborough* was badly mauled. 'A French 3-decker came under our stern,' reads the ship's log, 'and heaving his main topsail to the mast, raked us which wounded Captain Berkeley severely, carried away our 3 masts and did other considerable damage. Made the signal for assistance, but it was almost instantly shot away. Hoisted it again on a boat's mast.'[29] The second signal was seen by the *Aquilon* who 'bore down to the assistance of the stricken ship' and took her in tow not long before the firing ceased. 'After the smoke cleared away', Francis saw '9 French ships dismasted, two 3-deck ships with their main and mizzen masts gone, others much disabled in rigging and sails'. As the French fleet limped away to leeward, their damaged ships in tow, Admiral Howe raised Signal 102: 'To close and join the Admiral forthwith.' The battle was over and, although the French fleet was crippled but not destroyed and the grain convoy escaped and reached Brest safely, Britain claimed 'The Glorious First of June' as a great victory.

The fleet returned to Spithead to great rejoicing. Again with his royal connections, Captain Stopford and the *Aquilon* were chosen to entertain the royal party for the official celebrations. The frigate was scrubbed and polished and scrubbed again. She was dressed all over with flags. Finally, on 29 June at '1 PM manned ship, and fired 21 guns on His Majesty passing the

Queen Charlotte'. Ten minutes later, the royal barge slid alongside the *Aquilon* and King George III and Queen Charlotte were piped aboard with their old '*Aquilon* hand', Prince Augustus Frederick, his brother Prince Ernest and five of the Princesses. The Royal Standard broke out at the masthead and after the party had inspected the ship, they went below to dine with the Captain and the senior officers. That afternoon, the *Aquilon*, escorted by the *Niger* 'ran down to Cowes [Isle of Wight]. At 4, hauled the wind and worked back towards Spithead with the flood tide.'[30] To the ship's deep embarrassment, the Master, apparently drunk, put the *Aquilon* aground on the Mother Bank between Cowes and Ryde at 5 p.m. The stern and kedge anchors were put out astern and after two and a half hours, she was finally worked off. The *Aquilon* returned to Portsmouth and the royal party was rowed ashore in the ship's boats. According to Lady Mary Howe, the Admiral's second daughter and lady-in-waiting to Queen Charlotte, they returned 'having passed the most delightful day, and in the finest weather possible'.

The experience cannot have been too much of an ordeal, as the royal party returned the next day. But to their further shame, she 'broke all capstan bars trying to weigh anchor'[31] and the cable had to be cut – fortunately minutes before their guests came aboard. The victory celebrations drew to a close when the *Aquilon* sailed them to Southampton, and after the Royal party were safely in their carriages, Lady Mary Howe and her mother returned to the ship 'when the wind, which had been quite favourable to carry them on, shifted exactly round, and brought us home in 3 hours, the most delightful sail down the Southampton river in boats I ever went'.[32]

At that time, Francis had nearly completed six years as a midshipman. He had served commendably well and fought in a major action – long before he died, he was the last surviving officer to have taken part in the 'Glorious First of June'. The war with France was escalating. New ships were being built, and old ships being brought back in commission. At twenty, Beaufort's prospects for a brilliant career in the Navy had never looked better.

CHAPTER 5

Lieutenant Beaufort RN

FRANCIS BEAUFORT was in the main top as dawn broke. Below, Captain Robert Stopford paced up and down on the windward side of the quarterdeck of his new command, HMS *Phaeton*, a 38-gun frigate. As signal midshipman, Beaufort trained his glass on the *Royal Sovereign*, Vice Admiral the Honourable William Cornwallis' flagship, and his squadron of three 74s and a frigate following some way behind. On the horizon, he could just make out Penmark Point in the Bay of Biscay. He kept his eye too on the *Triumph*, a 74-gun ship-of-the-line and the gun-brig sloop *Kingfisher* just two cables to windward, all making the most of the fresh breezes and clear skies as they forged ahead bearing north-north by west. 'At 10 h. 30m. AM [8 June 1795] the *Triumph* threw out the signal for six sail east by north.'[1] Beaufort repeated the signal back to the

Admiral. What they had discovered was a small French squadron with a convoy under the command of Rear Admiral Vence bound for Brest. On seeing the British squadron, the enemy ran up their colours, turned tail and 'at about noon, stood away for Belle-Isle, under a press of sail'.[2]

HMS *Phaeton* too made all sail and cleared for action. Beaufort did not need his signal book to recognise Cornwallis' signal No. 5, a single red and white quartered flag standing for 'Engage the Enemy' followed by signal No. 40: 'Engage the enemy on arrival up with them in succession.' He repeated them for the *Triumph*, then acknowledged them back to the Admiral. The *Phaeton* set all her topgallant sails and went after the first ship, an 84-gun ship-of the-line, as she scurried away. From time to time she 'engaged the enemy's rear, yawing occasionally to fire'[3] her guns at the stern of the retreating ship, the enemy returning their fire ineffectually from her stern chasers. As they rounded the Pawlin Head, Beaufort could see nine more ships-of the-line at anchor in the Palais Road, Belle Isle. He signalled their number and position back to Admiral Cornwallis who was still too far behind to reach the French before they made the shelter of the island. The chase was over, and the *Phaeton* hauled her wind and stood four miles off Belle Isle. Beaufort simply wrote to his mother: 'Fired a great deal at them. If supported, we would have cut her off.'[4]

But the action was not over for the day. Two more French frigates, one with a Dutch merchantman in tow, were sighted. The *Phaeton* and *Triumph*, lying two cables astern of her, were ordered after them. As *Phaeton* hauled close to Point Canon, the shore battery fired at her as she gained on the French frigates. The French abandoned their prize while the *Phaeton* hauled her wind after the weathermost frigate, firing her bow chasers continually. They 'got up close under her quarter' and were 'just on the point of taking her, all life, spirits, joy,' Beaufort recalled in a letter home, when they found themselves too close into the bay 'and the infamous dog of a pilot said there was danger of shoaling'.[5] As they retreated, Beaufort made 'the signal for the danger'. As a final act, the *Phaeton* wore round and fired a devastating broadside into the stern of the frigate that 'you might have driven a coach and six into'. The Dutch prize was taken in tow, and along with seven other prizes laden with wine, the British squadron sailed north to the Channel. Meanwhile, the *Phaeton* was ordered back to Palais Road to report the movement of the French squadron. On the way, she came on to an armed brig and managed a single broadside as the brig fled behind Belle Isle. When the *Phaeton* went in to cut her out, the wind dropped and, as the *Phaeton* drifted under the lee of the three shore batteries, she was pounded mercilessly. The frigate received 'several shot in her hull and by which 2 guns were disabled, 1 man killed and seven wounded'.[6] Eventually, the ship's boats were lowered and the *Phaeton* was pulled away from danger. 'Our ships were never intended to go against stone walls,' Beaufort commented. By way of compensation, two more prizes were taken.

The first prizes safe in English waters with the *Kingfisher*, Cornwallis turned and sailed southeast hoping to find Vence at sea. By that time, intelligence reports had reached Admiral Villaret-Joyeuse in Brest that Vence and his squadron were blockaded at Belle Isle by Cornwallis, and he set off immediately with a large fleet to 'rescue' them. On the morning of 15 June, Villaret-Joyeuse, aboard his 120-gun flag ship *Peuple*, fell in with the untroubled Vence to make an imposing French fleet of eleven 74-gun ships-of-the-line, eleven frigates and sundry support vessels.

The next day, the steady breeze came over the starboard quarter of the *Phaeton* allowing her to carry all sail. Acting as Cornwallis' lookout frigate, she was so far ahead of the squadron that she shortened sail by taking in the first and second reefs until the squadron came back into signal distance. She was then ordered into Belle Isle where again she bore up and 'set her royals and studdingsails'. With the Penmark Rocks in sight, the lookout saw a 'strange fleet 5 miles to starboard'. Frantic signalling followed the sighting, Beaufort conveying its position and the number of sail – signal No. 26, a blue flag over a red and white flag – to the *Royal George*. He then hoisted signal No. 71 to say that the *Phaeton* was shortening sail. The fact that no signal was sent to say that the 'strange fleet' was the enemy, added to the fact that the *Phaeton* did not return to the squadron, led Cornwallis to assume that the signal merely referred to a number of sail (most likely merchantmen), rather than a strong enemy fleet, and he pressed on. By 11 o'clock, all became apparent. The squadron 'hauled to the wind on the starboard tack under all sail, and formed in line ahead: *Brunswick, Royal Sovereign, Bellerophon, Triumph*, and *Mars*'.[7] In the afternoon, the French fleet separated into two divisions, one going north, the other continuing south. The wind fell and veered to the northward off the land, 'allowing the north division to weather, and the southern division to lie well up for the British squadron'.[8] To add to Cornwallis' problems, the *Brunswick* and the *Bellerophon,* normally considered good sailers, were out of trim due to an error in their stowage and so held the rest of the squadron back.

At daybreak, Admiral Cornwallis called for the signal midshipman of the *Phaeton*, and Beaufort was pulled across to receive orders for Captain Stopford. Back on board, the *Phaeton* then headed off while 'the van of the strange fleet lay SE by S, 3 miles distant, and hoisted French colours'. From the deck of the *Phaeton*, they witnessed the ferocious engagement as the *Mars* was attacked. The squadron edged away, virtually surrounded by a vastly superior French fleet that kept up a constant fire for most of the day. Cornwallis signalled the

Bellerophon to join the *Brunswick* to leeward, and together with the *Triumph* returned the fire with their stern chasers as they came to bear. The *Mars* badly crippled, Cornwallis brought the *Royal Sovereign* and the *Triumph* down to her. With powerful broadsides, they fought off the four French frigates saving her from capture. 'A partial firing continued until 6h. 10 m. P.M., when it entirely ceased.'[9] In another half-hour, the French fleet shortened sail and stood out to the east, and 'at sunset were nearly hull-down in the northeast'.[10]

The extraordinary and rapid departure of the French was entirely due to the action of the *Phaeton* carrying out Admiral Cornwallis' orders. That morning, she had sailed off to the northwest and at '40 m. past 10, made the signal to the Admiral of a strange sail to the west-north-west'. This was followed by another signal that they had seen four more sail, and finally, at '55 m. past 10 [the *Phaeton*] let fly with Top gallant sheets and fired 2 guns 20 secs. apart'[11] – the signal (known to the French) for the sighting of a fleet. Although she was some miles ahead of the squadron, the *Phaeton* then 'cut away the larboard bower anchor and cable and hauled 14 pigs of iron ballast overboard'. The French, keeping an eye on the *Phaeton* saw her make a private signal to the mythical fleet, followed by the tabular signals that told them that the fleet was British. To complete the *ruse de guerre* she signalled that the fleet was made up entirely of ships-of-the-line. Beaufort then repeated the signal, the Dutch ensign, from Cornwallis 'calling in the strange fleet'. By coincidence, a British fleet actually was on the horizon precisely where the *Phaeton* had signalled it. But it was the ruse that saved the day. As Beaufort wrote to his mother 'the French, the dastardly rascals, taking their a—s in their hand . . . tacked and left us'.[12] The *Phaeton* returned to the squadron and as they 'passed under the stern of the *Royal Sovereign* . . . gave her three most hearty cheers'.[13]

The engagement became known as 'Cornwallis' Retreat', and throughout his life, Beaufort was always justly proud of his part in the action. Years later he wrote 'in all the various services I had the good fortune to be connected with during that triumphant war, I look back with by far the most exultation to the honour of having shared in the glory of the 17 of June.'[14]

Beaufort's longed-for promotion finally came on 10 May 1796 with a velum commission signed by Earl Spencer, First Lord of the Admiralty. He had served just over six years as a midshipman (including the notional time in the *Colossus* but not including his time with the Honourable East India Company). The promotions board met in Portsmouth, and Beaufort presented himself at the Royal Naval Academy. For three hours, dressed in his best number one uniform, he sat with other hopeful candidates outside the main hall. He sat quietly, as family legend had it 'in a fright – as he was always very bashful and had, moreover, a very modest opinion of himself'.[15] His nervousness increased as each candidate emerged with accounts of harrowing interviews, but when he entered the vast hall he was relieved to see his own Captain Stopford, Captain Bertie, who had given him such a glowing testimonial from the *Latona*, and another. He presented his logbooks from his past cruises. They examined the neatly written pages, some illustrated with deft sketches. The drawings of 'The Hold of HMS *Phaeton* stowed May 1795' caught their eye, and they fell into a discussion as to how they themselves stowed their holds. Beaufort meekly sat in front of them until they were finished, when they merely asked him a couple of simple question on seamanship. 'Oh! This is a nice fellow,' declared Captain Bertie 'he may certainly pass.'

Just two weeks short of his twenty-second birthday, Francis Beaufort was appointed third lieutenant aboard the *Phaeton*, his 'apprenticeship' truly over. It was then entirely up to him how fast and how far he was to advance up the promotion ladder. But he knew, as did every officer in the Navy, that promotion for those without powerful patronage was solely gained through achieving 'glory' – daring deeds that brought their names to the notice of the Admiralty. Britain was at war with Revolutionary France and there should have been opportunity enough for the glory that Beaufort craved, but it was to be otherwise.

During the mid-1790s, there was no real defensive role for the French Navy in the Atlantic, save for the corn convoy from America to save a starving nation. The country was virtually bankrupt, and what money there was, was spent on the army fighting France's land enemies around her borders. So rather than risk another major confrontation with the British (and to save money), the Committee de la Marine kept the Atlantic French fleets in the comparative safety of their ports, leaving the task of harrying distant British colonies and merchant shipping to small squadrons or individual ships, in particular licensed privateers or *chasse marée*. The British retaliated by blockading the French ports, and attacking their ships at every possible opportunity. All merchantmen trading with France were deemed lawful prizes, and were taken, irrespective of nationality.

In the years 1794–99, the *Phaeton* was one of the most successful frigates in the Atlantic. In that time, she completed 15 cruises – from the north tip of Ireland to the south coast of Portugal – and took a remarkable number of prizes. A rich and successful ship is a happy ship, and Francis Beaufort in his own way contributed to her success. Stopford relied on him, so much so that he had wanted to promote him lieutenant eight months before his six years as a midshipman was up. His brother officers, in particular the first lieutenant James Hillyar, liked him well enough. As a master's mate, he had moved into the gunroom with the commissioned officers, with a small cabin of his own. With his promotion to lieutenant came the slightly larger third lieutenant's cabin. He was popular in the gunroom, holding his own with the best of them. Beaufort also held the regard of the non-commissioned officers and crew, who respected him as a person and acknowledged his seamanship and gunnery prowess. Nor was he lacking in courage, he just needed the right occasion to prove it.

The list of prizes taken by the *Phaeton* over the four-year period is impressive by any standard. The sheer volume of merchant shipping, nearly 30 vessels of varying size, and the tonnage of cargo taken, was vast. Then there were the privateers, some with prizes that were retaken and 'head money' (a sum paid for each prisoner taken at sea). But even with the most heavily armed *chasse marée* there was rarely any action. They relied on their speed to escape, but when pursued, sometimes over several days, and caught, their light guns proved no match for the heavy frigate. Their colours were invariably struck without a fight. Nor were the 16 French men-of-war that the *Phaeton* took or destroyed much of a match for her either.

The capture of the French corvette *La Bonne Citroyenne* with 20 nine-pound guns was typical of Beaufort's disappointment – although the prize money was welcome, he was primarily after the 'glory' that would secure his promotion. At midday 11 March 1796, a sail was sighted on the horizon and the *Phaeton* set all sails, including royals. There was a fresh breeze from the northwest, and in just over two hours she was near enough to 'fire a shot at the chase'.[16] The corvette hoisted her colours and shortened sail. A few minutes later, the *Phaeton* also shortened sail and *La Bonne Citroyenne* fired a broadside 'in the mêlée' and struck her colours. In another typical chase, *L'Actif*, a corsair of 18 guns, lightened ship by throwing half her guns overboard and cutting away part of her gunwales. She received several well-aimed shots from the *Phaeton* before striking her colours. At least Beaufort was appointed to her as prize master, his first command, and, with a party of seamen to sail her and marines to guard the prisoners, he took her back to Falmouth. Both ships were subsequently taken into service with the Royal Navy. *La Bonne Citroyenne* was renamed HMS *Speedy* and was later given to the maverick Thomas Cochrane as his first command. Cochrane and the *Speedy* were fictionalised in Patrick O'Brien's novels as Jack Aubrey and the sloop *Sophie*.

These prizes made Beaufort comparatively well off. In the capture of just three ships, *La Mercuse*, 18 guns, an American brig laden with sugar and coffee, and *L'Actif* he received £74 12s 10d after deductions from his prize agent, a Mr Druce, while his share of the prize money between 1797–99 amounted to £1,075.

Beaufort and his fellow officers lived particularly well in their mess, with good wines and tolerably fresh food – on one gunroom dinner, Beaufort recorded that he and 16 other officers and their guests drank 39 bottles of wine and port between them. Part of Beaufort's prize money was invested in consoles and other stocks (some Irish) and he made loans to his father and brother. On his rare visits to London, he indulged himself, not so much in high living like his brother officers, but with the likes of Edward Troughton, the leading scientific instrument maker of the day, where he bought a new sextant and surveying equipment. He spent large sums with his bookseller, adding more works on theology and philosophy to his library. Ever the dandy, he patronised his tailor, ordering new broadcloth uniform coats and breeches.

But despite this upturn in Beaufort's finances, he was still dissatisfied with his lot. He longed for *real* action, as opposed to the little skirmishes that had become almost a fortnightly occurrence. 'Other ships,' Beaufort remonstrated, 'are *drooping* beneath the weight of laurels, for I swear they are golden laurels, whilst others, and some of our consorts, have been so gallantly employed in the salvation of my country.'[17] He wrote to his father: 'The long and the short of it is that I want to get hold of a frigate of equal force, or perform some *valorous* deed or other.'[18] With such an action, the *Phaeton* would certainly come to the notice of the Admiralty. With such 'glory', promotion would undoubtedly come for both Captain Stopford and his first lieutenant, James Hillyar, into whose shoes Beaufort hoped to step, that being 'the only chance, I am afraid, that there is in getting one step higher in the ladder I have been this long time a-climbing, but a poor chance I doubt. I see I shall sit down at the end of the war as a half-pay lieutenant with my wife living on love and potatoes.'[19]

In the innumerable letters to his father at this time, Beaufort pretended that he was content. 'I am happy for I am resigned,' he wrote.[20] His father was taken in, once replying that Francis had the 'happy knack of seeing things *de bon côté*'.[21] Pages of code to his brother, however, tell a very different story. Inside his outward show of bravado and well-cut clothes, there lay a suppressed restlessness. There were flashes of wit. He could tell a very good story. But equally, his lack of self-confidence and self-effacing manner came out as seriousness. He often lapsed into fits of depression that he called his 'blue devils' or 'azure enemies'. In letters home, he would pass over (or even fail to mention) some action, but rail against his ill fortune when a similar prize escaped capture. To add to Beaufort's real and fancied woes, he developed the most awful skin problem.

In the summer of 1794, Beaufort mentioned that he was suffering from a mild skin complaint. At that time, such an affliction would have been quite unremarkable – most officers and crew experienced a variety of illnesses, from the bloody flux and scurvy to the gamut of sexually transmitted diseases that the port whores could supply. But within two years, Beaufort's 'cutaneous disorder' had become far worse, spreading from his hands to his arms, legs and feet. His hands cracked painfully, and the scabs became so large that they ran one into the other. At first, they were dry, peeling off in 'large flakes like whitebran',[22] but as the disease worsened and spread over his body, 'underneath those scales or scabs which used formerly to be almost dry,' he reported to his father, 'there is now a sensible quantity of glutinous matter, and under fine skin it is generally very tender'.[23] Nor did he have much faith in the diagnosis of the various naval and civilian doctors or their remedies. The Surgeon of the Fleet, Dr Trotter, prescribed a course of mercury having diagnosed a venereal disease, a charge that Beaufort vehemently denied. He also consulted a Dr Guck in London, and 'paid him a golden guinea. He called it the *lipra Græcia* of the Ancients.'[24] In other words, leprosy. This terrified Beaufort. He read and reread Leviticus chapter 13 that charts the symptoms and degrees of leprosy: 'the plague in the skin of the flesh, and when the hair is turned white, and the plague in the sight be deeper than the skin of his flesh, it is a plague of leprosy . . . and when raw flesh appeareth in him, he shall be unclean.'[25] They were exactly his own symptoms.

With no faith in the endless remedies – the likes of Gilbert's ointment, nitric acid, cold tar, hot and cold baths – that were prescribed to Beaufort, he was determined to fight his ailment from within. With his strong faith, he believed that this was God's punishment. 'By the grace of God my dependence on Him increased daily. He sent it to me, and he will take it away in due time.'[26] When Beaufort's condition worsened still, with painful swellings in his neck and chest, he merely put it down to God testing him further. 'How good is God!' he wrote to his father, 'he sends us afflictions and chastisement, to give us strength of mind enough, or more properly speaking resignation, to face them.'[27] By then, he believed that he was suffering from scrofula, the former King's Evil. What Beaufort actually had, in all likelihood, was symptomatic porphyria brought on by a metabolic malfunction. He had all the symptoms: 'cutaneous fragility and blistering of dorsal hands and arms, and sometimes of the face.'[28] What is more, Beaufort had endless opportunity to aggravate the disease – exposure to the sun, constant drenching in salt water, an unhealthy, often rich diet of red meat and above all, large quantities of alcohol. The cure for porphyria was bloodletting, a remedy that had been used for centuries as a panacea for practically every ailment. It was unfortunate for Beaufort that he was not bled medically, and had to wait to be cured in the line of battle.

At last Stopford came to the notice of the Admiralty and he was offered, and accepted, the *Excellent*, a 74-gun ship-of-the-line. In spite of his earlier unpopularity with his officers, he was a first-rate captain with a well-run ship, so much so that 'in 1797 he was present at Spithead during the mutiny, but to his credit, the crew of the *Phaeton* did not manifest the least symptoms of disaffection'.[29] With his transfer from the *Phaeton* came promotion for his officers. Stopford invited James Hillyar to go with him as first lieutenant, and Beaufort as second, the invitation issued 'in the most friendly manner'[30] he had ever 'experienced from him'. Despite what Beaufort described as '8½ years of servitude' he had 'no hesitation in readily and gratefully enclosing with his offer'.[31] Stopford was genuinely delighted. Beaufort 'made his bow', but the door was no sooner shut to the captain's cabin than the sacrifice he had made dawned on him. Hillyar was in a similar state. So Beaufort returned to the cabin 'emboldened by the friendly way' Stopford had treated him, and asked his candid advice on whether he should, after all, follow him to the *Excellent*. He explained that his acceptance might have been too hasty and over influenced by his regard for him and his family. Stopford was flattered by Beaufort's approach and on reflection 'he thought that a first lieutenant of a frigate was undoubtedly a preferred situation than a second on a 74,'[32] adding that his successor would be 'glad to have him'. Beaufort was delighted with Stopford's advice as being first lieutenant on the *Phaeton* was still, after all, 'his dearest wish'.

In hindsight, had he gone to the *Excellent*, Beaufort would have very soon been first lieutenant, for Hillyar was soon promoted captain. But as he was to admit to his father, he was still wracked with self-doubt. He was 'anxious as to the figure I shall cut in my present situation for knowing, dear father, that every day increased my doubts whether I shall ever make what I call a great officer. To be anything inferior to that, to trawl through my navy career in a middling way as a good-natured ass, is an ideal that wounds me to the quick.'[33] However, his new captain James Morris, 'late of the *Lively*' was particularly able and likeable. Again Beaufort veered between joy and irritation. He wrote to his sister that he was thrilled to be going to the Mediterranean 'the only part of the naval world where there is still a chance of service,' but 'alas, we are going with an intolerable cargo, Lord and Lady Elgin to Constantinople,'[34] he having been appointed British Ambassador to the Sublime Porte (the Ottoman Turkish Foreign Office).

The Elgins and their large and assorted party set off from Plymouth on 9 September 1799. The Earl and Countess took Captain Morris' cabins for themselves, and the rest of the party fitted in with the ship's company as and where they could. Beaufort was thrown in with them all, yet was oddly critical of the party that doubtless gave him the intellectual stimulation he lacked in the gunroom. Admittedly, he accused them of treating his ship 'like a stagecoach in which they had nothing to do but to take their places and be set down at their place of destination' and they teased him when he found their behaviour irritating. He liked Lord Elgin, whom he thought 'rather heavy, being apparently a sensible man unfashionably attached to his wife,' the marriage being a 'money one', while the Countess was a 'good-natured unaffected little woman, by no means handsome nor resembling an ambassadress'. Beaufort had her wrong for she was a spirited woman – she dressed up as a man when her husband presented his credentials to the Sultan. He disliked Mr Morrier, Elgin's secretary, and thought his chaplain, the Reverend P Hunt, a 'prig of a parson'. Beaufort also badly misjudged William Hamilton whom he found 'a civil and accommodating fellow', but accused him of not having 'even an ostensible employment' – he was in fact Elgin's political adviser and was to become a man of great distinction (it was he who secured the Rosetta Stone for the British Museum and was a fellow founder member with Beaufort of the Royal Geographical Society). Beaufort also enjoyed the company of J. D. Carlyle, 'a celebrated professor of Arabic in the University of Cambridge'. There were five servants out of livery and seven in, along with three maids whom Beaufort presumed were 'intentionally ugly for fear Selim [Sultan Selim III] should fancy any of them'.[35]

For landspeople, the journey was often rough, and Lady Elgin was constantly seasick. To Beaufort's annoyance, 'when the ship begins to kick, forsooth she must have a day or two' in port to recoup. Occasionally, the Elgins' sickness worked in Beaufort's favour. In early November, the *Phaeton* put into Palermo where Admiral Lord Nelson was on his flagship HMS *Foudroyant*. Beaufort went aboard and presented his letter of introduction from a mutual acquaintance, Richard Bulkeley. Beaufort must have impressed the Admiral greatly, and in return Nelson doubtless recognised someone of ability without influence at the Admiralty. He replied to Bulkeley soon after their meeting: 'Mr Beaufort gave me your letter a few days ago and I can assure you of my inclination to be useful to him. At present, he cannot be better off than 1st Lieutenant of so fine a frigate – it shall be my business to put her in way of meeting the Enemy where his promotion will of course follow.'[36] The Beaufort family greatly admired the sentiment, and Fanny thought it 'wonderfully well and distinctly written for a man who has lately lost both his right hand and right eye'.[37]

The cruise of the *Phaeton* with the Elgins continued uneventfully towards Constantinople. Once, in the waters of the Aegean, Lord Elgin demanded that they visit Ilium, the site of Troy. When they reached Alexandria Troas nearby, Beaufort was invited to join what he called the *cognoscenti* to view the ruins. Instantly, he was enthralled with the 'multitudes of broken columns of the most magnificent size, sarcophagi, bits of marble inscriptions, a theatre 120 yards in diameter, a place whose antiquity outstrips history'.[38] This first view of a classical site, that 'raised indescribable sensations' in his 'insensible breast', was to inspire him a dozen years later when he embarked on his survey of the southern coast of Turkey.

The *Phaeton* finally dropped her 'imprecatory' cargo at Constantinople, together with a few boxes of marble sculptures. Despite his initial reservations, the cruise must have been intellectually rewarding, as Lord Elgin gave Beaufort a glowing testimonial, written after two months' acquaintance: 'I have confidence in saying that I have seldom met with a better bred gentleman, one who possesses more information, or who had read more, or to better purpose. As first lieutenant of this ship he is called upon to do a great deal of duty: and the reliance placed in him by Captain Morris, & the ship's company justifies the character he bears of an excellent seaman. I have enjoyed a great deal of his society during our voyage and have found him a great resource.'[39] At last Beaufort's talents were being noticed in the right quarters.

For most of the next year (1800) the *Phaeton* was known as 'pride of the ocean'.[40] At that time, the French were being driven out of Italy by the Austrians, aided by the British. Lord Keith's Mediterranean Fleet, which *Phaeton* had joined, harried the retreating French supply lines and their shipping between

Genoa and Antibes. Beaufort was in his element. He commanded the boats in various coastal raids on artillery positions, he ferried supplies to the troops, and, on occasion, the *Phaeton* joined the blockades of Genoa and Toulon. The *Phaeton* took several small prizes with a few minor skirmishes, and in May received the approbation of General Melas, the Austrian commander, on their accurate fire during the siege of Genoa. A few days later, the Phaetons captured twenty grain ships and 'a depot of arms'.[41] But the good fortunes of the Anglo-Austrian forces did not last. Napoleon re-entered the scene, and after the Battle of Marengo, Italy fell to the French. The British Fleet retired to Gibraltar and the *Phaeton* was sent back to blockading duty off the French and Italian Rivieras, with the occasional foray into the Atlantic.

The *Phaeton* had been blockading the port of Cadiz since August as part of Admiral Sir Richard Bickerton's squadron. In early October, a Spanish cutter under a flag of truce hailed her and delivered a letter, smelling strongly of vinegar, from the governor saying that the city was rife with yellow fever. The main fleet arrived soon after, and the *Phaeton* was sent in to make soundings and to find a suitable landing spot for the proposed invasion force of 21,000 men. Beaufort himself went close inshore with the cutter and made his report to the Admiral. A landing place was agreed on (the wrong one according to Beaufort), then the whole operation was abandoned when it rained heavily. The commanders, to Beaufort's intense fury vented in his journal, blamed the plague for their incompetence in landing the troops. However, his irritation at the commanders of the British expeditionary force in their failure to capture Cadiz was short-lived, as he soon had his own engagement, one that nearly cost him his life.

On the morning of Tuesday 27 October 1800, a fresh wind came out of the north-northwest as HMS *Phaeton* sped along at a steady eight and a half knots. She stayed on the starboard tack, cutting through the short, choppy sea. The ship's company were in good spirits. They had left the Cadiz fiasco behind them and the Fleet in Gibraltar, and were on their own in a potentially rich cruising ground off southern Spain. The lookout hailed the deck having spied a strange sail on the horizon. The *Phaeton* immediately tacked, cleared for action, and put on more sail. The strange ship, a poleacre (a three-masted brig) hoisted Spanish colours, 'an ensign and a pennant' and headed for the comparative safety of the land. The *Phaeton* followed hard on her heels. The poleacre just managed to slip into the harbour of Fuengirola and anchor under the solid walls of the fortress. Captain Morris ordered the *Phaeton* about when he saw 'the livid waves on the shore, and as they were close into the surf and directly under the battery of fire of heavy guns, there was no prospect of bringing them off'.

The next day the *Phaeton* cruised up and down outside the harbour, venturing as far as Malaga where two Spanish gunboats lay in the harbour. As she passed, one of them fired two shots at the frigate, but the light ball fell far short of their mark and the *Phaeton* tacked out of the bay. The master was then sent in by the jolly boat to make soundings around Cape Molino, and the *Phaeton* hove-to off the coast while the ship's boats were lowered. All afternoon, Captain Morris and Beaufort poured over the charts and coastal views to work out how best to cut out the poleacre. Beaufort was to lead the expedition, but disagreed with Morris that he should have a heavy carronade, a type of naval mortar, in the launch to cover his retreat. Discussion was cut short when a sail was sighted in the distance, and the *Phaeton* was off again. She caught up with an American brig bound for Malaga from Lisbon. The two warning shots across her bows were enough to bring her to, and a boarding party was sent across to search her. Meanwhile, the Captain had his way and a carronade was lowered on to the launch and secured amidships, then the *Phaeton* made her way back towards the shore. It was a calm night with a fluky wind. The master ordered the third reef in the topsails, and then shortly before one o'clock in the morning, he brought her up into the wind.

On the hour, Beaufort said goodbye to his Captain on the quarterdeck, and gave him a letter addressed to his father. He then made his way down the gangway into the pinnace and settled in the stern sheets beside Lieutenant Duncan Campbell of the Marines. Resting his two loaded pistols on his lap, he pulled his boat cloak about him and laid his heavy cutlass on the bottom boards. The pinnace was cast off; the twelve oars held vertical in salute crashed down together as Beaufort gave the order to give way together. Two six-oared cutters and the launch with the carronade followed behind. The pinnace moved steadily through black water flecked with white, the boat crew pulling steadily towards the distant shore. After only a few minutes, the launch was far behind. Beaufort circled round and 'kept company with the launch'.[42] As he suspected, she was slow and unmanageable, particularly when he took her in tow. When a sudden rainsquall hit them, he abandoned the launch and continued with the two cutters to the land. For two and a half hours they rowed steadily, with short even strokes until the outline of the shore was just visible. They eased up in the calmer water, Beaufort intending to 'rest up the people's arms after so fatiguing a pull and to bale the boats being half full of water, and to repeat once more the particular stations and duty of each of my comrades'.[43] But it was not to be.

A flare went up on the headland and they were discovered. A beacon was lit on the beach, the orange light spreading out over the black oily water showing up the three boats in silhouette. The enemy on shore fired on them with muskets, so 'communicating their situation to the ship';[44] Beaufort urged his little flotilla forward as the whole place came alive. To his horror, he saw that a French privateer had slipped unseen into the port and was anchored between the poleacre and the fort. The three boats were pulling hard and were almost on the Spaniard when a volley of musket fire from the French schooner splattered around them. No one was hit and the fire only served to spur them on. An 'inspiring cheer' went up and Beaufort found himself under starboard forechains, while the green cutter under Lieutenant Huish crossed behind and went up to the larboard forechains. The black cutter, under the command of the gunner, Mr Dexgon, hooked on to the main chains.

At the same moment that the boats' crews and marines clambered up the ship's sides, Beaufort was leading his party up from the pinnace. He reached the deck first, cutlass in hand, pistols pushed into his belt. Again, the French schooner fired down on the attackers. A stray ball went through the throat of Able Seaman Peters, killing him instantly as he came up the side. Beaufort had hardly swung his leg over the gunwale when he received two quick sabre cuts to the head followed by one to the shin. The second cut, however, was partially deflected by a silk handkerchief he had folded in his hat. Blood poured out of his wounds as he staggered forward, only to be shot at almost point-blank range from a blunderbuss. Fortunately, Beaufort had turned at the last moment to take stock of their position – in fact the officers and crew of the poleacre had 'deserted the deck' leaving the defence of the ship to a body of around 20 marines – or he would have been killed instantly. As it happened, the irregular lead balls ripped into his left arm with a few in his chest. Some took fragments of his uniform deep into his flesh, but amazingly none of the shot severed anything too vital.

Despite the action of the Spanish marines, 'who indeed defended their ship bravely', the withering fire from the French privateer, and the shots from the shore battery, the poleacre was finally carried after the final charge led by the severely wounded Beaufort. Just when he knew that he had possession of her, he received yet another wound in his side, the force of the bullet spinning him round. He had just time to order Lieutenant Huish to cut the cables before collapsing in a dead faint. Huish obeyed, and the prize's 'sails were immediately loosed and she was soon out of reach of the fort who, however, continued firing'.[45] Meanwhile, Beaufort lay bleeding copiously, his blood spreading in pools over the deck. When he came round minutes later, he could hardly breathe from the mass of blood that had collected in his throat, nor had he the strength to spit it out. He fainted four more times, but eventually managed to clear his windpipe.

The *Phaeton*, standing-to off the coast waiting for the return of the boats, had seen the action and finally witnessed the prize sailing out of the harbour shortly after 5 o'clock that morning. She then spotted another Spaniard poleacre standing towards Malaga and, as the prize seemed perfectly under control, went after her. The shore battery at Cape Molino fired at the *Phaeton* 'without effect'. She then 'shortened sail and took possession of the Spanish brig' having firing several shots at her, then made all sail back towards the 'boat's prize', which she reached at eight o'clock that morning.

The 'boat's prize' that Beaufort had so gallantly captured, as Captain Morris reported to Lord Keith, 'proved to be His Most Catholic Majesty's armed ship, the *San Joseph* alias *L'Aiglia*, mounting two 24-pounders, two brass eighteen for the stern chase, four brass twelve and six swivel 4-pounders'. Beaufort noted that the 24-pounders were iron and of English manufacture, 'while all the rest were beautiful Spanish guns'. It was a gallant prize indeed and one that should have assured his future.

CHAPTER 6

Commander Beaufort RN, Half-pay

THE COT SWAYED GENTLY in the sick bay deep on the orlop deck of the *Phaeton* as she made her way back to Gibraltar accompanied by her two prizes. Francis Beaufort lay there weak and delirious from loss of blood, both from his wounds and the constant bleeding, a full 40 oz [2 pints] in two days, by the ship's surgeon. His brother officers called to see him. They looked into his ashen face and bandaged body and agreed that it was most unlikely that he would live. In one of his more lucid moments, Beaufort called to the loblolly boy for pen and ink and, with his left hand, just managed to scribble an account of the taking of the *San Joseph* to his father. It was a touching letter. He underplayed his own part in the action and made light of his injuries with 'I sank wounded in more places than one, but none are [*sic*] now dangerous.'[1] It was far from the truth.

Two days later Beaufort was in the hospital in Gibraltar where 'everything with all the skill and attention that they could direct has been done for me,'[2] he wrote to his brother William in early November. He watched as the bandages came off his head a few days later, and saw that his wounds from the razor-sharp Spanish sabre, amazingly, were nearly healed and with no ill effect. But his arms and chest were very badly wounded. He was in great pain. The surgeons operated a little at a time, encouraged that there was seemingly no infection. In all, they removed fifteen of the sixteen lead balls, some neatly wrapped in the broadcloth of his uniform; the last was bedded in his lung and was to remain there for the rest of his life. His whole body was a grizzly sight. The hole in his upper arm from where the majority of the 'slugs' were removed was so large that he felt he could 'just cram in my inkbottle',[3] while the wound in his hand numbed his fingers for months.

In the meantime, Captain Morris had been soliciting on behalf of Beaufort (whom he always found a 'most capable and zealous assistant'[4]) and his cutting out party. He gave a full account to Lord Keith and to Lord Spencer, First Lord of the Admiralty, extolling their actions. 'I am convinced that more determined bravery could not have been displayed than has been displayed by Lieutenants Beaufort and Huish, Lieutenant Duncan of the Marines, Messrs Hamilton and Stanton Midshipmen and Mr Dexgon, the gunner and the boats crews employed upon the service.'[5] This was Beaufort's main chance for promotion: 'I give your Lordship detail of this service feeling it incumbent on me to do so, to do justice to the parties employed upon it, humbly hoping that Mr Beaufort's conduct and wounds will entitle him to the protection given in the present war, to officers of distinguished merit.'[6]

Their lordships took immediate action. As he lay in hospital,

Francis Beaufort was promoted commander and appointed to the sloop HMS *Ferret*, a fire ship then stationed at Portsmouth. It was an appointment in name alone, and he never even saw his first official command. But again, Beaufort felt that he had been cheated of his due rewards. The *San Joseph* was immediately taken into service in the Royal Navy and renamed HMS *Calpe*, one of the Pillars of Hercules, the present Gibraltar. *Calpe* was refitted and given to a young lieutenant, George Dundas, a kinsman of Viscount Melville, Treasurer to the Navy. Patronage invariably paid off. But even if Beaufort had been appointed to the *Calpe*, which was his due, he could not actively have commanded her as he was still far from fit for service.

By mid-December it was thought better that Beaufort transfer to the Naval Hospital at Almade, just outside Lisbon. He sailed on the *Phoenix* and arrived on Christmas Day. With little else to occupy his mind, he became obsessed with his wounds and revelled in his ill health. He wrote a full account of his condition to his sister Louisa, even though he knew that she would have seen all his letters to his parents. He described how the holes in his arm had reduced to the size of a pea only to open up to resemble an oyster; he gave full reign to the effects of the damp sea air on his lungs. But most marked of all was the effect of his wounds on his advanced porphyria. More by chance than good doctoring, Beaufort lost enough blood to clear up his 'untoward' disease. In hospital he was fed a simple broth and so denied the rich food and red meat that had aggravated his complaint. The mild Portuguese winter sun healed rather than inflamed his skin. What was even more remarkable was that, as a result of his illness, although his hair remained white throughout his life, his skin healed completely, the six years of livid scabs leaving no marks. In a letter to his sister Harriet he wrote of his general improvement: 'still mending, healing, fattening, strengthening, lungs well, pains real and imaginary. A gloss of

health on my cheeks which you might think that I had stolen
from some pretty Portuguese milkmaid. The Portuguese milk-
maids have very nice cheeks and such as I hope my dearest girl
you possess.'

As the months of 1801 unfolded in Portugal, Beaufort
continued to improve. He bought a jackass to ride. He built up
his strength walking a 'mile or two at a time', later taking a gun
with him for some rough shooting. Here was a more relaxed
Beaufort. Even when a ship carrying his new orders was taken
by a French privateer, he merely remarked to his father that he
was 'a little curious' as to what they were, but assured him that
he had 'not abandoned all worldly and ambitious hopes'.[7]
Beaufort dallied in a boarding house run by an Englishwoman.
There was a note of envy in his letter as he wrote of the 'lucky
Dutchman' who had the 'moiety of her bed and profits for the
same reason that Kate the 2nd [Catherine the Great] preferred
that nation for her household officers!'[8] For the second time in
his life, Beaufort had courted death. The experience had left
him light headed, with a Devil-may-care attitude to life.

Another reason for Beaufort's great good humour was the
attachment he formed with a girl he identified in a single letter
to his brother William as his 'Dulcinia' – he professed love but
not so deeply that he could not 'shake off her yoke in a
moment'.[9] It appears that she was bright and witty, and stood to
inherit £6,000 or £7,000 from a maiden aunt who was nearly 80.
But Beaufort was rather cavalier about his relationship with 'La
Dulcinia' who swore her love for him. He could not believe that
any woman, least of all a pretty heiress, would even consider
him. His porphyria had made him unattractive to women in the
past and he remained uneasy in their company.

But slowly, his feeling of well-being leached away, and self-
doubt returned. His letters home now showed a desperate man,
one seeing life pass him by with no hope for the future. He

desperately missed the Navy and the exacting routine that produced an ordered life. When he was told that it would be advisable to give up the Service and remain in Portugal for at least a year to convalesce, he wrote in desperation to his father on his prospects 'without promotion, without pension, on my half-pay'. He was just 27 and felt washed up.

Realising that Portugal could do no more for his health, Beaufort returned to England on a passing frigate, HMS *Anson*, and arrived in London on 1 September to learn his fate. He was in a curious mood. On one hand he was still thirsting for honours and glory, performing all manner of heroic deeds in his troubled mind. 'I shut my book,' he wrote to his father, 'slouch my hat and strutting about the quarterdeck, in imagination take perhaps the combined fleet with a single ship.'[10] He was hoping against hope that the war with France would last long enough for him to make a full recovery and be passed fit by the Admiralty, as his chest was still giving him pain. Then his moral and serious side would take over. He abhorred the 'emptiness of ambition, the worthless praise of the mob'[11] of his daydreams. Then at times he was prepared to give up the Navy, and thought that possibly a country life would not be so bad after all. He had visions of building some 'nice little whitewashed cottage, covered with woodbines and jasmines, and bargaining for constant spring', there considering himself 'the happiest of mortals cultivating my cabbages on my half-pay!'[12]

But reality soon took over from such reveries. Beaufort presented himself at the Admiralty as the clock struck noon the day after his return. He paced up and down the antechamber to the rooms of the First Lord of the Admiralty, Admiral Earl St Vincent, along with a score of other hopefuls. After a six-hour wait, in which time he had examined each portrait minutely at least a dozen times, it was at last his turn. Beaufort was ushered into the room where the Admiral sat behind a large table. He was skimming through a sheaf of papers, one of which Beaufort recognised as Captain Morris' testimonial on the taking of the *San Joseph*. St Vincent looked up and examined Beaufort minutely. Despite his well-cut clothes and appearance of wealth, the Admiral recognised one of his own, a man of raw ability and courage but without the advantage of patronage. Beaufort immediately asked for a ship, as was his due, but greatly surprised the First Sea Lord by also asking to be made up to post captain, which was certainly not. St Vincent gently set him straight on that score, and although he sympathised and 'lamented' that as there were many ahead of him with as good or even better claims, Beaufort should bide his time and be patient. Considering his case and the impending peace with France, St Vincent advised Beaufort to apply for a pension as recompense for his wounds. Bravely, Beaufort remonstrated with the Admiral that that was not what he wanted, but the next day, he was at the Naval Surgeons Hall where his 'carcase was fingered in the buff'.[13]

In a factual petition to the King, Beaufort wrote of his action and had no compunction in exaggerating the extent of his wounds. It was sent to the Admiralty with his medical report, and was promptly lost. However, St Vincent took a different tack and turned down his request for the very pension that he himself had recommended Beaufort to apply for, saying that he had been more than compensated for his wounds with promotion, so why should he have a pension as well? Beaufort was indignant, and accused St Vincent (well known for his vindictiveness, especially to junior officers – one officer was so persistent that he had him press-ganged as he waited in the Admiralty for an audience) of double standards. He made a firm and lasting enemy of him, but in the end Beaufort received £45 12s 6d a year pension for the rest of his life along with his half-pay as a Commander RN.

★ ★ ★

It was a bright, crisp morning in February 1802 when the chaise was spotted coming over the bridge. By the time it had climbed the steep hill into Collon, turned right past Glebe Farm with its huge barns, and down the drive, the Beaufort family, flanked by a few servants, had assembled on the steps of the flag-decked rectory to welcome Francis back. It was a tearful homecoming – his mother and sisters fussing over his wounds, his father and brother William firing dozens of questions at him. They were all much changed. Beaufort had left a midshipman and returned a commander. Although he had seen his parents and brother in London on his infrequent leaves over the last 13 years, his sisters, Henrietta and Louisa who had grown from adolescent schoolgirls to young women, were virtual strangers.

The next few months were supremely happy for Beaufort. He was fairly well off with his prize money, half-pay and disability pension and lived reasonably well. He had asked his father to find him a servant, as he 'had grown bachelorish'.[14] The Rectory at Collon rang with their laughter and ragging, Mrs Beaufort once drawing the line at the brothers running around naked clad only in Persian rugs. Weeks at home turned into months. He made periodic visits to London to try for a ship but, despite the fragility of the Peace of Amiens, he met with no success, nor would he while St Vincent was First Sea Lord. He solicited the Earl of Courtown, but he was by then elderly and without influence. Beaufort thought of buying a farm with his prize money but could not find anything that he could afford – 'land at 1½ gns. per acre' was outside his reach. He spent two days at Packenham Hall as a guest of the Earl of Longford where he was 'received more than kindly'.[15] He asked to rent a farm, but the Earl could not 'promise him more than 120 acres'.[16] Beaufort also thought of becoming a land surveyor, a profession to which he was admirably suited. Again, he decided against it as not lucrative enough. He scoffed at the 50 gns. offered for surveying a new road in Galway. It was a bleak time for Beaufort's career. He had not given up hope of another ship, but equally was indecisive about finding alternative employment. He thought of spending the rest of his life 'in the bosom of his family', much to the chagrin of his cash-strapped, and by then distraught parents.

Their salvation (and their son's) came through Dr Beaufort's close friendship with one of the most remarkable men in Ireland at that time, Richard Lovell Edgeworth. Their friendship grew out of their many mutual interests. Both were men of science. They shared a passion for agriculture, mechanics and literature – Richard Edgeworth was the father of the celebrated novelist Maria Edgeworth. Not too distant geographical neighbours, their families came closer still when Edgeworth, divorced once and widowed for the second time, married Fanny Beaufort as his fourth wife. Francis Beaufort and Edgeworth admired each other from the very beginning, and a close friendship developed that was to last to the end of their lives. While Edgeworth recognised Beaufort as a kindred spirit and man with an ordered and scientific mind, Beaufort was truly captivated by Edgeworth. Ever active, Beaufort recalled him 'standing before the dining room fire, he made two steps forward and holding himself perfectly erect sprang right across the large oval table clear over all the bottles and glasses and lighted aplomb as light as a feather on the other side! – he once cutting a caper and clapping the soles of his feet together cracked a walnut between them! – it having been stuck on to his sole with wax.'[17] While nothing would diminish his father in his eyes, Beaufort looked upon Edgeworth as his mentor. While his father was essentially a pure scientist in the Enlightenment sense, Edgeworth took a more practical view. As such, he was a member of the famed Lunar Society of Birmingham,

along with such luminaries as Dr Erasmus Darwin, Matthew
Boulton, Josiah Wedgwood, James Watt and the chemist James
Kier, whose aims were to apply scientific investigation to
industrial problems.

Through Edgeworth, Beaufort entered a world that he had
only dreamt about, and between him and his daughter Maria, he
came into direct contact with all the scientific and literary
luminaries of the day. Nor was it a one-sided affair. Fanny wrote
to Mrs Ruxton, her sister-in-law, that 'Francis has pleased our
friends here much more than I ever expected after all the praise
that has been lavished on him. The more you see of him, the
more I flatter myself that you will like him – for his sentiments
resemble Mr E's so much that he seems but a part or a copy of
him.'[18]

But Beaufort had more to thank the Edgeworths for than
mere friendship and introduction to the literary and scientific
world – Richard Edgeworth gave him useful, though not
gainful, employment. Edgeworth had long conceived the idea
of a telegraph. It began as a bet in 1766 when a consortium,
led by the Earl of March, proposed a relay of fast horses so
that the result of a Classic race run at Newmarket in the
afternoon would arrive in London by 9 p.m., when they could
make their winning bets accordingly. Edgeworth then laid
£500 that he could name the winner by 5 p.m., whereupon his
raffish friend Sir Francis Delaval matched the sum. Edgeworth
tested his 'telograph', consisting of a large pointer on a tall
structure, between Delaval's London house in Downing Street
and Piccadilly. Certain of winning his wager, he hinted as
much to Lord March who naturally called off the bet,
thanking him 'for his candour'. Had the telegraph between
Newmarket and London been built, it would have well
pre-dated the French *télégraphe* invented by Claude Chappe.
In fact, Edgeworth accused Chappe of stealing his invention

after he demonstrated it at Collon in 1796 when 'somebody there described it in such a manner as to instruct the French how to emulate it, which they have since done'.[19]

Undaunted by the French machine, Edgeworth persevered with his own invention. In June 1795, he delivered a paper, *An Essay on the Art of Conveying Secret and Swift Intelligence*, to the Royal Irish Academy. In it he described his machine and gave an account of his three successful experiments, one of which was to convey a message across the Irish Sea. By 1803, Ireland was in a state of unease. The rebellion of 1798 and the subsequent Emmet uprising, combined with the persistent rumours of a French invasion, made the Protestant community jittery. So, after years of rebuff, this general unease was enough to persuade the Viceroy of Ireland and Lord Lieutenant, the Earl of Hardwicke, to adopt his proposal to build a telegraph across Ireland from Dublin Castle to Galway. Edgeworth was delighted and enlisted the help of Beaufort who 'declined remuneration for his services and applied himself to the task with vigour'. As Maria Edgeworth wrote to her sister-in-law: 'God speed them – & keep Bonaparte away until the giant isosceles is ready on the coast to meet them.'[20] But for two practical and gifted men, the scheme was ill conceived, totally flawed from the outset, and doomed to failure.

The 'giant isosceles' that Maria referred to were pointers made of light canvas stretched over a wooden frame. They were about 10 feet high, and so light that 'two men could, with ease, carry the whole paraphernalia of each station upon their shoulders'.[21] The pointers were mounted vertically on a portable wooden structure, with capstan bars attached to the axis to move the pointers manually. Other stations were permanent, being built on old windmills or new brick towers. The idea was that the pointer could be set momentarily in one of eight positions, 45° apart, each one representing a number – straight up was 0, 2 and

6 horizontal, 4 straight down, with 1, 3, 5 and 7 being the intermediates. Edgeworth and Beaufort concocted a numerical codebook where each set of four numbers represented either a word or a whole phrase.

After months of inactivity and rejection, Beaufort was happy doing something practical and challenging. Not only was he being employed, nominally as a captain in the Sea Fencibles, the local militia, he was also working with Edgeworth whom he admired, which in turn brought him into constant contact with his large and extended family. For Beaufort, it was like being back at sea. The winter of 1803 was hard. He supervised the construction of the first 15 positions and their attendant guardhouses, or spent hours drilling and schooling his unlikely telegraphers, mostly semi-literate tenants drawn from Edgeworth's estate at Edgeworthstown. But in addition, he had his usual gripe with authority over pay and conditions. As he wrote to his father, he had had 'six months' anxiety, six colds, six thoracic pains, six diarrhoeas – and denied six months' pay'.[22]

By March 1804, the first section of the telegraph from Dublin to Athlone was completed, and the initial transmissions showed up just how flawed the system was. Beaufort sent the first message that was received 11 minutes later by Henry Edgeworth, Richard's son. It made little sense, and even less sense when relayed back to him. Beaufort put it down to teething problems, but by the time the line was extended the 120 miles to Galway, the operation was no better. What these two learned men had not appreciated at the outset was the vagaries of the Irish weather and the difficulties of accurately interpreting the pointers positioned anything up to 20 miles apart. Not only were there days on end of mist and rain, there was also the 'casual smoke of Dublin' to combat. At last the day came for the official opening of the telegraph in Dublin by the Lord Lieutenant.

It was early July and near perfect weather when Beaufort sent a simple message to Galway. The crowds waited expectantly for the return. They trained their telescopes on the next tower, the pointer set up on a disused windmill on Cappa Hill. Twenty minutes passed, and the message came back. It was unintelligible. The whole project was a failure, and three weeks later it was taken out of Edgeworth's and Beaufort's hands and given to the military.

Beaufort was naturally disappointed – even more so as he was still waiting for his Sea Fencible pay – so he found being 'diplomatically thanked' by the Lord Lieutenant inadequate recompense for his labours. However, he had something far more important that occupied his every waking moment. He was deeply in love with Charlotte Edgeworth. Beaufort met her on 17 March 1802 when he first went to Edgeworthstown to see his sister Fanny. On Beaufort's part, it was love at first sight. By all accounts she was a great beauty. Marc-Auguste Pictet, Maria Edgeworth's Swiss publicist and editor of the scientific and literary journal *Bibilothèque Britanique* described her as 'a young girl of sixteen, pretty, fresh as a rose, her eyes full of intelligence',[23] while Fanny compared her to a sprig of Lily of the Valley or a 'May bush, so sweet, so neat, so white'. However, her milk-white complexion owed more to her ill health (there was a history of tuberculosis on her mother's side of the family) than the fashion of the day. Throughout that summer and the next, Beaufort made every excuse to visit Edgeworthstown to see his 'beloved', but so tortured was he with self-doubt that he could not bring himself to declare his love for her. It was only when Charlotte, accompanied by her father, Fanny and Maria, left for an extended visit to Paris in October 1802 that Beaufort even shared his secret with his brother William.

For the two years he was working on the telegraph, Beaufort contrived to see Charlotte at every possible moment, but still did not pronounce his love, nor ask her father for her hand. He wrote to his brother on the second anniversary of their first meeting, saying that he hoped that he would be wafted 'on the wings of love and harmony through life' or else 'the black and gathering storm' would 'rive and tear my firm soul'.[24] He assumed, correctly as it turned out, that Charlotte would have guessed that he was in love with her and, as she had not 'at once answered that she had opposite feelings',[25] he felt he would eventually marry her. But by the November of 1804, Beaufort, frustrated at the lack of response to his letters to the Admiralty asking for promotion and a ship, set off to London to present himself in person to Viscount Melville, the new First Lord of the Admiralty. As he was preparing to leave Collon in early December 1804, a messenger arrived with a letter from Edgeworthstown. He recognised Charlotte's hand, and broke the seal with anticipation.

My Dear Francis,

Though I should have regretted exceedingly not seeing you before you left Ireland and though there were many things I wished to say to you, yet I found it impossible to utter even kindnesses to you last night – but it has often been with me when the last moment arrives in which I could express what I wish – all recollection seems to forsake me and every idea seems for a time suspended.

But I cannot let you depart to enter on a life of danger thus. As I feel a sister's affection for you why may I not express a sister's feelings? Why may I not assure you I have and always shall set a high value on your friendship and why may I not thank you for the uniform and steady friendship I have experienced from you?

I am sorry you are going away but as my regard for you is sincere, I consider much more what may be for your advantage. I hope you may be placed in a situation where your talents and your merits may be rendered conspicuous and I truly hope you may return in Safety, to enjoy ease and happiness. I am much better this morning – and I shall ever be your sincere and

Affectionate friend,

Charlotte[26]

At first Beaufort thought that it was her way of letting him down gently, particularly the reference to her being like a 'sister' to him. Then, on closer examination, he read much more into it. In this beautifully constructed letter she reveals as much, but no more, than the manners of the time allowed. From it, Beaufort could see that she knew of his attachment for her, and that she too harboured strong feelings for him that she was unable to express in person. By describing herself as a 'sister', she could justifiably explain her obvious emotion without exceeding the bounds of propriety of early nineteenth century courtship. He was elated by the letter, and vowed to woo her even more ardently on his return from London. Beaufort now needed a gainful employment more than ever.

Two days later, dressed in his finest uniform, Beaufort presented himself at the Admiralty confident of his reception. Through working on the telegraph, he had ingratiated himself with the Earl of Hardwicke, who had promised to write to Lord Melville, St Vincent's successor. But Melville received him coldly. The promised letter of recommendation from Lord Hardwicke had not arrived. Beaufort stood motionless as Melville paced up and down the room rifling through his record of service. After what seemed 'like an age', the First Lord sneered at Beaufort: 'Are you not in a disagreeable position?' he asked. 'You have applied for orders and you avoided receiving them?' It was true. Beaufort had written to Admiral Whitshed, commander of the Sea Fencibles, for further orders but through frustration had not waited for a reply. Melville fumed at him, sending him off to the secretariat of the Admiralty to place himself on the active list.

Yet again, Beaufort railed against the injustice of the system. He had no influence at Court or at the Admiralty, and little money. In a letter to his brother he even accused Melville of bribery, believing that his 'right hand perhaps never signed a commission 'till he had value received in his left'. Shortly after Beaufort's meeting, Melville resigned after an investigation of his dubious time as Navy Treasurer. Beaufort was delighted with the news, declaring that he could not feel sorry for the man who had treated him 'with duplicity and contempt'. Nor did Beaufort have immediate satisfaction from Melville's successor, Lord Barnham, who merely stated that his name was on his list but that 'the number of candidates out of employ puts it out of my power to make any promises whatsoever'.[27]

Not for the first time, Beaufort was suffering from his blue devils. As his sister Fanny wrote to her sister-in-law, Mrs Ruxton: 'Poor Francis' New Year [1805] begins very much as the old one ended – and the old one ended just as the old one had begun – large claims on his part and foolish empty promises on that of a foolish government. I am afraid that he will not have gained much by his journey to London, and remains literally the Provoked Captain.'[28] He was, however, much encouraged by Charlotte's last letter, undoubtedly by reading more into it than was there. In the New Year, he travelled to Oxford and met her father at his old college, Corpus Christi. Richard Edgeworth was delighted to see him and not a little proud of his protégé. Later, they spoke of Charlotte at length. Beaufort declared that he had been in love with her for two years and formerly asked his permission to propose to her. Edgeworth was deeply upset. He was torn between his friend and his daughter. He had lost her mother to tuberculosis, and he feared that he was going to lose their daughter as well. He told poor Beaufort not to write to her, and on no account to propose to her as he felt certain that her health would not stand it. Beaufort was distraught. He wrote an agonising letter to his father, for the first time explaining his hopeless position. In his inimitable fashion, Dr Beaufort took up the cause and interceded on his son's behalf. He wrote to Francis stating that he was 'not surprised' at his passion and asked if he should talk to Charlotte. Then, without waiting for a reply, he went to Edgeworthstown to see Charlotte himself to ascertain the true position of her feelings towards his son.

Afterwards, in a carefully constructed letter, Dr Beaufort wrote to his son with sage advice. 'How I wish you were at my elbow for half an hour that I might clearly explain what I can but inexpertly explain on paper. She is a most amiable and superior character and I have often contemplated with great pleasure the probability of her becoming my daughter. And therefore I am not surprised at your passion though you cannot know her half so well as I do. And you certainly have had very little conversation with her individually.

'Now comes your dilemma, if you had spoken to her or written as it seems you intended, and that she approved of your addresses, you are bound to each other although much time may intervene and many things happen to postpone the completion of your wishes. If you had loved her in perfect silence and wait till a comfortable establishment should make you to propose for her, you were both at liberty to form any connection that might offer in the meantime but then she might be lost to you before that happened through ignorance of your attachment. In the present case, she is as much at liberty unless a mutual liking now concealed in her own breast should introduce her to reject other offers, but then how can she be certain that you will hold the same opinion of her that you do now? . . . If things succeed with you that a few years or less may bring you together, but if you should learn that the reverse is the case it would induce you to use your reason and strength of mind to overcome a hopeless passion, and not feeling yourself bound to anything. You might perhaps meet with a deserving object in time who might make you as happy.'[29]

His son merely replied that his love was constant, that if he was 'to swear by the whole firmament of stars that I could never change, you would only smile at the hyperbolic effusions of a lover'.[30]

With little hope of securing Charlotte as his wife, his finances in disarray, and constant rebuff from the Admiralty, Beaufort felt that his world was closing in. He wrote to his brother, 'I am 32 and with no employment, no wife, no shilling, and no hope.'[31] But then, on the very same day (5 June 1805) he received a letter from the Admiralty. He had at last been given a ship to command, the HMS *Woolwich*.

CHAPTER 7

Commander Beaufort RN

THERE WAS NO BOSUN'S CALL, no clash of rifles of
Marine sentries presenting arms as Francis Beaufort
saluted the quarterdeck of his new command, HMS
Woolwich. In their place, the caulkers' hammers rang out in a
steady rhythm as they chiselled oakum into the gaps between
the pitch pine decking. Beaufort stood there with his brother-
in-law, Richard Lovell Edgeworth, somewhat at a loss at what
to do. Eventually, the ship's carpenter appeared, blinked in the
morning sun, and unsteadily approached the two men. Beaufort
opened one of his sea chests and took out his pendant and
handed it to the carpenter. Beaufort and his friend watched the
long, thin streamer that distinguished the *Woolwich* as a man-of-
war (as opposed to a merchant ship) snaking its way aloft as the
old man hoisted it unceremoniously, hand over hand, up to the

very top of the main mast. It flapped gently in the faint breeze at the masthead then fluttered back down to the deck. The carpenter was too drunk even to belay the halyard. It was an inauspicious start.

Five days before, Beaufort had returned to his London lodgings at 69 Swallow Street off Regent Street from viewing a Dr Barney's 'most famous and interesting library'[1] to find a letter from the Secretary of the Admiralty announcing his appointment to the command of the store ship, HMS *Woolwich*. At first he was insulted. He railed against such an appointment, thinking that he deserved far better. 'Is it for the command of a store ship that I have spilled my blood, dragged out a tedious economy in foreign climates . . . for the honour of carrying new anchors abroad and old anchors home!'[2] Store ships, he argued in his journal, were the just reward of the sons of the First Sea Lord's housekeeper or bailiff or in return 'by the interest of some great Jew contractor for pursers' shirts or Dutch caps, or by any other backdoor means'[3] and not, as he unwisely pointed out in a letter to Lord Barnham, First Lord of the Admiralty, for the likes of him with his record of service. He saw his appointment without 'ambition, promotion, or riches – the three stimuli which singly must govern the mind of every sailor'.

But by the time he went to see 'the most insolent of all clerks, Mr Wright of the Admiralty' on 5 June 1805 to collect his commission (in return for a small fee to pay for the document), he had reconsidered his position. He realised that the alternatives were a great deal worse. At least he had a ship, and was thus gainfully employed. Having begged for a ship for so long, pointing out that he would accept anything, he realised that were he to turn the *Woolwich* down he would never be given another ship, let alone a *better* ship. Also, he had been kicking his heels in London with little money for the last seven months, 'laying about the Admiralty, the operas, the institutionals, the collections of paintings, Mrs This's squeeze, Miss That's piano makes the idea of a storeship appear a paradise'.[4] Above all, he hoped that this appointment would lead to his marriage to Charlotte Edgeworth.

Beaufort returned to Deptford to examine his new ship. The *Woolwich* was worse than he first feared. Although she had just come 'out of Lavender Dock, Mr Young's contract yard' where she had been partially repaired with 'doubled with fir plank of 3" at the brads and 1" on the Garboard streak and newly coppered'[5] the rest of her cabins, decks and combings were in 'a shameful and slovenly manner'. With a sinking heart he toured the ship with the carpenter, by then sober. Her bowsprit was a 'pathetic stick' while her fore, main and mizzenmasts were second-hand from the scrapped HMS *Argos*. Her foremast was so suspect that it had to be surveyed twice. But what worried Beaufort most was her lack of suitable armaments. The *Woolwich* had been built in the 1780s as a fifth-rate frigate, but her original 44 guns had been removed when she was converted to a store ship and not replaced. To his mind, the carronades on the new type of gun carriage he had inspected at the arsenal at Woolwich were ideal for close-order fighting – the *Woolwich* being slow and heavily laden would not be chasing an enemy, nor engaging at a distance. Also, carronades required a smaller gun crew to man, took up less space and, as they sat on the deck, did not need gun ports. However, the Admiralty in their wisdom refused Beaufort's request, supplying instead 24 assorted guns that neither fitted the existing gun ports nor used a standard shot, and used valuable cargo deck space.

By the end of August, Beaufort had received enough men (with the addition of some pensioners from the Royal Naval Hospital at Greenwich) to take the *Woolwich* downstream. She moored at Gravesend for further fitting out and to load the stores – mostly anchors, cables and canvas – that she was to carry to Bombay and Madras. Characteristically, he made a meticulous record of his cargo and stores, drawing to scale the position of the water casks and ballast in the holds. But no sooner had he tied up than he was beset with a catalogue of disasters. A seaman fell overboard and was carried away in the strong ebb tide. Two days later, John Flocket, a ship's boy fell from the rigging, and 'as he had received a concussion of the brain by the fall', Beaufort refrained from joining the rest of the Fleet in firing a 19-gun salute in celebration of the coronation of George III. Then HMS *Porpoise*, another store ship, tied up alongside the *Woolwich*. Her officer of the watch proceeded to 'clear the bower hawse'. By chance or design, the evil-smelling muck from the anchor cable that had collected around the hawsehole was washed out and landed square in Beaufort's own barge. Beaufort received a veiled apology from the officer, but still feeling slighted, brought up the iniquities of the *Porpoise* with Admiral Stanhope. The Admiral was duly sympathetic, then turned to an officer in the room. 'Captain Beaufort,' he said. 'I don't think you have met Captain Short of the *Porpoise*, your new commodore.'[6] Beaufort admitted in his journal that he had made an enemy of the man.

At last the *Woolwich* was ready to move down to Portsmouth, but Beaufort was still beset with problems. He learned that his two lieutenants were assigned to him as a form of punishment, 'sent to this new fashioned penitentiary house to do mortification for their wickedness'.[7] He began by loathing one of them, Lieutenant Macredie, but regretted his leaving a few weeks later. He was a classical scholar 'with the *Iliad* at his fingers' ends . . . and was far advanced in mathematics and geometry'. Beaufort knew that such a man would be a great asset in the long passage to India, where the usual conversation centred on 'the birds, the weather, the beauty of the dolphins, and the last sail seen'. Add to that misfortune, his by now considerable library had been held up in customs in Liverpool. The pilot, Alexander Cullum, came aboard and took the *Woolwich* down the Thames and anchored off the Nore. At noon the next day, 26 September, they weighed anchor. There was a light breeze and smooth water when Beaufort ordered the master to set all sails. Although there was room for great improvement, he was happy with the way his ship sailed. He was not, however, pleased with the 'old dog of a pilot', whose competence was seriously in doubt. The *Woolwich*, riding low in the water with her cargo, was bowling along over the Shivering Sands Flats on a flood tide at 8 knots when Beaufort 'suggested to the pilot the propriety of standing back again into deep water while yet the flood made up and while there was still wind'. But the pilot insisted on maintaining his course. As Beaufort predicted, the wind dropped as the tide turned. It was only a matter of time before she went aground. In a frenzy of activity, the topmasts were lowered to the deck and the jib booms made ready to shore up the ship. No sooner had she dropped an anchor than the wind picked up. Beaufort ordered the cable cut and all sail to be set, but the breeze only lasted ten minutes and 'she was brought by the sand, her heel gently caught'. The sails were furled and the topmasts and jib booms lashed on each side. There she remained, perfectly upright, until the tide turned and she floated off. Though embarrassed that he should be grounded on his first voyage (something that was not recorded in the ship's official log) he was delighted at the way his officers and crew reacted in an emergency, finding them 'all active, zealous and willing. They exerted themselves to their utmost and have given me the most flattering hopes for their future conduct'.[8] The disgraced pilot was put ashore at the Downs, and 'charming weather and a gay little breeze' brought the *Woolwich* to Spithead.

For the first few weeks, Spithead was an enjoyable time for Beaufort and the ship's company. Portsmouth was lively and entertaining, with a 'pleasing society' centred on the house of the Commander-in-Chief, Admiral Sir George Montagu, his wife, and two pretty daughters. Beaufort spent much time in the girls' company, both of whom he thought pretty and found lively. He 'chatted to them all day' and found 'sense and nonsense being equally acceptable to them'. At last he was content, but confided to his father that his time was 'constantly and pleasantly employed from 7 in the morning until 1 the next morning'.[9] But as the weeks of waiting turned into months, his frustration grew and his feeling of well-being faded. He wrote to his father he was sick of 'lying idle, inactive, disappointed and degraded'[10] while others, including those who had served under him, were 'gaining reputation, promotion and riches'. Beaufort's feelings of frustration were further tested by the 'intelligence distributed from the flagship of a most glorious victory obtained by Lord Nelson's fleet from the combined force of French and Spanish off Cadiz'.[11] As the home fleet fired a *feu de joie*, a thunderous roll of cannon fire that lasted throughout the day at the news, Beaufort ordered just three rounds of musketry in celebration. While he attended a dinner for the captains given by Admiral Sir Isaac Coffin, he ordered an extra allowance of grog for the crew of the *Woolwich*. But the victory celebrations were overshadowed by the death of Lord Nelson.

At noon on the morning of 8 November, Beaufort mustered the whole ship's company on deck. In a steady voice, he read the account of the battle and of the death of Lord Nelson from the *Gazette*. From his position on the quarterdeck, high above his men, he could 'hardly observe a countenance in which the flush of glory did not mount, nor in whose eye the tear of regret did not stand'.[12] Beaufort, too, was greatly affected by the death of the Admiral. 'Never had we such an illustrious commander!' he began the long eulogy sent to his father who, never one to waste anything, used it, word for word, in his own service of thanksgiving at Collon Church for the life of Nelson and his great victory. In early December, Beaufort watched HMS *Victory*, Nelson's flagship, return with his body aboard, followed, one by one, by the victorious ships of his fleet with mixed feelings of pride for the Service, and frustration at his own lack of action.

And so the *Woolwich* lay, the weed growing steadily on her bottom, rolling on her moorings for another six weeks. Beaufort, with time on his hands, railed against the incompetence of the Admiralty (in particular his old adversary Earl St Vincent) who kept him penned up in Spithead with a succession of adverse gales blowing up the Channel outside.

By mid-October it was reconfirmed that the *Woolwich* would be going to India and, to Beaufort's great dread, she was to sail as far as the Cape of Good Hope in convoy with Captain Short and Captain William Bligh, Governor designate of the penal colony of New South Wales. But after those weeks of waiting, the *Woolwich*'s stores were so low that Beaufort requested an audience with Admiral Sir George Montagu. He pointed out that 'That sagacious board yclept the Lord's Commissioners of the Admiralty forgot to order this ship to be victualled,'[13] to which the Admiral shrugged his shoulders and replied that there was nothing that he could do about it.

'But Sir,' Beaufort replied. 'Orders will come in a hurry, perhaps to sail with some ship. I shall be obliged to wait two or three days for my prog [provisions].'

'Well, well, I can't help it,' repeated the Admiral.

'But Sir. Suppose you were to mention it to them [the Admiralty] either privately or publicly? Consider how much my already long detention here may harm the Service in the East Indies.'

'No, Captain Beaufort, I will not say a word about you. I got twice a rap over the knuckles for interfering in what they call their own department, and I won't do it a third time.'

The Admiral dismissed him with a curt nod, but the request had been made. Beaufort then received orders from the Admiralty to temporarily transfer the *Woolwich* from Montagu's command to Admiral Sir John Borlaise Warren's squadron anchored at St Helen's Road on the Isle of Wight, where she completed her stores by 12 January. The intention, as Beaufort knew full well, was once provisioned to return to Spithead to wait for Captain Bligh to arrive. But those orders were not specified.

On the morning of 13 January 1806, Beaufort was woken at first light with a signal for a midshipman to repair on board Sir John Warren's flagship to receive orders. Sensing that the squadron was about set off, Beaufort ordered 'up the lower yards and topgallant masts'.[14] The midshipman returned without any orders for the *Woolwich* from the Admiral, but Beaufort still made himself ready to sail with the squadron. With a light heart, Beaufort answered Warren's signal to the whole squadron at 8 o'clock to unmoor, and even more enthusiastically answered the signal to make sail just two hours later. The moderate breeze, a little to the north of east, carried the *Woolwich* out to sea on her topsails alone. As she slipped steadily through the cold grey sea, after months of inactivity, Beaufort was supremely happy. He was leaving odious Captain Short behind and joining the squadron of a man with a high reputation for action and success. They were destined for the West Indies with a convoy, and then to cruise the Atlantic to harry the French. By 8 o'clock in the evening, the *Woolwich* was bowling along on a strong breeze at 8 knots with her foresail set, 'the Needles Light bearing NNE by E 24 miles'.[15]

That evening at sea, Beaufort dined alone. As was his custom, he wrote up his journal, seated at a plain table in the corner of his cabin lit by a single candle, the flame swaying with the roll of his ship. The entry for that day, 13 January 1806, was later to give him worldwide and everlasting recognition – far greater than any heroic sea battle or deed that would have brought him the promotion and riches he craved at the time. In his precise hand he wrote: 'Hereafter I shall estimate the force of the wind according to the following scale, as nothing can convey a more uncertain idea of wind and weather than the old expressions of moderate and cloudy, etc. etc.'[16] He began by numerating the force of the wind:

0	calm
1	Faint air just not calm
2	Light airs
3	Light breeze
4	Gentle breeze
5	Moderate breeze
6	Fresh breeze
7	Gentle steady gale
8	Moderate gale
9	Brisk gale
10	Fresh gale
11	Hard gale
12	Hard gale with heavy gusts
13	Storm

This was followed by: 'and the weather as follows etc.'

b	Blue skies
f	Fair Weather
d	Dry warm atmosphere
s	Sultry
p	Passing showers
c	Clear that is clear hard horizon but not blue sky

cl   Cloudy

w   Watery sky

wd   Wild, forked, confused threatening clouds

dk   Dark, heavy atmosphere

l   Lightning

t   Thunder

g   Gloomy dark weather

gr   Grey threatening appearance

h   Hazy

dp   Damp air

fg   Foggy

r   Rain

sr   Small rain

dr   Drizzling rain

hr   Hard rain

sh   Showers

hsh   Hard showers

sl$^{d.}$ Settled weather

sy   Steady breeze

sq   Squally

hsq   Hard squally

bk   Bleak horizon and clouds

thr.   Threatening appearance

What Beaufort had done was to record in his journal a scale of wind speed that he had merely copied from a *Memoir*, written in 1779 by Alexander Dalrymple (*see* Appendix 1), the same Hydrographer to the Honourable East India Company who had sent Lestock Wilson and the *Vansittart* through the Gaspar Straits. In fact, the only alteration Beaufort made to Dalrymple's scale was to insert a 'moderate breeze' at force 5, so moving the rest up a place. The shorthand to describe the weather was also taken from the *Memoir*, although here Beaufort has expanded the idea greatly. It was a clever system and worked well. With the use of a comma 'after any weather marked, implies that all the weather so separated by a comma are connected: thus *sq,r,th,l* implies squally with rain thunder and lightning'.[17]

Nor was this wind scale entirely the creation of Alexander Dalrymple either, for he had marginally adapted the idea worked out by John Smeaton, (1724–94) the great English civil engineer and Fellow of the Royal Society. In 1759, Smeaton delivered a paper to the Society entitled 'An experimental enquiry concerning water and wind to turn mills, and other machines, depending on a circular motion',[18] for which, with further research on windmills and waterwheels, he was awarded the Copley Medal. Smeaton could see the advantage to the owners of windmills that if they could accurately calibrate the speed of the wind they would automatically know how much sail their mill should carry – a Mr Rouse of Market Harborough in Leicestershire and a Mr Ellicott were working very effectively in the same area of research at exactly the same time, while a Dutch surveyor, Jan Noppen, had produced his own wind scale a little earlier in 1735.

Smeaton invented an instrument to measure wind speed. It was an ingenious device (see illustration) whereby an arm, fixed to a spindle, was mounted on a tripod. At one end of the arm were four wooden sails, mounted horizontally and counterbalanced by a weight at the other end. Through a series of pulleys, the cord attached to the axle of the sails moved a marker up a scale. To operate it, a rope was wound round the spindle, and by pulling steadily on the rope, the arm rotated causing the sails to turn. The faster the sails turned, the higher the pointer moved upwards. Comparative tests were made by altering the pitch of the sails and the speed at which the driving rope was pulled, and the results formulated.

Following these tests, Smeaton then experimented in the

Smeaton's ingenious machine for quantifying wind.

field. Using Authorpe Mill in Lincolnshire, whose 'length of the sails being 34 feet from the Centre; or 64 feet diameter' he worked out a table 'Containing the Velocity and Force of Wind'.[19] Not only did Smeaton measure the wind speed in miles per hour (also expressed in feet per second), he also worked out the 'perpendicular force on one foot area [of sail] in pounds *avoirdupois*'. Against these entries Smeaton entered the 'Common Appellation of the force of wind'. These ranged from 'Hardly Perceptible' at 1 mph, 'Gentle Pleasant Wind' at 4 mph, to 'A Great Storm' at 60 mph right up to 100 mph 'An Hurricane that Tears up Trees, carries buildings before it etc.'

Alexander Dalrymple was elected a fellow of the Royal Society in 1771 on the strength of his paper on discoveries in the South Pacific Ocean, and it was there that he met John Smeaton. With their common interests and like minds, he and 'the ingenious Mr Smeaton' soon became firm friends. One of Dalrymple's tasks as hydrographer to the East India Company was to ascertain the best times of the year and courses for their ships to sail out and back from the Far East. To this end, he minutely analysed the journals of the East India Company's ships, hoping to find some kind of a pattern. He also wrote to the hydrographer to the French Navy, as he knew that they had been analysing their ship's logs since the 1720s. However, as Dalrymple pointed out in his treatise entitled *Practical Navigation*,[20] he could not 'omit observing that having found on examining the India Sea-Journals a great want of perfection in the description of the winds'. This led him 'to an attempt for bringing the terms to a certain standard'.[21] Eventually, Dalrymple did come up with a plan which was 'to take all the terms I found in modern journals, and then to arrange them, numerically, according to my own judgement: from a *stark calm*, as sailors denominate a perfect calm, reckoning it as 0, to a *storm*, I found the graduations are 12'.

Having created a scale of his own, Dalrymple still needed some standard method of determining the terms while at sea. He dismissed the 'velocity or heel of the vessel' as 'incompetent', preferring to use 'the visible effects upon pendants, vanes, sails, sea etc.' To this end, he used a series of prints he had in his possession 'of sea pieces [the state of the sea] to explain the degrees and graduations of wind from a calm to a storm'[22] to illustrate his scale. That way he could 'teach the navigators, of all countries, the same language in describing winds'. The next step was to compare his scale and pictures with Smeaton's scale and 'common appellations'. Dalrymple was delighted with the result. 'Mr Smeaton's is not an *arbitrary*, or *fanciful scale*, but formed by proportionate work done by the mill; and it was satisfactory to find, that the sea-terms, in general, very readily compared with his scale.'[23] It is unclear if the French 'terms of winds' that he included in his comparative scale are mere translations, or if they too were divined by the same method from French ship's journals. As Dalrymple points out, the two scales drawn from totally different sources are remarkably similar (see Appendix 1).

Satisfied with his wind scale on paper, Dalrymple then set about having it adopted for general use by the East India Company. To this end, he devised a new format for the Company's ship's journal that was printed in his *Memoir*, (volume 4) amongst random instructions to ship's captains. It appears under the heading 'Explanation of the Columns in the Journal'.[24] The date, distance run, temperature, barometric pressure, position (including the difference between both longitude and latitude 'by account and observation') were required daily, while a record of the wind and weather in a standard form were to be entered four times throughout the day. The wind speeds in the *Memoir* correspond exactly to the scale in Dalrymple's treatise on *Practical Navigation*, and it was that very scale that Beaufort copied so faithfully into his journal that stormy night.

The wind and weather were only part of the reason for Alexander Dalrymple to undertake 'the very useful work of examining the Journals of Ships'.[25] The East India Company employed him to improve 'the Charts in the Navigation to the East-Indies' and to this end he relied largely on the service of competent ship's captains to conduct various surveys at his request. In 1795 Dalrymple was appointed Hydrographer to the Navy while still retaining the position of consultant hydrographer with the East India Company. In his new post his first action was to advise the Admiralty that it was 'highly important to the advancement of Nautical knowledge, and the safety of His Majesty's ships, that the reports of coasts, harbours etc. which the officers of his Majesty's Navy are directed to be transmitted to this [the Hydrographic] office'.[26] The response from the serving naval officers was derisory. Where he was used to civilian captains, like Lestock Wilson of the ill-fated *Vansittart*, going out of their way to cooperate and to send back the requested data, in the three years after 'their Lordship's orders for every Man of War to give in Reports under established Heads, only one had been sent to the Hydrographical Office under the enjoined heads, and that one of a well known part of the Coast of England.'[27] The single report was in fact a joke when one officer submitted extensive data on a popular South Coast resort. Dalrymple was disappointed with the response from the Royal Navy and the lack of cooperation from its serving officers. That was until he met Francis Beaufort.

The introduction, a month after Beaufort had been given the *Woolwich*, came through Lestock Wilson, one of the first to congratulate Beaufort on his new appointment. With his wife and daughter Alicia, Wilson had remained in close touch and he and Beaufort were firm friends. Wilson, by then a rich and successful ship owner, had also kept up his friendship with Dalrymple. It was an auspicious re-meeting for Beaufort, for as he wrote to his father, Dalrymple 'inquired after you, and was good enough to order me a complete set of his charts which will save me a vast deal of money'.[28] These charts, in four volumes, were Dalrymple's own from his days at the East India Company when he had allowed the Admiralty to reprint 100 sets. In addition, Wilson gave him many useful books, his 'sliding telescope' which Beaufort valued at £120, and indulged him with his chronometer for 40 guineas, which Wilson thought worth at least 90 guineas as it 'was better than new', although the maker, John Roger Arnold, 'valued the said chronometer N° 43/133 at 60 guineas which he would allow for it himself, was he to take it in exchange for one of superior quality'.[29]

Soon after his appointment to the *Woolwich*, Beaufort also applied to the Admiralty for a boxed chronometer. Dalrymple heard about the request from a Mr Alexander, a secretary at the Admiralty, and at his suggestion, canvassed Sir Andrew Hammond, Comptroller of the Navy, to intercede on Beaufort's behalf. He was given the very best one available at the time, No. 217 made in 1804 that had been under test at the Hydrographic Office for the last six months. It too had been built by John Roger Arnold who, with his father John, was considered amongst the finest chronometer-makers of their day. Chronometer No. 217 was finally withdrawn from service in 1930.

Even from their very first meeting, Dalrymple recognised in Beaufort a man of exceptional ability, more than fulfilling the criteria of a 'competent person' to be given a chronometer. He greatly admired his enthusiasm, his precision, and particularly his draughtsmanship, for apart from arranging for Beaufort to have a chronometer and charts, he gave him a quantity of his own published and unpublished material, including the all-important gift of the six-page *Memoir* containing the wind scale and the column heading for recording meteorological data. Since his first days at sea, Beaufort had religiously recorded the weather in his own journal, quite often at hourly intervals, for his own personal interest. When not on duty himself, he would take the information off the log-board kept by the officer of the watch, even when he was absent from his ship. He was to keep weather records every day, and only missed the last three weeks of his life. At last Dalrymple's scale could be put to use. It never caught on with the East India Company captains and he could not force them to use it – although they were required to submit their logs as proof of passage, the ships being chartered, the Company had no authority to dictate the *form* those journals took.

No sooner had the introduction been made, than Dalrymple assumed, rightly, that Beaufort would be a close ally and invaluable to the Hydrographical Office. Although both he and Beaufort knew that the *Woolwich* was most likely to be sent only as far as India, he wrote: 'Every nautical information will be useful to me. I am most especially in want of observations from

Point of Penang or Prince of Wales Island to Pergu; the charts of the islands to the southward of Mergui are extremely discordant; Forrest, as very careless, is not to be implicitly relied upon, though not wanting in ability, and a good draughtsman.'[30] More like a private treatise on surveying than a letter, Dalrymple gave Beaufort pages of advice, from taking lunar bearings to surveying at sea. However, by the gift of his *Memoirs*, Dalrymple could only hope that Beaufort would adopt some of his suggestions. By the time he died, two years later, Dalrymple had seen that his faith in Beaufort had not been misplaced.

Francis Beaufort was delighted with the scale that he had developed from Dalrymple's scale and was to retain it for his own personal use for the rest of his sea-going career. He was also pleased with his situation. The *Woolwich* was heading down the Channel, her main and fore-topgallant sails set. The mood of the whole ship's company (not least the captain's) had changed. On the orders of Admiral Warren, the guns of each ship in turn were exercised as the squadron passed 'the Bill of Portland'. But as was common throughout Beaufort's life, such moments of euphoria were swiftly followed by bad luck. Only three days out, the westerly gales returned. The *Woolwich* battled onwards. Her fore-topgallant yard was carried away and replaced in the teeth of the gale. Then came the signal that Beaufort was dreading. Warren ordered his squadron back to Spithead. No sooner had the *Woolwich* anchored than a signal went up for Beaufort to report to Admiral Montagu.

There was a high state of excitement when Beaufort stepped into the Admiral's chambers in Portsmouth. The clerks and staff officers had been on the receiving end of the Admiral's foul mood since the unscheduled departure of the *Woolwich*, and now it was Beaufort's turn. A lieutenant approached him.

'Oh, here is Captain Beaufort,' he exclaimed. 'The Admiral, sir, has been very anxious to see you again.'

Beaufort ignored him and spoke to a clerk. 'I am come to wait upon the Admiral, be so good as to inform him.'

Admiral Montagu turned on Beaufort as he was ushered into his rooms. 'Well, Captain Beaufort, where the deuce have you been?' he barked. 'It is very fortunate that you have been driven back. I am very glad to see you here again.'

Beaufort seized the initiative, 'In pursuance of orders forwarded to me by *you* a fortnight since,' he produced them from a piece of folded sailcloth, 'I went to sea with Sir John Warren. The winds have forced us back in spite of the Vice Admiral's endeavour to beat down. And I hope that you will pardon me when I say I am right sorry to find myself again under your flag.'

'Aye, aye, but the orders are nothing,' the Admiral continued. 'You know you were not going to go with Sir John.'

'I know nothing but my orders, Sir,' Beaufort provoked him. 'To put myself under the command of Sir J. Warren was the last order I received, and consequently I obeyed it.'

'But did Sir John ever give you any orders?' The Admiral thought that he had Beaufort there.

'Yes, Sir. An order about fresh beef.'

'Aye, but I mean did he ever give you sailing orders, or rendezvous, or . . .?' The Admiral hesitated. 'Well then, surely you know, Sir, you were not to accompany him. It was clear that if he meant to take you under his orders that he would have given you the usual ones. His not doing so spoke for itself.'

'What, Sir! Was it my business to remind him of his arrangements, or you or the Admiralty of my destination? But I beg leave to say that I received these orders to place myself under Sir John's orders, that I waited upon him, gave him my weekly accounts, answered all his signals at St Helens, followed all his motions – and on the twelfth if he did not intend that I should go with him would he not have answered the signal to unmoor, the signal to weigh, the signal to rendezvous off the Lizard, to the *Woolwich*, and particularly when he saw me not only answer them, with all the alertness of my little crew were capable of. I must repeat, Sir, that I obeyed the last order, indeed all the orders I received, that I think I acted for the good of the Service, and that I am sure I acted with perfect propriety.'

'Well, well, I believe Captain Beaufort,' the Admiral said smiling. 'I can make nothing of you.'

Beaufort was dismissed. He was genuinely thankful to be exonerated for his bold action, although this account of the interview with Admiral Montagu that appears in his journal may, however, be a little fanciful. He had so nearly succeeded, and it was with foreboding that he was handed orders from Captain Short. 'To be tied to that tub will be a devil, but I will keep with her as long as I can,' he confided to his journal.

By the end of January 1806, the *Woolwich* put to sea again, this time not only with Short and Bligh, but a vast convoy of nearly 300 merchantmen under the command of Rear Admiral Sir Richard Strachan. The Rear Admiral was a firebrand, and totally unsuited to convoy duty. Like Sir John Warren, he was keen to be rid of his convoy so that he too could find the French Fleet that had escaped the British blockade and was cruising in the North Atlantic. But before the convoy had battled half way down the Channel, Beaufort realised that he was commanded by a lunatic. Although one of the slowest sailers in the fleet, the *Woolwich* was ordered to bring up the rear of the convoy and take care of the storm-tossed and damaged stragglers. In vain, Beaufort tried to signal his Admiral that he was in danger of losing a significant part of his convoy. In reply, Admiral Strachan 'at 2 o'clock came up with his squadron carrying a press of sail and ran right through the middle of the poor astonished merchant vessels firing muskets at them on all sides to make them sheer out of the way!'[31]

Had Beaufort wished to 'escape', he could have easily done so during those first chaotic days, but he saw his duty was to stay with whichever merchantmen were around him, and he was stuck with them. He compared himself to an 'attentive shepherd', collecting up the stragglers whenever they appeared on the horizon. He continued with his 'little convoy of 14 sail', having lost Short, Bligh, and the rest of the convoy. Three ships departed for Gibraltar, and the remainder he took south to dispatch for the West Indies. On 19 February, Beaufort sailed ahead to Madeira, 'to make the land in order to obtain intelligence without delaying the convoy a moment. At daylight this morning, exactly as my excellent chronometer 217 announced, I saw Port Sarco.' Further south off Funchall, he met up with Sir John Warren and again hoped that he could transfer to his squadron. Warren dismissed his suggestion instantly, as well as his request for some Madeira, and ordered Beaufort to continue south for another week with his convoy.

Beaufort relished his position as captain, and the responsibilities that went with it. He had also become deeply attached to the *Woolwich* and the welfare of the officers and crew under his command. He was a practical sailor and spent days working out why his ship was sailing so 'diabolically, and continued to sail so'. Even in his first foray down the Channel with Warren, he could see the problem – 'that ugly toad Mr Andrews had stowed the ship at Woolwich and left her 3 feet by the stern instead of 10 inches, and secondly she is under jury masts and sails.' In the comparative calm of the Tropics, he conducted 'the arduous job of moving about 30 tons of stores, chiefly cordage, from the gunroom to the cable tiers: the result has answered my expectations from sailing the *worst* of any ship in the fleet, she now sails as well as the *Prioganti* [one of his convoy] if not better'.[32] He moved the warrant officers' cabins from the gunroom 'which will not only make them very happy but leave my gun deck very clear and also give much room and comfort to the people'.

'In the other misfortune *de rigueur*,' Beaufort, allowing himself a rare pun, wrote in his journal, 'I am also trying to lessen,'[33] and to restore the *Woolwich* to something approaching her original rig. For weeks he had been making notes and discussing his options with the ship's carpenter and sail maker. He began by moving the topsail sheet blocks out by two feet, and set the main topsail. Drawing on his large supply of spars and sailcloth, he rigged a new main topgallant mast, yard and sail, and both topgallant and royal masts, yards and 'thundering sails with a large reef' on the mizzenmast. In the light airs between the Tropics, he piled on all the canvas he could, extending the topsails and adding 'a large bonnet to the flying jib . . . and nine cloths in breadth and 4 feet hoist to a lower studding sail, and rigged a flying boom on each side, and a large top gallant studding sail for each top of 9 to 10 cloths – besides other supernumerary sails of less consequence'. Beaufort believed that he had done his best, and if she still would not sail, then 'why spiflicate her?'[34]

Pleased with his modifications, Beaufort continued south to the Cape of Good Hope. There was great excitement as the *Woolwich* overhauled and boarded the *Trio*, a cartel brig, an unarmed vessel used to exchange prisoners of war. She was 'carrying the ship's company of HM Sloop *Favourite* that had been captured by a French division from L'Orient'. Beaufort learned from the captain of the *Favourite* that the squadron consisted of 'regulars, a beautiful new 84, the *President*, a new flying 44, the *Sybelle* and a brig *Surillante*, commanded by Monsieur L'Hermite who sailed from L'Orient on 29 October'. Beaufort also learned that Commodore L'Hermite's squadron had been very successful, refitting and provisioning from the five prizes they had taken in four months, and that they were last seen heading for the Island of São Tomé off Gabon to water. From there it was obvious that the French were poised to harry British merchantmen bound for the East. Beaufort then 'thought it of importance to Sir John Warren to be made acquainted with this and therefore headed to the Canaries', first having taken five men off the *Trio* to complete the *Woolwich*'s complement. After four days of hard sailing on a north-northwest breeze, the *Woolwich* had covered nearly 600 miles when she 'shortened sail and spoke to the *Pelican*, an American brig out of Malta'.

The master of the *Woolwich* brought her up into the wind. But she was handling so well that her head came round too far, and her headsails backed. The captain of the *Pelican* saw what had happened and, seeing the *Woolwich* drifting astern, ordered his crew to luff up. He was too late. Painfully slowly, there was a dreadful crack as the American rammed the *Woolwich* on the starboard quarter. First to go was the store cutter hanging over the stern that broke into matchwood. Beaufort watched, horror-struck, as the *Pelican*'s bowsprit went through the midship's stern windows of his day cabin before tearing up a portion of the upper deck and destroying some gingerbread work on the gallery. Finally she came to rest, her bowsprit gone, mast jarred and a few sails torn. Beaufort felt partially responsible, and gave the *Pelican*'s Captain as much rope as he needed to lash a spare topmast to the stump for a bowsprit, and to secure her foremast. He asked the Captain to dine while the repairs were being made to both ships and there learned that the *Pelican* had spent four days passing through the Canaries and had seen nothing of Sir John Warren's squadron. Beaufort worked out that he might be cruising northwest of the Cape Verde Islands, so Beaufort 'bore up and made sail with studdingsails set' to look for him there.

After searching for a further three days, Beaufort decided to abandon his pursuit of Warren and once again headed south, calling in at the Cape Verde Islands. While the rest of the ship's company luxuriated in the warm weather and gentle sailing, their captain spent his time fixing the various islands and correcting Dalrymple's charts. The *Woolwich* anchored at Porto

Prago on São Vicente. While his first lieutenant, William Groabe, was sent ashore to buy the famous 'St Jago bulls, hundreds of oranges and thousands of bananas and yams', Beaufort 'amused himself taking angles and bearings for a sketch of the Road [a sheltered piece of water]'.[35]

As the *Woolwich* crossed the Equator, she received a visit from 'Neptune and the fair Amphrite, attended by a large concourse of tritons with long tails, black and yellow mermaids, sea monsters in all shapes and colours and not least in importance in the procession, Neptune's barber'. The crew had spent days perfecting their fantastical costumes made from coloured bunting and canvas painted in reds, yellows, white and black and shiny half boots painted on their legs in black varnish. Neptune and his court first paid their respects to Beaufort on the quarterdeck, then initiated twenty-three sailors, mostly midshipmen and ship's boys, ducking them in a studdingsail filled with seawater rigged on the deck, and ritually shaving their heads. After four hours, the ceremony was over and Neptune returned to 'the deep, the decks were scraped, the men's skins returned to their natural hue, tubs, gratings, chariots, lathering mops and razors restored to their proper places and silence and quiet was again the order of the day, and thus ended these nautical saturnalias without any improprieties or bad consequences'.[36]

While the rest of the ship's company fell in with the unalterable routine of a man-of-war at sea, their captain filled his day with recording the ship's progress, together with his own thoughts on everything from European colonisation and slavery in Africa to his longings for Charlotte Edgeworth. He made observations of the weather and the effect of the rain on the surface of the sea. He recorded the birds and even the fish that were caught. When in the southern Atlantic, he witnessed an extraordinary phenomenon. On the night of 13 April, 'there was no moon; the sky above us all round was obscured by the most dense black cloud that one could conceive. This was contrasted by the sea, which was an entire sheet of fire. A fresh gale kept it in continual agitation; each wave that broke had the appearance of an explosion or the irruption from a volcano and the ship, going with great rapidity, left a line of liquid fire from miles behind her and, breaking the water around her, threw up a light which was really dazzling; and the sails, strongly illuminated and opposed to the perfect black of the sky, was, I declare, terrifically grand and beautiful.'[37] Beaufort observed the strange phenomena from his Quarter Gallery, even reading a book from the reflected light from the wake. In that extraordinary light, the full sails looked concave. The crew could make nothing of it, some even climbing up the rigging to see them close to. 'This,' continued Beaufort in his journal, 'I conceive a solution of the case: when a sail is full, to an observer standing abaft it, it is very concave; therefore, as he is always used to the light coming from more or less above, the shadow is always (more or less sharply) situated under the upper part of the yard – thus:

but when before the sail, the light still from above, the shadow is consequently on the underside, thus:

though unconsciously in the minds of every sailor that when he sees a sail illuminated & shadowed like B when he knows that he is abaft of it, he cannot reconcile himself at first (nor indeed without reflection) to a contrary experience. Be this as it may, a more sublime, horrible and unique spectacle I never beheld.'[38] What Beaufort had in fact witnessed was the bioluminescence of the *dino flagellata*, most likely of a protozoon called *Noctiluca*.

The northeast trade winds had carried the *Woolwich* across the Atlantic to within a thousand miles of the Brazilian coast, then she beat down against the southeast trades to pick up the favourable westerlies to take her to the Cape of Good Hope. Having been driven down so far, Beaufort decided to 'haul up his course and run down a parallel a little to the windward of Tristan d'Acahna [Tristan da Cuhna]' as he wanted to see the island and fix its position. He also wanted to check his chronometers – if they were wrong it was better to know before he made landfall – and he was determined to see the little island of Saxenburg. But before he reached the island, the wind veered to the northeast and he was carried off course. That night he was dining with his officers in the gunroom when the lookout hailed the deck that he had spied an island. Greatly surprised, Beaufort and his officers rushed on deck, he climbing to the crosstrees of the mizzenmast with his night glass. Though the weather 'was thick and squally' the island appeared to be Saxenburg. Beaufort was delighted to have stumbled on the island as the charts 'had no other authority for its place of its discovery in 1607' and that with his accurate chronometer and relatively short distance from the Cape, he could fix its position accurately.

As they passed the island, Beaufort kept a sharp lookout for 'any smoke or signals of any forlorn brethren who might still be living in fond hope of being rescued'.[39] As they sailed eastwards, he fantasised at length in his journal how His Majesty's

Storeship *Woolwich* might rescue 'Amerable' Pérouse, the famous French explorer lost without trace at sea. Beaufort was wide of the mark as Pérouse was lost in the Pacific, not the Atlantic eighteen years before. Five days later the *Woolwich* was passing Tristan da Cuhna. Beaufort thought the islands bare and inhospitable, but to a shipwrecked sailor they would be paradise. Instead of flags and inscriptions when an island was claimed in the name of the Crown, Beaufort thought that it would be 'more rational' to populate the island with breeding pairs of pigs and goats. Although they did not land, the *Woolwich* circled the islands, Beaufort taking 'various cross bearings. Everyone has his hobby or his insanity,' he wrote in his journal. 'Mine I believe is taking bearings for charts and plans. I have indulged myself with a bushel at least this good morning.' What pleased him most was that his trusty chronometer 217 came up with exactly the same longitude of the main island that Aaron Arrowsmith had recorded on the chart that Dalrymple had supplied him.

The *Woolwich* made landfall in South Africa exactly where Beaufort calculated she would on 28 May 1806. Very gently, he eased past Grand Point into Table Bay, observing two ships sunk with only their mast above the water. There was an eerie silence. No salute. No colours hoisted from the fort. Beaufort assumed, correctly, that the British force thought the *Woolwich* a Dutch Indiaman and hoped to decoy her in. When the *Woolwich* had finally left England, the Cape of Good Hope was still in Dutch hands, but fortunately Beaufort had boarded an American whaler off Tristan da Cunha, who in turn had just left a British cartel with a number of Dutch prisoners aboard, and they confirmed that the Cape was indeed safely in British hands. The *Woolwich* sailed round into Simons Bay where Beaufort's high spirits left him as he made out the only two ships in the bay, the *Porpoise* and the *Lady Madeleine Sinclair* lying at anchor. He called for his master gunner to give a 13-gun salute to Captain Short, his commodore. His salute was answered, and a gig pulled across with orders for the *Woolwich* to anchor.

The two ships had, amazingly, only arrived two days before the *Woolwich*, but as Beaufort was to find out, he was fortunate to have lost them so early on the voyage. 'Throughout the whole of the passage,' he wrote in his journal, 'Captain Bligh and Captain Short had been at daggers drawn. Each spoke in the most bitter terms of the other. Each had written the most violent representation to the Admiralty demanding the court martial of the other, and each claimed the command' in Simon's Bay when he arrived. The row had started soon after they had sailed from England. Bligh was senior to Short on the post captain's list, but Short had been given command of the *Porpoise* 'on all occasions in the absence of Captain Bligh'.[40] As Bligh travelled on the *Lady Madeleine Sinclair*, Short assumed that that was 'absence' enough and therefore he should have command of the convoy. That Short was dependent on Bligh for his new life in New South Wales – he was emigrating with his wife, seven children, stock and farm machinery – made no difference to the intensity he fought with Bligh, well known for his vindictive nature. At one point on the voyage south, Bligh altered course. Short signalled for him to resume his course. Bligh ignored the signal, whereupon Short ordered Lieutenant Putland, Bligh's son-in-law, to fire two shots, one ahead and one astern of the *Sinclair*, and then to prepare a third to actually hit her.

When Bligh returned to the *Lady Madeleine Sinclair* from an audience with General Baird, the Governor of the Cape, Beaufort was asked to adjudicate between him and Short. Having examined their respective commissions, Beaufort found that 'they were both wrong, both had acted intemperately and foolishly, both had laid themselves open to censure. I afterwards attempted to conciliate a little but in vain ... Flint and steel would be easier united. The first thing, however, was to decide on whose supremacy I was to acknowledge. I immediately pronounced for Captain Bligh [for] whatever I thought of their mutual conduct, I perceived that one was a man of talents and the other an ass.'[41] At the end of the sorry affair, Bligh saw that Short did not receive his grant of land in New South Wales, and that he was sent back to England having sold his stock and machinery at a loss. On the voyage home, his pregnant wife and one of his children died.

Governor Baird entertained Beaufort in Simonstown over the three days he needed to provision his ship, wishing him a good passage when he sailed for Bombay on 2 June 1806. As the *Woolwich* cleared Cape Hanglip, Beaufort wrote in his journal that 'Henceforward I decide to knot decimally so that 11 knots 2 fathoms would become 11.2.' Again at sea, Beaufort was supremely happy. He had picked up the northeast trades and 'experienced such heavenly weather as for this last fortnight – the thermometer never changing more than one degree from midday to midnight – the air clear and fresh – wind enough to soften the ardour of the sun, favourable to one's voyage and not enough to disturb the tranquil of the deep'. The *Woolwich*, formerly 'one of the best sailers in the Navy' was restored close to her prime, even recording a run of 241 miles in a day.

With the favourable winds, the *Woolwich* made Bombay in just four weeks. There, her 13-gun salute was answered by the British Fleet anchored around the bay. For three weeks she lay at anchor discharging cargo and doing 'routine maintenance, re-rigging, caulking and drying sails'. Again, Beaufort was in his element, sketching the harbour, taking bearings, making soundings around the bay. 'I seem to understand surveying harbours and shoals,' he wrote to his father, 'and what people do best they generally like best'. His rounds of dining aboard other ships of the Fleet, surveying, and leading a giddy life ashore ended abruptly when orders came overland from Rear Admiral Sir Edward Pellew for the *Woolwich* 'to repair to Madras' where she arrived ten days later.

As the *Woolwich* entered Madras Road, Pellew sent his own barge to show her where to moor and to bring Beaufort aboard the *Culloden*, his flagship. The Admiral was delighted to see Beaufort, for many reasons not least that he liked him. Pellew needed allies, even the captain of a store ship, and once again Beaufort had sailed into a political wrangle. The dispute had began two years before in Parliament where Pellew had made a bitter enemy of Pitt by supporting Lord St Vincent against the Prime Minister over the use of gunboats. As a result, he fully expected to be recalled from his new position as commander of the East Indies when Pitt returned to office, but instead the Admiralty divided up his station, giving the more lucrative part of the Indian Ocean to Admiral Sir Thomas Troubridge. Pellew also needed Beaufort for more practical reasons. He had been planning an attack on the Dutch in Batavia and could not spare a frigate to escort an East India Company convoy home. What Beaufort had hoped for finally came about when Pellew had the *Woolwich* reclassified as a frigate and him made up to an acting captain for the escort duty.

The two months spent in Madras were a hive of activity for the *Woolwich*. An army of carpenters were sent on board to prepare a cabin under the poop for Lord George Stuart, Captain of the *Duncan*, invalided home, 'with suitable accommodation for a lady with 4 children', while the displaced officers were moved to the lower gun deck. The *Woolwich* received tons of spent cannon for ballast and took on new armaments for her elevated position – four 24-pound carronades for the quarterdeck and six 18-pounders for the lower gun deck. Finally, an officer with fifty dragoons and seventy invalids from the Naval Hospital came on board, and the *Woolwich* was ready to sail with

Pellew's squadron by the end of October. At the exact rendezvous off Trincomalee, Sri Lanka, Beaufort met up with the 15
East Indiamen he was to escort, and turned for the Cape (along
with the *Duncan* also under his command) while Pellew sailed
eastwards to Batavia.

It took a whole month of hard sailing for the *Woolwich* to
reach Table Bay where once again he 'waited upon General
Baird'. There he learned that the garrison of St Helena was
starving, and he took it on himself to take his convoy there with
relief supplies of rice. Two days out, a tragedy struck which laid
all on board low: 'poor little Louisa Stuart, a charming little girl
of $2^1/_2$, daughter of Lord George Stuart, after a struggle of 4
months with a mistreatable dysentery sunk quietly into the arms
of Death. Her tiny body was committed to the deep from the
cabin window.'[42]

As the *Woolwich* and her convoy sailed into St Helena, an
11-gun salute was fired from the fort, followed by the arrival of
an ADC from the Governor who apologised to Beaufort for 'the
two guns too few' but they were conserving their powder. But
hard on Beaufort's heels was the frigate *Sampson* that had called
in at Simons Bay from Montevideo on her way back to England.
Baird had just received urgent dispatches from Sir Thomas
Maitland, the commander-in-chief of the forces in Ceylon,
concerning an insurrection on the west coast of India that he
feared would spread throughout the country. In fact, Maitland
over-reacted and the uprising was quelled with a few troops. But
Baird sent the dispatches on to Beaufort, with orders to leave
the convoy to the *Sampson* and head straight back to England
with all possible speed. Without hesitating, Beaufort left St
Helena to a 13-gun salute, which he returned. Throughout
February 1807, the *Woolwich* sailed north on 'smooth water and
all possible sail, including a beautiful new sky-sail, set'. Beaufort
smartened his ship up, blacking the yardarms and painting her

sides in readiness for her return to England.

Past the Equator, the fair weather turned and the *Woolwich* battled through heavy squalls. When she finally arrived off Lizard Point on 21 March 1806 her 'total log' since leaving Spithead was 33,313 miles. For a few hours, the *Woolwich* waited for a pilot to take her into Plymouth. Beaufort paid his respects to Admiral Sir Home Popham, and was sent with his dispatches to the Admiralty. He felt important as he left in a chaise with four horses that evening, and nearly 29 hours later he was standing in the rooms of the First Secretary, William Marsden, at the Admiralty. Precise as ever, he worked out that he had travelled in the chaise at an average of $7^1/_2$ miles an hour, including stops, at a cost of £41 10s. But the dash to England had cost him the usual gift of £500's worth of plate given by a grateful East India Company to the Captain for the safe delivery of a convoy. He never forgot the loss, even though he had previously railed against his brother officers who accepted 'emoluments from shopkeepers'.

After Beaufort had delivered the Maitland dispatches to Marsden, he 'begged to inform' the First Secretary of his own position. He discussed his temporary promotion from Pellew in the certain knowledge that the Admiralty would ratify it. Four days later, he returned to his ship lying in Plymouth, where he received a letter from Marsden: 'I have it in command to acquaint you that as Sir Edward Pellew had not received their Lordship's direction to alter the Establishment of the *Woolwich*; they cannot confirm the Appointment.'[43] Beaufort was devastated. True to form, he fired off dozens of letters to everyone of influence to intercede on his behalf. Countess Spencer, wife of a former First Lord of the Admiralty and great admirer of Beaufort, wrote back saying she could do nothing for him. His father wrote to his neighbour Mr Foster, asking him to influence Lord Mulgrave, the new First Lord, although he held out little hope as he believed that 'Sir E Pellew was attached to Mr Pitt and his friends and for that reason he would not confirm Francis' appointment'.[44] Other Irish neighbours, Lord Longford, the Earl of Courtown, and another Irish peer who was making a name for himself in politics, Lord Palmerston, were solicited but all with the same result.

But his lack of promotion was only the beginning of a string of misfortunes for Beaufort. He learned that the *Woolwich* was to be converted into a hospital ship, and his depression deepened. While at sea and actively engaged, Beaufort was in the best of spirits. He ran a good ship and cared deeply for the welfare of his crew. They were healthy and generally content – he believed that 'it is better to lose a dozen miles in a day's work than a dozen men in a long run.'[45] He was sure that he had given excellent service, and was mortified that even his ship was being taken away from him. But all that paled by comparison to a far greater tragedy. Dr Beaufort wrote to him to say that his beloved Charlotte was in the last stages of a terminal illness.

Three days later on 7 April, Charlotte died at Edgeworthstown. 'Alas, my dear Father,' Fanny wrote to Dr Beaufort, 'it is all over and Charlotte is no more. She died without a groan, laying her head back in her chair as if going to sleep and drawing her hand out of mine – and that at this instant she looks as placid as ever and like a beautiful figure of alabaster, smiling and unchanged – alas, alas, what a dreadful sorrow it is to part from those we love.

'Tell my mother that every day since the *Woolwich* came to England dear Charlotte expressed her astonishment at our not hearing from Francis – that she always expressed the greatest interest in his promotion – and yesterday said that she was very glad to find Lady Spencer was not faithless to her friend – that Francis' good fortune would come – but she had no hopes of Mr Foster for he is a selfish man who thinks only of his own interest.'[46]

In the midst of writing dozens of letters about his promotion, Beaufort wrote to Charlotte's father, his friend Richard Lovell Edgeworth, saying simply: 'Need I say more! God giveth and God taketh – Amen.' These were hardly the words of a bereaved suitor, but Beaufort was so consumed with his own misfortune that it excluded all else, including Charlotte. It is just possible that he had been delaying his contact with Charlotte until his promotion to post captain was confirmed.

Beaufort confined himself to his cabin. Just as his world was collapsing outside, so was his ship, as she swarmed with carpenters demolishing the bulkheads ready to take the sick and the wounded. 'All bulkheads being knocked down by 16 April,' Beaufort wrote in his journal, 'when it having been thought proper (by the same Board of the Admiralty) to send the *Woolwich* out immediately with provisions to the Rio de la Plata.' Over the next three weeks Beaufort supervised the shipwright, putting the bulkheads back entirely at 'his suggestion', creating comfortable cabins on the lower deck and a wardroom for his officers 'under the tiller'.

The provisions were finally loaded by 19 May and the *Woolwich* was off again to sea. She had been a happy ship on her last voyage, but no longer. Beaufort, the 'commander of a Pandora's box of miseries' had become morose. Floggings, formerly kept to a minimum, increased along with their severity – two men received '2 dozen lashes each for drunkenness', while the quartermaster received '4 dozen lashes for stealing spirits, neglect of duty, drunkenness and charging another man with his crime'. The voyage out was uneventful, apart from the two men falling overboard and three out of the tops. Every day, Beaufort entered up his private log with a record of the weather and position, often adding his lunar position in purple ink after he had worked them out at a later date.

The provisions aboard the *Woolwich* were for the British force

anchored in the River Plate. Their commander, Admiral Sir
Home Popham, had taken Montevideo and Buenos Aires from
the Spanish the year before in the mistaken belief that the
residents would support the expeditionary force. But no sooner
had he hoisted his flag, than the inhabitants, led by a French
colonel, ousted the invasion force, then withdrew to east of
Montevideo. A large relief contingent left shortly before the
Woolwich and by the time Beaufort's ship arrived, it had been
soundly defeated in Buenos Aires with the loss of 2,500 killed,
wounded or taken prisoner. The living were returned to the
Fleet on the assurance that the British would evacuate the River
Plate within two months.

Although Beaufort felt the defeat desperately, he at least had
a job to do that he enjoyed. He wrote to his sister Harriet 'There
is nothing to be seen here but wretchedness and disgrace,
nothing to be done here but to reflect either on my own miseries
or on those of my country.'[47] This was not entirely true, as he
had explicit instructions from Dalrymple to make as many
surveys as time allowed. Leaving the loading of the defeated and
wounded troops to his officers, he made a sketch of Montevideo
'chiefly determined by stepping the distances'. It is a remarkable
drawing, showing the streets and key buildings and defences of
'very solid mason work but unfinished'. He drew an elevation of
the city, and a plan of the adjacent harbour. Over the next few
weeks, he made other surveys of the approaches to the port,
shoals and islands in the river, liasing with another surveying
captain, Peter Heywood, the same midshipman who had stayed
with the mutineers on the *Bounty*. For some reason, Beaufort
used the backs of the charts that Dalrymple had given him to
draw up some of his surveys.

At last the *Woolwich* was ordered home. She left with her
invalids and troops on 15 September 'steering on the great circle
along latitude 35°'.[48] Still sailing well, she was bowling along on

the westerlies, often covering over 200 miles in a day and reached Table Bay in just 26 days. From there it was the old slog back to England with a convoy of seven Indiamen. She reached the Downs early in the New Year and returned to Gravesend where 'she carried away the *Calcutta*'s jib boom'. Once again the dockyard workers came aboard for a full refit.

Once ashore, Beaufort was on his old tack of lobbying friends and acquaintances to intercede on his behalf for promotion. Sir Edward Pellew was sympathetic. 'I know of no man who merits it more and with whom I would rather serve,' he wrote, but he was without influence. Stopford, by then an admiral, was the same. Yet Beaufort knew that 'without parliamentary or petti-coat interest' his chances were non-existent so long as Mulgrave was First Lord of the Admiralty.

Throughout March and April of 1808, Beaufort dined fre-quently with Alexander Dalrymple at the Royal Society, and the two become close friends. Dalrymple had recently proposed a survey of the banks and shoals between England and the coasts of Holland and Denmark and, impressed by Beaufort's surveys in the River Plate, wanted to use him. Dalrymple wrote to the Admiralty: 'It is fortunate that a Vessel most admirably adapted for the Service proposed is at present unemployed, and her Commander unquestionably fit as any man living to be entrusted with the execution of the service. I mean Captain Beaufort of his Majesty's ship *Woolwich*.'[49] Nothing came of the suggestion and the *Woolwich* returned to active service.

For the next year, the *Woolwich* was tramping up and down the Mediterranean, ferrying stores and supplies, and taking convoys back to England. At last the *Woolwich* returned to the Thames in April 1809 and her crew was paid off. Beaufort had sailed over 60,000 miles in the three years on the *Woolwich*, mostly with the same crew. As he said goodbye to them all, some had tears running down their 'course and rugged cheeks'.

He shook 'their tarry hands, and may I,' he confided to his journal, 'lose my power to squeeze whenever I am ashamed to do so, or whenever I shall feel more gratification in squeezing the delicate fingers of a virgin of nineteen than the rough but honest paw of a faithful, brave and warm-hearted shipmate.'[50]

By then, Beaufort was thoroughly dejected as he fully expected to haul down his pendant forever. He felt he had no prospects, no future in the Navy. He had been there before, but this time, the difference was that he did not care.

CHAPTER 8

Captain Beaufort RN, Rated Post

THE SCENE WAS ALL TOO FAMILIAR. The First Lord of the Admiralty, coat tails parted, stood warming his backside before the sea-coal fire in the Admiralty Boardroom. Over the marble chimneypiece, rolls of charts were mounted on the wall, while the gilt pointer of the huge wind dial at the end of the room showed the wind to be southeast by south. At the other end of the room was the precise carving of navigational instruments of the fifteenth, sixteenth and seventeenth centuries, said to be by Grinling Gibbons. Lord Mulgrave was clearly bored and wished to be shot of his visitor. But Captain Francis Beaufort was having none of it. He ignored the First Lord's look of 'cold-blooded apathy' and 'the fulsome and frivolous compliments' designed to cut him short as he pleaded his record of long service in the Navy, his character, his wounds, and his former promotions. At the mention of long service, Mulgrave, with a 'cold-freezing, unfeeling look' cut in and told him that 'Service was no claim nowadays to promotion.' Beaufort was indignant. He wrote to his father, 'if I obtain anything besides honour and credit in the service, it shall be by the means I achieved my first post, Industry.'[1] He hated 'begging for promotion' from Mulgrave, and despised those who relied solely on the 'system of Parliamentary influence and the corruption that deprived' him of advancement. As Mulgrave stepped over to the long boardroom table, leant over to pull the long silken rope hanging from the ceiling and rang the bell, Beaufort knew his interview, and possibly his sea-going career as well, was over.

But Beaufort had conveniently forgotten the dozens of letters he had written immediately after he hauled down his pendant from the *Woolwich* to those of rank and influence, the likes of Countess Spencer, Lord Stopford, brother of his captain on the *Aquilon*, and Admiral Hamilton, father of one of his former midshipmen. Although Beaufort continued to rail against the system, he did, however, have friends at the Admiralty who had noticed his considerable talent over many years. His greatest ally had been Alexander Dalrymple, who had loudly extolled Beaufort's surveys and charts of the mouth of the River Plate and the sketches of the fort at Montevideo as being the most 'exceptional work'. On the strength of them (and the many other surveys of Bombay, Madras, the Cape of Good Hope harbours and the South Atlantic) Dalrymple had written to the First Lord telling him that Beaufort's promotion was long overdue. His letter was endorsed by a testimonial from Duncombe Pleydell-Bouverie, another captain engaged in surveying during the same ill-fated expedition to South America. 'Captain Beaufort,' he wrote, 'did more in the month he was in the River Plate to acquire a correct knowledge of its dangers, than was done by everyone together before.'[2] Apart from the countless surveys, drawings and observations Beaufort had already submitted to the 'Hydrographical Office' over the years, he had also sent the Admiralty, scientists, and other scientific bodies an eclectic mix of ideas and data – from his observations of the diurnal variations of barometers to the presentation of a hitherto unknown 'light-giving animal' (a phosphorescent jelly-fish) from the Indian Ocean, which went to Sir Joseph Banks, President of the Royal Society. He had long had an admirer in Sir John Barrow, Second Secretary to the Admiralty and Secretary of the Chart Committee, who had fielded so many of Beaufort's improvements and ideas and had returned their 'Lordships' gratitude' for those submissions. In fact, at the time of his interview with Mulgrave Beaufort had recently prepared 'a list of the errata for the purpose of rendering the next edition of the general naval instructions more complete, and suggesting the utility of an alphabetical index for the same'.[3] He submitted this nine months later, and, to his irritation, it received greater approbation from 'their Lordships' than his survey of the River Plate.

The forces working on Beaufort's behalf finally triumphed, and in June 1809 Mulgrave reluctantly appointed Beaufort to HMS *Blossom*, an 18-gun sloop. Instead of being thoroughly delighted with his ship, he complained that his appointment was only made to 'throw dust in the eyes of my benefactors'[4] rather than given on his own merit. Mulgrave had in fact written to both Admiral Hamilton and Lord Stopford, playing one off against the other and saying that he alone was responsible for the appointment. Beaufort wrote to both men and heard that 'Lord S. was enraged and the Admiral couldn't care a damn'.[5] Beaufort held that a sloop was 'a commander's command', and thus could have been his for the asking at any time, but outwardly he 'considered being placed in a store ship a disgrace' and preferred to remain on the *Woolwich* 'until he was voluntarily removed'.[6]

His motives, however, were more calculated. Many commanders in a similar position and age to Beaufort preferred to remain on active service in command of their ships on full pay, rather than be promoted to post captain without a ship (and with little chance of being given one) and therefore be reduced to half-pay. Once on the post captain's list, a captain would move up automatically to admiral, but in the main the possibility of making it to the top was very remote indeed.

Beaufort declared the *Blossom* 'a fine sloop, tolerably well armed and reputed to sail well'[7] when, on 18 July, he saw her lying at the Nore, fully provisioned and ready for service. Within the hour, he had weighed anchor and set all sail to Portsmouth, where he waited for orders. But in the short voyage around the Kent coast, he found that his three-masted sloop *Blossom* was 'wretchedly crank, that is with any wind she leans over very much. I cannot say that I am much in love with her, but I am too much accustomed to larger ships and too tied to be being a commander to stomach this *con mucho gusto*.'[8] Despite these shortcomings, Beaufort the skilled seaman, made her sail 'decently enough'.

At last, Beaufort was commander of a man-of-war, the position he had been working towards for over twenty years. Britain was still at war, and despite her complete naval supremacy after Trafalgar, there was still the possibility of prize money and, more importantly, the 'glory' that he had craved for so long and had been denied as captain of a store ship. But the appointment had come too late. Although a dedicated serving naval officer and certainly not lacking in courage, Beaufort had had a change of heart. 'My soul sickens,' he wrote to his brother, 'at seeing all the world cutting or endeavouring to cut each other's throats, for what, they know not.'[9] So it was with no particular relish that he received his orders to sail for Corunna with a convoy carrying 10,000 reinforcements for General Sir

Arthur Wellesley for the start of his Peninsular campaign.

The voyage was uneventful. Beaufort had been told to be on the lookout for two French frigates that had run the blockade off Brest and were cruising in the North Atlantic, but he saw neither them nor indeed any other sail. When he arrived at Corunna and discharged the troops, the French had retreated. The *Blossom* was charged with carrying the 'detailed account of the complete evacuation of Corunna, Ferrol, and indeed all Galicia by Marshall Ney' to England which she managed 'at the rate of 10½ miles per hour'.[10] At Portsmouth, orders were waiting for him to take a convoy up the St Lawrence River to Quebec, giving him only three days to provision his ship.

Beaufort gathered up his convoy and headed west. As usual, they were a disparate group, with some good sailers and some that 'sailed like a haystack'. Beaufort ranted against the latter as he knew that they would shorten his time in North America, a country he was keen to experience. But on the long voyage he had time to rethink his career. Although he had grown accustomed to the *Blossom*, he still found her cramped and uncomfortable after the *Woolwich*. His decks were permanently wet, like 'a poor cracked pitcher'; the constant humidity below decks further aggravated his chest that still held the lead ball from the taking of the *San Joseph*. He felt that he was becoming old and wizened before his time. 'At 35½,' he saw 'life was passing him by' and realised that he had become disillusioned with the Navy. 'What object can I now have?' he wrote to his sister Frances. 'Riches? There is nothing more to be gained and if there were, to serve merely to fatten on plunder is really a base idea. Promotion? It is now too late to enjoy. Post me today, yet some years must pass before I could obtain a decent frigate.'[11] He was sure that he would never 'hoist his [Admiral's] flag' – he was already at the same age that both Nelson and Stopford had hoisted theirs – and if he did, he would be by then 'a morose and toothless old fellow'. In another letter to his father, he hinted that his body as well as his mind 'might be weaned from the Service'.[12] The two letters were sent from half way across the Atlantic by a merchant ship bound for Cork that was made to heave-to until they were written.

At last the slowest of the ships broke away for Nova Scotia and New Brunswick leaving the *Blossom* to hurry up the St Lawrence River. Beaufort was enthralled with everything he saw, his depression lifting as he took in every detail of the river and countryside. He admired the neat homesteads along the riverside, imagining himself finally leaving the Navy, emigrating to Canada, and taking on just such a farm – only to be put off the idea by the threat of a Canadian winter. The *Blossom* eventually anchored off Quebec '400 miles from the mouth of the St Lawrence and a thousand from its source'. With his enquiring mind, Beaufort took in the city and the surrounding countryside. He made copious notes of everything that caught his eye – the farm machinery and the agriculture, the forestry, 'the mineral productions, particularly in a geological point of view', the extremes of the climate, even the state of the native Indians which he found 'most distressing'. But strict orders to return immediately to England with a new convoy robbed him of further exploration.

Beaufort's obsessive compulsion for observation and recording natural phenomena had been fostered by his father from a very early age and honed throughout his career at sea. He was the typical Naval officer philosopher of his day, both by education and later by inclination, and as such, he was a true product of the Age of Enlightenment. Although his classical education at the hands of his grandfather, Daniel Cornelius Beaufort, was limited – his brother William, by contrast, went on to become a model classicist – Beaufort had excelled at pure mathematics (specially geometry) and astronomy, both core elements of the Enlightenment. Amongst the books that he first took to sea were mostly works of theology and philosophy, two of the major subjects that made up the eighteenth century view of the 'scientist'. His periods of disillusionment with the Established Church was also in keeping with the Enlightenment in England at that time. But Beaufort did more than just dabble in the study of philosophical curiosity like some gentleman scholar. As with other naval officers of the time, he was by necessity also skilled in what the English termed 'mixed mathematics', today's applied mathematics. These were the tools of the 'working scientist' – the navigator and the surveyor, the financier, the manufacturer, and the inventor. Thus, with his background and disciplines, Beaufort belonged to that breed of early nineteenth century naval officers who went far beyond mere observation for observation's sake, but observation for the advancement of every area of marine science. With his change of heart over promotion through glory, unwittingly he was on course for advancement through his interest in all things scientific.

Throughout his life, Beaufort was loyal to his officers, cared for the welfare of his men, and was invariably compassionate to those less fortunate than himself. Preparing to leave Quebec at the end of August 1809, he received a letter from a Maria Lennon, 'the widow of the late Mr Lennon, surgeon of the 29th regiment, who died two months before at Montreal and left three female children entirely unprovided for.'[13] Fearful of another Canadian winter, she begged for a passage back to England on the *Blossom* and explained how 'a faithless lackey' sent to buy provisions and bedding for their journey home had absconded with the remainder of her money. But no sooner had Beaufort arranged for Mrs Lennon and her children to be taken aboard the *William*, the largest of the merchantmen in his convoy, than the *Blossom* and the rest of the convoy sailed down the St Lawrence. Throughout the voyage, Beaufort continued to look after the widow and her children. Toys and dolls were sent across to the children, together with little gifts of books and delicacies from his private stores. His surgeon attended them when they were sick. He met her only once when he boarded the *William*. But she never forgot him. Throughout her lonely life in France, she often wrote to him remembering his 'never-failing humanity' to her and her 'helpless children'.[14]

The life of the Royal Navy captain at sea was necessarily solitary and lonely. Outside the running of his ship, he had little to do with his officers apart from the traditional Friday dinner in the wardroom, and the times when they in turn were invited to dine with their captain in his quarters. Captain Beaufort was no different. His long and uneventful sea passages, particularly in good weather, in the *Woolwich* to India and the Atlantic crossings in the *Blossom*, gave him unlimited opportunity to apply his mind to all manner of original thought and observation, and the time to analyse and record it. Nor was there any limit to his fertile and inventive mind. One day he was making observations on shaving – comparing the cutting properties of an upward, as opposed to a downward stroke and the sharpening of the razor on a variety of strops – the next he was working on an improvement of naval gun sights.

Here Beaufort was inspired. He knew that cannon on shore were 'pointed by means of the tangent scale which at once gives both that direction and elevation'.[15] This was possible on dry land, as the gun remained steady, so to fire 'the scale is removed and a match applied'. At sea, this was impractical through the motion of the ship and the sill of the porthole obscuring the target from the view of the 'zealous but clumsy seamen'. To site the naval cannon, the gunner alternatively squinted through the sight of the upper part of the gun lining it up with two small nicks in the muzzle rings for direction, and then along the side sights for the elevation, relying on 'a tolerable approximation to the required direction'. Beaufort proposed a cannon with a 'square breech, the same dimension as the muzzle ring, with a sight down the side'. That way, the line of sight would be parallel to the bore, both top and side. He drew up several variations, all ingenious and modified the *Blossom*'s guns with his new sight and a built-up breech. Sadly for Beaufort, a Major Dodd had already 'received a large award for the innovation of a gun with a square breech'. He was deeply disappointed, but was thankful that he learned about if before he submitted his scheme, there being nothing to him more 'hurtful as plagiarism'.

The right idea on paper, but totally unworkable in the field. Beaufort's idea for transporting a canon across marshy ground.

In Richard Lovell Edgeworth, the 'working' scientist and member of the Lunar Society, Beaufort invariably had the guidance, often the inspiration, for his thoughts and innovations. One such exchange was Beaufort's concept for 'a revolving platform for the transporting of artillery across marshy ground'. Years before, Edgeworth had shown Beaufort a working drawing he had made in 1770 of a portable railway 'consisting of a number of separate platforms, laid down before the carriage wheels, and picked up after they had passed by some sort of lever arrangement'[16] – the forerunner of the caterpillar track. Beaufort adapted the plan. His idea was to construct an octagon out of trussed planks, each side being about twice the length of the field piece. When the gun carriage was moved forward, 'so the next section falls and the last ascends'. It could also be used as a bridge by opening the octagon out and, with a series of chains, anchoring any combination of platforms together, it could be made to fit any width of stream to accommodate 'horses, baggage and artillery'. Beaufort thought that a hexagon might be simpler and wrote to Edgeworth with his sketches, asking if he had '8 minutes to spare' would he give it his consideration? Beaufort also took Simple Paddy, the telegraph they had developed in Ireland, and marginally adapted it for naval use, giving full credit to Edgeworth, and on his own account devised a whole new system of signalling with 'flags, pennants and balls'.

Sometimes the exchange of ideas was the other way round – Beaufort had the notion first and asked Edgeworth to develop it when he had 'pummelled and tried' his 'poor brain on the subject' and come up with no solution. They were a good combination. One such problem that Beaufort gave him was to design an efficient perpetual log or odometer for use at sea as none that he had 'yet seen described possessed the advantages to compensate for the defects' and that the 'scheme would be immediately patronised'. He gave practical advice on its positioning and suggested what form it might take – either 'one the existence of the water to some surface acted upon by weight, lever or spring, the second by revolution of wheelwork'.[17] Another brief was for Edgeworth to apply his mind to inventing an instrument that would measure current underwater and recommend an anemometer for use at sea. 'I am ashamed to say,' he wrote, 'that I have never made any experiments on the strength of the wind in different gales and at different heights from the water. One reason is I have never seen an anemometer described that would answer aboard a ship. Either they have been fluid which must presume its horizionatability [*sic*], or some perpendicular work which produces too much friction to move with truth.'[18]

It was an eventful time for the 'machine-making gentry', and both Beaufort and Edgeworth addressed the developments of their time. Beaufort declared himself 'wonderfully delighted by the passage [in 1809] of Sir George Caley on flying' and his full-scale model glider. Edgeworth claimed that he had worked out 'the whole problem to make a surface support a given weight by the application of power to the resistance of the air'[19] on a 'mathematical and physical basis' thirty years before, but had gone no further. Sir George could not care less about the claim and in 1852 went on to successfully fly a glider himself with his coachman (who promptly gave in his notice on landing) as passenger. Another area Beaufort applied himself to was the 'plan relating to the application of steam engines for vessels that are to use the high seas'.[20] There had been several successful schemes in the past – the canal tug *Charlotte Dundas* had towed two laden sloops 19 miles in 6 hours in 1801 – but try as he might, Beaufort could come up with nothing original. He did, however, duplicate many ideas, like a catamaran with a bank of paddlewheels mounted between the hulls, and wrote at length on the correct positioning and shape of a paddlewheel.

But it was as 'a meteorological philosopher' (as he described himself) that Beaufort had his greatest success in original thought, and again he canvassed Edgeworth for his comments. While in Canada, Beaufort observed a near perpendicular waterfall about 200 feet high. The water had created a deep basin at the bottom, and, as it crashed on to the rocks below it 'converted a large quantity of water into spray'. When the spray was blown from the fall, 'it had the appearance and velocity as

are manifested in a heavy squall, although the adjacent atmosphere is undisturbed by the lighter air at a small distance.
Whence then this wind? Evidently by the air compressed by the
falling masses of water.' He went on to observe that 'each little
sphere of water has little more gravity than is necessary to carry
it down,' but 'an infinite number of drops will produce an
aggregate of some value' – in other words, each drop on its own
is insignificant, but when they collide and combine, they become
a force, creating their own kinetic energy as they fall through
gravity. Without knowing it, Beaufort was observing at the base
of his Canadian waterfall the action within a cloud. He then
went on to observe that 'the constant effect of very heavy rain is
to lull the wind for a short time. And why? Because the violent
fall of the rain has accumulated an increased quantity of air.' As
the rain falls, Beaufort thought, it created 'a vacuum' and that
'the superfluous air has been itself drawn off to the equilibrium'
– in other words, a single rain drop falling automatically pushes
the air aside creating 'the vacuum', so a heavy fall of rain would
create a downdraught which would tend to quell the wind.

'I could, I think, apply this to other cases but having other
subjects for my remaining pages', Beaufort continued to
Edgeworth, 'I only mention that heavy rain always produces a
change of wind. If the wind is south and dry and the rain comes,
it veers to the westwards. If the wind is south-west and with it
generally rain, let the rain begin to pour and you may be sure of
its flying suddenly round to the north-west.' Beaufort had hit on
the idea of the passage of a warm front, although neither he nor
anyone else could explain it until the 1920s. Again Beaufort was
ahead of his times. He believed that with '1,000 vessels
employed in the king's service', depositing with the Admiralty
between two and eight logbooks a year containing an hourly
record of the wind and weather, from all around the world, could
give no better data to the 'patient meteorological philosopher',

and he felt certain that a captain would 'feel flattered if he was requested to keep a journal of the variations'. In 1809, Beaufort was advocating the founding of a meteorological office within the Admiralty, a body that was not created until 1854 by the Board of Trade 'in the interests of shipping'.

No sooner had the *Blossom* returned to England from Canada than orders were waiting for Beaufort to put himself under a Captain Lysaght of the *Jamaica*; once again the *Blossom* was back on convoy duty. In those early months of 1810, the *Blossom* ploughed between the Channel ports and the Mediterranean, escorting troop ships and convoys with supplies or bringing back dispatches, leaving little time for original thought or reflection. His life was mundane. He wrote to his sister Harriet that it was as if he was on a perpetual cruise 'from England to Cadiz, from Cadiz to Gibraltar, from Gibraltar to Lisbon, and Lisbon back to England only to begin it all over again'.[21] Apart from 'one miserable American recapture, there was neither frigate to smite, nor galleons to plunder, neither gold nor glory, neither promotion nor prize money to be picked up now, for the ocean is now a desert'.

Just when Beaufort was giving up hope of ever succeeding, 'General Lord Mulgrave, that callous and dull knave' was replaced as First Lord of the Admiralty by the enlightened politician, Charles Philip Yorke. Beaufort was delighted with the news. Then came word of his own promotion to post captain, one of the first of Yorke's appointments. Beaufort could not contain his excitement, nor his delight that was 'unspeakable, ineffable, sublime and almost passing comprehension of owing my promotion', he wrote to his father 'to my own character without the intervention of friends'.[22] When these friends, the likes of John Foster, continued to press John Croker on Beaufort's behalf, the Secretary of the Admiralty was obliged to tell them that the new First Lord had already 'gladly embraced the opportunity of rewarding so meritorious an officer. It really has never happened to one to hear a gentleman so generally and so highly commended as he has been, and I sincerely rejoice at his promotion.'[23] Further rewards were to come. On 30 May 1810 Beaufort received his commission to command HMS *Frederickssteen*, a 32-gun frigate, built in 1800 and captured by the British in 1807. At last Beaufort felt that his talents had been recognised. The *Frederickssteen* was classed a fifth-rate frigate, 'far above the rate generally conferred on a young post' and he revelled in the 'most gratifying confirmation of many mighty civil speeches that their Lordships have lately used about me. In my own opinion I am just what I was.'[24]

At the announcement of his promotion and subsequent appointment, Beaufort's life took on a whole new dimension. He began by proposing to Alicia Magdalena, Lestock Wilson's daughter. The bright, perky little girl of seven that he had first met just before he joined her father's ship the *Vansittart* twenty-one years before, had matured into a thoroughly sensible, pious, although somewhat dull, woman. Beaufort was hardly the gallant suitor. 'She is no beauty, but has a good though very delicate figure,' he wrote to his father. 'Her principles are incomparable, her education laboured though mismanaged, her temper excellent though quick, her head strong, but her heart weak as she has sacrificed it to me.'[25] There was certainly none of the passion for Alicia that he had held for Charlotte Edgeworth. But if it was not a marriage made in Heaven as far as Beaufort was concerned, it was at least one made in her parents' house.

During his infrequent leaves, Beaufort had used the Wilson's house as his own. Sharing a common interest in surveying and navigation, Lestock kept a fatherly eye on his protégé and took a great interest in his career. Bonne Wilson, Lestock's wife, had long been a confidante, with a frequent exchange of letters over the years. He was always a welcome guest, not just as a spare man for dinners, but as a useful escort for Alicia and her sisters. Alicia adored him, and let her affection be known as much as the rigid conventions of the day allowed. She was also the daughter of a very rich man. Lestock Wilson had prospered after the loss of the *Vansittart* and formed his own successful shipping company, Palmer, Wilson and Co. with another East India Captain. After Beaufort's marriage proposal was accepted, Lestock settled £5,000 on him (in two tranches). Although he had only a few pounds to his name, he declared that he was not 'marrying for monetary gain', as 'no one,' he declared, 'found money less indispensable to happiness than me'. Beaufort did, however, have the grace to describe his engagement as more important an event than his promotion.

Well-connected landed gentry, the Edgeworth family considered that Beaufort, a descendant of a nobleman of the Holy Roman Empire, was marrying beneath himself. Maria Edgeworth, who 'disliked vulgarity more than vice',[26] found Lestock Wilson coarse and unlettered and was irritated by Alicia's gushing when they met. She also disliked her way of saying 'Oy instead of I, although her faults were mild compared with those of her sisters'. Conversely Alicia, who had previously met Maria's cousins the two Miss Sneyds, had declared them the 'specimens of Irish tabbies'. However, whatever Beaufort felt for his fiancée at the outset, their marriage was to be supremely happy and over the 22 years they had together, his love deepened to an all-consuming adoration.

It was decided to delay the wedding until Beaufort had taken command of the *Frederickssteen* and completed his first tour of duty. He received orders from the Admiralty to take the *Blossom* to Cadiz and on to Gibraltar, then to put himself under the command of Admiral Sir Charles Cotton, commander of the Mediterranean Fleet. He also received sealed orders for when he took over the *Frederickssteen*. There was, however, a clue to what he might be doing in his new command in the Mediterranean when Thomas Hurd summoned him to the Hydrographical Office to issue him with not one but three chronometers – the tools of the surveyor.

Before he left England, he had time to sound out Edgeworth on his ingenious scheme for joining up a number of banks outside Portsmouth harbour with a series of locks to create a huge basin at high tide. With the water trapped inside, ships could then move more easily into and out of the dry docks. He also worked out that when the water was released, it would not only scour out the mud and effluent from the harbour bottom, but could also be harnessed to generate mechanical power. Nothing, of course, came of his suggestion.

As the *Blossom* headed for the Needles off the Isle of Wight to rendezvous with a convoy of '31 ships totalling 8869 tons',[27] Beaufort opened a brand new journal. On the first crisp sheet he wrote in his neat, precise handwriting:

Log of His Majesty's Sloop *Blossom*
Francis Beaufort, Commander.

Under that, he penned his wind scale, but this time he had developed it a stage further from the original (*see* Appendix 2). Where the nomenclature for the winds had remained virtually the same, he had qualified each wind force with a description of how much canvas a ship could carry. Thus Force 2 was 'a light breeze or that which will impel a man of war with all sails by the wind 3 or 4 knots',[28] while Force 6 was a 'Stiff Breeze or that which simple reefed topsails, fore-topgallant, courses, jib etc. would be just carried by the wind, by a wholesome frigate when fairly pressed in chase'. Force 10 became 'a whole gale or that where she would show no other canvas than a storm stay sail'.

This second scale went far beyond the straightforward affair that Beaufort had copied from Alexander Dalrymple nearly five years before. Where that relied on the individual's own opinion of the force of the wind, this revised scale was based on an unalterable standard – the amount of sail 'made in the normal way' that could be carried by a 'well-conditioned man-of-war', specifically a frigate. The concept could have been easily understood throughout the whole Royal Navy had it been adopted at that date. But the appellations of the winds had been in common use for two centuries – in 1606, a Captain Smith published a pamphlet *Assisting Young Seamen* that classified wind as 'a calme, a breeze, a fresh gayle, a pleasant gayle and a stiffe gayle'.[29] Nor was the idea of describing wind strength in terms of sail carried novel either. In *The Storm* – describing 'a collection of the most remarkable casualties and disasters which happened in the lat dreadful tempest both by sea and land' published in 1703 – Daniel Defoe 'set down sailors bald terms [for wind] in a table of degrees'. In the dozen entries, from Stark Calm to Tempest, 'A Top-sail Gale' (where only a top-sail is carried) came between a 'Fresh Gale' and 'Blows Fresh'. The term 'Top-sail Gale' remained in common usage in the Navy – when Beaufort took over the *Woolwich*, the shipwrights Omay and Druce advised him 'on her sailing qualities' and that 'in a Top-sail Gale, she behaves bearably well'.[30]

But what really made Beaufort's revised wind scale so functional was that it set out to measure the *force* of the wind, not the *speed* of the wind. At that time, it was virtually impossible to measure wind speed with any degree of accuracy at sea. For a start, there was no foolproof marine anemometer, and even if there were, the reading would have been inconclusive as the mean speed of the wind varies with the length of time over which it is taken. Also, the speed and the direction of the wind vary with its height above the water – the lookout in the crosstrees experiences almost double the amount of wind than the officer on the quarterdeck 120 feet below. Add to that, unlike on the land that is static, with a heaving deck in a rough sea, it would be impossible to specify a height above sea level at which a mean wind speed scale could be based. But with Beaufort's wind *force* scale, all trained observers would come up with exactly the same number on the scale merely by glancing at the sails and gauging the performance of the ship wherever they happen to be standing. The system worked equally well for ships other than frigates, as at that time officers of any rank would all have served some time on a frigate, and thus would know precisely what they were capable of carrying in a given wind. But despite the practicalities of Beaufort's scale, it was to be another 20 years before he himself had it officially adopted by the Admiralty.

The *Blossom* finally joined Admiral Sir Charles Cotton's Mediterranean fleet off Toulon, where Beaufort's replacement, a 'Captain Stewart came on board from the *San Joseph*'[31] to take command. Beaufort left his sloop with great regret – 'even the old wagger the *Woolwich* kept my eyes fixed on her for miles, much more my pretty little *Blossom*.'[32] He took with him five midshipmen, his clerk, coxswain and servant and repaired to the *San Joseph* to await passage to Smyrna, Turkey where the *Frederickssteen* lay. It was a profitable wait, for on 18 September 1810 the Admiral gave him the command 'for the time being' of the *Ville de Paris*, a 110-gun first-rate ship-of-the-line, one of the largest in the Navy. As she blockaded the port of Toulon, Beaufort dreamed of taking her into action against the French fleet, seemingly having forgotten his views on the futility of seeking glory. But the command was short-lived, and on

23 October, he joined the *Salsette*, commanded by Captain William Bathurst, parting 'company with the Fleet with a fresh NW gale'.

Beaufort's entry in his journal for 11 December 1810 reads: '3 ½ anchored off the English Consul's at Smyrna about a mile in 8 fathoms. Found her, the *Frederickssteen* and sundry merchant vessels.' The next and most important part of his life was about to unfold.

CHAPTER 9

Captain Beaufort RN, Surveyor

THE WEAK WINTER SUN filtered through the gallery windows throwing precise rectangular shadows over the painted canvas that resembled a chequer board on the deck of the cabin. Captain Francis Beaufort, in his library chair, the front legs raised by three inches with brass wheels, sat before a large dining table and surveyed his quarters in His Majesty's frigate *Frederickssteen* with satisfaction. His few possessions had been stowed by his servant exactly as his master's neat and methodical mind prescribed, but his precious new sextant, theodolite and microscope, recently purchased from leading scientific instrument maker of the day, Edward Troughton, he had secured himself. He had also personally arranged his expanding library in the bookshelves – some of the volumes dating back to his first voyage on the *Latona* – before fixing the rods that held the books in place in dirty weather. He was ready to read through his orders and the pile of papers left by Captain Joseph Norisse, her former commander.

Beaufort's appointment to the *Frederickssteen* was the result of much collusion in Whitehall. Although the First Lord of the Admiralty, Charles Yorke, was pleased to reward 'so meritorious an officer', it was John Barrow (in consultation with Captain Thomas Hurd, the Hydrographer to the Navy) who conceived the idea of a survey of the whole of the southern coast of Turkey. The timing was right too. Up to then, an alliance had existed between Britain and Russia against the Sublime Porte. When Napoleon forced the Tsar to abandon the treaty, it left the way free for Britain to mend the breach with her former adversary. Being a sensitive area, the Foreign Office was naturally included in the discussions over Beaufort's appointment and the survey. Their representative was none other than William Hamilton, Beaufort's ship-mate from the *Phaeton* twelve years before. Since leaving the employ of the Earl of Elgin in Constantinople, Hamilton's career had prospered in the Foreign Office and he had risen to become Under Secretary of State for Foreign Affairs. But he was also a passionate antiquarian and Patron of the Society of Dilettanti.

From his end, Hamilton was particularly keen that it was Beaufort who should be sent to Turkey. Although the classical sites of Europe were well known and visited by scholars and the tourists of the day on the Grand Tour throughout the eighteenth and early nineteenth centuries, information on the Greco-Roman sites in Asia Minor was virtually non-existent, other than what could be gleaned from the classical writings of the 'ancient geographers', the likes of Pliny, Herodotus, Ptolemy, Livy, and in particular, Strabo. Hamilton believed that with a coherent chart, the geographical co-ordinates of these sites could be fixed and identified later by classical scholars. Hamilton knew that Beaufort would deliver an excellent survey and description of the coast, what he could not have known was that it would also include a near complete account and correct identification of all those sites. When Beaufort received his commission, he had some idea of what was expected of him, which would explain the hand-written translation of Strabo's Book XIV chapter 5, the part that covered Southern Turkey, stowed in his library.*

But Beaufort's initial orders were to place himself in the service of Stratford Canning, the brilliant 24-year-old minister plenipotentiary at the British Embassy to the Sublime Porte. Canning had recently inherited the position from Sir Robert Adair, whom he had accompanied to Constantinople at the time of the diplomatic negotiations. Once this new treaty was signed, Canning stayed on in Constantinople to foster British influence in the Porte at the expense of the French, to promote British trade, and to protect her shipping against privateers. Then there was also the tricky question of Royal Navy deserters serving on Turkish ships on the pretext that they had become Moslems. Another area of conflict was the seizure of British ships caught smuggling grain. Britain maintained that the Turks could confiscate the cargoes but not impound the vessels as well, for 'His Majesty will never suffer any Power, at whatever distance from his dominions, to invade with impunity the right and property of his subjects.'[1] So Beaufort was appointed senior naval officer Smyrna 'to instil on the Porte an understanding of maritime law',[2] a post to be combined with the major survey expedition over the next two years.

So on the morning of 12 December 1810, the diminutive

---

* Strabo (circa 63 BC–21 AD) – the name means squint-eyed – was the author of an historical geography of the Roman Empire, all 17 volumes remarkably surviving virtually in tact.

figure of the *Fredericksteen*'s new captain stood on her quarter-deck and read his commission to all 214 men in the ship's company. Behind him, in their best uniforms, stood the three lieutenants, surgeon, purser and a bevy of midshipmen – the five from the *Blossom* eyeing the two left behind on the *Fredericks-teen* with suspicion. One of Beaufort's imports was William Henry Quinn, a clever farm boy from Edgeworthstown who made the transition to the quarterdeck. He had also served on the *Woolwich* and eventually rose to the rank of post captain.

Beaufort then made a full inspection of his new command. He was delighted with her and thought her admirable for the work in hand. Although 'a small ship,' he wrote in his journal, 'she has a great beam drawing only 15' 6" to 16".[3] The storerooms and water butts he found pitiful, but as they would rarely be out of reach of provisions on shore it would not present a problem. Her sails and standing rigging were the same as in 'the Danish service' – she had been captured in the Bay of Biscay in 1807 and, keeping her Danish name, she was immediately commissioned into the Royal Navy. What Beaufort particularly liked for his surveying work were her boats – 'one 8-oared, two six-oared, and one jolly boat' – a good start but he 'could do with one more'.

Canning began by sending Beaufort 'a description of two French privateers that are fitting out in this port [Pera] for a cruise in the archipelago'.[4] He had failed to persuade the Turkish Government to prevent their sailing, and dispatched the *Fredericksteen* to the Dardanelles to intercept them for if 'they get to sea, our trade will not fail to suffer'. He further hoped Beaufort 'would do a great service by taking these vessels and trust that you will find them sufficiently valuable to repay you for your trouble'. But bad weather kept the *Fredericksteen* in port and the privateers escaped, masquerading as Turkish vessels. On a personal level, Canning was delighted to see Beaufort as

A view of Gravesend, from where Beaufort left on his first voyage to the Far East.
Brown University Library, Providence, Rhode Island, USA/ Bridgeman Art Library)

THE INTERIOR OF A MIDSHIPMAN'S BIRTH

This colour print of a midshipman's berth by George Humphrey can have been little
different to Beaufort's own berths on *Latona* and *Aquilon* – 'a bear pit of a place'.
The National Maritime Museum)

The Reverend Dr Daniel Augustus Beaufort, always known as DAB. He could do no wrong in his son's eyes. (National Portrait Gallery)

Mary Beaufort, née Waller of Allenstown, Beaufort's mother. She brought stability (and much of the finances) to her husband and her family life. (National Portrait Gallery)

Richard Lovell Edgeworth – Beaufort's mentor, and both brother- and father-in-law. (National Portrait Gallery)

The Reverend William Beaufort, Beaufort's elder brother. They remained close throughout their lives.

'A Fleet of East Indiamen at Sea' by Nicholas Pocock. Beaufort first went to sea in the *Vansittart*, a generic East India Company ship similar to these. (The National Maritime Museum)

'Lord Howe's Victory, 1st June 1794', a colour engraving by Thomas Sutherland, 1816. Beaufort served as signal midshipman on *Aquilon* throughout the battle of the Glorious First of June. (Private Collection/ The Stapleton Collection/ Bridgeman Art Library)

A watercolour by Irwin Bevan of HMS *Phaeton*, one of the most successful frigates of her day. Beaufort was serving on her when *La Bonne Citroyenne* (the model for the fictional *Sophie*, Captain Jack Aubrey's first command in the Patrick O'Brien series) was captured (The National Maritime Museum)

A watercolour of Alaya (today's Alanya) by the antiquarian Charles Cockerell,
Beaufort's companion for much of his survey of the coast of southern Turkey.
(The British Museum)

Beaufort's watercolour of Bombay Harbour, 1806. This is a typical example of his skill
and unerring accuracy as a naval artist and draughtsman.
(Library of Congress, Washington)

Beaufort's Naval Service Medal with three clasps for his part in The Glorious First of June, Cornwallis's Retreat and the taking of a Spanish poleacre, *San Josef*. (Royal Naval Museum, Portsmouth)

The steam-assisted yatch *Fox* under the command of Captain McClintock was commissioned by Lady Franklin to discover the fate of her husband, Sir John, and his expedition in the search for the North-West Passage. The watercolour by Captain W.W. May is in the possession of a descendant of her family.

Captain Sir Edward Belcher's HMS *Assistance*, caught in the Arctic ice. A watercolour by Thomas Sewell Robins. (The National Maritime Museum)

'The Arctic Council' by Stephen Pearce, 1851. Standing, from left to right, are Back, Parry, Bird, Clark Ross, Barrow Jnr, Sabine, Baillie Hamilton, Richardson, with Beechey seated opposite Beaufort. In the portraits behind are Franklin, Fitzjames and Sir John Barrow. Crozier, captain of HMS *Terror*, who should have been there by rights, was thought not to be quite gentlemanly enough for inclusion. (National Portrait Gallery)

For his retirement portrait of Rear-Admiral Sir Francis Beaufort KCB, Stephen Pearce merely reproduced the portrait from his painting of the Arctic Council. The money left over from the subscription went to fund an annual prize for the Royal Navy Lieutenant who passes out top in navigation. (National Portrait Gallery)

visitors were few and far between and society was particularly limited – Canning's previous visitor had been Lord Byron whom he had last seen when playing in opposing sides of the Eton-Harrow cricket match.

At last the weather improved and the *Fredericksteen*, accompanied by the *Salsette* under Beaufort's overall command, began her cruise in the Aegean. Her first success was the taking of a poleacre, the *San Nicola*, with a French cargo valued at £8,000. But as with so much of Beaufort's life, nothing was straightforward. The captain of the poleacre had bribed the Bey of Rhodes to lie about the cargo, and this held up the procedure in the Prize Court in Malta. Beaufort, desperate for the award, went to see the Bey, where he was received in a dirty room and with a 'dignity that the better kind of Turks possess'. He threatened to tell the Porte that he had been accepting bribes and the Bey immediately retracted his evidence. On leaving, he informed Beaufort that no salute was necessary, as they should both keep their 'powder for their enemies'. Beaufort was fortunate that the Bey of so powerful an island as Rhodes could be threatened with action from the Porte. The Ottoman Empire had been on the decline since the sixteenth century, and its power, even within Turkey, was patchy. Local warlords ruled autonomously, and Beaufort was to find that his *ferman* (right of passage) issued from Constantinople was not always recognised.

Time and again he was dogged by bad luck. Beaufort learned that a rich Maltese brig had been captured by a Neapolitan privateer and that the two ships were heading for the island of Syra (Siros). Beaufort arrived after the cargo had been landed, and was about to impound it and both ships when a Turkish frigate intervened, the captain being technically the 'temporary governor'. Beaufort 'sealed up the cargo' and decided to withdraw to Smyrna for advice. Then he returned to Syra 'a wretched looking island yet it has three advantages: it has a very snug port for a few vessels, it had a grape that makes good wine, and it has no Turk resident on the island'.[5] Not surprisingly, there was no sign of ships or cargo. In his time in Turkey, Beaufort found the Turks 'capricious, rude and uncivilised; but they are brave and frank, and, when their suspicions or bigotry are not excited, they are hospitable and generous'.[6] In return, the Turks dismissed him as an infidel and a Frank, and invariably regarded him with deep suspicion.

With the near total lack of success of the *Frederickssteen* in the Aegean, both Canning and Beaufort considered it a waste of time and energy to continue. In July 1811, she was ordered out of Smyrna to begin her other commission, the survey of the southern coast of Turkey. In old age Beaufort told his children that he had lost £20,000 by giving up the 'lucrative post of senior naval officer Smyrna', which was not true. But the effect of his subsequent survey of what he was to call 'Karamania', the medieval term for Asia Minor, was to be far greater and longer lasting than a list of captured privateers or any amount of prize money. *Karamania*, the account of his journey, together with his exemplary charts were to assure him a place amongst the scientific luminaries of the day.

At the beginning of the nineteenth century, Turkey was virtually unknown territory to the European traveller. A few had touched the western ports on their way to Egypt, and some had taken the overland road from Constantinople to Syria that cut across her eastern extremity. The main cities in the hinterland were known by name only, but as Beaufort wrote in *Karamania*, 'of the remainder of this great range of country, the only accounts extant were those left by the ancient geographers; and there was no nautical description of the coast, nor any charts whatever by which the mariner could steer'[7] – that was until Beaufort entered 'this unknown land' with his marine survey and geographical observations.

The survey of the coast began at Bodrum and ended in the Bay of Iskenderun opposite the Syrian border eighteen months later. In that time, Beaufort vowed 'to see every place and obtain a complete knowledge of the whole of my own observations'.[8] He was supremely happy and uniquely qualified for the job in hand. Under his leadership, the *Frederickssteen*'s ship's company worked well together as a team, quickly falling into a regular daily routine. Beaufort had begun by instructing his seven midshipmen. While larger ships-of-the-line had their own schoolmasters, in the smaller frigates much of the midshipmen's teaching, especially mathematics, navigation and surveying, devolved upon the captain. Beaufort held regular classes soon after his appointment to the *Frederickssteen*. Three times a week at 6.30 in the morning, the bleary-eyed midshipmen turned up in the captain's cabin for instruction. He was an enthusiastic teacher and made his subject lively.

Beaufort began with the theory behind the system known as a 'running survey', taken from Murdoch Mackenzie's *A Treatise on Marine Surveying* published in 1777. On a large blackboard, he drew a wavy coastline, and, in his artistic hand, drew some feature on each promontory – a lighthouse, a temple, a castle, a rocky headland, and the like. He then drew the *Frederickssteen* off the coast, telling his 'young gentlemen' that her position should be fixed accurately by astronomical surveys. Then, with screeching chalk that set the midshipmen's teeth on edge, he drew in lines to represent the bearings of each point on the coastline taken from the ship both by compass and angles taken with a horizontally-held sextant. Beaufort then drew the *Frederickssteen* in a new position along the mythical coast, and told them that her new position should be fixed again as before, or by dead reckoning, accurately recording the distance and bearing from the first position.

More screeching chalk represented the back bearings to the original points, and more forward, to establish the next prominent positions. Crowding round the chart table, the midshipmen strained to watch their captain plot the results on a large sheet of paper with a station pointer – a fine brass instrument from Edward Troughton with one fixed arm and two moveable arms with semi-circular scales on top to measure the angles between them and the fixed arm, all mounted on a central axis. The bearings between the points on the headlands were then set on the scale, and the axis placed on a dot on the paper that represented the ship's position. Beaufort then drew in the bearings along the arms. He repeated the exercise from the second ship's position, and where the lines crossed marked the headland, castle or whatever. He then drew in the intervening coastline by eye. But Beaufort was a stickler for accuracy, and, as he explained to his pupils, running surveys were only acceptable when time was short or it was impractical to use the boats for close inshore work.

Back to the blackboard, he scratched out the theory of surveying short stretches of coastline from boats and the shore, the midshipmen religiously copying the diagrams into their journals. Beaufort showed them the steel chain, exactly 100 yards long. This, he explained, was laid on the shore to create a baseline, each end being marked with poles and flags, about ten feet high, that could be seen from both the boats and the ship out to sea. A triangle was formed on the baseline with another flag and recorded by measuring the internal angles, then doubled into a quadrilateral with the addition of another pole. From there, a series of triangles was built up to fix every salient point on the shore. When coast-lining, the fine detail of the actual coastline was plotted by taking horizontal sextant angles from previously determined points on the foreshore to the mean high water line. Beaufort told of the painstaking task ahead of them, and promised his midshipmen that they would all get very wet surveying – either riding the surf to establish survey marks ashore, or in the boats taking soundings.

At last the theory was put to the test. The midshipmen were seconded to the surveyors as Beaufort divided up the duties between himself and his officers. The first lieutenant, William Gammon, was primarily engaged in the administration of the *Fredrickssteen* and the running surveys. Beaufort himself led the teams working from the boats and the shore. There was the master, 'a tried and trusted officer' who worked from a gig scrounged from the wharf in Smyrna and rebuilt by the ship's carpenter for his use. There were two lieutenants, and Dr Hugh Stewart whom Beaufort considered 'a better surveyor than ship's surgeon'. Traditionally, the ship's surgeon doubled as naturalist on such expeditions, but with Stewart it was surveying that he 'embraced with enthusiasm'.

Every day was punishing for Beaufort and the boat crews. He breakfasted 'often by candlelight, always by 5,' he noted in his journal, 'and took the boats' crews' dinners with me, or appointed a fresh boat's crew to meet me at noon'.[9] Their work ended at sunset, but the day was often extended when the evening sea breeze that 'did not lull until 8 or 9' at night prevented them returning to the ship. The survey, hampered through shortage of time, nonetheless went fast and well. However, when the *Fredrickssteen* reached the ancient city of Patara, the whole tenor of the operation changed. Beaufort anchored off in a deep bay at the mouth of the River Xanthus and was pulled ashore with his officers in his own gig. They ran the surf, beached the boat and clambered over the burning sand. They had all heard tell of 'Apollo's famous oracle', and, 'beneath a tranquil sky without a cloud or breeze',[10] spent the day clambering over the ruins like overexcited small boys. It was a source of wonder to them all as they pulled the undergrowth away from fallen masonry to reveal columns and pediments, carved friezes and the occasional statue not seen by any European since the Crusades.

The Gate of Patara illustrated in *Karamania* from an accomplished pen-and-ink sketch made by Beaufort in his journal.

As a true gentleman scientist, Beaufort spent his time measuring and recording his findings. He was delighted that he was able to identify the name PATARA on several columns and pediments. He made an accomplished pen and ink sketch in his journal of the magnificent city gate with its three arches known as the Great Gate, and, with his portable theodolite, measured the theatre 'somewhat more than a semi-circle, whose external diameter is about 200 feet; and contains thirty-four rows of marble seats, few of which have been disturbed'.[11] He marvelled at the preservation of the proscenium and the temple nearby. But it was the 'deep circular pit of singular appearance' that excited him most. 'A flight of steps,' he wrote, 'leads to the bottom, and from the centre a square pillar may have supported the statue of the deity, and the pit may have afforded some secret means of communication for the priest.' However, he speculated (rightly as it turned out) that it might just be a cistern and the pillar a nilometer. It was a long and fulfilling day for them all, as they had neither eaten nor drunk, and their clothes were torn to shreds from creeping through the brushwood. Their 'shoes cut on the rocks, soaked by the quagmires, or burned in the red-hot sands were of but little use'. With their bodies 'nearly exhausted by the copious penetration and exercise'[12] and bitten by mosquitoes, they returned to the gig. By the time they reached their 'floating house', Beaufort admitted that he and his officers were all 'committed antiquarians'.

That night, Beaufort joined his officers in the gunroom. They dined well on the wild boar that Mr Gammon had bought from a Turkish peasant while watering the ship the day before, and drank Sicilian wine. The fish had been caught over the side. It was a particularly pleasant evening as they discussed the adventures of the day. They compared their notes and the Latin and Greek inscriptions they had copied out, and speculated mostly on the temple which 'from the frequent recurrence of the word ZEYE was probably dedicated to Jupiter'.[13] A large hand, with nine-inch-long fingers 'in the act of grasping, perhaps a thunderbolt' was found amongst the debris. Beaufort had made a sketch of the whole area from the hill overlooking the site, and they were able to identify the harbour, by then a marsh, from Strabo's account. As the *Fredericksteen* was anchored in Kalamaki Bay (Strabo's Port Phoenicus) – 'a large, gloomy bay in which the Roman fleet anchored previously to the attack on Patara' – there was a lively debate on the likely tactics of the commanders and the methods they would have employed. Fired with their new-found 'true antiquarian taste', they begged to be allowed to explore the city of Xanthus, described by Strabo as the largest city in Lycia, six hours up-country – distances were measured by the 'number of hours which a caravan of camels employs in performing a journey [about 2 ½ miles per hour]'. Beaufort demurred, reminding his officers that they were there to survey the coast and not to explore ruins. Also, the further inland they ventured, the more dangerous and 'barbaric' the Turks. They were all disappointed, but none more than he.

The *Fredericksteen* returned briefly to Rhodes to check the bank of chronometers that Beaufort had been given, and then returned to the mainland coast. Nothing escaped his keen eye; no detail was too small. Just as each physical detail of the coastline was recorded, so was every aspect of the country, particularly its nomenclature. He became obsessed with identifying every site, point, and river with both its ancient and local names. He looked into subsequent appellations, such as Kastellórizon (Pliny's Megiste), drawn from the Frankish name of Castel Rosso after the red veins in the limestone cliffs of the island, or Kekova (Strabo's Dolchiste) after the Mycenaean word for partridge, 'truly well named for such flocks abound – in one cove, not less than 300 started up as the bowman jumped on shore. They are the red legged species, a large but not so well-flavoured bird as the grey and extremely fast and very wary.'[14] The area and islands known as *Chelidoniæ*, between Finike and Antalya Bays was named from the swallows that lighted there on their migration north. Although too late in the year for swallows then, they had met with vast 'flights of these birds, as if coming from Africa'.[15] At sunset they had perched on the *Fredrickssteen*'s yards and rigging, some even flopping exhausted into the cabins.

The destruction of the majority of the tombs and the ruins greatly upset Beaufort. He railed against the tomb robbers: 'what barbarous Greeks are these Turks! See their sarcophagi are prey to their cupidity. Look at these columns and temples, trampled under their profane feet or carried away to build their hovels.'[16] He did, however, admit that it would be hard for any Turk to take any interest in Roman or Greek civilisations, let alone their culture, when rich treasure and a ready supply of building material was there for the taking. He reserved his scorn for those 'educated in the highest veneration for the ancient Greeks and Romans' – the likes of the Earl of Elgin – who rob and pillage 'to gratify a momentary whim or childish caprice'.[17] Beaufort was also in a difficult position. He only had to admire a statue to arouse 'a jealous and ferocious' outburst from the Turks. At

Phineka, one of the mob exclaimed that 'if the infidels are attracted here by these blasphemous figures, the temptation shall soon cease; for when that dog is gone, I will destroy them. A Mohammedan considers all imitations of the human figure to be impious, and the admiration of them idolatrous.'[18] Even worse was to come at Side where many of the columns had been cut up and rounded 'into balls, such as the Turks use in their immense cannon at the Dardanelles and at Smyrna'.[19]

From Kekova, where Beaufort noticed that the canon on the tumbledown fort 'would be destructive to those only who might fire them',[20] the survey continued round Cape Chelidonia on the tip of the Promontorium Sacrum or Sacred Promontory, Beaufort was taking 'as many soundings as the master and myself could obtain, and as many angles as was necessary to give a general idea of an intricate piece of coast that would take a month to survey accurately'.[21] He began to spend more time ashore, where he sketched, observed and recorded, even camping for the night when he needed a star sight to fix a particular position.

Pages of Beaufort's journal were given over to conjecture of everything, from geological observation to natural phenomena. Passing the five barren Chelidonian islands off the Cape, he speculated over their formation through earthquake. He marvelled at the 'little stream of excellent water which bursts out of so sharp and barren a ridge', the source of which must be in the mountains on the mainland so 'its channel of communication must pass under the bed of the sea, which is 170 feet deep'.[22] He tried to fathom the strong, but irregular currents that swept the whole coastline, particularly around the islands, that came from the eastern end of the Mediterranean. He reasoned that there could not be an 'influx from the Atlantic, as it is not felt along the coast of Barbary, nor could it be the water of the Nile, as one could not possibly expect its influence so far'.[23] Rivers and rain were dismissed as 'trifling'. He hoped to discover the cause in the course of his 'peregrinations'.

The *Frederickssteen* settled down to a daily routine – Beaufort and the master now doing the soundings, while 'the good doctor and a marine officer are good enough to go search on shore for whatever can be discovered however modern or antiquarian',[24] while one of the pilots sought out the 'names in Greek and Turkish of the places, ports and islands'. The purser and a translator bought fresh beef and vegetables. When they reached Deliktaş, or 'Perforated Rock, so called from the natural gateway' in the mountains behind, Beaufort and a party of officers all went to explore. Amongst the ancient remains, 'of very different character from those already mentioned', was a ruined temple. When they turned over a pedestal, they found a 'perfectly fresh' Greek inscription that confirmed that they had indeed found Olympus.

The *yanar* – the natural gas flame on Mount Olympus. The locals claimed it would not cook meat that was stolen.

That night, anchored at the other end of the bay beyond Olympus, the ship's company were intrigued by 'a small but steady light among the hills'. The shore hunting party had reported sundry ruins in a little inlet abreast of the ship, and that an hour's ride from them was a small volcano. The local aga, who had come to inspect the ship, supplied the horses, and ten of the ship's company set off at daybreak along the fertile plain and up into the hills. They followed a well-worn track up a rocky ravine, through thick pinewoods (said to be 'unctuous wood that is highly inflammable') and parched scrub to a collection of small, ruined buildings. In the corner of one of them was the site of the 'volcano' – a small 'vivid flame from a hole like the mouth of an oven'. The Turks called the flame *yanar*. Beaufort tried to throw a stone in the flame but was beaten back by the heat. He was amazed that there was no soot, 'nor smoke, nor noxious vapours, nothing but a brilliant perpetual flame, that no water could quench'.[25] The guide told them that the shepherds cook their food on the flame but it would not cook meat that was stolen. Beaufort later worked out that he had found Pliny's Mount Chimæra,[26] home of the fabled Chimæra, the mythical beast with the head of a lion, the body of a goat and the tail of a dragon. According to legend, she vomited horrible flames. The personification of the storm cloud, Chimæra was eventually slain by Bellerophon, who, mounted on his horse Pegasus, filled her mouth with a large ball of lead that melted in the flames and killed her when she swallowed it. Another theory was that Moses fled from Egypt and lived near Deliktaş, the *yanar* being the burning bush. However, what Beaufort and his companions witnessed was not mythical nor Biblical, but merely natural gas leakage. While the rest explored the other ruins, including a church, Beaufort made a sketch of the flame in its house. The drawing from his journal appeared in *Karamania* and on many editions of his printed chart of the area.

The party returned by another route through a Turkish village, which Beaufort uncharacteristically admired, to the beach where another local aga was waiting 'in high dudgeon'. He had been invited on board, but had assumed that Lieutenant Seymour was the Captain. He took great umbrage at the slight, but a gun salute and a pouch of gunpowder 'completed the reconciliation'.

A little further north, there was another delight for the new 'antiquarian-minded' crew of the *Frederickssteen* – the ancient city of Phaselis with its three ports. While the massive stone pier of the principal port had fallen into the sea, and another was just a narrow opening, the masonry of the third was 'still nearly perfect'. Beaufort with his officers and boats' crews tied up alongside it, again conscious that they were the first Europeans to land there for centuries. They sauntered down the 'straight avenue flagged with marble' as far as the theatre, in a fair state of decay, and the Temple of Minerva, which was reputed to have held Achilles' spear. They marvelled at the aqueduct and explored the ruined houses on the plateau. Again Beaufort sketched and recorded, measured and copied inscriptions. He made a detailed survey of the whole promontory that, like the *yanar*, appeared on all but the latest editions of the Admiralty charts of the area.

But what excited them most were the unopened sarcophagi partially hidden on the beach. Notwithstanding Beaufort's aversion to grave robbers, he sent his gig back to fetch tools to open them. They were of 'the whitest marble and of very neat workmanship'. Unlike others on the coast with a single-slab Gothic top, these were flat carved with a recumbent figure and the sides 'richly ornamented' with fruit and flowers, a funeral procession, or 'a chace in which figures of the rhinoceros, and the elephant were manifest'.[27] As the carpenter prised open one sarcophagus, the assembled company's curiosity was

Beaufort's plan of Phaselis. So experienced a surveyor was he that this plan was executed in an afternoon.

'wound up to a high pitch' as the lid was removed to reveal '... nothing. There was neither medals nor treasures, nor indeed anything'[28] but the bones of one skeleton. Marbles were moved, their inscriptions copied, and replaced 'in the same situations in which they had been found: or rather, they were put into positions as appeared best calculated for their preservation for the benefit of future travellers'.[29]

Beaufort had always planned to set up a little observatory on the Island of Rashat close by Adalia (the modern Antalya) for the 'occulation of a star and a lunar eclipse', vital observations in determining the longitude of the 'principal city of the whole coast'. Nearly there, he learned from a passing ship that the canon fire he had heard the night before was an uprising in the city led by the Pasha's brother. Shortly after, the rightful governor of Antalya retook his city and the rebels fled. Beaufort anchored the

Frederickssteen in a small creek some 30 miles to the west in the hope that she would remain 'unperceived and undisturbed' for the last thing he needed was to become involved in a local dispute. It was a vain hope, and the next day a party of the rival Bey's supporters appeared on the beach, and begged for protection from the watering party. Beaufort refused, having no wish to interfere in their disputes, nor to 'involve His Majesty's flag, or to expose our operations to interruption or failure' as the Pasha's rule extended far along the coast in both directions.

But Beaufort's compassion for his fellow man had the better of him, and he gave them bread while the ship's surgeon patched up the wounded. He urged them to escape to the woods where the cavalry, who had by then entered the plain, could not pursue them, but they demurred saying that there were no roads, they had no allies, there was a price on their heads, and anyway, their God would provide. Their God did provide, in the form of an abandoned sailing vessel that was seen drifting out to sea. The coxswain retrieved the boat, and even though Beaufort offered to repair and provision it, still they declined on the premise that none of them was a seaman. When one of the Pasha's cruisers appeared round the headland and the cavalry had surrounded the fugitives Beaufort 'could not stand by and see them butchered in cold blood' and so dispatched his boats to pick them up from the shore. They found them sitting under some bushes quite resigned to their fate. When the 60 'souls' were brought aboard, they stood on the quarterdeck 'displaying neither exultation nor joy'. Beaufort thought that they might at least have shown a little gratitude, but he was still an infidel in their eyes and 'though the immediate preservers of their lives, we were but tools in the hands of their prophet'.[30]

Having saved their lives, Beaufort's own problems were just beginning. There he was, anchored off the beach in 5 fathoms of water, his quarterdeck full of rebels, with a cruiser belonging to the

Pasha of Antalya bearing down on him. For the sake of his survey, he could not afford to offend the Pasha. There was a chance that the revolt had been ordered by Constantinople, but the Pasha might complain to the Porte who would naturally wish to distance themselves from the failed plot by admonishing Beaufort. The Admiralty, too, would have words of their own on his conduct. But Beaufort's luck for once held. He sent Lieutenant Gammon across to the cruiser, but before he was half way over a small cannon ball landed only a few feet short of the cutter drenching them with its spray. This was clearly an act of aggression, and changed the whole situation. Beaufort was in a fury: 'in my rage, I swore by the beard of their rascally prophet that he should pay for such a wanton and impertinent aggression,'[31] but with his long glass he could see that his first lieutenant was well received and welcomed aboard her quarterdeck 'with a profusion of respect'. The rebels were quartered below decks before the Pasha's envoys returned to the *Frederickssteen* and were ushered into the Captain's cabin. Beaufort had furnished it in the Turkish manner with large cushions around a low table on a Kelim rug. Coffee, the 'precursor of all business' was brought and the series of negotiations began. No, we did not know that one of His esteemed Majesty's frigates was in our waters, but had you come to the city first . . . We know that you would never 'condescend to be interested in our local affairs . . . Although we know that 'the remnant of the band of robbers, of whom we were in pursuit' could not possibly be on board . . . The Porte's displeasure . . . But Beaufort sat in stony silence until at last they demanded the return of the rebels. When he realised that 'nothing but their indiscriminate slaughter would satisfy their vindictive master' he 'civilly dismissed them'. As they left, they offered the interpreter a large sum to give up the Bin Bashy (leader) and begged for some coffee and rum – the Turks drank rum without compunction as law prohibited only spirits distilled from the grape.

After the fracas with the Pasha's envoys, the *Frederickssteen* weighed anchor and made for Kaş for the lunar observations and the occulation of a star (that did not happen) and to deposit her cargo of Turks. But the port was within the pashalik of Antalya so the rebels could not be landed, and the unexpected arrival of two of the Pasha's ships in the harbour sent Beaufort back to sea. He headed for Rhodes, but news of his involvement with the uprising preceded him. Eventually, Beaufort made for the island of Kos. His 'passengers' were so disenchanted with their 'cruise' and, with Ramadan approaching, decided to jump ship, any fate being better than the lower decks of the *Frederickssteen*. As Beaufort put it, he was finally 'disembarrassed of our perplexing companions'.[32]

Despite the fiasco in Antalya, Beaufort was in his element. He spent days exploring Kos, taking in as much of the town and fort as the locals would allow. Here, his normal, conscientious nature for surveying gave way to his passion of seeking out antiquities over the rest of the island. However, he did make an exacting survey of a spit of fine sand formed where one current from the Dardanelles met one from southern Turkey, and identified it as Strabo's *Scandaria*. He made notes of the interior, of the good wine to be had, the kind climate and the benefits of appointing a good British Consul to promote trade from the island. His further sightseeing was interrupted by reports that a French privateer was about to dispose of her prize in Bodrum, and he felt that he should 'show the flag' to the 'governor of that town'.

By then, Beaufort had the measure of the Turks, or so he thought. On entering the harbour, he made a present of a 'little fine powder tied up in green ribbon in velum paper and inscribed in Turkish 'The King's own Powder' which pleased him vastly'.[33] He had heard that there were fine marbles in the Crusader castle of St Paul and asked to be allowed to see them.

The governor demurred and extracted some more powder from Beaufort. Still permission was refused. When in the past, a French captain, armed with a *ferman* from the Porte, requested to see the marbles, the governor put the document to his forehead saying that he had orders to let him in, 'which must be obeyed, but 'it contains no directions about your coming out again'.[34] Beaufort, thoroughly thwarted, 'hove up his anchor' and made sail from Bodrum. He did, however, leave with a fine survey of the harbour, and a good series of observations for his book.

The *Frederickssteen*, in desperate need of a refit, was taken to Malta. Ships from the Levant needed 18 days' quarantine, but typically Beaufort served most of them 'examining the coast and islands to the westward [of Bodrum]. Landing only on detached rocks, or on the solitary beach, to obtain our angles, we avoided all intercourse with the inhabitants, and every temptation to visit the ruins that we passed.'[35] At the end of the fortnight, Beaufort 'quitted the shores of Asia and made sail for the island of Malta'.[36] With the rest of his crew, he found it strange to be in an English-speaking environment, but their three-week visit was made even more pleasant by the payment of prize money from the *San Nicolo* and another two prizes that they had picked up over the year.

The New Year saw the *Frederickssteen* back in Smyrna. The weather was still too foul to even think of resuming his survey and instead Beaufort joined Captain Henry Hope of the *Salsette*, his replacement as senior naval officer Smyrna. They sailed for Rhodes and there called on Lady Hester Stanhope who had 'lost everything but her life by shipwreck'.[37] They had admonished the governor, Hassan Bey for not 'having treated her with more gallantry and hospitality' – she was after all the niece and close confidante of the late Prime Minister William Pitt. Hope's offer to take her to Alexandria (that she was also a close friend of

Lord Mulgrave was not lost on either captain) was reluctantly declined as she had to wait for her physician, Charles Lewis Meryon 'who had not yet returned with her ladyship's garments' from Smyrna.

Beaufort went to Smyrna himself as the British trading station was threatened by a local Pasha, but the sight of an armed British frigate was enough to deter the insurgents. The *Frederickssteen* was anchored within the mole that protected the harbour. It was bitterly cold, the water a flat, oily black. Forward, the sounds of the crew dancing filtered aft to the captain's cabin, but that happy sound was nearly drowned by the raucous laughter coming from the gunroom. Beaufort tried to concentrate on a treatise he was writing on the beauties and the geographical features of the coast of Turkey. The purple prose ebbed and flowed, like the tides he was describing. But he was lonely and felt thoroughly dejected. When he could bear it no longer, he called for his gig and was rowed ashore, cocooned in his boat cloak, his hat pulled low. He wandered round the streets behind the port until he identified the brothel that he had heard one of his midshipmen bragging about. Inside, it was stiflingly hot, the air filled with the heady scent of attar of roses and sweet-smelling tobacco smoke. Voluptuous women lay around on velvet cushions. It was all too much for Beaufort, starved of female company and lonely, as he was led away by not one but two *houris*. However pleasurable the liaisons were at the time, Beaufort was wracked with guilt when he returned to his ship. Using his childhood code, he confided his shame to his journal:

Oh Smyrna, what have I suffered within your walls! The beastly lasciviousness and acute cunning of one woman, the seductive charms, the dangerous follies of another and the strange mixture of my own vices, virtues and weaknesses have thrown my mind and body into a state when they must have long to emerge. Oh God, let me turn to this bitter lesson to account, to reclaim the one, and forgive the other, heal me, oh God.[38]

Beaufort carried his guilt for years, so much so that any major disaster was seen as God's punishment for his deed, or rather deeds. However, he was given orders to sail to Athens to liaise with Sir William Gell, the classicist, archaeologist and traveller. Ostensibly there at the direction of the Prince Regent, William Hamilton had requested that Beaufort assist Gell in his visit to Karamania. Beaufort disliked him on sight – he agreed with Byron's sobriquet 'coxcomb Gell' in his *English Bards and Scotch Reviewers* – and was suitably evasive on his own findings. He and his officers took in the 'sights' like latter-day tourists and were spared any further contact with Gell when the foremast of the *Frederickssteen* was struck by lightning and she left immediately for Malta for repairs. The mast was restored, but the work revealed that the *Frederickssteen* was in a sorry state, her bow timbers being condemned as 'mere dust'. Beaufort thought that she might survive the summer but should return to England before the winter, whatever the state of his survey.

It was mid-April before Beaufort could return to the Turkish coast to continue the survey, taking it up at Cape Avova, the point 'where its progress had been arrested the preceding year by the troublesome adventure with the fugitive Turks'.[39] William Hamilton had alerted Beaufort that Charles Robert Cockerell, the distinguished antiquarian, would be somewhere along the coast and should be given 'every assistance'. When the *caique* Cockerell had chartered in Athens spotted the *Frederickssteen*, she scurried away while a boat pulled ashore in order to bury their corn money in the sand. Her Greek captain knew only too well that a Turkish frigate would have plundered her, a Barbary cruiser would have pillaged her and then enslaved the crew, while a Greek poleacre would have arbitrarily taken her cargo at her own price – 'in all climates slave and tyrant are exchangeable terms'.[40] Once their identity was established, Cockerell needed little persuasion to repair to the *Frederickssteen* to 'pursue his researches with less hazard, and with come degree of comfort' and not to say a great measure of intelligent companionship for Beaufort.

Cockerell made the whole difference to Beaufort's life. They were a good partnership, one complementing the other. Although his officers were enthusiastic, they did not have Cockerell's background. At last, Beaufort had found a soul mate, someone to share his discoveries and thoughts. Passing Phaselis, for example, they discussed Arrian's epic account of Alexander's march along the shore, where a provident north wind held the water back long enough for the army to wade round the projecting cliffs.

No sooner had the *Frederickssteen* dropped her anchor outside the harbour of Antalya than one of the envoys Beaufort recognised from the year before came on board. From him he learned that old Pasha was dead and that he had been succeeded by his son, Hadgy Mehemmet. But the Porte had still to ratify his claim and invest 'him with the three [horse] tails of a Pasha'.[41] Thus, when Beaufort arrived from Smyrna, he was viewed with even deeper suspicion than normal. The envoy asked to view the ship and searched all the cabins and storerooms, apprehensive that behind every door a new Pasha, or worse a *Kapoojy Bashy* (executioner) would pop out. A lieutenant was sent back with the envoy to negotiate a suitable gun salute – they agreed eleven – and to arrange the exchange of presents. Bullocks, chickens, goats and vegetables came on board, a cask of gunpowder, a hundred quail, some beer and some trinkets, wrapped in green cloth (the sacred colour of Turkey) were borne ashore on poles by 'ten of the most athletic and handsome men of the crew, calculated to enhance the value of the present'. The first meeting between the young Bey and Beaufort was polite but suspicious. Slowly, Beaufort's diplomacy won the Bey round, but still he was refused permission to explore the inner city and so had to content himself with a view from the outer wall. On his last visit to the Bey, 'his increased serenity was apparent; yet even then, he could scarcely repress his joy when the day of departure was announced' as he wished him a safe passage along the coast.

Yet for someone who was denied access to the city, Beaufort acquired a remarkable insight into Antalya. He wrote at length on the architecture and the inhabitants, the mosques and the gardens, and made a fine pencil sketch of the city from his anchorage. Finally, he identified the fortress city as Strabo's Olbia, from the adjective 'blessed' or 'happy'. It was, however, with little regret on both sides that the *Fredericksteen* sailed eastward out of the bay on an offshore wind.

It can only have been torture for Beaufort and Cockerell to miss the glorious ruins of Perge and Aspendus. The *Fredericksteen* had anchored off the mouths of the rivers Aksu (Strabo's Cestrus) and the Köprüçay (Eurymedon). Although wide and deep, a large sandbar made entry difficult, but the boats were hauled over it to the river on the other side. As they were pulled up the Eurymedon, Cockerell regaled Beaufort on how Cimon destroyed the Persian fleet at the mouth of the river in 467 BC. He described the Rhodian fleet putting into the river with 'thirty-two quodriremes and four triremes'[42] fresh from their narrow victory over Hannibal in 190 BC, where 550 galleys fought outside the city of Side. However, the currents and lack of knowledge of the river, but mostly time, robbed them of some of the finest remains in Asia Minor – the vast theatre, nymphaeum and aqueduct at Aspendus; the stadium, towers and colonnaded avenue of Perge. However, what they missed there, they made up for in Side.

From the moment that Beaufort sprang ashore where 'the first

Fig.3.
Profile of the Seats enlarged.

Corridor

Corridor

Diazomatos

Area
(filled up with
ruins and bushes)

a

b

Proscenion
(ruined)

Fig.1.
A portion of the Plan
with part of the Seats removed
to shew the Corridors and Stairs.

10 0 10 20 30 40 50 60 70 80 90 100 10 20 30 40 50
Scale of Feet

23 Seats

Diazomatos

26 Seats

Area

Surface of the Ground

Fig.2.
Part of the Interior Elevation with a Section on the line a.b.
c.c.c. Corridors.
d.d. Doors Corresponding with the upper Corridor.

F. Bedford, del.

Spence Nicol f.

THEATRE of SIDÈ.

thing observed upon the beach was an inscription on a broken pedestal, beginning with the word ΣΙΔΗΤΗΣ'[43] (Side) he was captivated. The place was deserted, which added to its charm, and for five days he and Cockerell systematically took in and recorded every detail of 'the profusion of interesting objects which arrested the eye at every step' throughout the ancient harbour and city. Beaufort began by making an exacting survey of the whole promontory, plotting the harbour and moles, the city gates, walls and towers. He drew in the Agora, with its double row of bases for columns long fallen and central pedestal for 'a colossal statue'. On one side, the ruined temple faced the theatre, two truly magnificent structures that enthralled both Beaufort and Cockerell. Beaufort took five pages in *Karamania* to describe it in minute detail. He made a precise drawing in his journal, and, having measured the seats, worked out that if the 'ancients' did not cross their legs as was the contemporary fashion and sat with them 'pendant', then the theatre would hold 15,240 spectators.

Further excitements included a ruin of a circular building 'in some manner dedicated to astronomy', complete with a series of figures that represented the signs of the zodiac. They found pieces of sculpture amongst the brambles, and in one house, the interior was 'profusely ornamented' with warriors, colossal females, and mythological subjects that included the Rape of Proserpine, Diana and Endymion. Both men puzzled over the nymphaeum, the city's ceremonial water works, Beaufort could not 'form a guess as to its purpose', while Cockerell dismissed it in his travel journal as a piece of 'absurd architecture'.[44] Cockerell also recorded that the local aga offered 2,000 piastres for one of the midshipmen, a fact that Beaufort chose to overlook.

When the *Frederickssteen* sailed on 10 May, Beaufort was confident that he had done enough with his survey, plans and drawings, along with Cockerell's fine watercolours, for others to follow in his wake to explore the ruins of Side properly. Life was particularly pleasant and the weather kind. After the excitement of Side, they soon settled back into their routine, surveying the coast towards Alaya. Beaufort rose at 4 a.m. and left the ship as soon as he could see, 'to pursue the operations along shore'. At noon, the boat's crew returned while Beaufort observed the latitude, before a fresh crew arrived and they continued with their 'angles and bearings' until sunset. He dined with Cockerell at 8 p.m. and then 'snored until the next morning'. He invariably carried his double-barrelled fowling piece, once recording without shame that he shot and roasted a hawk and some sand larks for lunch.

They reached Alaya (today's Alanya) and anchored to a six-gun salute, which was duly returned, and, the next morning, the ritual exchange of presents took place amicably. At noon they returned to the shore, the gatekeeper offered the party of officers (that included Beaufort) coffee. To refuse would have been a gross insult, but by accepting, it was seen that 'the infidels were stopped at the gate and rigidly examined' before they were allowed to enter the city. As the party mounted the hill, a group of small boys began chanting *ghiäoor* (infidel) and soon there was an angry mob baying and throwing stones at them. Their guide hurried them down the hill, insults and stones still raining about their heads. They took to the boats and immediately landed the present of six bullocks on the shore. An envoy came on board with profuse apologies. The mob was barbarian. They had already been 'seized and *bastinadoed*' (caned on the soles of the feet). Would the captain care to inflict further punishment? The officers, this time without Beaufort but with the envoy, returned to the city and found there was little there 'to repay their toil'. Antiquarians to a man, they dismissed one of the finest examples of Seljuk military architecture in Turkey as being too modern. Beaufort's part in the affair was shaming and there is no mention that he was there in *Karamania*. However, under the circumstances retreat, though ignominious, was undoubtedly the wiser option. The rock of Alaya was to haunt him 'every night'.

Other 'modern' castles were the two at Anamour (today's Anamur) that 'stood on the edge of the sea, and in general appearance strongly resemble some of the ancient castles of Great Britain'.[45] That they were the first Europeans to see it since the Crusaders left was not lost on Beaufort and Cockerell, and with the blessing of the friendly aga, they took an informed interest in it. Beaufort clambered over the battlements and the 'dodecagonal, octagonal square, round and half-round' towers, even copying Arabic scripts over the gateway precariously balanced on a portable ladder. He gave all the outward appearances of enjoying himself. The survey was going well, and there was still plenty of time for him, Cockerell, and what he called his 'groper' officers to explore on shore. Yet Beaufort, presumably for the benefit of his family who were to read his journal, laments that his toil and labour were of no account, and that he should forgo 'those amusements of antiquity-hunting'.[46] Judging from that same journal and *Karamania* that came out of it, this is patently not the case. There is no detail of any site, ruin, or inscription, nor any geological feature or natural phenomena along the rest of the coast that he wrote about from there on that was patently not observed at first hand.

The two exceptions that followed the outburst in his journal occurred when Beaufort carried on surveying while a party of officers went to see the city of Tarsus, and before that, the visit to the extensive ruins at Seleucia, the modern Silifke. When the shore party returned, the *Frederickssteen* had gone in pursuit of a pirate. She was a galley that 'rowed fast, possessed a swivel gun and twenty muskets, and with the forty ferocious looking villains who manned her, might have carried the largest merchant ship on the Mediterranean'.[47] Unfortunately, she escaped 'when the weather became hazy'. The fortresses of Korghos Kalaler (the modern Kiz Kalesi) at Korykos being uninhabited and with only a few ancient columns, did not hold Beaufort for long, although he made a separate survey of the island castle, with a note that one of the most romantic places in all Asia Minor would make a good lighthouse.

Beaufort was an excellent captain. He led by example and his officers and crew respected him greatly. His authority was absolute and fair, so much so that there was only one flogging throughout the whole of the second voyage. By comparison, the life of the crew was considerably better than in other ships-of-the-line, like those on blockade duty in the North Atlantic. Sometimes it was pleasurable for all, like the afternoon spent by the mouth of a stream near Lamas. There, in a copse each tree had a family of rooks, the fledglings being easily caught by the boats' crews and tamed as pets back on board. The sailors gathered shellfish amongst the rocks, samphire on the cliffs, and birds' eggs in the bushes. There was wild sage for tea, grass for the ship's goats and myrtle for brooms – 'every place furnished its employment'.[48] Further on, they bathed in the river Cydnus, whose 'extreme coldness is said to have occasioned the death of Frederick Barbarossa and have proved nearly fatal to Alexander [the Great]'.[49]

On the morning of 12 June, the *Frederickssteen* anchored in the bay of Soli (the ancient Pompeiopolis, named after Pompey the Great). Beaufort and Cockerell had dined in the gunroom the night before, where they were all 'looking forward to the place with eagerness'.[50] Nor were they disappointed by what they saw, standing on the quarterdeck, their telescopes trained on the city. Excitement mounted as slowly they made out the mole in the harbour, then 'a lofty theatre appeared over the trees that had usurped the place of houses' followed by a long row of

Corinthian columns. They went ashore and Beaufort and his gropers once again systematically explored the city. Again he recorded every detail, speculating on the avenue of double columns that led from the harbour through a portico at the end, a site that even 'the most illiterate seaman in the ship could not behold it without emotion, even in its present state of wreck'.[51]

At last the *Frederickssteen* rounded Cape Karataş into the Gulf of Iskenderun, and, with the end of the survey nearly in sight, the mood of the ship became quite light-hearted. Beaufort went ashore where he met an old black man with his middle-aged wife and their very pretty daughter of about seventeen. Neither was wearing her veil, and the three of them 'diverted' Beaufort in conversation. The old man examined Beaufort's gun and clothes, then gave him 'a good deal of information, and what was very singular (as 48 hours afterwards proved) advised us to beware of the inhabitants to the eastwards and addressing himself to me, "Tell your Captain not to trust himself on shore, for he will not be the first that they have killed or carried away".'[52] Sailing into Ayas Bay, they found 'the greatest number of fish and fowl' they had seen anywhere along the coast. Great flocks of pelicans, swans, geese, ducks and gulls swarmed over the beach, shoals of fish darted around the shallow water. There were also a great number of green turtles that afforded the crew 'a great deal of amusement'. Some were 'upwards of 260 lb weight', and so strong that two men could not hold them, others were copulating which as Beaufort noted (in cipher) seemed 'a very slow affair'. They took 26 of them back to the ship, which nearly swamped the boat. The next day, Beaufort was rather shamefaced over 'sacrificing' so many of them, and believed that their death for his and his crew's amusement was an ill omen for the future.

The next morning, 20 June 1812, was flat calm and hazy. Knowing that there was not enough wind to blow out a candle, let alone move the *Fredericksteen*, Beaufort was pulled across to the eastern side of the long, narrow gulf at daylight. Shortly after, the pinnace under Lieutenant Lane left the ship and followed the gig. They were all strong oarsmen, in high good humour as they raced each other across the smooth water, dead heating at a deserted round tower on the other side of the bay. Beaufort sent Mr Yhary, his interpreter, up the portable ladder to read the Turkish inscription over the door, while he copied two Greek ones on a fallen pillar nearby. Beaufort sent his gig on to Ayas with his instruments, ready to make the survey of the little port, while he walked the 'few cables toward the large castle'.

The lane, strewn with the shrivelled remains of the spring flowers, was dusty but the air was fresh. On either side, Turks were cultivating their strips of land. When Beaufort arrived at the town, his coxswain had already landed his instruments ready to survey the little cove, and to fix the position of the castle. Standing on a rock, he took his last set of bearings when a crowd appeared on the cliff above 'accompanied by an old and ill-looking Dervish'.[53] He did not need his interpreter, who by then was with another party on shore, to gauge their feeling towards him – as he put it, 'their voice and gestures and some abusive expression that I could not understand was sufficiently indicative of their hostile feelings'. They were all armed, but as every Turkish man bore arms Beaufort was not unduly alarmed. Also, Cockerell and the watering party of the night before had reported that the inhabitants seemed particularly friendly. Beaufort just kept a wary eye on them as the instruments were loaded into the boat, but such was the weight of all his surveying equipment he could not carry much more than his 'double-barrelled fowling piece and one musket, with a couple of cutlasses', no match against the mob, all 'armed up to their teeth'. His 'little store of friendly words and signs seemed to irritate, rather than appease them'.[54] Then he just ignored them.

Nonchalantly, Beaufort wandered along the shore and, as he stepped into the boat, the cries from the mob became shriller as they descended to the beach. As the gig shoved off, they levelled their muskets at Beaufort and his crew who pulled frantically for the narrow opening in the bay. Beaufort brought out his fowling piece. The mob seemed surprised, but the old Dervish urged them on with wild cries of 'Infidel'. Then Beaufort 'holding the gun elevated very high' to show that he did not 'intend to strike them', fired over their heads. The effect was instantaneous. Most sank on the ground at the report, some, including the Dervish, slunk away, but one more 'resolute and rascally fellow' jumped behind a rock that hid him completely. Just as the gig was clearing the surrounding rocks of the cove, Beaufort stood up in the stern sheets and fired his second barrel. The 'ruffian' behind the rock took 'deliberate aim' at him and fired. Fortunately, the ball struck the stern first, which deflected it a little. So, instead of shattering his groin, it entered the middle of his thigh, striking the femur close to the hip joint before passing through the leg muscles, then 'penetrating above 10 inches of flesh' to make its exit 'about an inch from the rectum'. The gig was out of range by the time the other Turks had stood up, otherwise the rest of the crew would certainly have perished.

Fortunately, the pinnace was within signal distance, and Beaufort called her in to collect the rest of the shore party before fainting from loss of blood. But before the pinnace could reach an outlying party, the mob turned on the other boat that was waiting to pick them up. The midshipman, a Mr Olphert, was killed outright. The pinnace, with 19 armed men under the 'cool and steady conduct of Lt E. Lane' collected the rest of the officers and men, and it was with difficulty that 'the natural fury of the boats' crews' was curbed from dealing 'a wholesome lesson in retaliation'. The blood-soaked Beaufort was rowed the five miles to the *Frederickssteen*, hoisted aboard and taken down to his cabin. As the surgeon prodded and poked, Cockerell declared that his friend was fortunate that his wound was not worse, but was amazed at 'his coolness and moderation even in this extremity'. When Beaufort learned of the death of Olphert, he wept being, as Cockerell noted, 'more affected by that blow than his own'.[55]

Eventually, a light breeze sprang up and the becalmed *Frederickssteen* made it across the gulf to anchor off the castle. The villagers feared 'a dreadful retribution' and insisted that the mob had come from the hills. They promised to 'seize and deliver, if possible, the principal offenders to the Ahga'. To their great relief, the *Frederickssteen* sailed for Iskenderun, where Olphert was interred in the burial ground that had formerly belonged to the British Factory. Beaufort, though severely wounded, was still in command of his senses and his ship. He sent a strong letter to the Pasha of Iskenderun, who insisted that Ayas was in the Pasheric of Adana and not his, and that 'every exertion should be made to bring the assassins to justice'. But Beaufort was having none of it. He told the Pasha that a British squadron would soon arrive for the 'punishment of the offenders', and it was only 'in consideration alone for the friendship which exists between my most powerful King and the Sublime Porte that I have not burned the castle, destroyed the country, exterminated the inhabitants of a place which treated us as enemies and you will I am sure be sensible of this moderation'.[56]

The *Frederickssteen* put to sea and soon fell in with Captain Hope and the *Salsette*. 'The whole transaction was reported to him' and he repaired to Iskenderun to administer such measures of retribution as he thought appropriate. It was a delicate mission. The Sublime Porte had fully declared for Britain against France, and Stratford Canning had given orders that Hope was not to antagonise the Turks. Beaufort, too, was having second thoughts on his own actions. He later admitted to his father that as he had fired the first shot, he was therefore the first aggressor. So in the end, nothing was done.

The fresh breezes that carried the *Frederickssteen* towards Malta and the 'unwearied attention' of Dr Stewart were not enough to aid Beaufort's recovery. Infection set in in the wound and Beaufort relinquished his command to Lieutenant Gammon. Fearing the worst, he wrote his will which he sent to his 'dear and excellent friend' Lestock Wilson. Although he had 'the strongest dependence and assurance upon the Almighty and Merciful',[57] he strongly believed that it was Divine punishment for his 'many sins' – not least the night in the brothel in Smyrna. He begged that Wilson should tell his fiancée Alicia of his wounds gently, and that he should visit Ireland to 'impart the fatal intelligence to my dear and excellent friends'. He ended his letter with 'may we meet again if not here, hereafter'. In his will, everything connected with the survey was to go to Thomas Hurd, Hydrographer to the Navy, at the Admiralty, while his library and a small pocket telescope he bequeathed to Alicia, with specific requests for his other instruments to be divided amongst other members of the Wilson, Beaufort, and Edgeworth families.

But in Malta, Beaufort made a swift recovery and was soon hobbling around on crutches. Orders came for him to return to England with a convoy. He arrived in mid-October and the *Frederickssteen* was paid off and immediately condemned. Deeply sad, Beaufort brought her up the Thames to Deptford to the breaker's yard with his faithful ship's company. There he ended his sea-going career, just five miles up-river from Gravesend where it began, 23 eventful years before.

CHAPTER 10

Captain Beaufort RN, Retired

FROM WHERE LESTOCK and Bonne Wilson stood in the parish church of St Mary Le Bone, London, on the morning of 3 December 1812, they looked a well-matched couple. To the left stood their daughter, Alicia Magdalena, still with 'her good, though very delicate figure', which perfectly suited the straight lines of the high-waisted dress of real Brussels lace over white satin with its pelisse of white satin trimmed with swansdown. Her light brown hair fell loose under a cottage bonnet of Brussels lace with two ostrich feathers at the back. Beside, and marginally above her, Francis Beaufort stood in the full number one dress uniform of a post captain: a coat of dark blue cloth with two gold epaulettes, a profusion of gold lace and white facings taut across his narrow back, nankeen breeches and silk stockings barely filled out by

his spindly legs, and silver buckled shoes. One hand rested
lightly on the lion pommel of his sword, the other more
heavily on a silver-topped cane. But the visiting officiating
minister, the Reverend John Maddy, had a different picture
once Alicia's deep lace veil had been removed. He looked into
her face, not pretty with her heavy features, but with a supreme
happiness that took on a beauty of its own. Beaufort was rather
more sombre. His prematurely white hair, tied back with a
black ribbon, had receded, making him look much older than
his 38 years. The vestiges of his nut-brown complexion from
his years in the sun were highlighted by pale smile lines. But it
was his piercing blue eyes that enlivened his bony face and
gave him the appearance of an alert and inquisitive bird.

When the marriage service – duly witnessed by Lestock and
Bonne Wilson – was over, the little wedding party (that also

The Parish Church of St Mary le Bone in Middlesex.

included the Griffiths, friends of Beaufort's mother), repaired around the corner to 31 Harley Street. Beaufort and his bride did not even wait for the wedding breakfast, for as soon as her 'travelling dress had been put on'[1] they were off to Lestock Wilson's other house, the Grove in Epping for their honeymoon. And there began their marriage of unqualified happiness that was to last up to her death nearly 23 years later.

The idea was that Beaufort and his new wife would return to London to stay with the Wilsons, and 'when they would be prevailed upon to let them go', he would take Alicia to introduce her to his friends and relations in Ireland. But it was not his parents-in-law that delayed the visit to Collon for a year but his work. For the next two years, he worked solidly on the charts and his book, *Karamania*, the former by day, the latter by night. He was as punctilious in his approach as he was painstaking in his execution of both. Although he had worked on the survey on a series of plotting sheets while the *Fredericksteen* went along the Turkish coast, for his final charts he began again from the very beginning with his own and his officers' original survey books, notes and sketches. It was exacting work. Often, if the coastline was particularly important or intricate, he would draw it in a larger scale, then reduce it to fit in with the general survey using a scale of two miles to the inch – this was done by drawing up squares on both surveys to scales, then transferring the detail by eye, square by square.

Much as he liked his parents-in-law, Beaufort played 'box and cox' with them between Harley Street and the Grove – when he and Alicia were at one, his in-laws were at the other. The arrangement suited Beaufort supremely well. The ignominy of not owning a home and providing for his wife was more than offset by the money he saved. The Wilson's two homes were comfortable, commodious, and well run. Both houses were fully staffed at all times, and the well-stocked cellar was at Beaufort's disposal, although after his last wounding, he drank in moderation for the rest of his life. He paid for nothing for the full ten years while his father-in-law was alive, and had all the space and peace for his work he needed at Epping, with a base in London for meetings and entertaining friends.

While the plotting and drawing of the survey was straightforward and merely time-consuming, Beaufort agonised over every word of *Karamania* – he even spent three months deciding on the title. He corresponded endlessly with his brother William over Greek and Latin inscriptions, discussing such matters as the finer points of Ptolemy. He frequently met with Cockerell, going over his text and comparing notes. Beaufort also badgered another classical scholar, the Reverend George Renouard, chaplain to the British Factory at Smyrna, who was also fluent in Turkish and had accompanied Beaufort for parts of the voyage. The help of other travellers was sought, notably Edward Clarke who knew parts of the coast and his friend Major James Rennell, former surveyor-general of Bengal. The French linguist Alexandre Zhary was consulted at length for translations of Arabic script. Every place name, its correct spelling, and attribution, and every translation was scrutinised, changed, and more often than not, changed back to the original. With the screeds of notes and translations from his brother William, and the proofreading by his father, *Karamania* developed into such a family work that they called it 'the Collon Committee'. Beaufort spent most of his time in Epping, content in his rigid routine of intense work, but his voluminous correspondence at least kept him in touch with the geographers and scholars of the day. But after several extracts of *Karamania* appeared in the *St James's Chronicle*, Beaufort was instantly recognised as the leading authority on Asia Minor. The result was that instead of consulting the scholars, it was they who came to him.

While his work was progressing at the speed of a Japanese Noh play, Beaufort's domestic life was changing. He was certainly not in love with Alicia when he proposed to her, but looked to her for material comfort and companionship on his return from Turkey. He saw her as an heiress, lamenting in a letter to his father that Lestock Wilson, although rich enough, had five children and was 'too English' to do much for an 'Irish Fortune Hunter', save come up with the promised dowry. But after Beaufort and Alicia were married and had settled down, he simply worshipped her throughout her life, and even more after her death. He delighted in her company, and could not bear to be parted from her.

Alicia was already six months pregnant when they made their long-awaited visit to Ireland where they were fêted by family and friends at Collon and Edgeworthstown. There were a few material changes in the four years Beaufort had been away, but the most remarkable was Dr Beaufort's ambitious scheme to rebuild Collon church in the style of King's College Chapel Cambridge, complete with fan vaulted ceilings. When Beaufort heard of the scheme during his refit in Malta, he immediately wrote to his father that had he known sooner, he could have brought back 'any number of marble columns' – so much for his high moral stand on the looting of antiquities.

At Edgeworthstown, Beaufort was reunited with his old friend and mentor Richard Lovell Edgeworth who delighted in showing him a letter from Sir Joseph Banks, President of the Royal Society. Edgeworth had sounded him out on the possibility of Beaufort being elected a member, to which Banks replied that 'no further recommendation can be wanted' by any candidate put up by him, and for someone of Captain Beaufort's standing, whose 'exertions in improving sincere and useful knowledge while employed in HM service are well known to the Royal Society',[2] little could 'stand in his way to election'. So with

Edgeworth to propose him, seconded by Dr Brinkley, the First Astronomer Royal of Ireland, and a Dr Barne, Beaufort's name went forward. He was in fact elected unanimously on 30 June 1814, 'with no black bean in the no box', and gazetted in November. Priggishly he told his father how an eminent Doctor of Divinity who came after him was blackballed 48 to 13.

On their way home to Epping in the New Year, the Beauforts made an emergency stop at the George Hotel in Woburn, where, on 10 February 1814, Alicia gave birth prematurely to a boy. The sickly baby was christened immediately – predictably Daniel Augustus – but before they had returned home, he had turned bright red with erysipelas. He recovered some months later to his parent's obvious relief. Added to that worry, Dr Beaufort, too ashamed to confess to his son during his visit, wrote to say that his finances were 'in bad shape'. Part of his problem was that some of his own money had been inadvertently siphoned off for the new church – on one occasion, he had asked the carpenter to go into the triple pulpit and say something so that he could test the acoustics. The carpenter climbed the stairs to the top and, hands on lectern, shouted, 'When are you going to pay me, Dr Beaufort?' Although that money was eventually made good, Dr Beaufort was still out of pocket in the building of the church, while the severe weather and severer economic climate left him with £600 of his tithe income in arrears. Added to that were various unwise investments, litigation and sundry debts which made his 'head giddy at the thought of the sheriff arriving to proclaim him to all the world a bankrupt'. Dr Beaufort, in his son's eyes, could still do no wrong. Beaufort arranged a loan of £3,000 from Lestock Wilson against a small estate belonging to William, but inevitably it was Beaufort who paid the interest charges. Beaufort needed every penny he could lay his hands on, particularly after the birth of his second child in 1815. They had hoped for a girl so that she could be called 'Anatolia' or 'Karamania', but it was a boy who was christened Francis Lestock.

The glorious day came on 27 April 1815 when Beaufort decided that his charts were as perfect as he could possibly make them, and the '12 charts, 24 plans and 26 views to which are added several other charts and plans in the Levant' landed on the First Secretary's desk at the Admiralty in a large folio. In all, there were 48 separate items. Using the Mercator projection (where the lines of longitude and latitude are drawn at right angles) Beaufort's survey consisted of eleven sheets of varying sizes. These were further condensed into six sheets using a scale of two miles to an inch. The index (shown on the end papers) drawn to the scale of 20 miles to the inch is a masterpiece of draughtsmanship. There were also separate sheets for harbours, anchorages and antiquarian sites. Normally, there would have been many more topographical sketches, but the *Frederickssteen* had hugged the coastline for most of the way so she was rarely far out enough at sea to record individual views properly. Beaufort's draughtsmanship was superb, and it did not take a skilled eye to actually 'see' the coast, with its cliffs and mountains behind. These were shown with his own form of hatching, beautifully executed, to represent the various inclinations of each elevation. Although he used contour lines to connect soundings of equal depth, mysteriously he failed to apply the same principal to elevations, as is the practice today.

An explanatory memoir written by Beaufort accompanied the charts. This was a set of comprehensive instructions and sailing directions with every fact that a mariner could possibly need in those waters. There were details of every anchorage, harbour, shoal and reef. There was an account of streams with good water and the availability of wood, in fact everything, right down to the temperament of the locals along the coast. The memoir also showed how he had fixed the whole survey on just three points –

Makry, Cape Avova and Anamour (Anamur). He explained how the longitude of each place had been determined by either observing Jupiter's satellites or the eclipse of the moon, and then was checked against the chronometers, while the longitude was deduced 'with an excellent circle of Troughton's',[3] The memoir was sent to his father asking that he 'criticise it largely and freely, particularly the Introduction,' which he intended 'should be the model of hydrographical prefaces'.[4]

Two days after the charts were delivered, Beaufort received an acknowledgement from the First Secretary to the Admiralty, John Wilson Croker. Croker had been commanded by the Lords Commissioners to say that 'on the slight inspection their lord-ships have been able to make, they were highly pleased'[5] with his work. Then came the news that Beaufort was not expecting. 'I am also happy to acquaint you,' Croker continued, 'that my Lords have given directions for your full pay being continued up to the date of your letter and the completion of your survey.'[6] Beaufort was outraged. In a fit of pique, he replied that while he was grateful for their lordships' approbation, he did think that he deserved better. He pointed out that he was 'Senior Naval Officer in the Archipelago', a potentially lucrative appointment, yet he 'instantly complied with their lordships' orders without murmur or stipulation'. He had carried out a survey that he considered was 'extra professional', one that was 'unusually confined to those who offer their services' specifically for it. Brazenly, he told their lordships that Captains engaged in survey work should receive at least two guineas a day extra, although at that date there was no precedent for it.

Under the circumstances, the Admiralty had treated Beaufort with great fairness considering what he later described as his 'bullying' tactics towards them. It was pointed out to him that the full pay was not a reward, but normal recompense for a Captain still on active service. Also, that serving officers go where they are ordered, and that included surveying and exploration duties. But it was still not good enough for Beaufort, who replied to Croker, 'In short sir, unless their lordships should be pleased to confer on me some recompense that would throw a lustre on my work and such as would not degrade me in the eyes of many other officers, I must beg permission to decline any further reward than their Lordships' gracious approbation and the proud consciousness of having contributed to the credit and resources of my country.' He was told that he could claim his out of pocket expenses as their 'Lordships never intended that you should defray them at your private cost'. Beaufort fired a parting shot at the Admiralty writing that he only hoped that his survey would prove as beneficial to the Service as 'it had been unproductive to me'. Richard Lovell Edgeworth was horrified at Beaufort's stance, thinking that he had taken his principles too far, particularly when he could ill-afford them.

Throughout his life, Beaufort was beset with endless loss-making schemes, partially brought about by his inability to deny anybody, particularly his family, any favour. His father persuaded him to bring over the library of a long-dead great uncle, Baron Louis de Beaufort, from Maastricht to sell in London. He had taken advice from an associate of Roland Hunter, his publisher, who advised him that the timing was right and the library would do well at the auctioneers, Leigh and Sotheby. The scheme was fated from the start. The transport costs, the duty of 14d a pound and a market flooded with continental volumes all conspired to leave a shortfall. Beaufort blamed himself, thinking that he should have been more selective in what was sold, and so picked up the balance himself. Against his better judgement, his father led him into another ill-fated scheme. Dr Beaufort asked his son to arrange for the publication of a silly novel written by a friend of his, a Miss Ennis. Beaufort went to his publisher (Hunter also published Maria Edgeworth). He knew that the

novel was perfectly dreadful, and when predictably it failed, he
ended up by picking up the cost of £124. It was a great deal of
money to come out of a Captain's half-pay.

Despite Beaufort's petulant dealings with the Admiralty,
Croker and their Lordships seemed well disposed towards him.
Croker wrote saying how sorry they all were that he was
dissatisfied with their offer of full pay, but accepted his reason-
ing. They offered to publish *Karamania* if he wished, but 'if you
wish to publish an account of the survey yourself,' Croker told
him, 'the Board can have no objection.'[7] They were also willing
to engrave the charts and illustrations, an offer Beaufort also
refused. The First Lord of the Admiralty Lord Melville, nephew
of Beaufort's old adversary, had also directed Croker to sound
Beaufort out on conducting a survey of the whole coast of
Ireland, as the present one was 'not to be depended upon'.
Acknowledging his talents, coupled with the fact that he was the
son of the maker of 'the first good map of Ireland ever made',[8]
they were keen to put his name forward for the commission.
Beaufort was naturally flattered at the offer, and considered it
long and hard. The survey would give him at least ten years of
gainful employment and in Ireland, the country of his family
and friends.

But Beaufort knew from the start that the proposed survey
was a waste of time, and as such it was certainly not for him.
Months later, he met with Croker to discuss the project. He told
him that there should be a land survey first, followed by the
marine survey, as was the case in England. He proposed that 'a
series of well-defined triangles, spreading from a base line in the
centre of the country towards its circumference would be laid
down in much less time and an infinitely greater number of
standard points would be fixed and with indisputable accuracy'.[9]
That way round, the marine survey would tie in the many
standard points, fixed by triangulation as opposed to the vagaries

of time-consuming celestial observation. The trigonomical survey of England was nearly finished, and sooner rather than later a survey of Ireland would inevitably follow. 'If we were now to proceed with the hydrography of that island founded on astronomical observations,' Beaufort told Croker 'we should be overtaken in a few years.'[10] Beaufort was too professional and too honest to take it on. He finally wrote to Croker that he was discarding from his mind 'every idea of present and personal advantage' but was flattered that he had been asked.

The year before, March 1815, Beaufort had written to John Barrow, Second Secretary to the Admiralty and Secretary of the Chart Committee, offering his services, which were 'duly noted'. Offers of employment came in, like a survey of part of the coast of West Africa, but he turned them all down on the pretext of health, which was partially the truth. The bullet lodged in his lungs was causing him trouble, and he had been spitting blood with his regular coughing fits. But the real reason was that he had become enamoured with home life. A voyage to some unknown and unhealthy part of the world held little attraction compared to the delights of the Grove.

By the end of May 1816, the agonising was finally over and Beaufort handed over the completed *Karamania* to Roland Hunter, his publisher. As with his reward from the Admiralty for the charts, he took the moral high ground over the book. He declined all payment, donating any profit to his publisher on the grounds that the information was gathered at the public's expense, so the price of the book to the public should not be further loaded with the author's royalties. He also believed that by not being paid for his work, he would be esteemed 'higher in the eyes of the world, but particularly those of my profession, by not appearing to make a trade of authorship'. Once again, Edgeworth thought that he was taking scholarship to 'idiotic extreme'. In fact, Beaufort did not believe that his work would succeed and that the rewards would be so meagre that they were not worth having, although 'a larger sum might prove a temptation'. *Karamania*, however, was well received when it was published a year later.

The agonising had paid off, and Beaufort basked in the universal admiration. The Admiralty were particularly pleased with it; Charles Yorke and John Croker both wrote to Beaufort favourably; John Barrow even went so far as to write in his autobiography that *Karamania* was 'a book superior to any of its kind in whatever language, and one which passed triumphantly through the ordeal of criticism in every nation of Europe'.[11] Friends and acquaintances, the likes of Cockerell, Marsden and Sir John Brinkley gave their constructive criticism and praise. It was also well reviewed, particularly in *The Times*. 'The interest of which a subject so described is susceptible, will speak for itself to the classical reader; and we shall merely observe, that it loses nothing in the hands of the gallant officer.'[12] As a piece of early nineteenth-century travel writing it succeeded on every level. It was a lively account of an unknown land that delighted the general public for its descriptive narrative and geographical information. As the Earl of Guildford wrote to him, 'It is an admirable work and I think that it not improbable that it should not be read with delight by every kind of reader from a professor to a fine lady.'[13] So wide was its appeal that it went into a second edition the next year. As a learned work, it spawned several archaeological expeditions for further exploration in Asia Minor purely on the strength of his descriptions – so much so that *Karamania* was singularly responsible for the filling of museums throughout all of Europe with their antiquities.

Just when everything was going well for Beaufort professionally, a series of family tragedies brought him up sharply. His third son, Alfred, was born in January 1817 with a severe mental disorder and nearly blind. For a few years Beaufort and Alicia struggled to keep the boy (whom Beaufort uncharacteristically referred to as either 'the dog' or 'my little half-wit') at home, but eventually his care was too much for them and he was sent to an asylum just outside London. His mind never developed beyond that of a six-year-old, but Beaufort and his children were very fond of him, visiting him regularly until he died at the age of fifty-two.

Later that same year of the publication of *Karamania* Beaufort's mentor, friend and brother-in-law Richard Lovell Edgeworth died aged seventy-three. Although he had been ill for some months, Beaufort was nonetheless totally devastated at the news. He wrote to his 'poor, dear, afflicted sister' Fanny lamenting the death of his 'warmest and most anxious friend' to whom he owed 'the power of thinking'. 'Whatever improvement I have made in my mind,' he continued, 'must be ascribed to the impact he gave it. It was he who taught me that the true education begins with the resolution to improve, and it was he alone of all my friends who tried to wind me up to that resolution and to sustain it.'[14] Edgeworth not only had appointed Beaufort as the executor of his will, but also his literary executor with express instructions to assist Maria in the completion and editing of his autobiography. The third tragedy to hit Beaufort and Alicia was the massive stroke that crippled her father at the end of the year. Lestock Wilson, always bluff and hearty, and a major influence in Beaufort's life for nearly 30 years, had become a mindless vegetable. He survived another four tortuous years at the Grove, requiring constant attention. Death came as a merciful relief to them all, but with his death came a great upheaval to Beaufort and his 'lamentably-growing' family – Sophia was born in 1819 and Rosalind Elizabeth a year later, while William Morris, named after the captain of the *Phaeton*, came in 1823, with the 'afterthought' Emily Anne three years later. But hardly had

Lestock Wilson been buried, than his son requested that Beaufort and his sister quit the Grove and the house in Harley Street. And all that was on top of the death of his beloved father.

In financial terms, Dr Beaufort died not a minute too soon. When his creditors openly threatened to sue the year before, he left Collon 'with its greenhouses, its walled vegetable and fruit gardens and colourful beds of auriculars, pansies and gentians so long and lovingly tended by Mary Beaufort and her daughters'[15] to live with William in County Cork. After a series of disasters, not all of his own making, where he was 'deceived in every speculation which relied on honesty and honour', Dr Beaufort was about to be made bankrupt. His sons were unable to help him financially, and seriously considered shipping him off to France to escape his creditors. But he died on 17 May 1821 before the 'army of unpaid stonemasons' and other sundry creditors could get to him, creditors whom Beaufort eventually paid off himself over many years.

Beaufort had experienced many troughs in his life, but none was deeper than that year. After the success of *Karamania* and the execution of his charts, he believed that his career would take off, but nothing came of it. Alicia had written to her sister-in-law Fanny, 'I cannot bear that his fine talents, enterprising spirit and noble principles should be left in oblivion and inaction. His ambition, like his patriotism, is of the true sort, ardent yet chastened.'[16] Yet with the deaths of the three men, Edgeworth, Wilson and his father, on all of whom he had relied for advice and direction, Beaufort surprisingly emerged with a new vigour. He set about finding a house in London in the New Year and settled on 51 Manchester Street in the West End. It was a commodious house, with a decent drawing room with a bow front on the first floor, and enough bedrooms for his family and his two Edgeworth nephews whose education Fanny had entrusted to him. His gesture of economy was only to employ female staff.

As he wrote to his brother, Beaufort was living on £700 a year made up of his half-pay, pension for his wounds, and the income of his marriage settlement. This was supplemented by a few directorships of various utility companies, such as the United Gas Company, based in the City of London, but these consumed more of his time than he gained in remuneration. Other ventures he tried were typically doomed to failure through lack of judgement or plain bad luck, usually both. His investment in an Irish slate quarry was shortly followed by a building slump in Ireland, and the price of slate did not even cover the transport costs. He poured money into a revolutionary machine for refining sugar, but it never went into production. Worse, he persuaded members of his family to follow his advice and they too lost money. Typically, he made it up to them all as and when his finances allowed.

Throughout this time of financial hardship, there were many demands on Beaufort's income, yet he was as free with his money as he was with his time. When the wife of William's agent absconded with her lover and his tithe income to America, Beaufort sent him £50 on the proviso he told no one. School fees for the boys accounted for £100 a year, his mother and sister another £100. He was generous to a fault. Duncan Campbell, the Captain of Marines who accompanied him on the assault on the *San Joseph*, asked for £140 to emigrate to Cape Province. Beaufort wrote back immediately that he did not have the money but that he would have it by the time it was needed. Fortunately, Campbell raised the money elsewhere. Throughout his life, Beaufort was always busy, more often than not in the service of others. He gave his time freely. He cared for the needs of his friends and family, performing every imaginable service for them – from finding an asylum for the demented William Edgeworth to purchasing bee-keeping equipment for the Ruxtons, his sister Fanny's in-laws. After the death of Dr Beaufort, Maria Edgeworth used Beaufort as her agent when dealing with their publisher and he became the major critic of her work. But she implored him to 'spare himself the trouble of so fully illustrating and illuminating his observations. This is love's labours lost with me, for I assure you I am not attached to my errors and have no affection for my own sentences.'[17]

After years of waiting, Beaufort at last saw his opening when Captain Thomas Hurd, Hydrographer to the Navy, died – or if legend is to be believed, he walked out from where he was staying and was never seen again. The very next day, 30 April 1823, Beaufort wrote to Lord Melville: 'Some years ago I received a hint at the Admiralty that I was there considered an eligible person to succeed Captain Hurd in case of a vacancy in the Hydrographical Office. That vacancy having occurred, it became my duty to present myself immediately to Mr Croker in order to state that I was ready to accept the office if their Lordships should still consider me in the same favourable light.'[18] Ten days later Beaufort received a reply from Melville advising him that he could 'not hold out to you any expectation' to the post, as it was 'not intended to fill up that appointment for a considerable time'.[19] Despite Melville's peremptory refusal, Beaufort had been seriously considered for the post – Croker had replied tersely in his own hand to a Dr Young soliciting for an Army surveyor for the post: 'I am afraid that the Naval Service which includes such men as Beaufort, Parry, Lyon, Smith, etc. etc. would be justly disappointed if a Major Kates would be selected to be the Naval Hydrographer.'[20] Beaufort was greatly disappointed by his rejection, but typically pretended that his disappointment was for his friends and not himself. 'Being confined to an office,' he maintained, would be 'a heavy drag' around his neck.

Beaufort's rejection was political and largely of John Croker's making. Croker had the reputation that he was no friend of the Hydrographic Office, there being none 'holding so prominent a position' amongst its many detractors within the Admiralty. He had his own detractors, too. There was a rumour that Benjamin Disraeli later used him as the model for his character Rigsby in his novel *Corningsby*. He described him as 'a man who possessed in a very remarkable degree, a restless instinct for adroit baseness'. Croker had often clashed with Hurd, and was in no hurry to appoint a successor for repeat performances. He well knew of Beaufort's zeal and dedication, and could see that his appointment would inevitably lead to friction, however much he liked and admired him as a person. Croker saw the Hydrographic Office as an expensive waste of Admiralty resources and wished to restrict its activity. He frequently reminded the Board of the Admiralty that if ships could navigate without scientific charts before, 'why then should not the navy of the period, and posterity, do the same?'[21] Some six months later, Croker came up with what he thought was the solution to running down the activities of the Hydrographic Office – the appointment of Captain William Edward Parry.

Croker knew that 'Parry of the Arctic' had been selected to lead an expedition to search for the North West Passage while still remaining at the head of the list of prospective candidates for the post of Hydrographer to the Navy. At the end of November, Melville summoned Parry to the Admiralty and offered him 'first in a very handsome manner, the situation of Hydrographer, stating that the former Hydrographer had not fulfilled his duties of his station satisfactorily' and that he had kept the post open for him. The conversation then turned to the North West Passage, to which Parry immediately offered his services, not hesitating a moment 'in declining the other situation, and giving the preference to the more active employment'.

But as Parry wrote to his brother, 'Lord Melville said and done so handsomely about the Hydrographer's situation, insisting on keeping it open for me, even during an expedition, that I have literally accepted it.'[22] Under the circumstances, it was probably as well that Beaufort was not appointed Hydrographer at that time. Croker saw to it in Parry's absence that the Hydrographic Office became merely a depôt for issuing charts to the Fleet and, to this end, appointed Lieutenant Alexander Becher to catalogue and index the published charts and to unravel the mess left by Hurd. On Parry's return in 1826, the in-fighting within the Admiralty began all over again, particularly when he requested that Becher be retained to index the thousands of Remark Books sent in to the Admiralty over the years from which he wanted to prepare Sailing Directions for the Fleet. Croker sourly replied that the indexing was so much part of 'the Hydrographic Department work' that he saw no reason to retain Becher. Beaufort, with his mercurial temperament, was well out of it.

Whatever his reasons, Croker kept in touch with Beaufort. He wrote offering him the job of Inspector of the Greenwich Pensioners, but the offer was withdrawn when Beaufort failed to respond in time. Later Croker offered him a splendid commission – to make a study of the whole of the Gulf Stream. Beaufort was well suited to the task with his interest in tides. Ten years before, he had contributed to Major James Rennell's paper on the 'Florida Stream'. It was Rennell who suggested that he was just the man to conduct the new survey. Beaufort was delighted at the prospect, but typically thought that 'it should be placed in more skilful hands',[23] while at the same time detailing his plan of action using three vessels 'who should endeavour to keep on the edges and in the centre of the current' to make the survey. Again Beaufort turned Croker down. The thought of going back to sea and the rigours of the North Atlantic after an absence of sixteen years, leaving his growing family, adored wife and close friends was too much for a man in his early fifties. And it was a truly contented and loving home that he and Alicia had created in their house in Manchester Street.

Beaufort had come from a large, intellectual and sociable family, and he in turn was at pains to do the same for his own large family. He wrote inspiring letters weekly to his boys, Daniel Augustus and Francis Lestock, at Bedford School. When he was away, he wrote endearing letters to Alicia, the girls, and particularly 'little Morry' his favourite. During the school holidays, the children were always brought down to tea in the bow-fronted drawing room, whoever had been invited. Although it was quite noisy – there was a carriageway to a mews beyond underneath the room – it was well furnished. Some pieces had been bought at auction from the Grove, some inherited from Collon. When there were guests, the children were encouraged to converse with them, but on their own, there were family games and projects. One such exercise was keeping up to date a booklet entitled *Remarkable People Constantly at the House*. The cover is in Beaufort's own hand, but the entries are all written by his children. By modern standards, it sounds like the account of a conceited social climber, but it was kept at a time when lists were the norm and everything was recorded. This little booklet was solely for their own amusement. Moreover, this large and learned group of influential friends gives a valuable insight into Beaufort's life since leaving the Navy. By any standard, it is an impressive list, but for one who was totally self-taught in the midshipman's berth it is quite remarkable. What is more, having been entertained at his house *constantly* meant that they were friends rather than mere acquaintances.

Over the four years of the account, the guests fall into well-defined categories. There were, of course, the many Service friends of Beaufort's who had done well, including the likes of

Peter Heywood and Henry Foster who were gifted surveyors like
him. George Everest, surveyor general of India after whom the
mountain was named, and Major James Rennell were two more.
Others who remained close friends included Charles Cockerell,
soon to be celebrated as the architect of the Fitzwilliam Museum
in Cambridge. Another archaeologist was Edward Daniell. Not
all were from the world of science – Thomas Hofland the painter
and Thomas Bellamy the singer were frequent visitors. But the
majority of his friends came through Beaufort's fellowship of the
Royal Society where he had taken a very active part in its affairs
and served on the Council. He had made a particular friend of
the president, the great chemist Sir Humphrey Davy as well as
his successor Davies Gilbert. Also on the list was one of the
secretaries, Dr Peter Mark Roget, physician, and later compiler
of a *Thesaurus of English Words and Phrases* that went into 28
editions in his lifetime, and the chemist and physicist William
Wollaston, a past secretary.

Throughout his life, Beaufort was seen as a man who could
always be relied upon, who never refused any offer of service or to
serve on a committee. Consequently, there were ceaseless
demands on his time and expertise. When the Royal Society
needed someone to inspect their estates and properties, it was
Beaufort who was appointed. When the post of Secretary became
vacant, it was Beaufort they offered it to. He was greatly flattered
and thought it a great honour, but realised that he could not
afford the time that the job would demand and so turned it down.
He wrote to his brother with false modesty that he did not feel he
was up to the post, although he knew he was better qualified than
some of the former secretaries. He also hinted that the meagre
salary of £100 was not the reason to decline the offer, as money
was not what philosophy was about and 'science was not a trade'.

While the money was obviously a consideration, the real
reason he declined was that he was about to cross swords with the

newly elected president Davies Gilbert. While serving on the Council, Beaufort was invited by the astronomers James South and John Herschel together with the mathematician Charles Babbage (all on 'the list') to join a committee to look into 'the best means of limiting the membership of the Royal Society'. During the long and benign presidency of Sir Humphrey Davy, virtually everyone proposed for membership of the Royal Society was elected. Consequently, the membership was predominated by those whom Beaufort described as 'dunces' with 'venal motives' to 'increase their professional practice, or give *éclat* to some silly book by the imposing appendage to their names of FRS'.[24] These members, at best with an old-fashioned Enlightenment view of science, dominated the Society at the expense of the true scientists. Beaufort drafted the proposal to limit the membership to four true scientists a year, but Gilbert saw that the motion was defeated. Beaufort was furious, and when Gilbert asked him to continue on the Council he refused, his seat being taken by Sir John Franklin. The debacle at the Royal Society put Beaufort firmly in the camp of the 'Cambridge Network' of these scientists and mathematicians, the likes of Babbage, Peacock, Herschel and Airy, a relationship that was to develop to their mutual benefit over the years.

The astronomers on the list of *Remarkable People* naturally included *confrères* from the Royal Society, South, Herschel, Airy and Baily, and much later William Jacob, who, from his observatory in India catalogued 244 double stars and corrected 317 stars from the *British Association Catalogue*. Beaufort had been an ardent astronomer since his time with Dr Ussher in Dublin as a boy, and its fascination had only increased while he was at sea. When he came ashore, James South gave him free rein in his own observatory in London. It was a measure of the depth of his astronomical knowledge that Bishop John Brinkley, the first Astronomer Royal of Ireland, corresponded with him over many years on the complex question of the double parallax of áLyrae that Brinkley claimed to have discovered.

The final group that were *Constantly at the House*, apart from the titled folk who peppered the account, were the eminent polar explorers, amongst them Sir James Clark Ross, Sir John Franklin, George Lyon and Sir William Parry, all scientists to a man. There is no direct evidence of Beaufort's involvement in the three Arctic expeditions other than his undoubted friendship with their captains, but there are frequent references to summonses by Croker to the Admiralty that exactly coincide with the planning meetings of the expeditions. The Admiralty and the Royal Society worked closely together, both with the common goals of geographic and scientific exploration. Beaufort, at that time the key member of the Meteorological Committee of the Royal Society, had to be the link between the two.

The first of the four voyages of discovery in search of the North West Passage in the 1820s was led by William Edward Parry. Beaufort had written to him twice before he left 'on the subject of the barometer'[25] and its diurnal (daily) variation. Parry replied to his friend from his ship, HMS *Hecla* in the Davis Straits (between Greenland and Baffin Island) that he found his readings 'as curious as it was new that there was only one rise and one fall of the barometer in the 24 hours'. He promised to read the barometer twice daily, four times 'in the winter where there is less to employ and distract the attention of us all'. On his return, he gave Beaufort screeds of his observations taken from 'the first barometer deserving the name'. Parry's orders were to proceed from the Davis Strait up through Lancaster Sound, then head south through Prince Regent Inlet to meet up with another of Beaufort's correspondents, Commander George Lyon aboard HMS *Gripper*. A letter found its way back from him in the Hudson Strait promising Beaufort that he too would take barometric readings, but the weather was against him and the expedition was abandoned after only five months.

On the other side of the Canadian Arctic, Sir John Franklin was having a comparatively easier time travelling overland from the United States, past Lake Athabasca and the Great Slave Lake, where he stopped for the winter of 1825 at what is now Fort Franklin. He too corresponded at length with Beaufort, who sent him news and journals and requests for meteorological data. Franklin, referring to him as 'My dear Friend', described his frozen existence and lamented that his barometers had been broken. What he did manage to supply, however, was an account of the effect of atmospheric changes on a compass needle. Franklin noted that an easterly gale 'produced an increase of variation as shown by the needle which was placed on the Magnetic Meridian' and that it returned to its original position when the wind subsided or changed direction. Franklin put this down, rightly, to 'the state of electricity in the atmosphere being changed', a state that probably accounted for the easterly gale as well. Franklin's plan was to travel down the Mackenzie River to what is now the Beaufort Sea, and journey west to where he would hopefully join up with Captain Frederick William Beechey who, in Beaufort's old command HMS *Blossom*, had sailed round Cape Horn, and up through the Pacific to the Bering Straits. They missed each other by just 160 miles as the winter, the ice and the weather forced them away in opposite directions.

After Parry's return to the Hydrographic Office in 1826, the Admiralty was approached by the Royal Society with the idea of a scientific world cruise. The Royal Society Committee under the chairmanship of their President, Sir Humphrey Davy, had eight members that included Beaufort – again he was an obvious choice with his interests and strong ties with the Admiralty. A number of scientists and scientifically minded naval officers were canvassed by the committee and it was decided that the expedition should first observe longitude at salient points, then take 'more observations for the length of a second pendulum so that a true Figure of the Earth might be finally established'[26] (to determine the ellipticity of the Earth). In addition, they were to research 'the laws of the variation of gravity in different points on its surface', as well as the usual wind and current observations and measurements of tides and tidal streams. It was a commission that would so well have suited Beaufort himself, but his sea-going days were now long past and it was given to Commander Henry Foster of HMS *Chanticleer*. The expedition was ready by the spring of 1828, and in the months that followed, reams of scientific data filtered back from the South Atlantic to be assessed by the Admiralty and the Committee of the Royal Society. But three years later, Foster was drowned in a river in Panama, and with his death the Service lost a particularly gifted astronomer and scientist and Beaufort one of his closest friends.

At about the same time, another request that Beaufort could not refuse was made by Henry Brougham (later Lord Brougham and Vaux, the remarkable lawyer, educator, and philanthropist) to join his founding committee of the Society for the Diffusion of Useful Knowledge (SDUK). Its aim was to provide 'a mass readership with cheap but authoritative printed material',[27] that would fulfil the 'want of the better kind of artisans', especially 'the inferior workmen'.[28] With Beaufort's expertise, he was naturally nominated to oversee the production of the maps, a project that particularly appealed, and he applied himself to it with his usual excessive zeal. As cost was the essence of the operation, he and the map committee looked into ways of producing the maps as cheaply as possible. Beaufort suggested using lithography – reproducing from stone rather than copper engraving – but the general committee thought it 'inexpedient to sacrifice any of the beauty of the maps'.[29] In the end they thought, rightly as it turned out, that huge sales would keep down the unit cost. Beaufort typically gave his time for free. Family legend had it that the maps would have cost a shilling, but without the cost of a draughtsman they could be sold for sixpence. But the mathematics do not add up as no draughtsman would have been paid an average of £500 to prepare a map. Each sheet containing two maps was sold for one shilling. The maps could be collected singly, then bound into an atlas which Beaufort could see 'finding its way into every house in the Empire, and would not this be diffusing real tangible knowledge?'[30]

For the next fifteen years, Beaufort rose at 5 a.m. to work on the maps himself. The first of the series was of Southern Greece, both ancient and modern. The initial idea was for 60 maps to be produced over four years, but Beaufort spent so long perfecting each one that the project dragged on. Under his care and direction, they were often the most complete and up-to-date maps of their day – for the map of South Africa, Beaufort wrote to all the missionary societies to ask them to lend him 'their maps or other documents by which we might correctly place their stations'.[31] So accurate were they that no ship in the United States Navy went to sea without a complete set of SDUK maps. Sometimes he would delay publication for many months, as in the case of the map of Ireland, while he waited for the Ordinance Survey to be completed. He was incapable of compromising his high standards of excellence, which worried the General Committee when the long delays 'alienated sub-scribers and hurt sales'. Between 1829 and 1844, 106 double maps were produced, the vast majority drawn by Beaufort himself. More than 3 million individual maps, the equivalent of 15,000 complete atlases, were sold and constituted the major source of income for the Society.

Just when Beaufort was despairing that he could make no further contribution to society, and that he was not able to provide for his still young family adequately, fortune for once favoured him. Sir William Parry resigned as Hydrographer to the Navy on 12 May 1829. He was just 38 years old. Parry and the Hydrographic Office had prospered under the brief patronage of the Duke of Clarence during his tenure as Lord High Admiral, but he too was frustrated by the stranglehold of the administration orchestrated by Croker and resigned in 1828. So when Parry returned from his overland expedition to the North Pole from Spitzbergen he had found on his return that once again he had been relegated, as he put it, to 'a director of a Chart Depôt for the Admiralty rather than a guide and originator of Marine Surveys'. Thus it was not a hard decision for him to accept the offer of the Australian Agricultural Company 'to superintend the colonisation of a million of acres at Port Stevens, a little to the northward of Botany Bay'[32] at a salary of £2,000 per annum and a pension of £300 a year for life.

Beaufort had heard the rumour that the post was vacant again, but he bided his time. Two days later, Lord Melville summoned him to the Admiralty where Beaufort 'waited upon him' and, as he wrote to his brother William, Melville offered him 'the vacant office with a few kind words which were a great deal for a cold person like him. And I accepted at once.'[33] Nothing was ever straightforward with all of Beaufort's dealings with the Admiralty over money, and this time it was no different. He was offered £500 per annum, but Beaufort realised that by accepting a civil appointment, his half pay would be forfeited. Squaring up to Melville, he said, 'Now my Lord, I closed with your offer without hesitation because I never refused any service which it is possible for me to perform and if the appointment were but £50 a year I would work as zealously and cheerfully as if it were 500 – but I think to one who has made the sacrifices that I have etc. etc. that that order in Council which prohibits an officer receiving his $1/2$ pay who takes a civil office is most cruel.'[34] With Beaufort, his reported speech with powerful figures always tended to be exaggerated. However, Melville demurred and 'reasoned' that he 'should have a dispensating order'. Good as his word, the next day Beaufort received a short letter from Barrow: 'My Lords Commissioners of the Admiralty have been pleased to appoint you Hydrographer to this office',[35] his salary and his half-pay intact. Later, he was given a house, 7 Somerset Place, owned by the Admiralty, worth a further £300 a year.

Beaufort was naturally ecstatic at the appointment. At one stroke, he had solved all his money troubles – 'it will enable me to educate my children without robbing them,' he declared. At the age of fifty-five (the age when the Hydrographer retires today), he found himself 'absolutely at the head of a department, and that in a country which places its hydrographical department at the head of all others'.[36] It was a position that he had achieved by his own merit, 'without intrigue, or even asking'. In fact, the post had been offered to Beaufort's friend, Captain Peter Heywood but as he had turned it down he stated 'that Captain Beaufort was the fittest person to fill it'.[37] Barrow had no doubts on Beaufort's suitability either, declaring that 'we had little or no hesitation in assigning the palm to Captain Beaufort. It could not be otherwise.'[38] Nor did it take long for Barrow to find out just how right he was, for 'sometimes in history the right man fills the right post at the right time and no more perfect example could be found than the appointment of Francis Beaufort to be hydrographer'.[39]

CHAPTER 11

Captain Beaufort RN, Hydrographer to the Navy

N O SOONER HAD CAPTAIN FRANCIS BEAUFORT left Lord Melville, First Lord of the Admiralty, than he trotted along the passages to the back of the building and entered the rooms given over to the Hydrographic Department. He knew the way instinctively, having been there countless times over the years. Inside, it was a gloomy set of four rooms; the windows looking out on to a dingy passage, the skylight caked in dirt. As he entered the drawing office, the meagre staff stood up. He knew them all from old, particularly John Walker, who had been in the department since Alexander Dalrymple's day – it was he who had salvaged many of Dalrymple's chart plates that were being sold off for scrap copper that was to form the basis of the newly formed Hydrographic Office chart collection. As he had been with

Dalrymple and Hurd, Walker was now Beaufort's assistant hydrographer, and he introduced him to the other three draughtsmen – his third son Thomas, then William Higgins and John Tucker, before leading him through their office, with the huge tables strewn with half-drawn charts and broad shelves bulging with charts still to be worked on. Outside in the corridor, the two packers, Anderson and Nye, were boxing up charts for dispatch, there being no room for them to work anywhere else in the department. Beyond the two storerooms where the finished charts were kept, was the office of the three Naval Assistants. Lieutenant Alexander Becher, who had had a reprieve from Sir John Croker's vindictive cuts, introduced Beaufort to his two assistants, Lieutenants Barnett and Dessiou. Remark Books, some 80 years old, were piled like stalagmites everywhere – on the floor, the chart chests and the run of tables down the centre of the room where the three of them 'digested the information communicated in them sent home by every ship in commission'.[1] At last Beaufort made it to his own room. It was a good size with a high ceiling and, although there were no windows, it was filled with natural light from a belvedere immediately above his desk and drawing table. As he sat at his desk for the first time, he allowed himself a moment of self-satisfaction as he glanced at the Letters Out Book on his desk, open at the last entry. It was a circular stating: 'Captain Beaufort having been appointed to succeed me as Hydrographer to the Admiralty, I request you will in future address to that officer all communications usually made to the Hydrographer, I am etc. E W Parry Captain RN.'[2] Little did he realise then that he was about to spend a very large part of the next 26 years of his life in that very room.

As was by now his manner, Beaufort was soberly dressed in a black frock coat, velvet waistcoat and tight trousers. Inside the coat was a pocket specially made to fit the same type of

Morocco leather diary that he kept every year for the last 50 years of his life. That morning, Beaufort opened his diary and, in his small, neat and precise hand, wrote, on the page of 12 May 1829, in the purple ink that he kept for special occasions: 'Took possession of my new Hydrographer's room. May it be a new era of industrious and zealous efforts to do my duty with sincerity, impartiality and suavity . . . not for worldly motives but from a sense of a far higher duty I owe to that Providence who placed me in this vocation.'[3]

Always a creature of habit, Beaufort began the next day as he would for the rest of his working life. He rose at 5 o'clock in the morning, shaved himself, dressed, then worked on the SDUK maps until breakfast (after 1844, this period was spent on correspondence). He then walked, whatever the weather, on the same route to the Admiralty, arriving precisely at 9 o'clock. He carried a little portmanteau with his own writing paper, pens and sealing wax for his personal correspondence – the seal on his watch chain bore the cipher of the Beaufort crest. Sitting at his desk that first working day, Beaufort took stock of his situation. Parry was underestimating his position when he said that he was a mere 'director of a chart depôt', for although a large part of the Hydrographic Department's operation was 'issuing sets of charts to every ship and receiving back old sets'[4] there were at that time a dozen surveys in progress. Most of the surveyors were engaged in home waters – Mr Thomas in the *Investigator* was at Lerwick in the Shetland Islands, Captain White in Jersey, with Commander Mudge surveying the approaches to Dublin harbour and Lieutenant Slater in the *Blyth* working near Newcastle – others were far flung around the world. Commander Copeland in the *Mastiff* was fitting out in Malta ready for the Greek Archipelago, Commander Bayfield was in the St Lawrence River as far as Quebec while Commander Henry Boteler was surveying off Sierra Leone in HMS *Hecla*. Farthest away was Commander

King in HMS *Adventure* off Montevideo, waters that Beaufort knew well. He scanned the list of charts in Becher's index, with the works of Cook in New Zealand, Beechey in America, Owen in Africa, Flinders in Australia, King in South America, Smyth in the Mediterranean (and of course his own in Southern Turkey), but if all 883 existing charts were plotted on a map of the world, it would have been littered with what he termed 'woeful blank spaces'. Their accuracy was questionable too, 'there being scarcely what could be termed a correct chart of any portion of the globe in existence'.[5] Apart from the English Channel, even the home waters were inadequately charted. Beaufort could see the daunting task ahead of him, but knew that with his administrative skill, dedication, and the current team he could accomplish a very great deal. More important, he had the advantage of taking office at exactly the right time.

After the final defeat of Napoleon, the Fleet was drastically reduced – between 1814 and 1820, more than 550 ships were scrapped, leaving only 127 sea-going vessels. 'To what purpose could a portion of our naval force be, at any time,' wrote John Barrow in 1816, 'but more especially in time of profound peace, more honourably or more usefully employed than in completing those details of geographical and hydrographical science of which the grand outlines have been boldly and broadly sketched by Cook, Vancouver and Flinders and others of our countrymen?'[6] But that was just Barrow's personal view. However, within a year of Beaufort's appointment, Sir John Croker, that indefatigable opponent of the Hydrographic Department, resigned. Beaufort had inherited what was still 'a hybrid institution, the one branch of it inviting as it were the opposition of the civil element at Whitehall, the other calculated to encounter the ill-will of authorities afloat'.[7] The position improved when the Admiralty decided to form a Scientific Branch, made up of the Hydrographic Department, the Royal Observatory at

Greenwich and the Cape Observatory, the Nautical Almanac and the Chronometer Offices at Devonport and Portsmouth. Although ultimately responsible to the First Lord, for the first time the Hydrographer acted independently of the Admiralty Board and was responsible for its estimates – Beaufort's first return was a mere £9,746 for 1831. As head of his own department, it was left to Beaufort alone to decide which part of the world should be surveyed, by whom, and for how long.

His decision was initially influenced, however, by defence and the needs of the Royal Navy. By the 1840s, for example, the Opium Wars prompted the charting of China, French activity in the Pacific and the claiming of a part of New Zealand incited a survey there. But equally important were the needs of the Industrial Revolution, the expansion of British trade and necessity to secure overseas markets. For this, 'passages to existing markets had to be made safe, and routes opened up to navigation in fresh areas of trade';[8] and, with the import of raw materials, it meant that the 'surveyor and the merchant went hand in hand'. It was a period of great change, the like of which had not been seen before. At sea, the merchant fleet was expanding rapidly, iron ships were being built and propelled by steam. Britain's Maritime Empire was expanding. Safe and accurate charts were needed more than ever. And so under Beaufort's leadership of an independent body, it was inevitable that the Hydrographical Department (or just the Hydrographic Office as it became known after 1839) expanded and grew in stature to meet those vital needs.

Of all Beaufort's multifarious functions as Hydrographer to the Navy, his principal duty was, of course, to direct and examine 'the construction of new charts of all parts of the world'.[9] In his 26 years in office, he produced 1437 charts in 113 separate surveys – an average of more than one a week. But the road to the finished chart was long, often dangerous, and required his constant attention at every single stage. In the main, the exact location for a proposed survey was decided by Beaufort himself. Sometimes a directive came through Sir John Barrow, at other times a specific request for a survey came from an individual, such as Sir James Brooke, the White Raja of Sarawak, who pointed out the need to chart Sarawak and Borneo for its 'commercial and strategic importance', or the legislative bodies of Nova Scotia and New Brunswick who claimed that the charting of their coasts 'was long overdue'. When the Gold Rush hit Australia in 1851, charts were needed and surveys ordered of the eastern approaches with its islands and reefs to guide the spate of ships that sailed from Great Britain and California.

In the past, Beaufort had been the conduit between the Royal Society and other scientific bodies and the Admiralty, but in his new position as Hydrographer he consulted – or indeed was consulted by – the Council officially. He held a unique position, for often he himself was serving on the very body that was lobbying the Admiralty for some scientific research project. What is more, he was in a position to deliver, as he directed his surveying officers to 'observe, record, and collect' for every branch of known science, including geodesy, meteorology, oceanography, astronomy, geology and geography, as well as zoology and botany, even anthropology. The input of these various scientific bodies (mostly the Royal Society and the Royal Geographical Society) to a given survey varied from requesting some specialist data to a whole new area of research, as with, say, the tides in the North Sea. As the gathering of this data was entirely at the expense of the Admiralty, it made them the principal backers of British science at that time, and Beaufort 'the authorised organ of scientific communication in England'[10] – the Army's research was limited, and the universities only funded their own in-house projects of pure science. With the aims of the proposed project in mind, Beaufort then assigned the most apposite of his surveying officers to a suitable ship given over to his department. He then went to the Board of the Admiralty for them to agree the survey, and to commission the officers and the ship. With the rare exception, (his request for a fast frigate for tidal observations in the North Atlantic was refused on the grounds that it would cost £10,000) his proposal was invariably ratified.

Weeks of planning followed. Beaufort took immeasurable care and trouble over his officers and the vessels in his service, and before each voyage, the ship was refitted and supplied to his exacting specification. Everything to do with the survey went through the Hydrographic Office (which meant Beaufort himself), including the issue of chronometers and all instruments, even the supply of stationery right down to '2 pieces of India rubber and 1 lb. of sealing wax'.[11] He sent each captain detailed orders for his proposed survey, and the copy was entered in the Hydrographic Office Minute Book. One such example amongst scores of orders is that dated 3 November 1834 for Lieutenant William Arlett to survey the Canary Islands and the West Coast of Africa. Arlett had distinguished himself commanding the cutter *Raven*, the tender to HMS *Etna* under Captain Skyring, who 'was foully murdered by the natives at Caches River near Cape Roxo,'[12] Gambia, while conducting a survey of the coast of West Africa – the place is still called Murder Bay. Arlett returned to England with both ships, and was rewarded by Beaufort with the command of the *Etna* and the order to resume the survey.

In compiling surveyor's orders, Beaufort spent weeks pouring over existing charts and examining the Remark Books of the area. The general orders for Arlett were straightforward enough, but were amplified by more detailed hydrographic instructions. 'You are hereby directed and required to take the *Raven* [commanded by Lt Hilliard] under your orders,' they began, 'and when that vessel and the *Etna* are in all respects ready, you are to put to sea . . .'[13] He was required to identify a shoal 'called the Eight Stones' off Madeira, then put in there to rectify the chronometers, or to push on to Tenerife to 'devote 5 or 6 days to the settlement of their rate at the Lanzarotte'. The fixing of the survey naturally depended on the accuracy of the chronometers and, throughout the directions, Arlett was repeatedly ordered into Santa Cruz, Tangier or Gibraltar to check them.

It would appear that Beaufort on this occasion had not involved the Foreign Office as was usual in more sensitive political waters, for Arlett was merely told to obtain the consent of the Governor of the Canary Islands 'to gain free access to any or to all the Canary Islands as points to be used for triangulation along the coast' and to notify him of the proposed survey of 'the north coast of Africa to the north of Bajador' in the Spanish Sahara, right up to Cape Spartel by the Straits of Gibraltar. Arlett was also to be 'most careful to consolidate not only the authorities, but also the inhabitants and especially the fishermen who seem from a distinct tribe who may be of instable service to the survey in pointing out banks and dangers'. After surveying the Canary Islands, he was to proceed to the mainland, but was ordered to 'have no communication with it except in cases where the operations of the survey render it indispensable' because of the surf and 'the inhabitants who are Moors and are recognised as being particularly treacherous and savage'. He was told to 'correspond on all the details connected with the survey' and to send tracings back whenever convenient, and continue 'this service until it has been completed', then return immediately to Spithead.

The hydrographic instructions for Lieutenant Arlett, as indeed for every other survey, were an extension of the general instructions, but a great deal more detailed. They filled anything up to 20 pages in the Minute Book. Throughout all the instructions it can be seen that Beaufort knew exactly what was required of his surveyors, and he gave advice on how they could achieve it. For Arlett to determine 'the correct triangulation of the remarkable peaks on these Canary Islands' (without interfering with the prejudice of the islanders), Beaufort advised that he would 'have an excellent opportunity of measuring by sound and flash a long base, assuming the whole velocity of the latter being 1,170 feet per second. But to establish such a base satisfactorily, the mean must be taken of many observations made with great care and if possible under a variety of circumstances of the wind, weather, and state of the atmosphere.'[14]

Arlett's instructions continued. Views of the coast – detailed drawings made from the sea for 'the stranger recognising the land' – were required, as was the perpendicular height of all the hills and mountains with advice on how best to determine them. 'With respect to the nomenclature, the name that has been most generally adopted in the English charts should be retained.' He was against change and respected the right of other nations to name their own discoveries and colonies – in a letter to Captain Beechey he wrote, 'you place San Francisco in New Albion. Is it not a Spanish settlement? Have not the Spaniards a right to call their colonies what name they please: do not they call it Neuva California?'[15]

As in Southern Turkey, Beaufort was a purist on nomenclature. Although he held that the 'name stamped on a place by the first discoverer should be held sacred by the common consent of all nations', he urged his captains to adopt a name that would 'convey some idea of the sense of the place, or some allusion to the inhabitants, or better still to adopt the native appellation, than to exhaust the catalogue of public characters and private friends'.[16] But for most surveying captains, the naming of their discoveries after some influential person who could advance their careers was too good an opportunity to miss. In the gazetteers, there are dozens of entries for Melville, Barrow, Peel,

Croker, and of course Beaufort, as in the Beaufort Islands in the Antarctic and the Beaufort Sea in the Arctic. Fitzroy also named two bays in Chile after him. Beaufort did, however, change Captain Horatio Austin's 'Beaufort Land' to 'Queen's Land' it being 'too presumptuous to let a humble hydrographer's cog-nomen stand'.[17] Later, it became common practice for his surveyors to call any particularly adroit native guide or pilot 'Beaufort', and their descendants who kept the name can be found in many parts of the world today, particularly in China and Borneo.

For all of Beaufort's captains, it was obviously not enough merely to chart some home or foreign shore, nor did any of them expect to confine their duties to mere surveying. Beaufort required, and indeed received, every kind of scientific data from each voyage. 'The magnetic variation appears to be rather ambiguous along the whole interval of coast between Cape Spartel and Cape Bojador,' Arlett was informed, 'and it will be therefore one object of great importance to obtain the variation.' This, as with all other surveys, was to be duly recorded with a mass of other data. 'A minute examination' of tides was also required, 'including set, force and duration, their rise at springs and neaps, and the extent by which they are influenced by the periodic winds and sea currents.' These were to be 'punctiliously' recorded in a meteorological register devised by Beaufort, along with the recordings of the 'height of the barometer at 4 regular periods over 24 hours' in another column, beside details of the wind and weather in two more columns.

As with all other surveyors, Beaufort furnished Arlett his own wind scale and weather shorthand 'by which the force of the wind is to be assessed and certain abbreviations by which the weather may be described'. As Hydrographer to the Navy, he was in a position to revive his scale, by then marginally adapted, and to require that all his surveying captains use it. The first was

Commander Robert Fitzroy, who on his second voyage of the *Beagle* to South America received with his orders sheaves of specially printed paper to use as his meteorological register. In this register, designed by Beaufort, 'the state of the wind and weather will, of course, be inserted; but some intelligible scale should be assumed, to indicate the force of the former, instead of the ambiguous terms "fresh", "moderate", etc. in using which, no two people agree; and some concise method should also be employed for expressing the state of the weather.'[18] In fact, the Beaufort Scale had been used outside the Hydrographic Office by the whole of Admiral Sir George Cockburn's squadron in America and the West Indies where his officers found that it 'answered perfectly'.[19]

The final branches of science that Beaufort called for in his 'hydrographic instructions' were geology and natural history. With Arlett, he recognised that 'the heavy surf which beats upon the coast of West Africa' would prevent him landing, 'and therefore no collection of natural history or geological arrangements can be expected, although the medical officers of both the vessels will no doubt be anxious to contribute their share to the scientific character of the survey'.[20] While most surveys returned little or no naturalistic data, others produced a wealth of material, particularly through those who began their distinguished careers as surgeon naturalists aboard a survey vessel. One such was Thomas Huxley who served on the *Rattlesnake* as an assistant 'surgeon naturalist as a curtain-raiser to his life's work in marine biology'.[21] Another was Joseph Hooker, son of Sir William Hooker, the Director of Kew Gardens, whom Beaufort sent to the Antarctic and the Antipodes with James Clark Ross on the *Erebus*. The result was six volumes of the flora of Australia and New Zealand. Others had no medical knowledge, like the naturalist Edward Forbes who sailed with Thomas Graves on the *Beacon* in his survey of the Greek

Archipelago – when Commander Copeland commanded her, he took the 'classical traveller', Robert Pashley from Cambridge to help identify the classical sites.

But the best known of all the naturalists attached to a survey was Charles Darwin, who famously sailed with Fitzroy on his second voyage to South America in the *Beagle*. Fitzroy, who had already made extensive surveys of Patagonia, saw the advantage of having a trained naturalist on board and wrote to Beaufort asking if he could recommend anyone who would be prepared to accompany him without salary. Beaufort called on the 'Cambridge Network' and wrote to his friend and fellow astronomer Thomas Peacock, who in turn contacted the mineralogist John Stephen Henslow. 'An offer has been made to me to recommend a proper person to go out as naturalist to this [South American] expedition;' he wrote. 'He will be treated with every consideration. The Captain is a young man of very pleasing manners (a nephew of the Duke of Grafton), of great zeal in his profession, and who is highly spoken of. Is there any person whom you could recommend? He must be such a person who would do credit to our recommendation.'[22] Henslow came up with Charles Darwin, and Beaufort replied to Fitzroy that he had found a 'savant' for him, 'a Mr Darwin, grandson of the well known philosopher and poet'.[23] Fitzroy and Darwin took to each other on sight, but after the meetings they had with Beaufort, Darwin declared him 'too deep a fish' for him to make out. Whether he liked him or not, Beaufort arranging for him to sail on the *Beagle* led to one of the most revolutionary theories of the nineteenth century.

In a separate letter, Beaufort instructed Arlett to take 'the utmost care not to arouse suspicion' in assessing the 'native fortifications of the African tribes, the range commanded by its guns, and the supply of water etc.' together with an appraisal of where to land troops and 'field pieces required to attack any fortified place'. The information gathered in the course of his expedition was 'to be committed in a separate communication' to Lords Commissioners of the Admiralty. But whatever else the Hydrographic Office was under Beaufort, it is unlikely that it acted as a serious intelligence front, unlike under his successor, Captain John Washington, who effectively combined both operations.

Having completed the survey of the Canary Islands by March 1835, Lieutenant William Arlett spent the next five months charting the Moroccan coast between Cape Bojador and Cape Spartel, a distance of 750 miles. The *Etna* and the *Raven* then returned to Spithead. He had been away for inside of a year, a very short trip by comparison to some which lasted up to five or six years. Arlett complied with his instructions and handed over to Beaufort the account of his survey and his meteorological journal, together with 'the logs and sailing descriptions, with the nautical descriptions of the places confined within the lines of the survey, and clear directions of the ports and the dangers for seamen'. The fair charts – drawn up to Beaufort's directions to the scales of '1 inch to the nautical mile for its headlands and bays, and 3 inches to the mile wherever rock shoals or other intricate matters occur' – were delivered in early October 1835 to the Hydrographic Office. On receiving them, Beaufort congratulated Arlett on their quality and hoped that the success of the survey would ensure his promotion.

There was no one at the Admiralty who pushed harder for the promotion of his officers than Beaufort, nor fought for the extra pay (that he himself was denied) for surveying duties. News of promotion sometime came in a bizarre fashion, as with a Lieutenant Pullen of the *Plover* on the shores of the Great Slave Lake in Northern Canada. During an expedition searching for Sir John Franklin he was hailed by two Indians in a canoe bearing a letter from Beaufort, confirming his promotion as Commander.

To all his officers, Beaufort was 'a protective and fatherly figure'.[24] Throughout the whole of his time as Hydrographer he was fiercely loyal and protective of them all. Kind and thoughtful letters to every one of his surveying captains and their officers survive. They are filled with advice, encouragement and praise (conversely, he was not short on stinging censure when deserved). One example of his thoughtfulness amongst scores is the letter to Captain Copeland written shortly after taking up his appointment in Greece: 'Having severely felt the want of books relating to ancient geography when I was surveying the southern shores of Asia Minor,'[25] he began, then enclosed a copy of *A Description of Ancient Greece* by the Reverend J. A. Cramer, justifying the expense to the Admiralty as an 'aide to correct nomenclature'. He invariably passed on news of one voyage to another when he knew that officers had served together, or that some piece of information would be useful to them, both personal and professional – Captain Owen of the *Blossom* was sent details of the 'Sargasso Weed' found in an old Remark Book when Beaufort realised that he would pass close by the Sargasso Sea. Frequently, as in Arlett's instructions, Beaufort suggested that his department be used as a post office for forwarding mail to and from his surveyors.

Once Beaufort had made a professional and personal friend of an officer, he would stand by him whatever the cost. One such was Captain Edward Belcher. He was so unpopular with his officers that a midshipman once threw him overboard – 'How unfortunate it is,' wrote Charles Bethune, an officer who had served under Belcher, 'that such a capital fellow for work should be the devil incarnate with his officers'.[26] But Beaufort defended him against all odds in a public trial where his wife accused him of infecting her with venereal disease. Belcher wrote expressing his gratitude for his 'preserving kindness' adding 'to yourself, I look with the affection of a son'. Beaufort admired him greatly for his scientific and surveying skills, but such esteem did not save even him from a later rebuke. He was one of Beaufort's most prolific surveyors, charting the West Coast of Africa (before Arlett in the *Etna*), Central and North America, the Pacific, China, and the East Indies. A colourful character, his exploits read like a series of *Boy's Own* adventure stories – mediating between rival families in Portugal, rescuing ship-wrecked sailors from natives in Sarawak, becoming embroiled in the affairs of its 'White Rajah', James Brooke, storming Canton in the Opium Wars, and fighting pirates. On one occasion he was up the mast of a captured pirate junk taking bearings with his sextant while the ship burned below. But for Beaufort, these heroic deeds were interfering with the real purpose of the voyage, surveying: 'Your last letter is really all Hebrew to me:' he wrote, 'ransoms and dollars, queens; treaties and negotiations? What have I to do with these awful things; they far transcend my limited chart-making facilities however well suited they be to Admiralty Lords, to Commander in Chiefs, to Governors of Colonies and to you; and with them my very good friend you must arrange your diplomatic enterprises and then you must look for applause. That you have been doing good service to the country I will not deny, but the harvest that I look for at your hands does not stretch beyond the reach of a deep sea-line and all the credit I crave for you, and through you for myself, must be won in the Kingdoms of science and reaped in hydrographic fields. As I have no late drawings from you I have no critical remarks to offer.'[27] Later, he was to rebuke his surveying captains for asking permission to break off from a home survey for a few days leave to visit the Great Exhibition in 1851. Another captain was admonished for working on a Sunday, a day 'sacred to religion and rest'.[28]

As with all surveys, Arlett's charts joined the pile in Beaufort's office in line for his meticulous checking before handing them over to the draughtsmen. As the years went by, the pile waiting for his attention grew larger and larger as Beaufort would trust no one but himself to check every single detail. Like with the SDUK, his detractors invariably complained that he was over zealous, and that his caution held up the rate of production of much-needed charts. So much so, the huge backlog of 135 charts was published the year after his retirement. Beaufort demanded the same exacting standards of his surveyors as his own, and expected that they should mirror his own zeal, energy and enthusiasm. Depending on the survey, Beaufort worked on each chart for anything from one to six days. Again, praise was given where it was due, but slipshod work earned his rebuke – proof charts were sent back for correction, letters for clarification of some point, some even with a flash of humour. When Lieutenant Spearman referred to a distance as a 'handspike's length', Beaufort replied, 'For heaven's sake avoid such expressions. I wish some of these handspike gentlemen would tell us where the handspike is to be placed.'[29]

Arlett's charts of Cape Spartel to Azamor were passed by Beaufort after just three days checking, then sent in the middle of April 1835 to Purdy, the new draughtsman, who spent a further week working on them. The reduced charts were then sent on to the engravers, Messrs Walker of Holborn, a firm run by two of old John Walker's four sons, another John and Charles. John Walker had died in 1831 having worked at the Hydrographic Office for 31 years and had been replaced by his second son Michael as Beaufort's assistant hydrographer. If the Hydrographic Office was slow, Messrs Walker was even slower. The engraved copper plates were still not back a year later when Purdy and Higgins were working on Arlett's next set of charts. In December 1838 the plates were finally returned and the charts printed 'in a garret' in the Admiralty. Nearly six years after the original conception of the survey, the charts of the Canary Islands and the West Coast of

Africa were ready for distribution to the Fleet and for sale to the general public through the Admiralty agent, Messrs R. B. Bate. The cost varied with the size: 'The largest sizes of charts engraved, viz. antiquarian or double elephant, were then generally sold for 3s [shillings], the next size 2s, and so on down to 6d [pence].'[30]

However good his charts were, Beaufort knew that it was virtually impossible to keep them up to date with the constantly changing 'hidden maritime dangers, too often fatal to ships, statements of changes in lighthouses, position of buoys, and the condition of channels',[31] and to keep all mariners up to date about when new charts became available for issue or for sale. To this end, in 1834 Beaufort introduced a monthly publication called *Notices to Mariners* for 'there are no charts of any part of the world so accurate, and no directions so perfect as not to furnish frequent occasion for revision and amendment'.[32] This publication replaced a section in the *Nautical Magazine*, founded by Beaufort's worthy naval assistant Lieutenant Alexander Becher two years earlier and funded by a grant from the Admiralty and the Mercantile Marine Fund. Becher was to edit the magazine for 39 years. Its aim was 'the advancement of Hydrography by the diffusion of useful information' and solicited 'communications on the subject, however trifling, from the numerous intelligent seamen of the royal and mercantile Navy of Great Britain'.[33] In an early edition, Becher wrote an article (entitled *The Log Book*) that reported the difficulties of recording weather at sea and suggested the use of a system of letters and numbers that had 'originated with Captain Beaufort' – a clear case of in-house collusion designed to influence 'their Lordships' on the value of his Wind Scale. The Admiralty eventually answered the call, and the Beaufort Scale and the 'Letters to denote the state of the Weather' were officially adopted for general use in the Royal Navy through a *Memorandum* dated

28 December 1838. The Merchant Navy was slower off the mark and the first Board of Trade publication to mention the Beaufort Scale was the *Barometer Manual* in 1862.

In the intervening years, Beaufort was determined to foster meteorology as a science within the Navy. The Fleet was scattered all over the world, and naval officers 'trained from an early age, to take accurate readings using precision instruments, and to keep careful records in his journal'[34] made near ideal scientific observers. However, as the majority of his own suggestions for various improvements were inevitably ignored by the Board of the Admiralty, he approached the Royal Society 'to work out a scheme for promoting meteorological observations on a wide scale'[35] within the Navy. The advice (formulated by Beaufort himself) of the Royal Society was soon adopted by the Admiralty, and shortly afterwards their Lordships instructed the Hydrographic Office to implement Beaufort's own suggestions. An immediate result was the issue of marine barometers to the Fleet. It was Beaufort, too, who pioneered the research into the relationship between pressure and meteorological phenomena by commissioning a Reverend Dr Robinson 'to undertake experiments to assign the pressure in pounds to each of the figures in his scale'.[36]

The *Nautical Magazine* was also a useful organ for the surveying captains and their officers to publicise their voyages and findings, although some of the longer surveys, such as Fitzroy's voyage in the *Beagle*, King's in the *Adventure* to South America and Belcher's *Narrative of a Voyage around the World in HMS* Sulphur, merited volumes in their own right. Another useful publication that was widely used by Beaufort to bring the activities of his department and captains to the notice of a like-minded public was the *Proceedings* section of the *Journal of the Royal Geographical Society*.

The Royal Geographical Society had been founded in 1830,

although it had taken two years to form since it was first suggested in a letter to the *Literary Gazette* by a member of the Asiatic Society. It was, however, the natural arm of the Raleigh Travellers Club, a dining club founded by a retired army captain and traveller, Sir Arthur de Capel Brooke aiming 'at the attainment at modest expense of an agreeable, friendly and rational society formed by persons who have visited every part of the globe'.[37] Beaufort was one such member along with other Navy Captains, Basil Hall, Frederick Marryat, Sir John Franklin, Sir Edward Parry, and William H. Smyth, as well as friends like William Hamilton, and the Reverend George Renouard, late of Smyrna. The 'genial atmosphere of the Raleigh Club was in its earlier days enriched by the amiable custom of its members contributing to the dinners viands and drinks brought from far away, such as haunch of venison from Lapland, winged game from remote parts of Europe, hams from Mexico, bread baked from wheat grown on the shores of the Dead Sea, and curiously named wines and spirits'.[38]

It was Beaufort's closest friend, Captain W. H. Smyth, who co-opted him on to a steering committee of the proposed geographical society, along with the likes of Francis Baily, the President of the Royal Astronomical Society, but it was Beaufort himself who 'enlisted Barrow's interest' and proposed that he should take the chair at the inaugural meeting, there being no 'more desirable person to preside over the resolutions'.[39] Barrow proposed that 'a society was needed whose sole object should be the promotion and diffusion of that most important and entertaining branch of knowledge – geography – and that a useful Society might therefore be formed, under the name of the Geographical Society of London'.[40] Beaufort served many times on the committee, then made up mostly of like-minded naval officers, but later declined the presidency pleading lack of time. Another resolution of the new society was 'to facilitate the voyages of any explorers who came forward with good ideas as to how that branch might be extended'. Barrow had cleverly engineered it that he had complete control of every exploratory venture, either through the Royal Geographical Society, of which he became vice-president, through the Admiralty, where he was second secretary, or by way of Beaufort and the Hydrographic Office.

On 12 January 1820, Sir John Herschel dined at the Freemason's Tavern near Lincoln's Inn Fields, London with a learned group 'to take into consideration the proprietary and expediency of establishing a society for the encouragement and promotion of Astronomy'.[41] Although Beaufort was not amongst that august group of founder members, some of his fellow members of the Royal Society were. They immediately put his name forward, and he was unanimously elected a fellow of The Royal Astronomical Society in 1820. It was not long before he was serving on the Council (from 1824–38) and was elected vice-president six times between 1826 and 1834. Here, too, was another case of Beaufort using his dual role of Hydrographer and officer of a scientific body to the advantage of both. The Royal Astronomical Society was frequently consulted by the Admiralty, not least in its responsibility for the Greenwich Observatory and the Cape Observatory in South Africa, both institutions falling within Beaufort's aegis for administration and budgets under the new Scientific Branch of the Admiralty. The direction of the Observatories' policy and scientific programme was in the hands of their Board of Visitors, 12 luminaries appointed by the Royal Society until 1830, when their responsibility devolved on to The Royal Astronomical Society. Beaufort was their chief nominee, and served as a Visitor continuously until 1854.

Every year on the first Saturday in June, Beaufort and his family assembled at Westminster Pier to take the ferry to

Greenwich. It was an outing that they all looked forward to, Beaufort to confer with the Astronomer Royal and his fellow Visitors, his family to be with their father and to be shown yet again the Royal Observatory. Once there, they went their separate ways. The Visitors and the Astronomer Royal worked out their aims and scientific objectives for the coming year. Then, business over, Beaufort took his family off for a picnic tea, then returned to London. The next week, Beaufort went through what he and his fellow Visitors had agreed and, in his position as Hydrographer, drafted the estimates for the Greenwich Observatory for the Admiralty, who in turn presented them to Parliament to finance the year's programme. It was another case of the mild-mannered, slight, and pernickety Beaufort being a person with far greater influence than ever appeared on the surface.

The dual role of the Hydrographer could have led to difficulties in his dealings with Sir George Biddell Airy for the two decades that they overlapped as Visitor and Astronomer Royal, but such was Beaufort's tact and reputation, the two worked in harmony and became close, personal friends. Airy was a great innovator and found the perfect ally in Beaufort when reorganising the Greenwich Observatory. Their voluminous correspondence shows a mutual respect, of advice being sought and freely given. Airy used him as a sounding board for his discovery of the errors in planetary theory in terms of the motion of the Earth and Venus, as well as his other great discovery, the determination of the mass of the Earth from gravity measurements in mines. At times there was friction between them. Airy frequently complained to Beaufort, his titular head, of the 'fearful burden' that the repair, checking and issue of the Admiralty's chronometers put on his staff at the Observatory. The self-taught Beaufort, in turn, was slightly in awe of Airy, the Lucasian professor of mathematics at Trinity

College Cambridge: 'I left the field to him and his worshippers, discussion being useless when common sense is sacrificed at the shrine of great talents'[42] was one diary entry in response to some disagreement. Airy established 'a new meridian at Greenwich by the instillation of his transit circle, and it was this meridian that was to become the prime meridian of the world'.[43] It is extraordinary that Beaufort 'could see no good use for the conveyance of Greenwich time throughout the Kingdom',[44] (or as it was also known, 'railway time'), as opposed to local time, when the sun was directly overhead at noon, which, of course, varied. When asked to advise what time a new clock for Devonport Naval Dockyard should show, he suggested a clock with two minute hands, similar to the one today over the Exchange in Corn Street, Bristol, where one hand shows 'Bristol Time' and the other, eleven minutes later, 'Great Western Railway Time'. Presumably Beaufort felt that the Devonport dockyard hands could make up their own minds as to which time they kept.

In fact, Beaufort's sphere of astronomical influence extended a great deal further than just the Greenwich Observatory. In 1830, the Admiralty asked the Royal Astronomical Society if, considering the great expense, it was necessary to keep up two observatories at the Cape and at Paramatta, Australia (founded by Sir Thomas Brisbane and recently handed over to the Government). Again Beaufort sat on the committee and pointed out that the Cape Observatory was vital, being near the same meridian as most of the European observatories in the Southern Hemisphere, while Paramatta, on a far longitude with a different climate, was essential for comparison. Also, little was known of the 'southern heavens' and an observatory there would be 'of importance to geographical and hydrographical surveys'.[45] It made sense, too, having all observatories, including those in St Helena and Mauritius under the same 'dome' so that their operations could be coordinated. As a dedicated astronomer, Beaufort was deeply committed furthering its appeal amongst colleagues and amateurs alike, and gave his time equally to both.

Beaufort could never be accused of empire building, but with the ongoing difficulties within the Nautical Almanac Office he was on the committee that arranged for control to pass from the Royal Observatory to the Hydrographic Office. The *Nautical Almanac and Astronomical Ephemeris* was instituted in 1767 by the Astronomer Royal, Nevil Maskelyne and published by order of the Commissioners for Longitude. In it, the distances between the moon, the sun and nine other selected stars were projected for every three hours at Greenwich over the year. The positions of other stars and planets were added from time to time. The navigator, taking what are known as 'Lunars', measured the angle between the moon and a given star with a quadrant, and, by referring to the relevant table on that date in the *Nautical Almanac*, could work out his longitudinal position in reference to Greenwich. It was, however, a laborious and inaccurate system. When Maskelyne died in 1811, the *Nautical Almanac* declined sharply, and was marginally rescued under its new superintendent, Thomas Young, an expert in hieroglyphics (he translated the demotic part of the Rosetta Stone) but with little knowledge of astronomy or navigation, 'who improved its accuracy but set his face against reform'. The *Almanac* also had many errors and thus could not be relied upon – so much so that in a pamphlet by Sir James South attacking Young, South quoted the case of Beaufort's friend Captain W. H. Smyth, who was 'obliged to use the ephemeredes of Paris, Milan, Bologna and Florence on account of the omissions and errors of the *Nautical Almanac* (this Smyth in a letter certifies to be true). But wishing to show civility to a Spanish captain, he presented him with his copies of the *Nautical Almanac* for the current and subsequent years. Captain Smyth with his foreign ephemeredes found his way to England; but there is an awkward story afloat that the Spanish captain has not been heard of.'[46] The astronomers felt the *Almanac*'s lack of accuracy as much as the navigators. A committee for reform, that included Beaufort, was set up at the request of the Admiralty, and a Lieutenant Stratford was appointed superintendent to the *Nautical Almanac* under the direction of the Hydrographer. The Hydrographic Office was then able to implement the majority of the improvements recommended by the Royal Astronomical Society to the benefit of all.

When Beaufort took office as Hydrographer, 'the study of tides had been allowed to lag behind other branches of astronomy',[47] but he had always held a deep fascination for the subject. He had kept Major Rennell supplied with temperatures and information on the Gulf Stream, and during the voyage of the *Fredrickssteen*, he had stumbled on the remarkable effect of the sea's density with depth while taking soundings off Turkey.

The early work on tides, mostly by the French, had been largely confined to oceanography and various suppositions, with little to support mostly erroneous theory. There were published tide tables for London, but these were privately printed and their computation and research kept secret. When their inaccuracy was pointed out in an article by the Society for the Diffusion of Useful Knowledge, one of Beaufort's fellow members, John William Lubbock, took up the challenge to produce an accurate set of tables. Lubbock was an ideal person. He had studied physical astronomy under William Whewell, Master of Trinity College, Cambridge. He was a keen scientist, rich (a partner in his father's bank) and later a vice-president and treasurer of the Royal Society. By chance, he found that high water had been recorded day and night at London Docks for the last 30 years. When Beaufort heard of his plan to analyse the records, he gave him the services of one of his able naval assistants, Lieutenant Joseph Dessiou. The result of their joint labour was a set of tide tables for London that were published in the *British Almanac* for 1830. Lubbock then set out to record the 'heights and times of high water over a long period to calculate the different variations to be detected in the tides, the semi-diurnal rise and fall, the twice monthly springs and neaps, the alterations caused by the variation in the moon's orbit, and to relate them to the astronomical forces which had caused them'.[48] Again Beaufort smoothed his path – at his suggestion, the Royal Society approached the Admiralty who agreed to install automatic tide gauges to the dockyards at Sheerness, Portsmouth, Plymouth, and two in London. The result of their findings appeared in the first *Admiralty Tide Tables* published in 1833.

Throughout these experiments, Beaufort kept in close touch with Lubbock. In over 40 letters he gave advice and encouragement: 'I assured him,' he wrote, 'as I do you, that no one can be impressed with a stronger conviction than myself of the urgent necessity of acquiring proper data for the construction of Tide Tables, that I consider it to be a national object, and that Government should take it in hand when they found a person qualified like you, disposed to undertake a principal part of the labour without expense to the Country.'[49]

However well received Lubbock's research was 'from seaman and scientist alike', with the backing of the Admiralty (as it did not involve them in much expense), the results were largely confined to harbours, not the open sea. However, his Cambridge tutor, William Whewell, became involved and widened the field of research to 'discover the general pattern of tides throughout the world'. He worked on 'co-tidal' lines, imaginary lines 'joining points reached simultaneously by the crest of the tide wave'. For this, he gleaned information from the Hydrographic Office –

through Beaufort, all his surveyors were by then reporting on tides – and attempted to draw co-tidal lines for the world's oceans. Again, he co-opted Beaufort's help in arranging for the 'Preventative Service' (coastguards) around Great Britain and Ireland to record high and low water during a fortnight in June 1834. The success of that survey prompted them to expand their observations worldwide, and Beaufort went to the Admiralty, who in turn approached the Foreign Secretary, the Duke of Wellington, to make the necessary arrangements with foreign governments for a series of simultaneous observations. The date was set for June 1835 and readings were taken 'for a fortnight on both sides of the Atlantic, at 28 or more places on the American and European coasts, between Florida and Nova Scotia and from the Straits of Gibraltar to North Cape, and at over 500 points on the coast of Great Britain'.[50] The results were as surprising as they were revealing – for example it was always thought that the tide flowed in opposite directions on the English and Belgian coasts – that is, when the tide ebbed off the English Coast it flowed off Belgium. This survey showed how the two tides were connected and how they fitted into the general tidal pattern. It was also revealed that the co-tidal lines in the North Sea were not straight, but convex.

Whewell also decided that the North Sea was oscillating, like water in a basin, high on one side, low on the other, with a mid-point that did not change in depth. He worked out exactly where the amphidrome (where there was almost no rise and fall) would lie and took his findings to Beaufort. In a typical manoeuvre, Beaufort went to the Royal Society, the Royal Society went to the Admiralty and the Admiralty directed Beaufort to put Whewell's theory to the test. Beaufort charged Captain Hewett of the *Fairy*, his most experienced surveyor in the North Sea, to find the amphidromic point. In August 1840, he replied that he had found the point near where Whewell predicted.

Beaufort was indefatigable in his quest for knowledge of tides, both in home waters and around the world – he even designed a form for anyone interested in recording tidal observations for analysis at the Hydrographic Office. Although he had the backing of the Royal Society, not all the Council shared his enthusiasm: Sir John Herschel who supervised the observations at the Cape Observatory wrote miserably to Beaufort, 'Observing tides is the greatest bore on earth, or upon the waters, and the greatest exhauster of a man's patience and trial of his temper.'[51] And all because he fell into the water while observing a current.

As the years went by, Beaufort's prowess in the scientific field was increasingly recognised. Back in 1825 he had gone to *L'Académie des Sciences de l'Institut de France*, the equivalent of the Royal Society as a guest of Sir James South. There he was surprised to be placed as 'a distinguished foreigner', but 'delighted' to be introduced to La Place, the great French mathematician. In fact, at that time Beaufort had not achieved much in his own right and had every reason to be surprised. But fifteen years later he was made an actual member of *L'Académie*. Other honours had already come his way – he was elected a member of the United States Lyceum and the Philadelphia Philosophical Society in 1832. Nearer to home, in the same year he was elected to the Royal Irish Academy that his father had helped to found, and, for some reason, the Royal Society for Literature. He was an avid reader and appreciated fine literature, but, other than advising Maria Edgeworth, he made no other contribution. Other honours from abroad came to him. The King of Denmark arranged for him to receive a chronometer and a gold medal, which is understandable; less so is the Indo-Persian scimitar, with ivory handle and curved blade, that he received from the Imam of Muscat, as Beaufort had no direct dealings with the man, his country, or littoral. Beaufort accepted the sword gladly, expressing 'his deep sense of gratitude, which has been excited by this flattering compliment, allow me to assume your Majesty that the sword shall be preserved in my family as one of the proudest distinctions of my life, and that I shall always be ready to unsheathe it not only in defence of his Majesty's person, but in support of those nobler principles which have thrown such lustre on his Majesty's throne'.[52]

It was also a measure of the respect that Beaufort commanded within the Royal Society and the Royal Astronomical Society that he could call on any of the luminaries for advice, ask them to submit papers or to serve on a committee, just as they frequently called upon him for the same. One undertaking entirely of Beaufort's making was the *Manual of Scientific Enquiry* that was 'prepared for the use of Officers in His Majesty's Navy'[53] (as well as for 'Travellers in General') edited, at his invitation, by Sir John Herschel. Recalling his own limited education and quest for knowledge, Beaufort lobbied The Lords Commissioners of the Admiralty to produce a work that 'would be an honour and advantage of the Navy, and conduce to the general interest of science if new facilities and encouragement were given to the collection of information upon scientific subjects by the officers, and more particularly by the medical officers, of Her Majesty's Navy, when upon foreign service'.

Beaufort called on the services of his friends to collaborate on the work. It was an impressive list headed by Sir George Airy writing on astronomy, Sir William Hooker (in later editions, his son Joseph) on botany while William Hamilton wrote on geography and hydrography. Sir Henry de la Beche, the great geologist, wrote the section on mineralogy and General Sir Edward Sabine, a President of the Royal Society and foremost authority on terrestrial magnetism, submitted a piece on his subject. The essay on meteorology was provided by Sir John Herschel himself, with a contribution on tides by Sir George Darwin, a professor of astronomy at Cambridge. The article on zoology was written by Professor Richard Owen. The *Manual of Scientific Enquiry* was distributed through the Fleet, and went into four editions with minor variations. The Navy was still at the forefront of scientific enquiry, and the *Manual* reflected the thinking of Naval officers at that time, as can be gauged by the number and variety of scientific papers that filled the scientific journals of the day.

Another of Beaufort's contributions to society probably came through his association with Charles Babbage and the other Cambridge mathematicians, although this one, 'the Beaufort Cipher', was decidedly less good than his other innovations. His interest in steganography (cryptography) began with the simple substitution method he had used since childhood with his brother William, and possibly Fanny as well. In 1855, Commander Becher published an account of 'Sir Francis Beaufort's Plan for Secret Correspondence' in his *Nautical Magazine*, which outlined his system of encoding a message using polyalphabets in conjunction with a keyword. Then, shortly after Beaufort's death, his son William Morris Beaufort published the code and instructions for its use on folding, A6-sized card that sold for sixpence. The cover stated that it had been 'adapted for telegrams and postage cards', and that as both had become widely used, they were nonetheless 'prey to prying eyes'.

The Beaufort Cipher was made up of 26 standard alphabets, each slid one space to the left of the one above, with a normal alphabet on the top, for the plain text, and another down the side, for the key (*see* p. 254). The system was simple though time-consuming to use. The sender and the recipient agreed on the key, a word, a line of poetry or 'the name of some

a	b	c	d	e	f	g	h	i	j	k	l	m	n	o	p	q	r	s	t	u	v	w	x	y	z
b	c	d	e	f	g	h	i	j	k	l	m	n	o	p	q	r	s	t	u	v	w	x	y	z	a
c	d	e	f	g	h	i	j	k	l	m	n	o	p	q	r	s	t	u	v	w	x	y	z	a	b
d	e	f	g	h	i	j	k	l	m	n	o	p	q	r	s	t	u	v	w	x	y	z	a	b	c
e	f	g	h	i	j	k	l	m	n	o	p	q	r	s	t	u	v	w	x	y	z	a	b	c	d
f	g	h	i	j	k	l	m	n	o	p	q	r	s	t	u	v	w	x	y	z	a	b	c	d	e
g	h	i	j	k	l	m	n	o	p	q	r	s	t	u	v	w	x	y	z	a	b	c	d	e	f
h	i	j	k	l	m	n	o	p	q	r	s	t	u	v	w	x	y	z	a	b	c	d	e	f	g
i	j	k	l	m	n	o	p	q	r	s	t	u	v	w	x	y	z	a	b	c	d	e	f	g	h
j	k	l	m	n	o	p	q	r	s	t	u	v	w	x	y	z	a	b	c	d	e	f	g	h	i
k	l	m	n	o	p	q	r	s	t	u	v	w	x	y	z	a	b	c	d	e	f	g	h	i	j
l	m	n	o	p	q	r	s	t	u	v	w	x	y	z	a	b	c	d	e	f	g	h	i	j	k
m	n	o	p	q	r	s	t	u	v	w	x	y	z	a	b	c	d	e	f	g	h	i	j	k	l
n	o	p	q	r	s	t	u	v	w	x	y	z	a	b	c	d	e	f	g	h	i	j	k	l	m
o	p	q	r	s	t	u	v	w	x	y	z	a	b	c	d	e	f	g	h	i	j	k	l	m	n
p	q	r	s	t	u	v	w	x	y	z	a	b	c	d	e	f	g	h	i	j	k	l	m	n	o
q	r	s	t	u	v	w	x	y	z	a	b	c	d	e	f	g	h	i	j	k	l	m	n	o	p
r	s	t	u	v	w	x	y	z	a	b	c	d	e	f	g	h	i	j	k	l	m	n	o	p	q
s	t	u	v	w	x	y	z	a	b	c	d	e	f	g	h	i	j	k	l	m	n	o	p	q	r
t	u	v	w	x	y	z	a	b	c	d	e	f	g	h	i	j	k	l	m	n	o	p	q	r	s
u	v	w	x	y	z	a	b	c	d	e	f	g	h	i	j	k	l	m	n	o	p	q	r	s	t
v	w	x	y	z	a	b	c	d	e	f	g	h	i	j	k	l	m	n	o	p	q	r	s	t	u
w	x	y	z	a	b	c	d	e	f	g	h	i	j	k	l	m	n	o	p	q	r	s	t	u	v
x	y	z	a	b	c	d	e	f	g	h	i	j	k	l	m	n	o	p	q	r	s	t	u	v	w
y	z	a	b	c	d	e	f	g	h	i	j	k	l	m	n	o	p	q	r	s	t	u	v	w	x
z	a	b	c	d	e	f	g	h	i	j	k	l	m	n	o	p	q	r	s	t	u	v	w	x	y
a	b	c	d	e	f	g	h	i	j	k	l	m	n	o	p	q	r	s	t	u	v	w	x	y	z

memorable person or place'. The key was written out and repeated as often as required to cover the number of letters in the message, which was then entered below the key. By running across from the first letter of the text on the vertical alphabet to the first letter of the key on the horizontal alphabet, where these columns meet is the cipher letter. For example, taking 'Manners maketh man' as the key:

key   M A N N E R S M A K E T H M A N M A N N E R S
message   A R R I V I N G B Y T R A I N S A T U R D A Y
cipher   M R E V Z Z F S B I X K H U N E A G G R Q N C

In its day, it was moderately advanced, but not as advanced as when it was first formulated by a French cryptographer, Blaise de Vigenère in 1586 as 'probably the most famous cipher of all time'.[54] In 1710, it was revised by another cryptographer, Giovanni Sestri, but it faded into obscurity until Beaufort published his version. However, Beaufort was not a plagiarist, and to pass off someone else's work as his own would have been unthinkable. But he was a friend of Charles Babbage who dabbled in cryptography, and of the remarkably gifted Sir Charles Wheatstone (famous as the inventor of the Wheatstone Bridge that measures electrical resistance, and the concertina), who had produced a cipher machine. If Beaufort had been discussing cryptography with his friends, they could easily have sown the seeds in his mind for the *Beaufort Cipher*. However, as it is so similar to Vigenère's cipher, it is more likely that he did copy and amend it slightly for his own amusement. Becher could have found it and assumed it was original when he published the account, followed by William Morris Beaufort who compounded the error.

In the 1920s, Rupert Gould, the self-taught horologist who repaired the famous John Harrison chronometers, attempted a history of the Hydrographic Department. He managed just two chapters, but when he came to the Beaufort era he abandoned the project as 'the canvas had become too vast for him to cover. There are masses of facts and figures available, but to get them into any order, chronological, historical or even alphabetical is like trying to unscramble a scrambled egg.'[55] The 'masses of facts and figures' were accumulated through the intense activity and advancements of the age in Britain, most of which seemed, in some form or other, to land up on Beaufort's desk, some-times as there seemed no other logical place to put them, but more often as Beaufort was *exactly* the right person to deal with them.

As early as 1830, Beaufort could foresee the problems to the coast and harbours arising from the rapidly expanding railway system and canvassed the Admiralty accordingly. It was he who was consulted on each Railway Bill laid before Parliament, until the task became so great, even for Beaufort, that he requested an assistant, 'an officer of respectability sufficient acquainted with science and practice not to be imposed upon by specious representations'. A special Harbour and Railway Department was set up in 1846 under a Captain Charles Bethune, the appointed assistant, to deal with 'all questions relating to rail-ways, bridges, and other works that may interfere with, or injuriously affect, the harbours, rivers, and navigable rivers of the United Kingdom'. By 1853, the department was scaled down and once again its responsibility devolved on to Beaufort.

Nor did it seem that any maritime committee was complete without Beaufort. He sat on such obscure bodies as the Committee on Lifesaving Rockets and the Harbours-of-Refuge Commission. As a Commissioner of Pilotage, he was responsible for pilot's rates; he was a natural choice for Trinity House to consult on lighthouses, at home and abroad, and was responsible for the installation and siting of the lighthouses in the Orkney and Shetland Islands. This was extended to marking the 'approaches to all harbours with beacons, buoys and lights'. With the advent of steam propulsion, he instantly became the Admiralty's authority to be consulted on the alteration and building of new harbours to take steam-propelled ships. He noted, too, that with steam power, the smaller creeks and rivers on the south coast of England would be navigable and therefore should be charted, as they 'could be used for smuggling and hostile purposes',[56] – charts obviously more beneficial to the smuggler than the Preventive Service.

To add to Beaufort's workload came the solving of the problem of how to correct a compass in iron ships, and those powered by steam. Again, it was he who foresaw how the iron would affect the compass and the ship's chronometers and approached the Admiralty with a view to setting up a committee. In July 1837, they gave their consent and the committee, headed by him, looked into how to correct the errors of the Fleet's compasses. Five years later, the Compass Branch was formed under Beaufort's supervision, and the method of 'swinging a ship to determine compass error' was first adopted.

Nor did it take long for others outside the Admiralty to realise that Beaufort's dispassionate advice was worth seeking. He claimed to be apolitical – in a letter to his brother he wrote that 'one half of my friends revile me for being a Whig and a Radical, and the other half despise me for being an old womanish Tory' – and consequently, both parties consulted him. But he found serving on Thomas Drummond's Boundary Commission that redefined Parliamentary constituencies 'a duty less agreeable to me'. He could not, however, refuse the assignment as it came through Sir James Graham, the new First Lord of the Admiralty and member of the Prime Minister's committee to draft the Reform Bill of 1832. Another committee he served on more willingly was the Senate of the new University College, London through its founder, Lord Brougham.

The old cry of 'Ask Dr Beaufort' in response to the perennial requests for information on the most diverse topics was inherited by his son the moment he walked into his office as Hydrographer. Just as the Hydrographic Office became a clearinghouse for objects and ideas from around the world, so Beaufort's immense knowledge on seemingly every subject was tapped by all and sundry, even on the most trivial matters like the best shape for a ship's biscuit or the cost of the pens in his drawing office. Who better to advise on what lights a steam vessel should carry, or what books should be put into the library of the Fleet, or indeed what coaling facilities were required for Portsmouth, Dover and Newhaven? Despite the huge demands on Beaufort's time, he diligently applied himself to each appeal.

There seemed to be no limit to the requests. Thomas Arnold, the headmaster of Rugby (who had also tutored Beaufort's two eldest sons), wrote to ask if he had 'any good charts of the Bay of Tunis with so much of the coast given in detail to assist in understanding the Geography of ancient Carthage'. Being puzzled by the position of Libytean, he wondered whether 'there is nothing fuller on the West Coast of Sicily', and could Beaufort throw any light on Minoan Crete? Another classical request came from the antiquarian George Long who wanted to know where Caesar landed, while Sir George Airy needed to know the exact route that Agathocles took in the Punic Wars. Sir John Croker called for Beaufort's advice on the demarcation line drawn by Pope Alexander VI in the New World ceding the territories to Spain and Portugal.

Queen Victoria and the Prince Consort also drew on Beaufort's knowledge and expertise. Prince Albert requested, and received, a chronometer. He then asked for advice on where to site what was to become Osborne House, their proposed home on the Isle of Wight. When the house was built, Beaufort was consulted again on the best place for a private landing stage so that they did not have to pass through Cowes and bear the 'inquisitive stares' of the crowd. Beaufort was commanded to make the arrangements for the voyage of the Royal Yacht *Victoria and Albert* to France for the Queen's historic meeting with Louis Philippe. For this, he went to Windsor Castle where he discussed the arrangements with the Prince, then according to his diary he 'sauntered about the castle and town and read till dressing and at 8 assembled in the drawing room. At 8¹/₂ the Queen swept in with all her train, bowed to all and at once proceeded to the dinner table. 26 in all. H M sat but a short time after dinner and we hove [followed] too after her. Royal round game and 2 whist tables.' He found himself at the same table as 'Her Majesty of Great Britain, and though ensconced in the form of a little woman, still it was majesty'.[57] The party broke up at about 11 when the Queen 'retired and I followed not her but her example' to his room in the York Tower.

It seems that Beaufort had also become a depository for information that either needed to be recorded, or passed on to the most advantageous quarter. Sir James Brooke, the White Rajah of Sarawak, sent a paper to Beaufort on the Dyaks of Borneo, and hoped that it would 'prove interesting'. Algernon Horsey 'having been employed 19 months on the Columbia River on HM sloop *Moderate* in conjunction with Mr Montgomerie also of that ship had the opportunity of acquiring a knowledge of that language spoken by the natives or the barkers of that river'. He made a vocabulary that he sent to Beaufort on the chance that it 'may be useful'. The explorer Macgregor Laird advised Beaufort that it 'is not to be expected that Europeans would settle at Cameroon's, they will naturally prefer a healthy tropical country for that purpose – nor will Africans, the climate of the low grounds will not injure them'.[58] The Scottish Astronomer Royal, Thomas Henderson, wrote a description of Halley's Comet that 'appeared as a nebulous mass extremely faint like Eucke's Comet that was last observed in 1832'.[59] Captain Fitzroy argued that Port Arthur in the Falklands was the best place to set up a meteorological station and that 'without easy and frequent intercourse with ships the Falklands are not worth notice. With that they are invaluable.'

Francis Beaufort had indeed become a worthy successor to his father, 'little Dr Beaufort'.

CHAPTER 12

Captain Beaufort RN, Surveyor to the World

THE MORNING OF 14 NOVEMBER 1840 was still and clear, the kind of morning with an intensely blue sky that follows a violent storm. As usual, Francis Beaufort entered the Admiralty at 9 o'clock precisely and walked up the stairs to his office. Lieutenant Dessiou, looking grave, was waiting for him by the door and followed him into the room. There he told Beaufort of the terrible storm in the North Sea the night before, and the news that had just come in that HMS *Fairy* had not reached Yarmouth, where her commander, Captain Hewett had been heading to demonstrate his new invention for dredging, before lying up for the winter at Woolwich. Beaufort was not unduly worried. The *Fairy* was a seaworthy brig, the sister ship to the *Beagle* that had survived the gales of Cape Horn, and Hewett was an excellent seaman. He knew the

North Sea better than any man, for at Beaufort's direction, he had surveyed the whole of the southern portion drawn up in a notable 'chart number 1406 of the North Sea from Dover to Calais and Orfordness to Scheveningen'.[1] A week later, Beaufort read in *The Times* that fishermen returning to Yarmouth had seen a three-masted vessel founder in the gale. Still, Beaufort refused to believe that it was the *Fairy*. A reward was offered for information of her whereabouts; he even wrote to the Admiralty in Norway in the hope that she had run for shelter in some fjord. It was not until 10 February 1841 that the wreck of the *Fairy* was found off Lowestoft. Beaufort was devastated, and instituted a fund for the widows and children of the lost hands. When Belcher heard of the death of Hewett, he wrote to Beaufort, 'a very steady, hard working fellow not to be replaced by any of the feather bed crew about Charing Cross [the Admiralty]. You can fill his vacancy but it will not get one to stand the North Sea work as he did, although he was said to be too much in port. I know what the weather is around Great Britain, and he must be very fond of ducking who keeps his vessel on the move.'[2]

Hewett's survey of the North Sea was a part of Beaufort's 'Grand Survey of the British Isles' that he inherited from Hurd, then Parry, which was completed in 1855, the year of his retirement. It was a great achievement, considerably aided by the introduction of paddle steamers, or paddlers as they were known, into the surveying service. Lieutenant Frederick Bullock had commanded a small paddler, HMS *Echo* in 1829 to survey the Thames, but it was not until 1837 when Parry returned from his lucrative post in Australia to take up the position of 'Comptroller of Steam Machinery' at the Admiralty that Beaufort felt he 'had a friend at court'. The *Fairy* was replaced in 1841 by HMS *Shearwater* under the command of Captain John Washington (he was to succeed Beaufort as

Hydrographer), along with five other paddlers for surveying home waters. Replacing a motley selection of hired boats, these paddlers were ideal. They drew less water so could go nearer to the shore; they were easily manoeuvred to an exact position for taking a bearing or lines of soundings. Also, they could operate in calm or rough weather and could put out and return to port at will. But it was not to last. Just when all of Beaufort's surveys were going so well, his steamers were withdrawn from his service in 1848 for famine relief on the west coasts of Ireland and Scotland.

A further blow to Beaufort's surveying schedule was the cut of £10,000 from his budget of £70,000 in 1851. Yet again, he railed against the Admiralty, ending his letter 'I will not trifle with your time by repeating here any hackneyed truisms about the comparative expense to the country in the cost of surveys or the loss of ships and cargoes, but I will entreat you to weigh the small sum you propose to save against the large amount of mischief which may result.'[3] Nor did the steamers come back into his surveying service. 'The natural tendency of men is to undervalue what they cannot understand' was a frequent cry from Beaufort when thwarted by higher authority.

Yet despite these setbacks, the whole of the coast of the British Isles was surveyed under Beaufort's direction (*see* Appendix 4). He inherited George Thomas, master of the brig *Investigator*, the first ship ever purpose-built for surveying. In 25 years, he literally wore her out in surveying in the English Channel, the North Sea, the east coast, and ending up in the Orkney and Shetland Islands. She was decommissioned in 1836 and sold to the Thames River Police. The *Investigator* was replaced by the *Mastiff* and Thomas continued in her for another ten years, dying on board on his last voyage before retirement. Another good surveyor who died 'in harness' was Commander Michael Slater, who had trained under Captain William H. Smyth. He had already surveyed the northeast coast of England, was working his way round from the River Tay to the Thurso on the north coast of Scotland, when in February 1842 he slipped on the rocks and fell to his death at Holbourn Head while setting up a theodolite station. Captain Henry Otter in the ketch *Sparrow* (later the two paddlers, *Avon* and *Comet*) continued from the spot where Slater died, and for the next 17 years surveyed all the Outer and Inner Hebrides right down to the Isle of Mull.

Otter's survey joined up with another prolific surveyor's work, Captain Frederick Beechey who spent eight years surveying the Irish Sea and the Severn Estuary, while his brother, Richard Beechey (a fine marine watercolour artist), charted much of the west and north coasts of Ireland. Again under Beaufort's directions, Beechey's surveys tied in with the existing work on Dublin Bay started by Commander Mudge, which he had inherited, and Lieutenant George Frazer continued the survey of Ireland round to Cork. It was fitting that this survey that tied in with the Ordinance Survey of Ireland was completed under Beaufort's direction, he having turned it down so honourably in 1815. Captains William Sheringham and George Williams completed the Grand Survey between 1843 and 1855 with the charting of the south coast of England and the west and north coasts of Wales, the Solway Firth and Land's End, including the Isles of Scilly.

It was a measure of Beaufort's leadership qualities that he kept the loyalty and consistently high standard of his home water surveyors for so long. Commander Frederick Bullock spent 26 years surveying the River Thames and far out into the North Sea. As ships became larger with a greater draught, so they required deeper channels, and the Thames Estuary was in danger of becoming unnavigable to these larger ships. But Bullock resurveyed all the approaches and in the Estuary found a deeper channel and (taking no notice of Beaufort's nomenclative directive) called it Bullock Sound. Renamed 'The Duke of Edinburgh Channel', it is the present entry to the Port of London. Bullock's North Sea Survey covered the Goodwin Sands, where he established a permanent survey point with a covered platform to take his bearings. In it, he left a stock of biscuits and a gallon of rum for shipwrecked sailors. Likewise, it was Lieutenant Henry Denham who found the 'New Channel' in the River Mersey when the two existing channels were silting up and threatening the existence of Liverpool as a port, with its eleven thousand ships arriving and leaving each year. Denham, promoted to captain, went on to spend six years surveying Fiji and the coast of Australia.

Throughout his long tenure as Hydrographer, Beaufort invariably sent out the right man in the right ship for the job – 'surveyors are scarce, especially when other qualities than mere professional talent is required' he wrote to Fitzroy in 1847 when faced with a tricky situation for the proposed survey in New Zealand. To a man, his surveying captains shared his enthusiasm in the knowledge that they were contributing to the safety of the sea and the advancement of scientific knowledge. Some paid with their lives. Apart from Skyring, 'foully murdered by the natives', the West African coast also claimed the lives of Commanders Bird Allen, 'who fell victim to the climate' and Thomas Boteler. Lieutenant Lawrence died of fever surveying the Leeward Islands in the West Indies, while Lieutenant David Gordon 'was hurried to the grave' in Borneo by a fever that 'naturally undermined a robust constitution'. Another was Captain Owen Stanley, the veteran of 25 years surveying, from the Mediterranean to the Straits of Magellan to Australia and New Guinea, in his command HMS *Rattlesnake*. 'His health had been declining under the fatigues and anxieties attendant upon the arduous labour of surveying in tropical climates among coral reefs, strange currents and many physical and moral evils.'[4] He died in Sydney not quite 39 years old. Others met violent deaths, like Captain Thomas Graves, who was assassinated by a disaffected boatman in Malta where he had retired as Port Officer.

Graves, a fellow officer of Owen Stanley on Captain Philip King's survey of South America, had been given the command of *Mastiff* to survey the Grecian Archipelago, moving on to the *Beacon* when his commodore, Commander Copeland retired a sick man – Graves found him 'looking miserably ill and more interested in brandy and water than in writing sailing directions'.[5] Beaufort gave Graves every encouragement and greatly admired his work. Like him, Graves was a fine watercolourist and competent antiquarian. Thus, he in command of the *Beacon* was the natural choice to take Sir Charles Fellows back to Xanthus in Southern Turkey to collect the magnificent Xantian Marbles that he had discovered two years previously. Beaufort, who had been within 30 miles of Xanthus, had taken a particular interest in Fellows' travels, as he knew that his *Karamania* had been his inspiration. At Xanthus, a fierce argument broke out between Graves and Fellows over how the monuments, which included the famous Harpy Tomb and the Nereid Monument, were to be dismantled. Graves gave orders that no one was to touch them until he had further instructions from Whitehall, and, after months of delay, they were transported to the British Museum in London. After nearly 100 separate surveys conducted over ten years, Graves' commission was 'suddenly put a stop to on the score of economy by orders from the Admiralty'. Beaufort was not consulted, and, a master of the understatement, he found their Lordships' peremptory behaviour an 'inscrutable measure'.

Although the Hydrographic Office was an easy target for the cost-conscious Admiralty, Beaufort fought single-handedly for his department, his surveyors and his survey vessels. After just ten years in office, his expenditure had increased six-fold, to nearly £60,000, while the number of ships engaged in surveying rose from twelve to twenty-one. With Beaufort's management, the Admiralty received full value for their money. During that time, the *Beagle* under Captain Fitzroy had made her epic voyage around the world between 1831 and 1836. Fitzroy tied in with the existing surveys of South America begun by Captain Parker King in the *Adventure*, charting the coast from the River Plate to Cape Horn and taking in the Falkland Islands. Surveying the Straits of Magellan, he then worked up the Chilean and Peruvian coasts, 'where no port or roadstead was omitted'.[6] Parts of the survey were original, parts were correcting the Spanish charts – in some cases over 25 miles out of latitude. He went up as far as Ecuador, before heading off to the Galapagos Islands and across the Pacific. The return journey was taken up with measuring meridian distances and setting up fixing stations along the way. For this he took 22 chronometers and on his return after five years, 'the whole chain of meridian distances round the world exceeded 24 hours by 33 seconds only'.[7] Fitzroy was assisted by his able officers who surveyed whole sections of the coasts in chartered vessels, or in ships bought by Fitzroy out of his own pocket.

During Beaufort's period as Hydrographer, it was the norm for surveying captains to teach their junior officers their craft and to advance them up the Navy List. Over and again, the names of officers reappear, first as midshipmen, then lieutenants, then in command of tenders, moving up to commands in their own right, while they, in turn, brought on the next generation of surveyors. A prime example was Fitzroy's midshipman, John Lort Stokes who advanced through the system fostered by a dogged determination and the overall guidance of Beaufort. From midshipman on the *Beagle*, Stokes rose to mate and assistant surveyor, then lieutenant to Captain Wickham who took over from Fitzroy in 1837. When Wickham was 'severely wounded in an affray with the natives', Stokes assumed command, which was later confirmed. It was Beaufort who, in 1848, appointed him to HMS *Acheron*, barque-rigged with an auxiliary steam engine driving paddle wheels, for the first proper survey of New Zealand since Captain Cook. By chance, Stoke's second in command, Commander George Richards, and the mate, Frederick Evans, both went on to become Hydrographers to the Navy after Captain John Washington, another of Beaufort's protégés. After three years surveying in dreadful conditions, Stokes was recalled and his project finished by Captain Byron Drury in a sailing brig, the 400-ton *Pandora*.

Another name, that of Henry Kellett, is written large throughout the whole of the Beaufort period. He began under Captain William Owen on the West African coast around Fernando Po, where promotion came through the fever that wiped out most of the officers. He returned to the west coast of Africa as first lieutenant to Edward Belcher, then his successor, William Skyring, followed by the command of the *Raven* under Lieutenant Arlett. He was then appointed to his own command, the 105-ton cutter *Starling* and sent to survey the west coast of South America, before being ordered on to China, where once again he came under the command of Captain Belcher. There they 'joined in the warfare then commencing against the Chinese in which he bore a very eminent part'.[8] With Lieutenant Richard Collinson, the 'surveying officer to the fleet', he charted the necessary channels that led to the capture of Canton, 'thoroughly sounding between the ships and the shore and thus enabling the *Cornwallis*, *Blonde* and *Modeste*, while the troops were landing, to take up excellent positions against the sea batteries'.[9] Promotion followed on his return to England. Beaufort then sent him back to the Pacific in *Herald* to survey parts of Chile and Columbia as far as Panama, 'till then only known from the accounts of Dampier and older authors'. As Vice Admiral, he was Commander-in-Chief of the China Station but returned after three years to England 'much debilitated in constitution from the effects of the climate'. But when Kellett was surveying the coast of California, again in the *Herald*, he received new orders from Beaufort dated March 1848. Although it was 'vexatious' for Beaufort to take him away from his sacred surveying duties, even he 'could not even grumble', for Kellett was being sent to search for Sir John Franklin, lost in his quest for the North West Passage three years before. 'Any effort on behalf of poor Franklin,' Beaufort continued, 'and his anxious friends here no one with any heart can grudge. Besides which, there is no one on that station who has the resources of mind and the physical activity you have.' On receipt of Beaufort's letter, Kellett could only think back to May 1845 when, moored off Chatham, he and the crews of *Herald* and her tender *Pandora* had cheered the *Erebus* and *Terror* at the very start of their fateful voyage.

Although Polar expeditions were exclusively initiated by the Admiralty, and thus were outside the budget and control of the Hydrographic Office, Beaufort, in his position as Hydrographer and member of the Royal Society and the Royal Geographical Society contributed to the directions of the exploration, and naturally benefited from the results on its return. Since the early 1820s, he had been in close contact with the great Arctic explorers of the day – Parry, Lyon and Franklin – even then in his unofficial capacity gleaning much magnetic and meteorological information. Letters passed between them. In 1819–20, Parry in HMS *Hecla* had managed to penetrate as far east as Melville Island before being frozen in at Winter Harbour. Then in 1829–33 in an expedition privately funded by the distiller Sir Felix Booth, Sir John Ross aboard *Victory* reached as far west as Felix Harbour by way of Prince Regent Inlet from Baffin Bay – it was on this expedition that his nephew and second-in-command,

Commander James Clark Ross made various sledging trips, one of which was westward across 'the isthmus to Spence Bay and the north coast of King William Island as far west at Victory Point'.[10] In another sledge journey, he discovered the North Magnetic Pole, which he marked 'with the Union Flag'.[11]

Eventually, Ross abandoned his ship and made his way north overland by sledge and boat where he was rescued by the whaling ship *Isabella* and returned to England. Although Beaufort had first-hand accounts of these expeditions, Ross's *failure* to find the North West Passage bizarrely seemed proof of its existence, and nothing could convince him that its discovery was not within easy reach. On the cover of one of his annual letters from the frozen-in *Victory*, Beaufort even wrote 'affords abundant proof of what may be affected by resolution, perseverance and unanimity'.[12] His friend Colonel Edward Sabine (who had accompanied both Parry and Ross as astronomer on their Arctic expeditions) agreed with him too. 'I feel more confident,' Beaufort wrote to James Clark Ross on his return in December 1833, 'than I have ever previously ventured to feel that the probability of accomplishing a passage is now so great as fully to justify the attempt.'[13] He had become totally obsessed with the project, not for himself (he was not a vain man looking for personal glory), but he could see the advantage to Britain's trade were the Atlantic and the Pacific joined by a route other than round Cape Horn.

So, spurred on by Barrow and other Arctic explorers James Clark Ross, John Franklin, George Back and Dr John Richardson, Beaufort lobbied the Royal Society to set up a committee to influence the Admiralty for a final assault on the North West Passage. To the Royal Geographical Society, he wrote 'that there is an open and, at times, a navigable sea passage between the Straits of Davis and Behring [*sic*] there can be no doubt in the mind of any person who has duly weighed the evidence; and it is equally certain that it would be an intolerable disgrace to this country were the flag of any other nation to be borne through it before our own'.[14] And that was before the Hudson Bay Company mounted a boat-borne expedition, led by Peter Dease and Dr Thomas Simpson, eastwards from the mouth of the Coppermine River along the northern Canadian coast. In the summer of 1839 they passed through what they named Simpson Strait, then along the southern shore of King William Island to the west coast of Boothia Peninsular, visiting Montreal Island. When they erected a large cairn at Cape John Herschel, they were about 70 miles to the south of Victory Point, the same that James Clark Ross had reached.

At eighty, Sir John Barrow knew his long reign at the Admiralty was coming to a close. Like Beaufort, the discovery of the North West Passage had become an obsession to him, and national honour was at stake. 'If the completion of the passage be left to be performed by some other power,' he wrote, 'England, by her neglect of it, after having opened the East and West doors, would be laughed at by all the world for having hesitated to cross the threshold.'[15] With the wholehearted and active support of Beaufort, Barrow initiated the project in that well-tried and tested way of making the Royal Geographical Society approach the Admiralty. He then solicited the opinions of the seasoned Arctic explorers, the likes of Back, Franklin, Beechey and James Clark Ross. Armed with Beaufort's and their written testimonials, Barrow went to the Prime Minister, Sir Robert Peel to pre-empt the Admiralty. He presented his case well, citing the huge public interest in the project and the minimal cost for mounting such an expedition by sending the *Erebus* and the *Terror*, recently returned from circumnavigating Antarctica under the command of James Clark Ross. In fact, the ships were ideal, being converted bomb vessels constructed with extraordinary strength to withstand the shock of heavy mortars fired from amidships. The Admiralty could do nothing but agree to Barrow's last proposal in his long and distinguished career.

With Admiralty approval, the next step was to find someone to lead the expedition. James Clark Ross was the obvious choice but he turned it down saying that he was too old at forty-four and anyway, he had promised his wife that his days of exploration were over. Also, he had a serious drink problem. Crozier, the former captain of the *Terror*, also turned it down on the grounds that he could not stand the hardship, while 'Parry of the Arctic' hinted to Beaufort that he might come out of retirement. But nothing came of that, either. No one wanted Sir John Ross, which left just one candidate in Barrow's stable, Beaufort's great friend Sir John Franklin. Franklin, who had been monstrously treated as Governor of Tasmania, was eager to restore his name and reputation. But just short of sixty, he was far too old for the assignment. Although sympathetic to his friend, Beaufort knew Franklin was the wrong choice and begged James Clark Ross to reconsider. Others thought so too, and Ross was offered many *douceurs* to change his mind – a pension, a baronetcy and a year to dry out. They counted for nothing, and Ross refused all inducements leaving the way clear for Franklin to command the expedition.

The *Erebus* and the *Terror* were then completely refitted and overhauled, the existing bow timbers being further strengthened and armour-plated. Steam engines, bought from the Greenwich Railway Company, were installed to drive two-bladed propellers that could be withdrawn inside the hull. Unheard of luxuries, like a desalination plant and a central heating system for the living quarters, were also added. The ships carried three years of provisions that included 48 tonnes of meat, 3,684 gallons of liquor, 3.5 tonnes of tobacco and lemon and cranberry juice for scurvy. The combined complement of 134 officers and men (all on double pay) were also carefully chosen, the men (mostly whalers) coming from the north, the officers with Arctic experience. Captain Francis Crozier, a veteran of two of Parry's Arctic expeditions, again commanded the *Terror*, Commander James Fitzjames, a newcomer to the Arctic, the *Erebus*.

Sir John Franklin's general orders from the Admiralty were straightforward enough – to sail 'through the North West Passage from Baffin Bay to the Bering Strait, then proceed to the Sandwich Islands (Hawaii) and return to Britain via Cape Horn'.[16] To achieve this they suggested that he sailed west through Lancaster Sound and Barrow Strait as far as Cape Walker, then head south and west towards the Bering Strait in as straight a course as the 'ice and unknown land' would allow. If his passage was blocked, he was to return to Cape Walker and head north through Wellington Channel between Cornwallis and Devon Islands before turning west. In July 1845 the *Erebus* and *Terror* entered Melville Sound and sailed for a few days alongside two whalers, the *Enterprise* and the *Prince of Wales*. Their crews were the last Europeans to see any of Franklin's expedition alive.

As the *Erebus* and *Terror* were fitting out, Sir John Ross had been disparaging about the whole expedition – the ships, with a 19-foot draught were too large and drew too much water. He had then told Franklin that if nothing had been heard of him by the February of 1847, then he, Ross would come personally and rescue him. Nothing was heard of Franklin for the rest of 1845 and all 1846, but then nothing was expected. As promised, in February 1847 Ross turned up at the Admiralty with his plan to rescue Franklin, and was peremptorily sent away. The expedition was not lost, they maintained, and therefore there were no plans for its rescue. But the month before Beaufort had also had his fears for Franklin's safety. He wrote to James Clark Ross, 'Though I would not let a whisper of anxiety escape from me, one must perceive that if he be not forthcoming by next winter, some substantive steps must be taken in 1848 – and for that step, certain measures must be set on foot in 1847.'[17]

When Franklin did not materialise by the spring of 1848, a three-pronged rescue mission was launched. Besides Kellett being ordered north from the Pacific by Beaufort to rendezvous with HMS *Plover* in Kotzebue Sound, the Admiralty sent James Clark Ross (flattered out of retirement by Beaufort with the line 'to no other person would the country be satisfied to delegate that exploit') in the *Enterprise*, and Captain Bird in *Investigator* to search from the east. An overland expedition led by Sir John Richardson and Dr John Rae, a Hudson Bay Company man, was sent down the Mackenzie River to search the shore eastwards from the Coppermine River. No trace was found by any of them, and, after wintering on Somerset Island, Ross returned to England empty-handed. Having mounted one abortive rescue attempt, the Admiralty had little enthusiasm in continuing the search. But public opinion could not be ignored. By way of a compromise, they offered large rewards for Franklin's rescue (£20,000), the discovery of the *Erebus* and the *Terror* (£10,000) and a further £10,000 for the discovery of the North West Passage. With that they handed the responsibility over to the Arctic Council so completely that Commander Leopold McCormick recorded that 'Could you point out the very spot where you could put your hand on Franklin they would not listen to it at the Admiralty, everything being left to the Arctic Council.'[18]

The Arctic Council was a nebulous organisation that had been founded in the 1830s to monitor attempts on the North West Passage. It was another of John Barrow's committees of which he was naturally the head and its members were predictably drawn from his scientific friends that included such luminaries as Beaufort, Parry, Beechey, Sabine, James Clark Ross, Back, and Bird. After Barrow's death, his place was filled by his genial son, also called John Barrow, while Beaufort assumed the role of foreman or chairman. Beaufort threw himself into his new duties with exaggerated energy on several counts. He had certainly played a major role in commissioning Franklin's ill-fated voyage of discovery, and partially blamed himself for his plight. Sir John Franklin was a very old friend, but he also could see that any rescue attempt would certainly yield some very useful surveys and research. Added to that, the second Lady Franklin was a close friend, too, and very forceful – she was to call Beaufort her 'wisest councillor' and to virtually the day he died she was to enlist his help in all but the last of her privately funded rescue missions.

Under Beaufort's direction, the Arctic Council was galvanised into action. From 1849 for ten years, the Arctic Archipelago teemed with ships and overland rescue attempts. With no Polar experience to draw on, Beaufort had to rely on others in the Arctic Council who had. But no one could agree where to search. Nor would they, or the Admiralty, listen to other opinions – Dr Richard King, the surgeon who had accompanied Captain Back down the Back River said that the search should (rightly as it turned out) start from there and go north, but his demeanour was so offensive that no one, not even Lady Franklin, listened to him. Later Beechey, who was actually serving on the Arctic Council, and Lieutenant Sherard Osborn, one of Beaufort's surveyors, held a similar view, but they too were overruled.

What Franklin had actually done was to obey orders, but the exceptional weather in 1845–6 meant that he could begin to carry them out, to his cost. The first season went particularly well. Franklin entered Lancaster Sound, heading up Wellington Channel to latitude 77° North, until ice forced him back down and around Cornwallis Island to Barrow Strait to winter in Erebus Bay on Beechey Island. With the break up of the ice the next year, Franklin headed south and west through Peel Strait (renamed Franklin Strait) between Somerset and Prince of Wales Islands heading for what he thought was familiar territory from his 1825 expedition. The waters were unusually free of ice as he pressed on to the west of King William Island to complete what he thought was the North West Passage. But once there, the *Erebus* and *Terror* entered the trap that was to spring shut tightly behind them – the unending wall of crushing ice, pushed from the open sea and squeezed through McClintock Channel cut them off. Slowly, the ice closed around them. The ships' companies spent their second ice-bound winter, looking forward to the summer. But before the expected break-up came, on 11 June 1847 Sir John Franklin died. But the awaited break-up never came that summer, and after the next winter frozen to the same spot, the strengthened timbers and the iron cladding were no longer a match for the crushing power of the sea ice. As *Erebus* and *Terror* began to break up, the ships' companies, led by Crozier, abandoned both ships on 22 April 1848 and made their way over the ice to King William Island.

In England, plans for searches continued, and Beaufort went back to Franklin's original orders for some clue as to where they might explore next. 'Sir John Franklin,' he wrote, 'is not a man to treat his orders with levity, and therefore his first attempt was undoubtedly made in the direction of Melville Island and out to the westward.'[19] And so the rescue parties continued to search too far to the west. But Franklin had also been ordered south. Rescuers had noted that Peel Sound was blocked and so the south option was overruled, and again the search parties were directed too far to the north. So in the summer of 1849 Beaufort, still convinced that Franklin had made it to the west, ordered Kellett back through the Bering Straits, in the company of *Plover* and the Royal Thames Yacht Club schooner, *Nancy Dawson*, to continue his search. Amazingly, at Kotzebue Sound, Kellett gave a dinner for the officers of the three ships serving bread, pies and pudding made from flour left by Beechey 23 years before. The early ice forced the *Herald*, *Plover* and *Nancy Dawson* to retreat south, but Kellett made a survey of northern Siberia on the way. They were, however, ordered back the next summer to resume the search.

The total lack of success only fuelled public interest. The search for Franklin had become something of a national crusade and, fostered by Lady Franklin, it spread to the United States. When Beaufort heard that two American ships were being fitted by private subscription, he exclaimed, 'What we are to do is now the question, for we must not be behind the feeling manifested throughout our own country or suffer ourselves to be eclipsed by the humane enthusiasm in America.' By the summer of 1850, there were no fewer than ten ships in the Arctic eastern approaches. Captain Horatio Austin aboard HMS *Resolute* commanded a squadron of four ships (Captain Ommanney of the *Assistance* with two tenders, *Intrepid* and *Pioneer*) taking them to Barrow Strait where they were held up by ice. There were two American brigs, *Advance* and *Rescue*, sent by the US Navy and financed by the philanthropist Henry Grinnell (at the request of Lady Franklin) who searched the Wellington Channel to the north. But most extraordinary was the presence of Sir John Ross in the steam yacht *Felix* (named after his sponsor Sir Felix Booth) and her tender, the 12-ton yacht *Mary*, financed by the Hudson Bay Company and public subscription. Although Ross was no favourite of the Admiralty, he did at least have the support of Beaufort who recorded his approval of the 73-year-old Arctic veteran: 'He is well acquainted with the management of steam. He possesses a singularly hearty constitution. He has acquired much dear bought experience in the ice, is full of inventive resources and would feel a degree of pride in carrying out this, his favourite scheme, which supported by an intrepid and dogged resolution would probably do more in surmounting the difficulties and dangers of this sacred cause than would be achieved by officers of far more brilliant talents.'[20] There were two more Admiralty-chartered ships sent by the Arctic Council, the *Lady Franklin* and the *Sophia* under the command of Captain William Penny, a dour whaling captain from Aberdeenshire but a favourite of Jane Franklin. The *Lady Franklin* had an appropriate figurehead, that of Hope leaning on her symbol, an anchor.

Lady Franklin mounted and sponsored her own rescue attempts, using her own funds and those she raised publicly – McCormick told a story that when once sharing a cab with her, she suddenly ordered the driver to stop in St Paul's. Jumping out, she ran into Mr Dolland's shop and reappeared a few minutes later clutching a draft for £100. The money had come from Mr Dolland, she explained to a startled McCormick, on the strength of him being Franklin's optician. In the autumn of 1850, she sent the *Prince Albert*, a schooner of 80 tons commanded by Captain Charles Forsyth with orders drafted by herself and Beaufort. The *Prince Albert* was to sail down Prince Regent Islet, to cross North Somerset and to continue down Peel Sound. It was the right direction, but as with James Clark Ross's expedition two years before, a wall of ice forced her back after just 70 miles. But on her return to England, she took with her the first tangible evidence of Franklin's expedition, the location of his first (1845–6) winter quarters on Beechey Island found by William Penny. The news was greeted with great excitement in all quarters – Queen Victoria herself asked Beaufort to prepare a chart of Beechey Island and Wellington Sound to show the exact spot where the remains were found.

Armed with this new piece of information, Beaufort then sat down on his own to rationally rethink the whole of the Arctic Council's disjointed policy, then communicated his thoughts to the Admiralty. The *Erebus* and *Terror* could have caught fire or struck a rock and sunk, but that was unlikely as one or other might have come to grief but not both. It was also unlikely that either had capsized in a heavy sea, as the Arctic waters were laden with ice that would prevent a swell. If both ships were caught in the ice, the most likely option, then the crews would have taken to the boats (at best) or sledges if they left it too late and made for the shore, where they would have been rescued. Had they foundered north, they would have made their way back to Lancaster Sound or Barrow Strait and been rescued there; if they had reached Victoria Island, then the Inuit around the mouth of the Mackenzie River would know about them. If they had gone up Wellington Channel, as the sledge tracks from the Beechey Island encampment indicated, then there would have been some reference to it in a cairn. There was none. So where had he gone?

To Beaufort, there was only one possible solution. He must be in some undiscovered archipelago to the west of Melville Island having sailed through some uncharted islet beyond Cape Walker, and then turned south or southwest as ordered. If they had foundered then, as indeed they must from the length of time since anyone had heard from them, then they must be to the south, towards the Mackenzie River but not as far east as Back River, or even Coppermine River. Beaufort was right in one premise, that if an entrapped Franklin could not send word *back* to Barrow Strait, then there was little point in starting the rescue missions *from* there. 'In the fifth year of their absence,' he wrote to McCormick, 'every place should be searched'.[21] The inlets off Wellington Channel and Smith Sound were searched, and, to no one's surprise, they revealed nothing.

It was Beaufort's own plan, therefore, to mount another expedition from the west in the hope of meeting Franklin as he journeyed east. James Clark Ross's ships were available after his final voyage, and Beaufort chose Richard Collinson, one of his best surveyors, to captain the *Enterprise* and lead the expedition, with Commander Robert McClure, an old Arctic hand under James Clark Ross, as captain of the *Investigator*. For the last weeks of 1849, Beaufort worked on what he called his 'Behring Straight affair' to the exclusion of all else. He poured over the existing charts, he consulted his fellow members of the Arctic Council, namely Ross, Beechey, Back and Richardson. He lobbied the Admiralty. Eventually, his scheme was approved. Collinson would sail eastwards along the north coast of Alaska, then head northeast towards Banks Land and eventually Melville Island.

There was also a plan to send Dr John Rae to tackle the western Arctic from northern Canada using boats, but if the coast became impassable, he was to fall back westward to the Mackenzie River.

In the flood of excitement in sending off his expedition, Beaufort lost none of his inventive flair and interest in new technology. He looked into the possibility of supplying Collinson 'with a balloon to carry him half a mile high from whence with a good telescope he could see ships, huts, smoke or flags for many miles'.[22] The balloon, however, was too bulky to take, while the proposal for a powered balloon was dismissed as 'totally absurd'. He also experimented with paper balloons with tails of slow-burning fuses to which bundles of papers with information for the rescue party were attached. As the fuse burnt down, so the papers were released from a mile high where 'they will fly to dispersing to a great distance'. The idea actually worked when a balloon was sent up from a ship in the Thames and 'half Woolwich Common confessed the shower'.[23] Beaufort had come a long way from James Clark Ross's 'Two penny postmen' – Arctic foxes released with metal collars stamped with rescue information.

Beaufort went to the Portsmouth to see the *Enterprise* and the *Investigator* off, telling their captains that he had arranged for them to be towed by Royal Navy steam tugs through the

Strait of Magellan to make up for lost time. In the journey north in the Pacific, the two ships became separated, McClure reaching the Bering Straits first. There he met Kellett who advised him to wait for Collinson but the headstrong McClure carried on, as Pim, one of Kellett's lieutenants recorded in his journal: '*Investigator* intends to take the pack at any risk.' Running east by squeezing between the fast ice and the pack as far as Banks Island, he inched his way north through Prince of Wales Strait before being forced south to winter at Princess Royal Islands. The next spring, 1851, he sent out sledging parties and explored the western coasts of Victoria Island, and after his ship was released from the ice, continued around Banks Island until he was forced to winter in Mercy Bay, off McClure Strait. There the *Investigator* remained embedded in the ice for that winter and the following summer (1852) and the next spring, McClure was about to abandon his ship when Lieutenant Pim arrived informing him he was saved – Captain Henry Kellett of the *Resolute* was anchored off Dearly Island across McClure Strait in company of the *Intrepid* under Commander McClintock. The whole ship's company sledged across to the *Resolute* and, after another winter, their fourth, McClure and the '*Investigator*s' sledged back to Beechey Island when both ships were abandoned. Both crews then returned to England in the summer of 1854.

But Collinson's voyage was no less remarkable. The month that he was behind McClure entering the Bering Straits made all the difference. He was driven back by the ice, retreated to the Pacific and spent the first winter in Hong Kong. Back again the next year, he followed McClure's passage heading up into Prince of Wales Strait before being forced south again to winter on the southwest corner of Victoria Island. To his fury, Collinson's sledging parties criss-crossed those of McClure around Victoria Island. Then, in the summer of 1852, he took the *Enterprise* south and east through the narrow waters of Dolphin and Union Strait, Coronation Gulf and Dease Strait, ending up at Cambridge Bay for the winter. Early the next spring, 1853, Collinson took a sledge party to explore the southeast and east coast of Victoria Island where he found evidence of Dr John Rae's overland expedition from the summer of 1851. It was tragic, however, that he did not know that at one point he was within 100 kilometres from the spot where *Erebus* and *Terror* had been abandoned. McClure had disobeyed orders; he pressed on in order to find the North West Passage and so claim the £10,000 reward. Had he stuck with Collinson, the interpreter aboard *Investigator* (who should have been transferred across) would have understood the Inuit encountered on the mainland. They would doubtless have sent them over to the northwest coast of King William Island, where they would have come across the remains of Franklin's party. Collinson retraced his passage and spent another icebound winter before returning to England by Hong Kong and the Cape of Good Hope with nothing but a few good charts to show for his five-year voyage.

While Collinson and McClure were battling it out with the western Arctic, and later with each other, the mood at home had changed little. The Admiralty wished to draw a line under the whole affair, but the Arctic Council (and certainly Lady Franklin in whose house they often met) wished to keep it going. They also had public opinion on their side. No one now cared a fig for the North West Passage, but they did care about what had happened to Franklin and his crew. An editorial in *The Times* pointed out that 'we do not think the geographical importance of these expeditions commensurate with the cost or exposure of a single sloop's crew, but it does impinge most emphatically on our national honour that we should ascertain the fate of our missing countrymen and redeem them, if living, from the dangers to which they have been consigned'.[24] And so yet more expeditions were put together in 1852, the one mounted by the Admiralty being led by Captain Sir Edward Belcher. Within the Arctic Council, Beaufort alone appears to be responsible for his appointment, and was thus blamed when it went so disastrously wrong. Although he had no first hand experience in Polar Regions himself, Beaufort was consorting with those who had, and thus should have been advised on the special qualities needed to command a ship, let alone a squadron, in Arctic waters. Having no Polar experience either, Belcher could not have been a worse choice – his understated entry in the *Dictionary of National Biography* read, 'Perhaps no officer of equal ability has ever succeeded in inspiring so much personal dislike, and the customary exercise of his authority did not make Arctic service less trying.'[25] Yet Beaufort knew his limitations only too well and still he had him appointed to the post. In orders dated 16 April 1852, Belcher was given command of a squadron comprising his own ship HMS *Assistance*, with Lieutenant Sherard Osborn aboard the tender *Pioneer*, and Captain Henry Kellett of HMS *Resolute* and Commander Francis McClintock aboard the *Intrepid*, along with a depot ship *North Star* under the command of Captain William Pullen.

It can be no coincidence that this squadron contained two of Beaufort's most able surveyors, Belcher and Kellett. By the time they were dispatched to the eastern Arctic, his own theory of Franklin stranded in the west had still not been disproved by Collinson and McClure. While Beaufort was at the forefront of the quest for Franklin, he still was Hydrographer to the Navy. Before the Franklin expedition, the charts of the Arctic and known scientific data were rudimentary and sketchy. As each search expedition returned, so the knowledge and the charts of the Arctic built up. In hindsight, many of the orders that captains received would appear to have more to do with surveying than rescue.

Belcher's squadron reached Beechey Island in August 1852 and immediately split into three. Leaving *North Star* there, he headed north with *Pioneer* searching Wellington Channel where he wintered in Northumberland Sound on the northwest coast of Devon Island. Kellett, along with *Intrepid*, moved west along Parry Channel until blocked by ice when he retreated to Dealy Island on the south coast of Melville Island. In the spring, Kellett sent out sledging parties to explore the western and northern parts of Melville Island (where Pim discovered McClure), with Belcher's sledges working in the northeastern section along Grinnell Peninsular and Bathurst Island. Another year passed and with both pairs of ships frozen in during the whole summer, Belcher gave orders that all four should be abandoned and retreated by sledge (with the crew of the *Investigator*) to the *North Star* at their base at Beechey Island. With the help of two supply vessels, *Phoenix* and *Talbot*, the crews of all five vessels were taken back to England. The recriminations were predictable, and Belcher only just survived his court martial for the total loss of his squadron.

The fate of Franklin was finally solved – as far as it will ever be fully solved – by Dr John Rae who, in 1853, was sent by the Hudson Bay Company on a surveying expedition of the relatively short uncharted stretch of the mainland between the Castor and Pollux River and the Bellot* Straits. The party consisted of twelve men including two Inuit interpreters. The expedition spilled over into the next year, Rae over-wintering in Repulse Bay where they built a snow house and lived off the game, including '109 caribou, one musk ox, 106 ptarmigan and

---

* Joseph Réné Bellot was a lieutenant who had served with distinction with the French Navy before volunteering for the second privately funded voyage of the Prince Albert under Captain Kennedy. He disappeared into the ice while carrying a message to Belcher.

54 salmon'.[26] At the end of March 1854, Rae set off to chart the west coast of Boothia where he met an Inuk wearing a gold cap band. He said that it had come from 'a number of Whites who were dying a long way to the west'[27] but he himself had not been there. Rae bought the cap band and proceeded with his survey. He reached the cairn erected by Dease and Simpson at the mouth of the Castor and Pollux River, and returned to his winter quarters where a group of Inuit were also camped. From them, Rae bought a silver fork and a spoon with the initials F.R.M.C. [Francis Rawdon Moira Crozier] scratched on the handle. Over the next two months, Rae pieced together the story of how Inuit families hunting seals off the north coast of King William Island reported seeing about forty white men hauling a boat and sledges. But before returning south, these Inuit had later discovered about thirty-five corpses and some graves 'about a long day's journey to the northwest of the mouth of a large stream [Back River]'.[28] Also second-hand, Rae learned from them that 'from the mutilated state of many of the bodies and the contents of the kettles, it is evident that our wretched Countrymen had been driven to the last alternatives, as a means of sustaining life'.[29] Rae returned to York Factory with other articles from Franklin's expedition, including a silver salver engraved with 'Sir John Franklin K O H', then sailed to England to report his findings to the Admiralty. But far from being lauded with his discoveries, Rae was vilified on two counts – the reports of the cannibalism and the fact that he did not immediately go himself to find the graves. Rae's charge of cannibalism was proved a century and a half later when the bones were found with cut marks 'consistent with the removal of muscle tissue'. He did, however, receive the £10,000 reward for his findings.

On the charge of not going to the site immediately, Rae defended himself in a letter to *The Times* pointing out that he had hurried to England to stop further expeditions being sent to the wrong places. The Admiralty had had enough, and with this evidence declared Franklin and his crew dead. Beaufort had to tow the official line, but gave what help he could for private ventures even after he had retired as Hydrographer, in the main through the indomitable Lady Franklin. In fact one of his last acts as Hydrographer was to send charts and advice to Dr Elisha Kane who was about to lead another Grinnell-backed expedition, as proof of his 'earnest hopes' of his success. In the end, it was Commander Leopold McClintock, in the 177-ton screw yacht *Fox*, funded by Lady Franklin, who finally found the remains of her husband's expedition on King William Island. The news reached London late in 1859, but by that time, Beaufort was long dead.

One postscript to the whole sorry affair was of the *Resolute*, which broke free of the ice and was found drifting in the Davis Strait by the *George Henry*, an American whaler. Her captain, a James Buddington, was delighted with his find and sold her to the US Navy for $40,000. She was then restored to her former glory and sailed to Spithead where Captain Hartstein USN handed her over to Queen Victoria 'not only as an evidence of a friendly feeling to your Sovereignty, but as a token of love, admiration and respect to your Majesty personally'.[30] The story does not end there. When the *Resolute* was finally broken up in 1880, a six-by-four-foot desk was made out of the timbers and presented to the President of the United States. It was found in a storeroom and used in the Oval Office by President Kennedy, where it remains to this day.

CHAPTER 13

Rear-Admiral
Sir Francis Beaufort KCB

'MY DAYS AND ALMOST MY NIGHTS are occupied by a succession of business which I can neither avoid nor dismiss, indeed half execute,' Francis Beaufort wrote to his brother William. 'I am never more than $5^{1}/_{2}$ hours in bed, my meals are gobbled down with more voracious rapidity than when I was a midshipman, one job follows another like a showman's harangue, and whether at my house or my office everybody thinks that they are entitled to destroy as much of my time as they can in order to kill their own. I would fain have a little time to think for much of my business needs reflection, yet the only moment I have is washing and to and fro to the Admiralty, and that is too often curtailed by the necessity of taking a cab to expedite matters.'[1] The letter was actually written in 1831, but it would have been equally true at any time during his tenure as Hydrographer.

Nor would he have had it any other way, for the largest part of Beaufort's home life was merely an extension of his professional life. Besides his faithful Service associates, his circle of friends and acquaintances widened with his appointment as Hydrographer – the likes of the Babbages, the Souths and the Airys, with whom he shared a common interest in science or sat on the same committees, subsequently became close personal friends. Alicia was invariably out of her depth with these scientists, often their wives as well, but she kept a good house and was a charming hostess. At home, Beaufort relied on her implicitly. He sent her off (she willingly) to hunt for a new house when the lease on Manchester Street fell in – having eschewed Eaton Square, they settled on a large house in Cumberland Street which they just managed to afford with her inheritance and 'by letting the stables for £30 a year'.

Beaufort's love and admiration for Alicia as a wife and mother never waned. They delighted in each other's company, and shared the same ribbing humour. On their twentieth wedding anniversary, he commissioned a pair of silver candlesticks for her. In a letter to Alicia, he wrote: 'this tapered stand, tastefully fashioned as an emblem of her to whom it is sent. In its chaste and soft lustre of silver, we find your brilliant yet tender delicate mind – in its shape too, another resemblance is found, the base being broad, wide, spreading and round, the carriage erect and well developed above, *la taille* fine and svelte, all the form that I love, but the principal point of the parallel lies in the lighted supports – bright spreading eyes.'[2]

But soon after their 'china' wedding anniversary, a lump was discovered in Alicia's breast and cancer diagnosed six months later. While Beaufort was totally devastated, Alicia bore 'the march of her disease' stoically, maintaining until the last that it was ordained by God. As she wrote to William Beaufort, she could truly say that Heaven had taught her 'to rejoice in tribulation, for I have blessings without number – Oh! how many more than I deserve, and how doubly dear to me since I have the constant prospect of losing them'.[3] Right up to the end, nearly two years later, she was rarely free from pain. She was, however, sustained by her faith, 'the protecting love of a redeeming Providence', larger and larger doses of laudanum, and her husband for as much as his busy schedule allowed. She died, surrounded by her family, in the early morning of 27 August 1834. She was buried in a quiet ceremony in the cemetery of St John-at-Hackney, where both her parents were interred in a large 'table top' tomb. Beaufort was inconsolable, and emerged from her long illness and death 'so much changed that it seemed doubtful that he would ever regain his health and buoyant cheerfulness'.[4] But Alicia's dying wish was that he, her husband of over twenty-one years, should take care of himself 'for the sake of our children'.

When Alicia died, she left a young family. Daniel Augustus, then aged 20, had won an essay prize and a scholarship worth £80 to Trinity, Cambridge, his place being secured by Beaufort's friend, Thomas Peacock, while Francis Lestock at 19 was also offered a place at St John's, but opted for the East India Company College (the present Haileybury). Little 'Morry', his father's favourite, was just 11, the girls, Sophie aged 15, Rosalind 14, and the baby of the family, Emily was just eight. All were still at home and being educated at day schools. There was female staff in the house – a cook and two housemaids – who took charge of the young Morry and the girls, but Beaufort soon realised that with his demanding life he needed a stronger female presence. The obvious answer was for him to bring over his two spinster sisters, Henrietta, always known as Harriet or Harry, and Louisa, who shared a house in Dublin.

By this time, the Beaufort family had moved to a grace and favour house provided by the Admiralty at 7 Somerset Street in Westminster, and the sisters arrived in the summer of 1835. Their relationships with their brother were particularly close, but for different reasons. He admired Louisa as an author, her *Dialogues on Entomology* and essay on the round towers of Ireland earned her the membership of the Royal Irish Academy, a rare honour for a woman. Louisa had been born 'in exile' when the family were living in Wales, so Beaufort knew her since the day of her birth. Harriet, on the other hand, was left behind with relations in Ireland when she was just one year old. When the Beaufort family returned to Ireland, Harriet was six and her brother Francis ten. They had just four years together before Francis went to sea, and throughout that time, she idolised him. He was particularly fond of her and it was to Harriet that Francis wrote his most chatty letters throughout his sea career. In a revealing letter to him in 1825, she admonished him for not coming to see her to brighten what was a dreary life when he made a brief visit to Ireland. But despite 'all these lights and shadows, our friendship remains unclouded, unbroken,' she wrote, 'and you are still, as you say in your last command to me my old friend and brother and master – and when the vanities and flatteries of life have passed away, it will be one pleasure at least to us to look back on the unchanged affection of our whole lives'.[5]

The 'unchanged affection', however, was seemingly to go further. Having Harriet in the house, (probably in the only other room on his bedroom floor of the tall terraced house) was too great a temptation. Although it appears completely out of character for a God-fearing man of such a high moral calibre as Beaufort, it would appear from the ciphered entries in his private diary that he entered into some close relationship with his sister. He was sixty-one, she fifty-seven. The first entry, over the Saturday and Sunday 26 November 1837, 'Fresh horrors with Harriet, O Lord forgive us', presupposes that whatever the relationship between them was, something had happened earlier. She always appears a willing partner. The entries continue at irregular intervals – 'and yet H[arriet] – I have sinned again this night' is recorded two days after he 'visited my beloved wife's shrine and renewed my vow of virtue', followed a week later with 'H – I sinned again', and a week after that, 'Wicked Sunday'. Other later entries read 'By HB. Wretched man that I am indeed' and 'Did it to Harriet'. That same year, 1837, also in a ciphered entry, on 27 August he records, the anniversary of Alicia's death: 'Absolutely forgot this sad day'. Throughout that relationship, Beaufort was wracked with guilt. The entry for 16 December 1837 (again a Saturday night) reads, 'My poor sister again tempted by me but the shame I now feel will I hope preserve forever from further temptation. O Lord assist me to receive Thy Holy Sacrament worthily.' The relationship ended a month after he proposed, and was accepted by, Honora Edgeworth, the daughter of Richard Lovell Edgeworth and his third wife, Elizabeth Sneyd. In a plain entry in his diary for 1 October 1838, 'Long conversation with H[arriet] B[eaufort] about – and I did very wrong. Heaven have mercy on me.' Immediately after the wedding, Harriet and her sister returned to Dublin.

The marriage between Beaufort and Honora took place at Edgeworthstown on 8 November 1838. He had known her since she was a slight 'slip of a girl' of eleven, when he first went to see her father, and later, to pay court to her half-sister Charlotte. At 14, she had accompanied her Sneyd aunts to see him on the *Woolwich* when he declared 'little Honora, if I mistake not, will one day be the heroine of a more interesting tale than this'.[6] But even in the intervening 33 years when she was looking after an aged aunt, Beaufort never forgot her. He rarely failed to inquire after her in his letters to his sister Fanny, referring to Honora in such terms as 'that tender plant' or the 'amiable and affectionate friend'. He took the keenest interest in all her many ailments, going to great lengths to find the right cures for her heart murmurs, deaf ear, and stomach disorders. Beaufort fixed on her with a passion and began his courtship two years after the death of his 'beloved Alicia'. But despite her miserable lot in Ireland, Beaufort's path to her was crossed by doubt (guilt over the memory of Alicia) and rejection. She wrote to their mutual friend, Thomas Robinson, for advice and his opinion on the proposed marriage. He replied that 'in him alone is the high tome of moral feeling. He is indeed, as the novel has it, a one in a thousand, and you should be most happy in your choice.'[7] And indeed she was.

At last he won through and 'secured a friend to himself and his daughters for many of the later years of his life'. But they made for an odd couple. He was 64, she twenty years younger. Not long before her marriage she was described as 'the tall, thin, elegant looking young lady with a high colour and with such a remarkable lady-like manner'[8] (although she described herself as being 'as grey as a badger'[9]), while Beaufort, pale through over-work and showing his age, declared himself her 'devoted little man'. Although they shared many of the same characteristics – she was 'dependable' with the 'strong judgement' of her father – they had little in common. But those interests that she did not share with Beaufort, like music and dancing, were, however, much to the liking of his daughters.

The marriage by Victorian standards was agreeable enough, and even after five years Beaufort could claim that 'neither unkind word or look have escaped either of us'. He was bereft when Honora went on a visit to her family in Ireland. He wrote touchingly while she was away – 'Midnight. It is either very late or very early to begin a letter, but no hour can be too early or too late to whisper my love to my dear little wife,' ending with, 'you are seldom absent from my thoughts where you are the master.'[10] They soon settled down into a routine that altered little. To Beaufort's irritation, Honora was intensely social. During the London Season, they attended balls and dinners – Beaufort once confiding to his diary 'how horrid dining abroad every day, wasting time, learning nothing, seeing less, eating and drinking too much, talking nonsense.'[11] They entertained new and old friends at their new house, 11 Gloucester Place, Marylebone, sometimes with as many as 20 seated for dinner, or they dined with friends. Beaufort often dined out, either at one of the many societies and committees like the Senate of University College, Trinity House, or the First Lord of the Admiralty's dinner to mark the Queen's birthday. When he was working late at the Admiralty, he dined at the Athenaeum, the club founded by Sir John Croker for 'the association of individuals, known for their scientific or literary attainments', of which Beaufort was amongst the original members.

Sundays, unless prevented by sickness that was rarely absent in one or more members of the Beaufort household, was a day of unalterable routine. The family attended the Portman Chapel where Daniel Augustus Beaufort, newly ordained, was curate. When he preached the sermon at evensong, the family returned to hear him, Beaufort recording the subject and quality of the sermon in his diary. As regular as church on Sundays were the annual six-week holidays in August and September. Sometimes Beaufort took his family to the Continent, either Germany or France, but more often they toured parts of Great Britain. One year they went to the Lake District and called on Wordsworth (he was out), another year it was Yorkshire and Northumberland, another the Scottish Highlands. But every year the holiday was the same – sightseeing, painting, sketching and recording, particularly the journey times of the trains.

In October 1842, Beaufort gloomily wrote to his brother, 'I believe that both happiness, and its more humble dependant pleasure, consists far more in expectation or anticipation than in actual enjoyment.'[12] But apart from the odd interminable dinner, dance or concert that Honora and his daughters dragged him to, his life was totally enjoyable – he was fulfilled at the Admiralty (although here too he complained of overwork) and he lived in, and was party to, an exciting scientific age. More often, however, it was he who dragged his family to exhibitions to see such innovations as John Ericsson's propeller, a new steam engine, or to see the new electric lights in Trafalgar Square. Isambard Kingdom Brunel himself showed them his Thames tunnel at Greenwich, Sir William Hooker took them around Kew Gardens, while Beaufort and Honora met Charles Darwin by chance in Regent's Park who 'introduced' them 'to some curious facts about the bumble bee'.[13]

In 1844, Beaufort celebrated his seventieth birthday. His health, never robust, was not any worse than it had been earlier in his life, considering he was still carrying a lead ball in his chest. But his wounds, age, and overwork were beginning to catch up with him. A slipped disc caused painful sciatica for which the doctor prescribed cold baths and long walks, a regime he kept to the end of his life. He frequently suffered from chronic gastritis, and later prostate trouble. Once, when walking home, he was knocked over by a runaway post office van. Although badly injured, he spent just three days in bed. Even when he had a mild heart attack at his desk, he walked home that night.

Nor was the family doctor often out of the Beaufort house. Once one of the children had some ailment that even required a visit from Sir James Clark, the Queen's physician. There are frequent references in Beaufort's diary to his daughters' fits of hysteria – Rosalind's being brought on by excessive smoking of

Indian hemp. In true Victorian fashion, the youngest daughter Emily was also prone to fits of hysteria and bouts of dizziness quickly cured when some entertainment was on offer. But it was Honora, however, who required his services the most. Two months after their wedding she had suffered a mild stroke from which she fully recovered, but she had another seven years later when she fell over and broke her hip. An infection set in which left her hopelessly crippled, and from then on, she slowly deteriorated in mind and body.

Around this period too, there are various coded entries in Beaufort's diaries of a sexual nature that show a tortured soul riddled in guilt. There is no evidence to suggest what he was doing that caused him such remorse, but whatever it was, he was not doing it with Honora as, for the most part the entries are at times when she was away in Ireland with her family, in ill health, or when he was absent from home. The first entry is for June 1844 – 'Deliberately sinned again. Shame' and a month later, 'In despair again'. In February 1847 he recorded that 'The Devil again tempted me so I punished myself by taking no tobacco through the day.' After that, the entries are sporadic over the next three years, such as 'wretch that I am' and 'Again at 8, and the worst form. Lord have mercy on me.' There are no entries after 1853 when he was in his eightieth year.

Throughout their lives, Beaufort tried to recognise his adored Alicia in his daughters. When too enfeebled to visit her grave, he wrote in his diary how 'every successive year brings out in stronger light the virtues she possessed and which I have lost! and which 'til that loss I never knew how to appreciate. The Lord bountifully gives and indignantly takes away.'[14] In a way, he found a little of Alicia in each of his daughters, and they, particularly Rosalind, were a great solace to him throughout his life. He frequently alluded to their 'excellence' in his diary. He particularly liked his son-in-law, Reverend William Palmer whom Sophia, the eldest daughter married in 1838. After their father's death, Rosalind and Emily travelled widely in the Levant, where they met the linguist, Viscount Strangford whom Emily married. She was to die of apoplexy on the *Lusitania* in the Mediterranean in 1887 on her way to found a hospital in Jerusalem.

If his daughters were a comfort to him, his sons were a trial, although Beaufort was always at pains to see the best in them. To his dying day he blamed himself for Alfred's mental condition, 'a melancholy victim, no doubt, of my sins'. Daniel Augustus was also a disappointment to him. As curate of the Portman Chapel, he was just passable as a clergyman, and when the incumbent William Bennett moved to a new parish, Beaufort bought the chapel (for £2,901) for his son. Daniel Augustus struggled on for five years but finally gave up when his congregation all but deserted him. Nothing was ever proved but there was talk of an 'unsuitable liaison' with the daughter of his housekeeper. But Beaufort never gave up on anybody, least of all his sons. He sent Daniel Augustus to Italy where he remained for eight months. On his return, Beaufort noted that he 'had improved in mind and body, but not much in estate'. But he ended up well enough as rector of Lymm cum Warburton in Cheshire where he remained for 22 years. He married Emily, daughter of Sir John Davis, who held the advowson of his parish.

Nor was Francis Lestock Beaufort much of a success in his early life either. Soon after the death of his mother, he stole one of her rings and pawned it at Cameron's in the Strand. His father 'taxed him with the robbery and he confessed all'.[15] Beaufort went himself the next day and redeemed it for thirty shillings. Although Francis Lestock 'seemed truly penitent', Beaufort was in a dilemma. He believed that he should expose him as a thief, as he thought that it would be 'criminal' of him to let him go to India 'to possibly sit in judgement there as a judge'. For four days he agonised about what he should do, finally making up his mind 'not to disgrace him out of the Civil Service. Oh Heaven, what a question for a father.' At the same time, he was kept down a year at the East India College, but graduated the next year with honours in Hindustani and Classics. He is next found in India, but three years later was charged with embezzlement of company funds. Beaufort used all his influence to save his son. The charge was reduced from dishonesty to one of incompetence and gross neglect of which he was found guilty. He survived the disgrace, and rose steadily through the East India Company to become Attorney General in Bengal. His legacy was a work entitled *Digest of Criminal Law and Procedure in Bengal*.

'Little Morry', William Morris Beaufort followed his brother to Bedford School and then into the Indian Civil Service where he did little to distinguish himself. He remained his father's favourite to the very end. On his first return home in twelve years, Beaufort was overjoyed to see him, remarking that he appeared 'much oldened and yellowed, but his heart in the same spot, his spirits as buoyant and his disposition as full of integrity and good feeling, without a grain of affectation or vanity as the day he left us'.[16] He returned home for good three years after that and spent the rest of his life compiling a book on the Beaufort pedigree, *The Family of de Beaufort*.

Despite the odd bouts of self-doubt and frustration experienced from the authorities above, generally the Lords of the Admiralty, Beaufort knew that his talents were widely appreciated and that he had made significant contributions to the society in which he lived. Occasionally, the odd moment of pique crept back when particularly crossed or he did not get his own way – 'thus I labour every day turned over by caprice and ignorance' was a typical reaction. He often threatened to resign, but always reconsidered, his employment and position being too valuable to him. In his office, he commanded genuine respect both from above and from his subordinates, but, as Sir George Back was quick to point out in his obituary of him, Beaufort was 'susceptible to flattery'. The diary entries like 'the worthlessness of my long life' do not really hold true. But like so much in his life, even the joy in his final promotion was overshadowed with controversy.

By 1846, Beaufort had risen nearly to the top of the Admiralty's active service list of post captains and was therefore due for promotion to rear admiral. This prompted some official to point out that a serving admiral could not head what was largely a civilian post within the Admiralty. Beaufort therefore had to decide whether he wanted to remain on the active list or resign, and continue as Hydrographer to the Navy. He was naturally furious that he should be put into such a position and immediately offered his resignation. Their Lordships begged him to reconsider and it was only after the intervention of the First Lord of the Admiralty, Lord Auckland, that he finally agreed to stay and go on to the retired list. The next day, 31 October 1846, Beaufort was gazetted Rear Admiral on the retired list. 'In short,' he wrote to his brother, 'there is some mystery and all mysteries are dirty, and at the end of it is that this day I am a YELLOW ADMIRAL.'

But official recognition did come eventually in the form of a knighthood when, on 28 April 1848, he was gazetted Knight Commander of the Bath, second class. In a true piece of genuine Beaufort modesty, he wrote in his diary, 'of the many unexpected events that have taken place in my life whether of good or evil this has been the most unlooked for and I can say the most uncoveted.'[17] Beaufort was no stranger to Buckingham Palace – he had once spent the whole of one ball eating ice cream in the tent that had once belonged to Tipu Sultan, which had been captured at the siege of Seringapatam. The ceremony, which clearly touched him, was recorded in a letter to his sister Harriet, written in purple ink to match the wonderful piece of overblown purple prose: 'That knightly and distinguished person who was yesterday invested by the dear and delicate fingers of Her sacred Majesty with the insignia of the Most Honourable Order of the Bath,' he began. He went on to describe how he was dubbed 'in the most sentimental manner' and the pleasure of receiving 'the glittering star which thenceforward was destined not only to dignify my left breast but to derive fresh dignity from the devoted heart which was then (somewhat uneasily) beating in that breast'. He kissed 'her august (but plump) little hand' twice before his 'first proof of true knightly skill – in retreating backwards from the presence'. There was a moment of angst when his sword was 'boldly endeavouring to insinuate itself between' his legs as he negotiated the 40 feet of red carpet lined with the old Grand Cross Knights. He managed it without 'fall or fatal trip, which would have perhaps excited a smile on the royal but compassionate features, and so terminated a wonderful and unsought page'[18] of his life. To his surprise, Beaufort had to pay 12 guineas for the order and miniature.

If Beaufort was flattered by the Queen and his Order of the Bath, it was a different honour that he received from the First Lord of the Admiralty in March 1854 when he tried to resign his post of Hydrographer. Beaufort had served 25 years in the post and was worn out. He was deaf, enfeebled and in constant pain from his back. He asked to retire, which he thought, under the circumstances, was his due. Messages of congratulation flooded in from the likes of Parry and Airy. But war with Russia was imminent and Beaufort could not be spared. The First Lord of the Admiralty himself persuaded him to change his mind – 'Sir James Graham tells me I must not go yet,' he wrote in his diary. 'Rather a nondescript position for me, but things had better be left to take their course.'[19] The Crimean War had given Beaufort the reprieve that he did not want, but after he saw what lay in store for him in retirement, he was grateful for the extra year.

Again, Beaufort was in his element, and the whole of the next year he spent producing charts and sailing directions, almost exclusively of Russian waters. In the past, he had had close ties with his opposite number in St Petersburg, and the information and charts that had been sent to him in the past were updated and reproduced for the use of the Fleet against Britain's former ally. New charts of the Baltic and the Black Sea were hurriedly made; Beaufort sent Captain Thomas Spratt to survey the Dardanelles from the Grecian Archipelago.

Finally, at the end of January 1855, Beaufort was literally worn out like an old survey vessel kept in service too long. He wrote to the Admiralty: 'Having been in HM Naval Service upwards of 67 years, 25 [sic] of which I have been employed in this laborious office, I feel that advancing age and severe infirmities make it my duty to retire, and to leave its labours and its responsibilities to younger and more active hands.'[20] The Admiralty finally agreed and the next month was spent handing over the office to Captain John Washington. He finished checking the charts around the White Sea, and the Norwegian and Swedish coasts. His last act was to send some Arctic charts to Henry Grinnell, advising him to look at the northwest corner of North Devon Island. It had been renamed 'Grinnell Land'. He then walked the two miles home, feeling rather lost.

After his retirement, there was a rather undignified squabble with the Treasury over his pension. Although he was officially due seven twelfths of his final salary, because of his 'meritorious services', they allowed him his full salary of £500 as a pension on top of his half-pay from the Admiralty and pension for his wounds. Undoubtedly prompted by Daniel Augustus, Beaufort claimed that his real salary was £800, as they had not taken the allowance of £300 for his house into account. Daniel Augustus embarrassed his father with the barrage of letters to Beaufort's friends and Members of both Houses of Parliament. Finally Beaufort had had enough – 'whatever have been my faults and follies, covetousness has never been one of them.' There the matter ended.

Beaufort's retirement from the Admiralty and the Hydrographic Office was marked by a subscription arranged by Washington, John Barrow and some of his old surveying captains. The 300 donors raised a total of £540. A portrait by Stephen Pearce was commissioned, but for the half-length canvas the artist merely repainted Beaufort from his sketches for the composition piece of the Arctic Council. Appropriately, it was hung in the Royal Observatory. The remainder of the money went into a trust fund for an annual prize for the highest marks in navigation in the lieutenants' examination.

For Beaufort, it was a downhill slide after retirement. Without the stimulus of his daily toil, his days hung heavy and long. As Back observed in his obituary, he lived 'too long for many of his friendships'. But despite ill health, Beaufort conspired to keep active. He kept up a voluminous correspondence, including lobbying the Admiralty and the American public on behalf of Lady Franklin. Although Honora was a trial to him, he at least had his three daughters with him in the house. When the house in Gloucester Place became too much for him, he moved with Rosalind to a little cottage in Mills Terrace in Brighton. His mind wandered occasionally, but generally he remained lucid. He read continually and showed a keen interest in all around. Nor, in the spirit of the Age of the Enlightenment, did he lose the compulsion to observe, measure and record. He kept a meticulous weather journal for all his adult life, and during his last years, he also recorded the size, shape, consistency and colour of his stools.

By the middle of December 1857 Rosalind, fearing the worst, summoned the whole family to Brighton. On 15 December, the doctor came to see his patient and was amazed to witness Beaufort's 'wonderful clearness, memory, spirit and animation in the discussion of the book he was reading' and to debate what constituted a good historian. The next night, his children gathered at his bedside early as their father said that he was tired. They kissed him in turn, and left the room. He died in the early hours of the morning.

A fierce wind billowed the surplices of the two clergymen as they stood on the steps of St John-at-Hackney Church at noon on 22 December 1857. At last the hearse arrived, the horses blowing after the four-mile journey from Victoria Station. The pallbearers slid the coffin out of the back, then marched up the steps and through the north door. There they paused while William Morris Beaufort dressed the coffin. At the top on the centre of a red velvet cushion, he placed his father's Naval General Service Medal, with its three clasps for his part in The Glorious First of June, Cornwallis' Retreat and the cutting out of the *San Joseph*. He then arranged his Order of the Bath around it. Very carefully, the bearers hefted the coffin on to their shoulders, pausing while the two clergymen, Daniel August Beaufort and his brother-in-law William Palmer, led the way into the church.

In his will, Beaufort requested that his funeral service should be private. Only the three front pews were filled with family and a few of his closest friends, the little knot of mourners making the vast church appear even emptier than it really was. When the coffin was safely placed on the two stools in front of the altar, Daniel Augustus conducted the funeral service and gave a short address, while the Reverend William Palmer read the prayers and pronounced the blessing. The service over, William Morris removed the paraphernalia from the coffin and the pallbearers carried it outside and across to the centre of the graveyard. The top of the Wilson family tomb had just been rolled back by the two stonemasons who stood at a respectful distance beside the sexton, who had prepared the brick vault below the table tomb. The family gathered round as Daniel Augustus intoned the committal, and the mortal remains of Admiral Sir Francis Beaufort were lowered deep into the tomb, to lie beside those of his beloved Alicia.

This chronicle of Rear Admiral Sir Francis Beaufort KCB does not end with a crumbling grave in some forgotten churchyard in the East End of London, for the legacy of that talented man survives to this day. Most branches of science recognise his contribution to their advancement, none more so than the navies around the world who universally copied his systems and procedures when setting up their own hydro-graphic offices. As a practical surveyor, his charts of southern Turkey were truly exceptional, and served as an example of the standard of excellence he required of his own surveyors. The value of the surveys instituted by Beaufort during his tenure as Hydrographer is incalculable. Up to that time, in war more ships were lost through faulty charts (or indeed uncharted waters) than were ever sunk by enemy action. For the mercan-tile service, he provided safe routes around the world that enabled the Victorian Empire to expand and prosper. His legacy of producing accurate charts remains to the lasting benefit of all who sail the seas today, in whatever capacity.

As a scientist Beaufort never made any startling discoveries himself; but his lasting bequest was that he recognised those areas that needed to be explored and researched, and through his expertise, skill and energy, saw to it that they were carried out under the auspices of the Royal Navy. Beaufort had the advantage of being born at exactly the right time to make a very valid contribution to the scientific advances of his day. His precise manner and attention to detail, along with his acute powers of observation, recording and his encyclopaedic knowledge came from his early training in the twilight years of the Age of Enlightenment with its gentleman scholars. This he carried forward to great effect when he was at the very epicentre of all scientific experiment and discovery through his position as Hydrographer and in contact with all the scientific bodies around the world.

But it was the Wind Scale that he developed that rightly bears his name that is a lasting tribute to this remarkable man. During Beaufort's lifetime, he saw his Wind Scale adopted by the Royal Navy, and then worldwide. Admiral Frederick Beechey brought the news back from Brussels in 1853 from the first International Meteorological Conference, set up by Matthew Fontaine Maury, Beaufort's friend and opposite number in the United States. It was truly successful. The French claimed Beaufort as their own, and even today their shipping forecasts are punctuated with *Beaufort Cinq*, or *Beaufort Dix*.

Over the years, it has been necessary to tinker with the Scale. In 1874, it was modified slightly at the Maritime Congress when 'double topsails' entered the equation. But by then, the age of sail was slowly giving way to a new era of power-driven vessels, and the appellations of how much sail a frigate would carry in a chase had little relevance. Slowly, the sails criteria gave way to the state of the sea, returning to Alexander Dalrymple's original thought. Beaufort's descriptive terms for the numbers 0 to 12, were also slightly altered – Beaufort's force 10, a 'whole gale', became a 'storm'.

Successive meteorologists the world over have continually tried to improve on the Scale, but try as they might with advanced anemometers and sophisticated instruments, they have found that nothing answers so well as Beaufort Wind Scale.

PRACTICAL NAVIGATION.

TABLE of COMPARISON of WINDS, from Ship's Journals, with Mr. SMEATON's Scale from Aufthorpe Mill, the Length of the *Sails* being 34 feet from the *Center*; or 68 feet diameter.

My Scale.	Mr. Smeaton's Scale and His Defcription.		French Terms.
0 Calm	0 Calm	The *Motion* of the *Air*, not felt	0 Calme.
1 Faint-Air, i.e. juft not quite calm	Scarce a Breeze	D?. . . . . . fcarcely felt	1 Petit fraicheur, ou feible.
2 Light-Air	Light breeze not working	The *Direction* of the *Wind*, fenfible, but infufficient to move the Mill, or under 6 turns in a *minute*	2 Fraicheur.
3 Light-Breeze	1 Light working Breeze	Juft fufficient to move the Mill 6 turns	3 Petit frais, ou petit brife.
4 Gentle-Breeze	2 Breeze	Sufficient to move the Branches of Trees, and Mill from 6 to 9 turns	4 Jolie brife ?
5 Frefh-Breeze / 6 Gentle-Gale	3 Frefh Breeze	Move the Boughs with fome noife, Mill 9 to 13 turns	5 Jolie frais ? / 6 Vent peu de frais.
7 Moderate-Gale			7 Vent moyenne frais.
8 Brifk-Gale	4 Frefh	Wind heard againft folid Objects and agitation of Trees, Mill from 13 to 18	8 Vent frais.
9 Frefh-Gale	5 Very frefh	Wind growing noify, and confiderable agitation of Trees, Mill 18 to ¼ Cloth	9 Bon frais.
10 Strong-Gale	6 Hard	Wind troublefome, larger Trees bend, ¼ to ½ Cloth	10 Grand frais.
11 Hard-Gale	7 Very hard	Wind very loud and troublefome, large Trees much agitated, Mill ½ Cloth to clofe ftruck	11 Vent fort.
12 Storm	8 Storm	Wind exceeding loud, Trees very much agitated and fome broke, Mill 25 to 30 turns without Cloth	12 Tempete.

Pamphlets by Alexander Dalrymple for East India Company captains, later adapted by Beaufort for his own wind scale.[1]

Explanation of the Columns in the Journal.

The *number* of *miles* on the *Log-Board*.

The *Day* of the *Week*, *Month* and *Moon*.

Thermometer, ⎫ defcribing, by a Mem. at the beginning of the
Barometer, ⎬ Journal, where placed; with fome defcription of
   the Inftrument.

The *Weather* and *Winds* in 4 lines ⎰ 1 from Noon to 6 P. M.
            2 - - 6 P. M. - - Midnight.
            3 - - Midnight - 6 A. M.
            4 - - 6 A. M. - - Noon.

  In the column of *Weather* c. denotes *cloudy*; f. *fair*; fg. *foggy*;
h. *hazy*; r. *rain*; hr. *hard rain*; sr. *fmall rain*; dr. *drizling rain*;
fh. *fhowers*; th. *thunder*; l. *lightning*; fq: *fqually*; and a comma
(,) after any *weather* marked, implies that all the *weather* fo
feparated by *comma*, are connected: thus fq, r, th, l. imply
fqually with *rain*, *thunder* and *lightning*; fq, r, th, l. imply *fqually*,
rain, and *thunder* and *lightning*, to have all been in the period of
fix hours, but not at the fame time: The *figures* under the *winds*
denote, 1. Faint Air, i. e. juft *not calm*. 2. Light Air. 3. Light
Breeze. 4. Gentle Breeze. 5. Frefh Breeze. 6. Gentle Gale.
7. Moderate Gale. 8. Brifk Gale. 9. Frefh Gale. 10. Strong
Gale. 11. Hard Gale. 12. Storm.

The Courfe corrected for Variation and Leeway, but without any
  allowance for currents.

The Diftance.

The Difference of Latitude in two columns; *Northing* being marked
  in one, *Southing* in the other.

The Departure,   ⎱each in two columns, *Eafting* being
The Difference of Longitude, ⎰
  marked in one, *Wefting* in the other.

The Daily Difference between the Latitude by Account and Obfervation; N denoting the *Obfervation* to be to the *Northward*, S to
  the *Southward* of *Account*.

The Daily Difference between the Longitude by Account and Time-
  keeper; E denoting the T K to be to the *Eaftward*, W to the
  Weftward of *Account*.

FIGURES

TO

DENOTE THE FORCE OF THE WIND.

0	CALM.	
1	LIGHT AIR, - - -	Or just sufficient to give steerage way.

2	LIGHT BREEZE, - -	Or that in which a well-conditioned man-of-war, with all sail set, and clean full, would go in smooth water, from - - - - -	1 to 2 knots.
3	GENTLE BREEZE, -		3 to 4 knots.
4	MODERATE BREEZE,		5 to 6 knots.

5	FRESH BREEZE, - -	Or that to which she could just carry in chance, full and by	Royals, &c.
6	STRONG BREEZE, -		Single-reefed topsails and topgallant sails.
7	MODERATE GALE, -		Double-reefed topsails, jib, &c.
8	FRESH GALE, - - -		Triple-reefed topsails, &c.
9	STRONG GALE, - -		Close-reefed topsails and courses.

10	WHOLE GALE, - -	Or that with which she could scarcely bear close-reefed maintopsail & reefed foresail.
11	STORM, - - - - - -	Or that which would reduce her to storm stay-sails.
12	HURRICANE, - - -	Or that which no canvas could withstand.

If the above mode were adopted, the state of the wind might be regularly marked, in a narrow column, on the log-board every hour.

LETTERS

TO

DENOTE THE STATE OF THE WEATHER.

b, BLUE SKY; whether clear or hazy atmosphere.

c CLOUDS; detached passing clouds.

d DRIZZLING RAIN.

f FOGGY—f Thick fog.

g GLOOMY dark weather.

h HAIL.

l LIGHTNING.

m MISTY hazy atmosphere.

o OVERCAST; or the whole sky covered with thick clouds.

p PASSING temporary SHOWERS.

q SQUALLY.

r RAIN; continued rain.

s SNOW.

t THUNDER.

u UGLY threatening appearances.

v VISIBLE clear atmosphere.

w WET DEW.

. Under any letter, indicates an extraordinary degree.

By the combination of these letters, all the ordinary phenomena of the weather may be expressed with facility and brevity. *Examples:*—Bcm, Blue sky, with passing clouds, and a hazy atmosphere. Gv, Gloomy dark weather, but distant objects remarkably visible. Qpdlt, Very hard squalls, with passing showers of drizzle, and accompanied by lightning, with very heavy thunder.

THE ARCTIC ARCHIPELAGO

GREENLAND

BAFFIN BAY

BYLOT
ISLAND

BAFFIN ISLAND

PRINCE
CHARLES
ISLAND

MELVILLE PENINSULA

FOXE
BASIN

HUDSON STRAIT

SOUTHAMPTON
ISLAND

HUDSON BAY

⊙ Victory Point
+ Magnetic North pole
★ Approximate location of
where *Erebus* and *Terror* foundered
✪ Cape Walker

200 miles

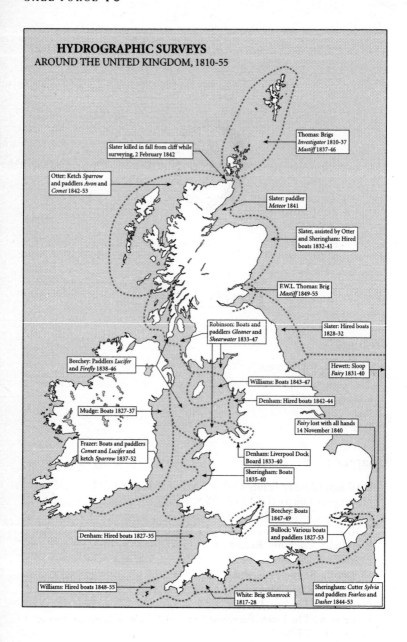

HYDROGRAPHIC SURVEYS
AROUND THE UNITED KINGDOM, 1810-55

Thomas: Brigs
Investigator 1810-37
Mastiff 1837-46

Slater killed in fall from cliff while
surveying, 2 February 1842

Otter: Ketch *Sparrow*
and paddlers *Avon* and
Comet 1842-53

Slater: paddler
Meteor 1841

Slater, assisted by Otter
and Sheringham: Hired
boats 1832-41

F.W.L. Thomas: Brig
Mastiff 1849-55

Robinson: Boats and
paddlers *Gleaner* and
Shearwater 1833-47

Slater: Hired boats
1828-32

Beechey: Paddlers *Lucifer*
and *Firefly* 1838-46

Hewett: Sloop
Fairy 1831-40

Williams: Boats 1843-47

Denham: Hired boats 1842-44

Mudge: Boats 1827-37

Fairy lost with all hands
14 November 1840

Frazer: Boats and paddlers
Comet and *Lucifer* and
ketch *Sparrow* 1837-52

Denham: Liverpool Dock
Board 1833-40

Sheringham: Boats
1835-40

Beechey: Boats
1847-49

Bullock: Various boats
and paddlers 1827-53

Denham: Hired boats 1827-35

Williams: Hired boats 1848-55

White: Brig *Shamrock*
1817-28

Sheringham: Cutter *Sylvia*
and paddlers *Fearless* and
Dasher 1844-53

Endnotes

Prologue

[1] *Penny Post*, 1 April 1868
[2] *The Gravesend Journal, Dartford Observer,* and *Country Intelligencer,* 6 December 1871
[3] Ibid.
[4] Ibid.

Chapter 1

[1] DAB Journal entry Trinity College, Dublin MS 4031 17 March 1789
[2] Huntington Library (HL) 1312 Alicia Beaufort's testimonial, undated
[3] East India Company Records L/MAR/C/506 20 March 1789
[4] DAB Journal entry Trinity College, Dublin MS 4031 20 March 1789
[5] East India Company Records L/MAR/C/506 Log of the chief mate 24 March 1789
[6] William L. Beaufort's autobiography, 1805
[7] Beaufort, William Morris, *The Family of de Beaufort in France, Holland, Germany and England,* London, 1886
[8] Letter to Sir Chichester Fortescue Journal 1797 Co. Kildare Architectural Society Vol. XII No.1

[9] Ellison, Canon C., *The Hopeful Traveller*, Ireland, 1987, p.xi
[10] Ibid., p.xi
[11] Ibid.
[12] Ibid.
[13] Ibid.
[14] HL FB 440 Testament c. 1801
[15] Ellison, p.25
[16] Ibid.
[17] DAB Journal entry Trinity College, Dublin MS 4031 12 October 1782
[18] Ibid.
[19] HL FB 198 17 July 1788
[20] Ellison, p.44
[21] DAB Journal entry Trinity College, Dublin MS 4031 30 January 1789
[22] Ibid., 20 July 1788
[23] Ibid., 7 March 1789

Chapter 2

[1] FB to DAB 4 April 1789
[2] Ibid.
[3] HL FB 178 FB to DAB 23 March 1789
[4] Ibid.
[5] Ibid.
[6] Ibid.
[7] East India Office, L/Mar/b/46H, Log of the *Vansittart* 11 July 1789
[8] Memoir of a Chart of the Passsage to the Eastward of Banka, New York Public Library Map Division, pub. 1806, seen India Office Library, London
[9] Ibid.
[10] HL FB 1687 Lestock Wilson to DAB 26 December 1801
[11] East India Office, L/Mar/b/46H, Log of the *Vansittart* 14 July 1789
[12] Ibid.
[13] HL FB to DAB 24 July 1789
[14] East India Office, L/Mar/b/46H, Log of the *Vansittart* 24 August 1789
[15] Ibid.
[16] Ibid.
[17] Ibid.
[18] Ibid., 26 August 1789
[19] Ibid., 7 September 1789

Chapter 3

1 HL FB to DAB 23 October 1790
2 Ibid., 27 June 1790
3 Leslie, Doris, *Royal William*, p.18
4 Masefield, John, *Sea Life in Nelson's Time*, p.38
5 HL FB 424 FB to DAB 23 September 1790
6 DNB entry for Earl Howe
7 HL FB 199 FB to DAB 6 August 1790
8 HL FB 205 FB to DAB 24 September 1791
9 Monk, William, *Euthanasia or Medical Treatments in Aids of Easy Dying*
10 Ibid.
11 HL FB 472 FB to WmB 8 January 1792
12 HL FB 11 FB Journal entry 28 June 1792
13 HL FB 215 FB to WB 24 September 1791
14 HL FB 217 FB to DAB 4 September 1792
15 Ibid.
16 FB 11 Journal entry 4 November 1791
17 Ibid., 25 January 1793
18 Ibid., 26 January 1793
19 Ibid., 10 January 1792
20 Ibid., February 1792
21 Ibid.
22 Ibid.
23 HL FB 256 FB to WmB 11 April 1792
24 Ibid., 5 February 1793
25 Ibid., 10 February 1793
26 HL FB 11 FB Journal entry 28 June 1792
27 Ibid., 23 February 1793
28 HL FB 219 FB to DAB 1 November 1792
29 Ibid.
30 Ibid.
31 HL FB 449 FB to Mary Beaufort 2 January 1793
32 HL FB 11 FB Journal entry 3 February 1793
33 Ibid.

Chapter 4

1 PRO ADM 51/54 24 February 1793
2 HL FB 12 FB Journal entry 24 February 1793
3 Ibid., 21 April 1793
4 Ibid.

5 HL FB 12 FB Journal entry 20 May 1793
6 HL FB 222 FB to DAB 9–25 June 1793
7 Ibid.
8 Ibid.
9 Ibid.
10 HL FB 221 FB to DAB 5 June 1793
11 Firth papers, Gillen, Mary, *Royal Duke*, p.72
12 HL FB 773 FB to Francis Edgeworth 19 September 1793
13 HL FB 12 Journal entry 2 September 1794
14 HL FB 230 FB to DAB 31 August 1792
15 Ibid.
16 Bouchier, Lady (ed.), *Memoir of the Life of Admiral Sir Edward Codrington*, Vol. 1, London, 1873, p.63
17 Ibid.
18 HL FB 246 FB to DAB 21 January – 5 February 1794
19 HL FB 247 FB to DAB 20 February 1794
20 HL FB 253 FB to DAB 6 March 1794
21 HL FB 256 FB to DAB 18 April 1794
22 HL FB 12 FB Journal entry between 19 May and 1 June 1794
23 Warner, Oliver, *The Glorious First of June*, p.32
24 HL FB 12 FB Journal entry between 19 May and 1 June 1794
25 HL FB 12 FB Journal entry 30 June 1794
26 PRO ADM 51/54 Captain's Log *Aquilon* 31 May 1794
27 Ibid.
28 Warner, p.35
29 PRO ADM 51/1151 Log of the *Marlborough* 1 June 1794
30 PRO ADM 51/54 Captain's Log *Aquilon* 29 June 1794
31 Ibid., 30 June 1794
32 Warner, p.148

Chapter 5

1 James, William, *The Naval History of Great Britain*, Vol.1, London, 1837, p.237
2 Ibid.
3 PRO ADM 51/1147 Captain's Log *Phaeton* 8 June 1794
4 HL FB 450 FB to Mary W. Beaufort 23 June 1795
5 Ibid.
6 PRO ADM 51/1147 Captain's Log *Phaeton* 8 June 1794
7 James, p.239
8 Ibid.

9   Ibid., p.241
10 Ibid.
11 PRO ADM 51/1147 Captain's Log *Phaeton* 17 June 1794
12 HL FB 450 FB to Mary W. Beaufort 23 June 1795
13 Ibid.
14 HL FB 963 FB to Sir Thomas Byam Martin 8 July 1848
15 HL FB 1284 Anecdote Book
16 Beaufort Journal entry 11 March 1796
17 HL FB 283 FB to DAB 6 November 1798
18 Ibid.
19 HL FB 275 FB to DAB 25 October 1797
20 Ibid.
21 HL FB 342 DAB to FB 26 January 1797
22 HL FB 279 FB to DAB 8 January 1797
23 HL FB 270 FB to DAB 28 June 1797
24 HL FB 271 FB to DAB 28 June 1797
25 Leviticus 13.3,14
26 HL FB 283 FB to DAB 25 October 1797
27 Ibid.
28 DeLoughery, Dr Thomas, Div. of Haematology, Portland, Oregon
29 O'Byrne, William, *A Naval Biographical Dictionary*, London, 1848, p. 1127
30 HL FB 288 8 July 1799
31 Ibid.
32 Ibid.
33 HL FB 289 FB to DAB 22 July 1799
34 HL FB 779 FB to Fanny Edgeworth 11 July 1799
35 HL FB 290 FB to DAB 14 September 1799
36 HL FB 1462 Admiral Lord Nelson to Richard Bulkeley 8 Nov 1799
37 NLI Edgeworth Papers 13176
38 HL typed sheet
39 HL FB 1128 Elgin to whom it may concern 1 November 1799
40 HO Letters In B-1411 11 April 1852
41 NRS Keith papers, 11, pp. 92–3
42 PRO ADM 51/1369
43 Ibid.
44 Ibid.
45 HL FB 313 FB to DAB 22 December 1800

Chapter 6

1   HL FB 293 FR to DAB 28 October 1800

[2] FB 294 FB to WB 2 November 1800
[3] Ibid.
[4] PRO ADM 1/403 Capt. J. Morris to Lord Keith 28 October 1800
[5] Ibid.
[6] Ibid.
[7] HL FB 296 FB to DAB 3 January 1801
[8] HL FB 472 FB to WmB 16 February 1801
[9] Ibid.
[10] HL FB 345 FB to DAB 17 June 1801
[11] Ibid.
[12] Ibid.
[13] HL FB 756 FB to Henrietta Beaufort 11 September 1801
[14] HL FB 299 FB to DAB 3 November 1801
[15] HL FB 478 FB to WmB 8 October 1802
[16] Ibid.
[17] Edgeworth, Richard Lovell, *Memoirs of RLE*, Vol. ii, pp.149–50
[18] NLI Edgeworth Papers MS 13176 (2) 409
[19] NLI Edgeworth Papers MS 12176
[20] Butler, Marilyn, *Maria Edgeworth*, p.203
[21] Edgeworth, Richard Lovell, *Memoirs of RLE*, Vol. ii, p.276
[22] HL FB 298 FB to DAB 29 February 1804
[23] Inglis-Jones, Elizabeth, *The Great Maria*, p.59
[24] HL FB 374 FB to WmB 8 April 1804
[25] Ibid.
[26] HL FB 1742 Charlotte Edgeworth to FB November 1804
[27] HL FB 1562 Lord Barnham to FB 28 May 1805
[28] LNI 446 MS 13176 446 Frances Edgeworth to Mrs Ruxton 9 January 1805
[29] HL FB 127 DAB to FB 18 July 1805
[30] HL FB 398 FB to DAB July 1805
[31] HL FB to WmB 8 April 1805

Chapter 7

[1] HL FB 14 FB Journal entry HMS *Woolwich* 5 June 1805
[2] Ibid., 10 June 1805
[3] Ibid.
[4] Ibid., p.4
[5] MO Beaufort Journal entry 6 June 1805
[6] Ibid., 12 August 1805
[7] Ibid., 24 September 1805

8 Ibid., 25 September 1805
9 Ibid., 5 October 1805
10 HL FB to DAB 9 November 1805
11 PRO ADM 51/1652
12 MO FB Journal entry 8 November 1805
13 MO FB Journal entry undated November 1806.
14 PRO ADM 52 379/1 12 January 1806
15 Ibid.
16 MO FB Journal entry 13 January 1806
17 *Memoir* TJ153 S62 Library of Congress, Washington DC
18 Ibid.
19 Ibid., Table VI
20 Dalrymple, Alexander, *Practical Navigation*, May 1779, Archives Nationales (Paris), p.29
21 Ibid.
22 B.10/3854
23 *Practical Navigation*, p.67
24 Dalrymple, Alexander, *Memoirs*, Vol. IV, section 5, p.5, May 1779
25 *Memoir*, p.1
26 PRO ADM 1/3522
27 Ibid.
28 HL FB 337 FB to DAB 19 July 1805
29 HL FB 77 John Roger Arnold to Lestock Wilson 16 July 1805
30 HL FB 1188 Alexander Dalrymple to FB 20 September 1805
31 MO FB Journal entry 9 February 1806
32 Ibid., 16 February 1806
33 HL FB 14 FB Journal entry 1 March 1806
34 Ibid.
35 Ibid., 21 March 1806
36 Ibid., 13 March 1806
37 Ibid., 13 April 1806
38 Ibid.
39 Ibid., 28 April 1806
40 HL MSA 84 p.127
41 HL FB 14 FB Journal entry 31 May 1806
42 MO FB Journal entry 25 November 1806
43 HL FB 1258 Marsden to FB 25 March 1807
44 TCD, DAB to Fanny Edgeworth, Beaufort papers MS 580 11 April 1807
45 HL FB 341 FB to DAB 9 November 1805
46 HL FB 982 Frances Edgeworth to DAB 7 April 1806
47 HL FB 762 FB to Harriet Beaufort July 1807

[48] HL FB 349 FB to DAB 19 April 1809
[49] PRO ADM 1/3523 9 April 1808
[50] HL FB 367 FB to DAB 4 July 1809

Chapter 8

[1] HL FB 367 FB to DAB 19 April 1809
[2] Fry, H. L., *The Emergence of the Beaufort Scale Mariner's Mirror*, 58, No. 4, 1967, p.312
[3] HL FB91 Sir John Barrow to FB 1827
[4] HL FB 936 FB to RLE 30 May 1809
[5] HL FB 350 FB to DAB 30 May 1809
[6] HL FB 936 FB to RLE 30 May 1809
[7] Ibid.
[8] HL FB 783 FB to Fanny Edgeworth 5 July 1809
[9] HL FB 504 FB to WmB 14 June 1808
[10] HL FB 351 FB to DAB 4 July 1809
[11] HL FB 788 FB to Frances Edgeworth October 1809
[12] DAB FB 353 2 August 1809
[13] HL FB 1396 Maria Lennon to FB 31 August 1809
[14] Ibid.
[15] HL FB 975 FB to RLE 5 January 1810
[16] Wood, Sir H. T., *History of the Royal Society*, London, p.248
[17] HL FB 937 FB to RLE 5 May 1808
[18] HL FB 367 FB to RLE 10 February 1810
[19] *Chambers Encyclopaedia*, 1958, Vol. 1, p.104
[20] HL FB 937 FB to RLE 9 December 1808
[21] HL FB to Harriet Beaufort 3 May 1809
[22] HL FB to DAB 20 May 1810
[23] NLI Edgeworth Papers MS 13176 (2) 755 Croker to Foster 21 May 1810
[24] HL FB 953 FB to RLE 17 June 1810
[25] HL FB 357 FB to DAB 13 June 1810
[26] Inglis-Jones, p.143
[27] MO FB Journal entry 1 July 1810
[28] Ibid.
[29] *Shorter Oxford Dictionary*
[30] HL FB 1476 Omay and Druce to FB 13 August 1805
[31] MO Beaufort Journal 1809–10
[32] HL FB 358 FB to DAB 23–30 September 1810

Chapter 9

1. HL FB 1145 Canning to FB 12 January 1811
2. Ibid.
3. MO Beaufort Journal entry 12 December 1810
4. HL FB 1143 Canning to FB 20 December 1810
5. HL FB Box 3 Journal entry 28 July 1810
6. Beaufort, Francis, *Memoir of a Survey of the Coast of Karamania*, 1817, p.vii
7. Ibid., p.viii
8. Ibid., p.xx
9. HL FB 15 Journal entry 13 August 1811
10. Ibid., 8 August 1811
11. *Karamania*, p.2
12. HL FB 15 Journal entry 8 August 1811
13. *Karamania*, p.4
14. HL FB 15 Journal entry p.102 17 August 1811
15. *Karamania*, p.39
16. HL FB 15 FB Journal entry 28 July 1811
17. Ibid.
18. *Karamania*, p.31
19. Ibid., p.161
20. *Karamania*, p.18
21. HL FB 15 Journal entry 25 August 1811
22. *Karamania*, p.41
23. HL FB 15 Journal entry 26 August 1811
24. Ibid., 1 September 1811
25. *Karamania*, p.49
26. Pliny, ii, p.106
27. *Karamania*, p.63
28. HL FB 15 Journal entry 30 August 1811
29. Ibid., p.70
30. Ibid., p.75
31. Ibid., 2 September 1811
32. *Karamania*, p.95
33. HL FB 15 Journal entry 21 September 1811
34. *Karamania*, p.106
35. Ibid., pp.107, 108
36. Ibid., p.112
37. HL FB 15 Journal entry 1 January 1812
38. Ibid., 3 February 1812
39. *Karamania*, p.113
40. Ibid., p.115

41 Ibid., p.118
42 Ibid., p.143
43 Ibid., p.146
44 BM Cockerell Travel Journal 1811–12
45 *Karamania*, p.203
46 HL FB 15 Journal entry 17 June 1812
47 *Karamania*, p.229
48 Ibid., p.259
49 *Karamania*, p.276
50 HL FB 15 Journal entry 12 June 1812
51 *Karamania*, p.261
52 HL FB 15 Journal entry 18 June 1812
53 Ibid., 20 June 1812
54 *Karamania*, p.303
55 Cockerell Travel Journal 1811–12
56 PRO ADM 1/423
57 HL FB 971 FB to Lestock Wilson 30 June 1812

Chapter 10

1 HL FB 1023 Mary Beaufort to Fanny Edgeworth 7 December 1812
2 HL FB 90 Sir Joseph Banks to REL 13 December 1813
3 HL FB Afc21
4 Ellison, p.116
5 HL FB 1174 Croker to FB 29 June 1815
6 Ibid.
7 HL FB 1178 Croker to FB 24 November 1815
8 Cain, Mead, *SDUK*, p.156
9 HL FB 814 FB to Fanny Edgeworth 23 February 1816
10 HL FB 748 FB to Croker 27 May 1816
11 Barrow, Sir John Bt, *An Autobiographical Memoir*, p.395
12 *The Times*, 3 September 1817
13 HL FB 1472 Guildford to FB 18 July 1817
14 HL FB 826 FB to Fanny Edgeworth 22 June 1817
15 Ellison, p.117
16 HL FB 1564 Alicia Beaufort to Frances Beaufort 3 October 1816
17 Butler, p.242
18 HL FB 771 FB to Lord Melville 30 April 1823
19 HL FB 1218 Melville to FB 9 May 1823
20 Board of Longitude RGO/43 p.41
21 Dawson, L. S., *Memoirs of Hydrography*, 1856, p.101

22 Ritchie, Adm G. S., *The Admiralty Chart*, p.175
23 HL FB 183 FB to Rennell 1817
24 Lyons, Sir Henry, *The Royal Society 1660–1940*, p.245
25 HL FB 1490 William Parry to FB 1 July 1824
26 *The Edinburgh New Philosophical Journal*, 1826, p.34
27 Cain, Mead, *Mappa Mundi* The Maps of the Society for the Diffusion of Useful Knowledge 1990
28 Minutes SDUK 6 November 1826
29 Ibid., 18 June 1829
30 Cain, Beaufort to Ker 21 April 1828 p.35
31 Ibid., Beaufort to Coates 7 October 1833
32 HL FB 616 FB to WmB 15 May 1829
33 Ibid.
34 Ibid.
35 HL FB 99 Sir John Barrow to FB 14 May 1829
36 HL FB 616 FB to WmB 9–19 October 1829
37 *London Daily News*, 26 January 1857
38 Barrow, Sir John Bt, p.395
39 Blewitt, Mary, *Surveys of the Sea*, p.34

Chapter 11

1   HL FB 616 FB to WmB 5 May 1829
2   HO Letter Book No.2 p.305
3   HL FB 17 Diary entry for 12 May 1829
4   HL FB 616 FB to WmB 5 May 1829
5   Richards, Adm George H., *Memoir of Hydrography*, p.9
6   Tuckey, J. H., *Narrative of an Expedition to Explore the River Zaire*, p.ii
7   Richards, pp.9, 10
8   Wyatt, A. G. N., *Charting the Seas in Peace and War*, p.12
9   HL FB 616 FB to WmB 5 May 1829
10 Cocks, Randolph, abstract of conference, *Science and the French and British Navies 1700–1850*, p.13
11 HO Letters Out 3 November 1834
12 Dawson L. S., p.24
13 HO Minute Book 3 November 1834
14 Ibid., 20 October 1834
15 HO Letters Out FB to Captain Beechey 8 December 1829
16 Ritchie, p.149
17 HO Letters Out 20 April 1852
18 HO Minute Book 11 November 1831

[19] HO Letters In C 720 Sir George Cockburn to FB 14 September 1833
[20] Ibid., 3 November 1834
[21] Day, Sir Archibald, *The Admiralty Hydrographic Service 1795–1919*, London, 1967, p.61
[22] Mellerish, H. E. L., *Fitzroy of the Beagle*, p.198
[23] HO Letter Book No. 3 1 September 1831
[24] Fisher, Susanna, *Aegean Seas through English Eyes*, p.23
[25] HO Letters Out 25 June 1829
[26] Day, p.65
[27] HO Letters Out 19 August 1845
[28] Collins, K. St B., *Admiral Sir Francis Beaufort, A centenary lecture by the Hydrographer to the Navy*, 20 December 1957, p.273
[29] HO Letters Out 8 October 1837
[30] Dawson, p.8
[31] Collins, p.278
[32] Title Page, the *Nautical Magazine*, 1832
[33] Prospectus, the *Nautical Magazine*, London 1832
[34] Cocks, p.13
[35] Collins, p.269
[36] Ibid., p.270
[37] Mill, Hugh R., *The Record of the Royal Geographical Society 1830–1930*, p.9
[38] Ibid., p.12
[39] Flemming, Fergus, *Barrow's Boys*, p.275
[40] Mill, p.23
[41] Dryer, J. L. E., and Turner, H. H., *History of the Royal Astronomical Society 1820–1920*, p.2
[42] HL FB 25 FB Diary entry 4 November 1841
[43] Personal comment Jonathan Betts, Curator of Horology Royal Observatory
[44] Collins, p.274
[45] Ibid., p.66
[46] Dryer, p.60
[47] Deacon, Margaret, *Scientists and the Sea, 1650–1900*, Aldershot, 1971, p.250
[48] Ibid., p.255
[49] HL FB to Lubbock 3 June 1832
[50] Deacon, p.269
[51] Collins, p.271
[52] HL FB 1838 FB to Harriet Beaufort 8 February 1838
[53] Frontispiece, *Manual of Scientific Enquiry*, 1849 edition
[54] Kahn, David, *The Codebreakers*, 1969, p.148
[55] Ritchie, p.210
[56] Day, p.59

57 HL FB 770 FB to Harriet Beaufort 7 May 1848
58 HO Letters In L 46
59 Ibid., H 319 Henderson to FB 29 August 1835

Chapter 12

1   Day, p.50
2   Ritchie, p.263
3   Ibid., p.217
4   Ibid., p.26
5   Fisher, p.18
6   Dawson, p.14
7   Ibid., p.16
8   Ibid., p.36
9   Ibid., p.48
10 Barr, William (ed.), *Searching for Franklin*, The Hakluyt Society, 1999, p.9
11 Ritchie, p.270
12 HO Lettters In C 342
13 Flemming, Fergus, *Barrow's Boys*, London, 1998, p.319
14 Neatby, L. H., *The Search for Franklin*, London, 1970, p.92
15 Flemming, p.365
16 Barr, p.1
17 Flemming, p.376
18 Ibid., p.382
19 Arctic Blue Book
20 HO 15 December 1849
21 HO Letters Out FB to Robert McCormick 17 January 1850
22 HL FB 632 FB to Louisa Beaufort 9 February 1850
23 Ibid.
24 Flemming, p.386
25 Lloyd, Christopher, *Mr Barrow of the Admiralty*, London, 1970, p.195
26 Barr, p.27
27 Ibid., p.13
28 Ibid., p.15
29 Ibid.
30 Ritchie, p.90

Chapter 13

1   HL FB 670 FB to WmB 26 June 1831
2   HL FB 193 FB to Alicia Beaufort 3 December 1832

[3] HL FB 115 Alicia Beaufort to WmB 5 May 1833
[4] Beaufort, William Morris, p.131
[5] HL FB 1513 Harriet Beaufort to FB 4 June 1825
[6] HL FB 14 FB Journal entry 4 July 1805
[7] HL FB 1650 Robins T to Honora Edgeworth 4 August 1838
[8] Colvin, Christina (ed.), *Maria Edgeworth, Letters from England*, p.454
[9] Ibid.
[10] HL FB 431 FB to Honora Beaufort 20 May 1840
[11] HL FB 24 16 March 1840
[12] HL FB 605 FB to WmB 18 October 1842
[13] HL FB 25 FB Diary entry 12 July 1841
[14] HL FB 18 FB Diary entry 3 May 1834
[15] HL FB 20 Diary entry 3 January 1837
[16] HL FB 38 FB Diary entry 1 December 1854
[17] HL FB 3028 April 1846
[18] HL FB 770 FB to Harriet Beaufort 7 May 1848
[19] HL FB 38 FB Diary entry for 3 March 1854
[20] HL FB 798 FB to Sir James Graham 29 January 1855

Appendix 1

[1] 'Practical Navigation' – reproduced from the National Library of Scotland, Nha.m90(3). 'Explanantion of the Columns in the Journal' – Library of Congress, Washington DC, Dalrymple, Alexander, *Memoirs*, Vol 4, p.1

Appendix 2

[1] The *Nautical Magazine*

Select Bibliography

Manuscript Sources

British Library – mostly India Office Library for East India Company papers including the log of the *Vansittart*

California State University, Northridge, California – Arnold Court papers

Duke University, North Carolina, USA – Beaufort account books

Huntington Library, San Marino, California – the Francis Beaufort Collection: private and sundry correspondence, diaries, journals and memorabilia etc.

Hydrographic Office, Taunton, Somerset – letters out and minute books, incoming letters etc.

Library of Congress, Washington DC, USA – Beaufort and Dalrymple papers

Meteorological Office, Bracknell, Berkshire – weather logs and journals of HMS *Woolwich* and the *Blossom*

National Library of Ireland, Dublin – Beaufort and Edgeworth papers

National Maritime Museum, Greenwich – Stopford papers

Public Records Office, Kew, Surrey – Admiralty papers

Royal Geographical Society, London

Royal Society, London – Beaufort, Herschel, Sabine and Lubbock correspondence

Scott Polar Research Institute, Cambridge – Beaufort, Franklin and Ross papers

Select Published Works

BARR, William (ed.), *Searching for Franklin: the Land Arctic Searching Expedition*, The Hakluyt Society, London, 1999

BARROW, Sir John, *An Autobiographical Memoir*, London, 1847

BEATTIE, Owen, *Frozen in Time: the fate of the Franklin Expedition*, London, 1987

BEAUFORT, Francis, *Karamania*, London, 1817; *Memoir of the Survey of the Coast of Karamania*, 1820

BEAUFORT, William Morris, *The Family of de Beaufort in France, Holland, Germany and England*, London, 1886

BERTON, Pierre, *The Arctic Grail*, New York, 1998

BLEWITT, Mary, *Surveys of the Sea*, London, 1957

BUTLER, Marilyn, *Maria Edgeworth: a Literary Biography*, Oxford, 1972

CLARKE, Desmond, *The Ingenious Mr Edgeworth*, London, 1965

COLLINS, K. St B., 'Admiral Sir Francis Beaufort', *Journal of the Institute of Navigation*, 1958

COTTON, Sir Edward, *East Indiamen*, London, 1949

COLVIN, Christina (ed.), *Maria Edgeworth, Letters from England*, London, 1971

DAY, Sir Archibald, *The Admiralty Hydographic Service, 1795–1919*, London, 1967

DEACON, Margaret, *Scientists and the Sea, 1650–1900*, London, 1971

De MORGAN, Augustus, *Midshipman's Three Dinners, Notes and Queries*, 2 October 1858

DREYER, J.L.E. and TURNER, H.H., *History of the Royal Astronomical Society*, London, 1923

ELLISON, Canon C.C., *The Hopeful Traveller*, Kilkenny, Ireland, 1987

FELLOWS, Sir Charles, *The Xanthian Marbles*, London, 1842

FITZROY, Robert, *Narrative of the Surveying Voyages of His Majesty's Ships* Adventure *and* Beagle, London, 1840

FLEMMING, Fergus, *Barrow's Boys*, London, 1998

FREELY, John, *The Eastern Mediterranean Coast of Turkey*, Istanbul, 1998

FRIENDLY, Alfred, *Beaufort of the Admiralty*, New York, 1977

FRY, H. T., *Alexander Dalrymple and the Expansion of British Trade*, London, 1963

GILLEN, Mary, *Royal Duke*, London, 1976

HERSHELL, Sir John (ed.), *The Manuel of Scientific Enquiry*, London, 1848

KHAN, David, *The Codebreakers*, New York, 1969

KING, Dean, *Harbours and High Seas*, New York, 1999

KINSMAN, Blair, *Who Put the Wind Speeds in Admiral Beaufort's Scale?*,

Oceans, New York, 2 August 1969; *Historical Notes on the Original Beaufort Scale*, Marine Observer, 1969

LEAKE, William Martin, *Journal of a Tour of Asia Minor*, London, 1824

LESLIE, Doris, *Royal William*, London, 1948

LLOYD, Christopher, *The British Seamen*, 1968; *Mr Barrow of the Admiralty*, 1970

MASEFIELD, John, *Sea Life in Nelson's Time*, London, 1905

MANDER, David, *St John-at-Hackney: the Story of a Church*, London, 1993

MILL, Hugh Robert, *The Record of the Royal Geographical Society 1830-1930*, London, 1930

MOORHEAD, Alan, *Darwin and the Beagle*, London, 1969

O'BYRNE, William, *A Naval Biographical Dictionary*, London, 1848

PARRY, Ann, *Parry of the Arctic*, London, 1963

RANDIER, Jean, *Marine Navigation Instruments*, London, 1980

RICHIE, G. S., *The Admiralty Chart*, Durham, 1995

RODGER, N.A.M., *The Wooden World*, London, 1986

SAVOURS, Ann, *The Search for the North West Passage*, London, 1999

SOUTHAM, Brian, *Jane Austin and the Navy*, London, 2000

ST CLAIR, William, *Lord Elgin and his Marbles*, London, 1997

STRABO, *Geography*, Book V, Jones, H. L. (ed.), London, 1923-28

WARNER, Oliver, *The Glorious First of June*, 1961

WHARTON, Sir William, *Hydrographical Surveying*, London, 1898

WOODWARD, Horace B., *The History of the Royal Geographical Society*, London, 1907

WORLD METEORLOGICAL ORGANISATION, *The Beaufort Scale of Wind Force, (Technical and Operational Aspects)*, Geneva, 1969

WYATT, A. G. N., *Charting the Seas in Peace and War*, London, 1947

Index

activities 244-8, 252; work on tides
248-51; honours and recognition
251-2; involvement with railways
256; politics 257; survey of British
Isles 262-5; education and
promotion of surveyors 267-8;
North West Passage and search for
Franklin 269-86; Alicia's death
288-9; relationship with Harriet
289-91; marriage to Honora and
family life 291-7, 301; poor health
294, 299; threatens to resign
297-8; promoted to Rear Admiral
298; knighted 298-9; retirement
299-301; death 302; legacy 303-5;
see also Beaufort Wind Scale
Beaufort, Francis Lestock (son)
202-3, 215, 289, 296-7
Beaufort, Henrietta ('Harriet')
(sister) 8, 9, 93, 138, 153, 299;
FB's relationship with 289-91
Beaufort, Honora (*née* Edgeworth;
second wife) 291-3, 295, 301
Beaufort, Louis de (great uncle) 205
Beaufort, Louisa Catherine (sister)
8-9, 89, 93, 289-90, 291
Beaufort, Mary (*née* Waller; mother)
5, 8, 9, 10, 26-7, 29, 93
Beaufort, Mary Anne (sister) 8, 9
Beaufort, Rosalind Elizabeth
(daughter) xii, 209, 215, 289,
294-5, 296, 302
Beaufort, Sophia *see* Palmer, Sophia
Beaufort, William Louis (brother) 7,
9, 44, 88, 93, 98, 202, 210, 211,
287; career 54; and cipher 36-7,
253; as classicist 146, 200
Beaufort, William Morris ('Morry')
(son) 209, 215, 289, 302, 303;
education and career 297;
publishes FB's cipher 253, 255
Beaufort Cipher 253-5

Beaufort family: crest 4; history 3-4,
297
Beaufort Islands 234
Beaufort Sea 234
Beaufort Wind Scale 112-14, 306,
308; first use and origins 112-21;
development 156-8; revived,
adapted and used in Hydrographic
Office surveys 234-5; used by
Cockburn's squadron 235;
recommended by *Nautical
Magazine* 241; official adoption by
Admiralty 241-2; adoption by
Merchant Navy 242; adopted
worldwide 304; later modifications
304-5
Becher, Alexander 214, 226, 228,
241, 253
Beechey, Frederick William 228, 233,
271, 274, 275, 277, 280, 304; as
captain of *Blossom* 219; survey of
Irish Sea 264
Beechey, Richard 264
Belcher, Edward 238-9, 242, 262,
268, 283, 284
Bellerophon, HMS 61, 70-1
Bertie, Albemarle 31, 35, 72
Bethune, Charles 238, 256
Bligh, William 26, 29, 111, 112, 123,
124, 131-2
Blossom, HMS 143-8, 153, 155,
156-8, 219, 238
Bonne Citroyenne, La (corvette) 74,
75
Borneo 230, 234, 259, 265
Boundary Commission 257
Branca 18, 20, 22, 24
Brinkley, John 202, 208, 217-18
British Almanac 249
Brooke, James 230, 239, 259
Brougham, Henry 220, 257
Brunswick, HMS 63, 70, 71
Bullock, Frederick 262, 264-5

SOUTH COAST OF ASIA MINOR
commonly called
KARAMANIA

CILICIA - TRACHEA.

ITCHI

ANAMOUR or MEMORYEH.

Snowy ridge.

Selinti Selinti

Aghalini

Port Cavaliere
Provençal I.
Cavaliere Pr.
Karpedon Pr.

Hamaxia
Selinty
sue Trajanopolis

Antiochia ad Cragum

Perhaps Nephelis Prom.
Kharadran
Chavadrus

Cape Anamour
Anemurilium Pr.

Agalini
Tryngasus Fl.

Anemoo

C. Kizilman

Melania

Chelindreh
Celenderis

Palmar
Papadoula I.

Aphrodisias

AILON CILICIUS

Crommyon Pr.

Part of